NAPOLEON

A remarkable figure in French public life, MAX GALLO is the author of eighty books – biographies, novels, historical novels, memoirs – which have sold in their hundreds of thousands. Formerly Professor of History at Nice University, he has been or continues to be an MEP, newspaper editor and éminence grise in the last French elections. He lives in Paris.

Also by Max Gallo from Macmillan

NAPOLEON: THE SONG OF DEPARTURE

NAPOLEON: THE SUN OF AUSTERLITZ

NAPOLEON: THE EMPEROR OF KINGS

MAX GALLO

NAPOLEON

The Immortal of St Helena

Translated from the French by William Hobson

PAN BOOKS

First published 2005 by Macmillan

First published in paperback 2005 by Pan Books
an imprint of Pan Macmillan Ltd
Pan Macmillan, 20 New Wharf Road, London N1 9RR
Basingstoke and Oxford
Associated companies throughout the world
www.panmacmillan.com

ISBN 0 330 49004 4

First published in French 1997 as *Napoléon: L'immortel de Sainte-Hélène*
by Editions Robert Laffont, Paris

1 3 5 7 9 8 6 4 2

A CIP catalogue record for this book is available from
the British Library.

Typeset by SetSystems Ltd, Saffron Walden, Essex
Printed and bound in Great Britain by
Mackays of Chatham plc, Chatham, Kent

For France, Monique and Gérard

Destiny has had to be stronger than me. And yet what
misfortune for France, for Europe . . . I became the arch
of the old and new alliance, the natural mediator between
the old and new order of things. I had the principles and the
confidence of one and I was identified with the other.
I belonged to both of them; in all conscience I could
have belonged to either . . . Europe would soon truly have
been one people and everybody, no matter where they
travelled, would always have found themselves in
a common country.

Napoleon at St Helena in the *Memorial*

If Napoleon's defeat did not destroy his legend, it is because
St Helena made him the companion of Prometheus.

André Malraux, *Fallen Oaks*

PART ONE

The sword is drawn.
We must drive them back
into their fields of ice

22 June 1812 to 14 September 1812

I

NAPOLEON PUSHES ON THROUGH the pine forest. Soldiers sheltering under the trees move out of his way, pulling aside the horses tethered to trunks and branches. Some rush to pick up their stacked muskets to salute the Emperor but, with a gesture, he brings them up short and stops anyone calling out. He jumps off his horse. Grand Equerry Caulaincourt, who is riding with Marshal Bessières and Grand Marshal Duroc, follows suit. Napoleon is brought a Polish lancer's cloak and a black silk forage cap. He quickly puts them on, leaves his hat, then remounts. Laying his cheek flat against his mount's neck, he gallops for the edge of the forest.

The trees thin out. The smell of sweat and stables that hung under the pines gradually gives way to a sweet scent of wet grass.

The Niemen is there, a few hundred metres below these bare hills that fall steeply down to its waters and tower over the Russian bank, a gentle slope covered in rye and wheat.

But that's what they have to hide from. Cossack patrols frequently sweep past, plunging through the crops at a gallop. They must not realize that this army of more than 600,000 men, this army of twenty nations, this army of Napoleon, is here, so close, lying in wait in the forests, choking the Polish roads, ready to cross the Niemen. The Russians must think that they're simply Polish lancers cavalcading along the river banks as usual.

Napoleon halts on the top of the slope. From this vantage point, he can see the meanders of the Niemen. He pushes his horse into a gallop towards the village of Poniemen which lies opposite the town of Kovno. There, in a bend in the river, the Polish bank curls round a spit of land jutting out from its Russian counterpart.

Napoleon goes down to the strand. The dark waters don't seem to be moving. Two hundred metres away lies the other bank; lies Russia; lies war.

Napoleon stays there for a few minutes. He remembers Tilsit

and the raft in the middle of the Niemen. He had met Tsar Alexander almost five years ago to the day, 25 June 1807. He believed in the alliance with Russia, in peace in Europe. Pure fantasy.

He waves his hand. The aides-de-camp accompanying him, also enveloped in Polish cloaks, come forward. The three bridges will be thrown here, he says, enabling the troops to cross. Inform General Éblé that he must build them tomorrow night.

Then he looks east for a long time. It is still oppressively hot, another annoyance like the swarms of mosquitoes that attack the horses and men's faces and get into the sleeves of one's coat. He hears a rumbling sound. A storm is brewing, zigzagging the red dusk sky with long flashes of lightning on this Monday, 22 June 1812.

Napoleon gallops through the gathering darkness towards his headquarters which have been established in the village of Naugardyski. On the roads beyond, the forest regiments are on the march. Further on, near the villages, soldiers are crowding around bread ovens built to supply the troops.

Napoleon yanks on the reins. Too much disorder: too many isolated soldiers, too many little bands of marauders. A quick glance is enough to tell him that. Military police courts of five officers must be set up to try pillagers and stragglers, and sentence them to death. Mobile columns must round up any soldiers who stray from their units. He communicates this to Marshal Berthier and to Davout. The Grand Army, of which almost 400,000 will cross the Niemen, comprises men from too many countries to stay together if there isn't strict discipline.

He bends over the maps in the dilapidated house that has been prepared as his headquarters.

The plan is simple, straightforward. Macdonald's troops, to the north, are marching on Riga.

'I am with Eugène in the centre; I am advancing on Vilna. My brother Jérôme is to the south with Davout. It is for them to attack the armies of General Bagration and Tormasov who hold the south. Once, with my assistance, they are destroyed we will turn back on General Barclay de Tolly's troops who are deploying towards the north of the Russian system.'

Running his hand over the map, he traces a line that splits the

Russian armies in two. They must cut Bagration and Barclay's armies off from each other and fight them in turn.

Then, suddenly, his voice is drowned out as the storm breaks. He sits down, his elbows resting on the map, so hunched forward he is almost lying on the table. And when the wind has died down, he announces that he wants to go down to the Niemen again, without an escort, just an aide-de-camp, Caulaincourt and General Haxo. He wants to take another look at the Niemen's banks in the company of Haxo, a graduate of the École Polytechnique who commands the engineers in Marshal Davout's corps. Every detail counts in a military operation.

HE HEADS BACK to the river bank. After the storm the ground is muddy, but the air is as stifling as ever and the atmosphere is clammy. In one of the villages he rides through Napoleon notices a light shining in the presbytery of a church around which cavalry units are bivouacking. He enters the little room. The curate is kneeling in prayer; he mumbles a few words in French.

'Who are you praying for? For me or for the Russians?'

The curate crosses himself. He is praying for His Majesty, he answers.

'You are right, as a Pole and as a Catholic.'

Napoleon pats the priest's neck and orders Caulaincourt to give him one hundred napoleons.

HE SETS OFF again in the dark and rides along the banks of the river, deep in thought. Every event, every encounter may be a sign, a portent, an omen. He is a man of reason and the Enlightenment. He is passionate about mathematics. But that does not illuminate all the truths of the universe; it does not explain the fact that destiny marks out certain beings and endows them with the energy to make their dreams a reality.

He lets himself be carried along, barely holding the reins, as his horse gallops through the ripe wheat. Suddenly his mount shies. He tries to hang on, slips in the saddle, spins and falls into the wheat. He hears a voice, Caulaincourt's perhaps, or Berthier's, or one of the officers who have caught them up, exclaim, 'A Roman would turn back; it's a bad omen.'

The aides-de-camp, generals and marshals leap off their horses. A hare ran between his mount's legs and startled it.

Napoleon says nothing and returns to headquarters.

I am a man of reason. I do not believe in omens.

But he looks around him at the faces of these generals and aides-de-camp and his secretary.

They saw it, or they've been told. They're worried, and I cannot shake off this sense of anxiety that presses down on me.

THEY HAVE NO knowledge of the Russian armies' movements on the other bank. No spy has offered to get him information.

Napoleon remembers what he was told by Count Narbonne, the last French diplomat to see Emperor Alexander.

'I am under no illusions,' the Tsar had said. 'I know how great a general the Emperor Napoleon is. But, you see, I have space and time on my side. There is no remote corner of this terrain, all of it hostile to you, to which I will not withdraw, no distant post that I will not defend, before I consent to a shameful peace. I won't attack, but I shall not lay down my arms as long as there is a foreign soldier in Russia.'

The Tsar pointed to the easternmost tip of the continent and added, 'If Napoleon makes war and fortune smiles on him, despite the Russians' legitimate aims, he will have to sign peace on the Bering Straits.'

NAPOLEON QUESTIONS CAULAINCOURT. Will the Russians join battle? Where? Outside Vilna? Caulaincourt murmurs that the Russians will not fight; they'll fall back, abandoning their cities.

'Then I have Poland,' replies Napoleon. 'And, in the eyes of the Poles, Alexander suffers from the ineradicable shame of losing their country without putting up a fight. He is losing Poland just by giving me Vilna.'

He must convince himself, and persuade the others, that the war will be short and victory quick.

'Within two months,' Napoleon goes on, 'Russia will be asking for peace. The grand seigneurs will be terrified, many of them ruined. The Emperor Alexander will be very embarrassed because, at heart, the Russians care little for the Poles and even less for being ruined for Poland's sake.'

He paces up and down, his hands crossed behind his back, taking frequent pinches of snuff. Then he stops in front of Caulaincourt and asks in a low voice, his face grave, whether they have been talking about his fall at headquarters.

Caulaincourt evades the question.

'The troops,' Napoleon declares in a peremptory voice, 'will start to cross the Niemen the moment the bridges are finished.'

HE SLEEPS SEVERAL hours, then at three in the morning on Wednesday, 24 June 1812, he gallops to the Niemen.

On the three bridges finished at midnight, the troops are slowly crossing; the discordant tramp of feet creates a muffled roar amplified by the river banks, like a wave breaking over and over.

He crosses the Niemen at five, then returns to his tent pitched on a hill on the left bank. Through his telescope he observes the three immense columns that diverge once they reach the left bank. The hills and valleys are covered with men and horses and wagons. The weaponry sparkles under a sky that is already dazzling bright. A pink dust starts to rise above the columns. The heat is oppressive. And the morning has only just started.

But what might, what an army! He slaps his riding boots with his crop and paces back and forth, humming, 'Marlbrough s'en va-t-en guerre'. Who could resist such a force on the move?

He rides back along the columns through the dust. Scouts inform him that they've had no sight of any Russians, just the odd glimpse of a Cossack here and there.

They cross another river, the Vilia. The advance guards have already entered Kovno. The Russians have fled. The road to Vilna is open. They must march, and keep on marching, and march fast.

He works all day, sees the scouts, the couriers, dictates his orders and then, at four in the morning on 25 June, is back in the saddle.

He sees horses lying on their sides, their bellies distended, dying, and collapsed soldiers, their arms stretched out in the sun. The animals have been fed green rye, and the young conscripts have died of exhaustion after a few hours of marching in this blazing sun.

He stops, walks a little way with Murat and Davout. They must move fast, he says, take the Russians by surprise, prevent them withdrawing, force them to join battle.

When night falls and a storm breaks, he takes shelter in a house in Kovno.

He is going to sleep on this narrow bed, in this stifling room. He thinks of nights in his palaces, of Marie Louise, of his son he doesn't see.

This must be a short war.

He writes to the Empress,

My friend,

I crossed the Niemen on the 24th at two o'clock in the morning. I crossed the Vilia in the evening. I am the master of Kovno. There's been no affair of significance. My health is good but the heat is extreme.

I am leaving tonight; I will be in Vilna the day after tomorrow. My affairs are going well.

Be gay, we will see each other when I promised we would.

Ever yours, your faithful husband,

Nap

II

NAPOLEON DRIVES TOWARDS VILNA. The Russians are still
refusing to fight. Their general, Barclay de Tolly, is retreating.

Napoleon leans out of his carriage. The dust gets under his
skin, sticks to his eyes. The heat reminds him of the Egyptian
deserts, but it seems even more suffocating, dirty and clammy.
And often at night cold rain turns the roads into muddy torrents.
Then in the morning a few hours are enough to dry the ground
and stir up the dust.

He passes the columns of troops and Würtemberger light
cavalry. Through the curtain of dust he sees the corpses of horses
covered in swarms of flies. He catches sight of isolated troopers
and infantrymen in the fields, probably looking for food because
the supply transports are not keeping up.

But they must push on, push on.

A few leagues from Vilna, on Sunday 28 June, he mounts his
horse.

THE CITY IS BEAUTIFUL, but the inhabitants, although Poles, do
not shout for joy. Where is the enthusiasm with which they were
met only a few days previously in the Polish towns west of the
Niemen? Are these Poles satisfied with their Russian masters?
Do they want a nation, yes or no? Let them show it then, and not
just by arguing endlessly in the Polish diet at Warsaw.

He enters the house occupied a few days before by Alexander,
who had established his headquarters in the midst of his troops.
He walks through the rooms and feels a sense of power, but no
joy.

Berthier reports that thousands of horses have died on the road
between Kovno and Vilna: the heat, the unripe rye, the exhaustion.
Perhaps 10,000. Overwhelmed by the marching, men have committed suicide. They are carrying thirty kilos; they can't breathe.
They're already suffering from dysentery; mosquitoes plague them
constantly. They have no bread.

Napoleon is furious. The generals have to get up at four in the morning, go to the mills and storehouses in person and make sure that thirty thousand rations are produced a day! If they just lie in bed and bemoan their lot, they'll achieve nothing!

He studies the maps, the regimental returns.

'We are losing so many horses here that we will have great trouble, even with all the reserves of France and Germany, keeping our current troop strength mounted,' he says.

What of the Guard? It must be protected at all costs. It must be guaranteed twenty days' supplies and, in turn, set an example of discipline.

He sends everyone out of his study except Caulaincourt and Berthier.

He sits down.

'These Poles in Vilna and Lithuania are not like their counterparts in Warsaw,' he mutters wearily.

He takes a pinch of snuff. Berthier has just announced that an envoy of Alexander's, General Balachov, his minister of police, is asking to be received by the Emperor so that he can deliver a letter from the Tsar.

Napoleon gets to his feet and begins to walk around the room.

'My brother Alexander, who gave himself such airs with Narbonne, already wants to come to terms,' he says. 'He's afraid. My manoeuvres have disconcerted the Russians. Within a month, they will be on their knees.'

But he must force them to negotiate. He will read Alexander's letter; he will receive Balachov, but first he will give his orders.

This news of the arrival of Alexander's envoy has given him ten times his usual energy. He doesn't even think of sleeping. He sends his aides out onto the roads. Davout and Jérôme must attack Bagration to the south. Advanced guards must be sent out from Vilna towards Glubokie and thus turn the fortifications the Russians have erected in Drissa, which they have transformed into a veritable fortified camp.

He questions his aides-de-camp.

'How many prisoners have we taken?'

It is the absence of Russian deserters and prisoners that worries him. He is sombre suddenly. Weakened armies disintegrate; their men surrender. He remembers Eylau and the fury of the Russian troops and, even at Friedland, how whole units sacrificed themselves.

He must keep peace a possibility; he mustn't allow a Polish state to be re-established immediately, and he must leave the door to negotiations open.

The other thing he could do, in this land of slaves, is emancipate the serfs and trigger a peasant revolt. In the Russian history books he has been reading for the last few months he has been fascinated by the character of Pugachev, the Cossack revolutionary who, barely thirty years previously, threatened Moscow at the head of his peasant army. But if he preaches the abolition of serfdom, who will be able to halt that conflagration? Who ever knows how far a revolution can go?

He is not just a conqueror who wants to bring down the Russians; he is also the Emperor of Kings. He wants victory and peace, but he also wants order.

He reads Alexander's letter.

What? Negotiations will be opened if my troops cross back over the Niemen? Is this what the Tsar is proposing?

'Alexander is mocking me,' he exclaims, brandishing the letter in front of Duroc and Berthier. 'Does he think I've come to Vilna to negotiate trade treaties? I have come to put an end once and for all to the barbarian colossus of the north. The sword is drawn. We must drive them back into their fields of ice so that they won't come and meddle in the affairs of civilized Europe for the next twenty-five years.'

He grimaces contemptuously.

'Now that Alexander sees it's serious and that his army is cut off, he is afraid and wants to come to terms. But Moscow is where I will sign the peace. Since Erfurt Alexander has given himself too many airs ... If he needs victories let him fight the Persians, but don't let him meddle in Europe.'

Then he goes out.

It's hot and dusty outside; the reddish-brown expanses are covered in a thick, almost sticky mist. He has decided to hold a review of divisions of infantry and dragoons a league and half from Vilna.

It is late afternoon but the air is still scalding hot. The troops march past for several hours. He remains motionless in the clammy haze. The moment the review ends, torrential rain sluices down.

Barbaric climate.

HE GOES INSIDE. He is going to have dinner, at seven on this Wednesday, 1 July, with M. Balachov. The Russian is a vigorous man with sharp eyes that he does not lower.

'What can you expect from this war?' Napoleon asks him. 'I have conquered an entire province without a fight. If it weren't for respect for your sovereign, who for two months has had his imperial headquarters at Vilna, you would have had to defend it. Now, when all Europe is behind me, how can you resist?'

'We shall do what we can, sire.'

Napoleon shrugs his shoulders.

'I am already in Vilna and I still don't know why we are fighting! Emperor Alexander is taking the responsibility for this war on himself, in front of his people . . .'

Balachov irritates him. This man has a sort of placid assurance that he must break.

'Which is the Moscow road?' Napoleon asks.

Balachov hesitates, then says in a calm voice, 'Sire, this question is designed to embarrass me somewhat. A Russian says, as the French do, that all roads lead to Rome. One can take whichever road to Moscow one wishes. Charles XII went by Poltava.'

He knows about that Swedish defeat. Do they think they're going to worry him? *Do Alexander and Balachov know who I am?*

He dictates a reply to Alexander.

Your Majesty has consistently refused to explain himself for the last eighteen months . . . War is therefore declared between us. God himself cannot make that which has been not have been. But my ear will always be open to negotiations for peace . . . A day will come when Your Majesty will confess that you were wanting in perseverance, confidence and, allow me to add, in sincerity. You have ruined your reign.

Alexander doesn't reply. He will only yield when he is beaten. Day after day Napoleon studies the maps, rides through the countryside around Vilna. No Russian prisoners, no trophies.

In the south, Jérôme, my brother Jérôme, has refused to heed the orders and counsel of Marshal Davout, and Bagration's Russians have managed to get away. And now Jérôme, my brother Jérôme, has left the army with his 40,000 Westphalian soldiers!

Napoleon flies into a rage. He holds it against Jérôme and Davout.

That night, to calm himself, he writes to Marie Louise.

The little king is in very good health. Vilna is a very beautiful city of 40,000 souls. I am staying in a rather fine house where a few days ago the Emperor Alexander was very far from thinking that I was so close to entering here . . . Storms and great heat alternate here; the harvest will be excellent. I envy the good fortune you will have of kissing the little king; kiss him for me. He will have grown already; tell me if he's started talking. *Addio, mio bene.* You know how much I love you.

     Ever yours,
      Nap

It rains, then is boiling hot, then rains again. Every day Napoleon is in the saddle for several hours.

On the Kovno road he watches two Bavarian divisions march past. The whole army has to regroup, and supplies, provisions and ammunition have to arrive. So they must wait, and he's already been in Vilna for seventeen days.

He should press on, but he does not want to be imprudent. He senses that those around him are watching him anxiously, awaiting orders for a battle that won't come. How is he to encircle the Russian army when it is constantly vanishing in the oceans of space that make up this vast country?

ON THURSDAY, 16 July 1812, when he returns to Vilna after inspecting some service corps regiments, Méneval brings him two dispatches from Murat, who is in command of the advance guard. The King of Naples reports that Russian troops have managed to surprise and capture a cavalry unit.

Surprise them! Murat is a fool!

The second dispatch announces that the Russians have evacuated the entrenched camp at Drissa on which they had been working for two years.

Napoleon doesn't hesitate. They have to give chase, seize them, reduce them to submission.

It is eleven in the evening on Thursday 16 July. He gets into his carriage. He is going to drive all night towards Glubokie.

Bivouac fires flicker here and there. He doesn't hear any shouting, any songs. The nights in this country are as cheerless as the days.

III

IT IS BETWEEN THREE and four in the afternoon. Napoleon is sitting in the dark vaulted hall of the Carmelite monastery in Glubokie. It is the time of day when the heat, in the second half of this July of 1812, is at its most intense. Even within these stone walls the atmosphere is suffocating. He dictates and writes, and that is enough to leave him drenched in sweat. Outside, the countryside bakes in the blinding light of a sun whose orb seems to fill the whole sky. The troops can't march in a furnace like that. Horses huddle together in the rare patches of shade; many rot, half-dismembered by the soldiers, at the roadside.

Napoleon writes. He will go out in an hour, when the sun starts to go down and relinquish part of the sky. He will visit the bread ovens, the artillery park and the hospitals. When it's dark he will go on reconnaissance to the east, towards Mohilev and Vitebsk. He will ride for part of the night and then review some Bavarian divisions or the Guard at dawn. Then he will come back here to study the dispatches, listen to his aides-de-camp and write.

My friend,

I am staying here in a Carmelite monastery in a very beautiful bit of country, and I am in good health. You will see that I am sixty leagues from Vilna and further from you. I assume you have reached St-Cloud. Kiss the little king twice for me; I am told he is charming. Tell me if he has affected you a great deal, if he's starting to talk, if he's walking and, last of all, if you are happy with his progress. My health is extremely good; I have nothing to wish for in that respect. I am in better health than in Paris.

I think it will be appropriate for you to go to Paris on my feast day, and do as I would by attending the public concert.

My affairs are progressing well; all I lack is my sweet Louise, but I am pleased to know she is with my son.

I am going to Mass; it is Sunday.

I hope you have been satisfied with Paris and France and that
the sight of it has given you pleasure.

Addio, mio bene, ever yours.

We will choose the heron you asked for and send it to you,
Nap

He remains motionless for a while. When will he see France,
Marie Louise and his son again? The Russians are withdrawing.
The heat and the distances are causing the Grand Army to melt
away. Supplies are not keeping up. Stragglers, runaways and
marauders are already in their tens of thousands. How many men
does he still have at his disposal – 200,000? Berthier is not even
capable of giving him exact figures.

Napoleon gets to his feet and starts to dictate,

Every day we lose large numbers through lack of order in
foraging procedures. It is urgent that the corps commanders
agree with one another on the measures to be taken to put an
end to a state of affairs that threatens the army with destruction; the number of prisoners taken by the enemy mounts by
several hundred every day.

In the twenty years I have commanded French armies, I
have never seen a more worthless military administration.
There is no one of any merit; everyone sent here lacks
aptitude and knowledge.

And then there's this. He rereads the text of the Russian appeal
to the soldiers of the Grand Army, written in several languages
and thrown into the advance posts.

Go back to your homes or, if you wish to find refuge in
Russia in the meantime, forget all about conscription and the
whole military tyranny that does not allow you to elude its
yoke for a moment.

He throws the leaflet away. His hands and mind feel soiled. Is
this a war between sovereigns?

'My brother Alexander is stopping at nothing now. I could call
on his peasants to claim their freedom too.'

But he refuses to do that. Along the roadside, in their hovels,
he has seen some of the muzhiks.

Eugène de Beauharnais has already come to urge him to abolish serfdom on several occasions. But what would this liberation of slaves lead to?

'I have seen the stupefied state of this sizeable class of the Russian people. I refuse to adopt a measure that would condemn a good many families to death and the most terrible suffering.'

Let there be no more discussion of the subject.

He turns to Caulaincourt, so long ambassador to Alexander's court where he was taken in by the Tsar. The grand equerry is still advocating a halt to the offensive. Not a day passes without him and Marshal Berthier speaking of losses from illness and desertion. The army's failure to scout their advance or take prisoners they put down to the horses' fatigue. They imply that Murat is pointlessly exhausting his squadrons by throwing them forward without thinking and submitting over-optimistic reports.

'Your Majesty must be told the truth,' they say. 'The cavalry is melting away fast; the overlong marches are grinding them down, and you can see brave souls being forced to hang back in charges because the horses can't get up enough pace.'

Berthier and Caulaincourt don't understand that peace will only be possible if Alexander is defeated.

Have they read the proclamation the Tsar has issued to his people?

People of Russia, more than once you have broken the teeth of lions and tigers as they sprung at you. Come together with a cross in your heart and a sword in your hand . . . Our goal is the destruction of the tyrant who wants to destroy the whole earth. Wherever he bends his step, let him find you inured to his treachery, despising his lies and treading his gold underfoot!

The tyrant is me!

Napoleon gestures scornfully. He takes Caulaincourt by the arm and leads him to one side.

'Your friend Alexander is a Greek – false. Anyway, I don't hold it against him. He has been deceived as to the strength of his army; he doesn't know how to lead it and he doesn't want to make peace; he is not a person of substance. When one is not the strongest, one must be the most political, and his politics should be to bring this to an end. When we can talk to each other, we will soon come to an agreement, because I am only waging a political war against him.'

BUT HE MUST force him to fight so that he will negotiate. And so he must push on.

They sleep under canvas. It's hot, then it rains. The villages are empty. No old men, no women, no children. The hovels are abandoned. What sort of nation is this, to obey an order of their Emperor like this?

These silent towns, these vast expanses sweltering in sun and heat, then drowned in torrential downpours, these armies of which they can only catch a few rearguard units or a handful of Cossack horsemen, and yet they sense are combat-ready and organized – all of it worries him.

They need to fight a battle in a circumscribed space, army to army.

He goes into his tent. It is midday on Saturday 25 July.

I don't want two days to pass without writing to you, my friend. It is raining a great deal; we're hot and we march constantly. I haven't had any couriers since yesterday; I have marched too hard. I am conducting a review this evening.

I have crossed the Dvina here; I am marching on Vitebsk, one of the large towns in this country. The harvests are superb, and look the finest.

I am waiting for news of the little king. You must have found him much grown. I am told he eats enough for four and is very greedy. My health is fairly good. My affairs are going well. Farewell, my friend, ever yours,

Nap

DAVOUT, MURAT AND Ney win victories at Ostronovo, but Bagration and Osterman's troops manage to avoid being surrounded. Rearguard actions enable them to withdraw.

They must be caught.

Napoleon is in the saddle for most of the night, then again at dawn, encouraging the troops. When he appears, the shouts of 'Long live the Emperor!' ring out again.

He stops at the top of a hill. Just a few hundred metres away squadrons of Russian cavalry are charging small units of voltigeurs. The isolated men fight back, standing back to back and awaiting each charge, which they repulse, for several hours.

As soon as the fighting ends Napoleon rides down to them. Some of the voltigeurs have even taken prisoners.

'All of you are brave lads and you all deserve the cross,' he calls.

The soldiers wave their muskets in the air and cheer the Emperor. Napoleon rides off, pushing his horse into a gallop.

This army is still full of ardour. All it's missing is a great battle, a real one, and a great victory.

But the plains are deserted. The plateau above Vitebsk and the Dvina, where the advance guard had reported the enemy, is empty. Napoleon walks his horse across it, digging in his spurs now and then, making the animal start.

He questions his aides-de-camp. Where are the Russians? Not a peasant, not a prisoner who can tell them the road taken by the enemy army.

He must return to Vitebsk. Napoleon takes up quarters in the palace of the governor of White Russia, the Prince of Würtemberg, a modest, dusty building. The vast town with its convents and churches is empty apart from some Jews who sell flour to the soldiers. A peasant found asleep under a bush is brought before the Emperor.

The man falls to his knees, stammering. The Russian army started moving out four days before, he says, along the Smolensk road.

Napoleon dismisses him. He wants a report from the corps commanders that evening.

'Perhaps Smolensk is where the Russians want to fight,' he says.

He questions the officers. Murat himself says the cavalry is 'on its uppers'.

Napoleon listens. Despite the troops' cheers he is well aware that the army is exhausted and that he must take it in hand so that it can be ready for a new leap forward for the decisive battle. To work! Parade every morning on the square at six. Reorganization of supplying, transports and hospitals. Daily reviews of units to be conducted by the Emperor.

He dismisses the corps commanders.

A FEW LINES to Marie Louise, same as every day. To breathe a different air than that of war.

> My friend,
>   The weather here is unbearably hot. We are suffocating.
> We are only a hundred leagues from Moscow.
>   Write to me from Paris of everything that comes to your notice and what people are saying.
>   The little king must be amusing you greatly if he is starting to talk and be aware. I am told he is a little devil and a good eater.
>   I know that you are in the habit of making good use of your time; it is a very precious and essential thing; it is one of your good qualities.
>   Your letter to the Pope is good, but you should end with the formula, 'Your dearest daughter'. That's the correct etiquette. I shall instruct Méneval to send you a model letter . . . I can't remember now what you asked me about the 120,000 pounds of presents. If it's the one's you have given your family, I think I've already ordered them. I don't know what the Dutch lace is either. In any event you will find enclosed the orders to settle all this. I defer to you.
>   Farewell, my friend; be in good health, kiss the little king for me, and never doubt your faithful
>   Nap

HE EXPLORES THE rooms of this modest building.

Since he is going to stay several days in Vitebsk he wants his living quarters organized, with his books, his maps and his little iron-framed bed. He establishes a daily routine. Up at five, review on the square in front of the palace (which seems cramped to him, so he orders the Guard's sappers to knock down houses and create a genuine esplanade), all the corps commanders and generals in the vicinity are to attend parades and present themselves to him.

He questions them, listens to their reports, their justifications, their protestations of devotion, their declarations of zeal and good intentions. He exclaims, 'All of this only matters to me if it results in success. We must succeed.'

He turns his back on them, and despite the heat, already intense at this early hour, he visits the cantonments, inspects the bread ovens again, and goes over the positions occupied by the Russian army. He leaps down from his horse, examines the traces left by the troops. How many were there? One army, two? Has Barclay been joined by Bagration?

It is nearly midday; he returns to Vitebsk.

HE SEES MARSHAL OUDINOT, who has just defeated Wittgenstein's Russians at Jaboukowo but, instead of pursuing the enemy, has fallen back as if terrified by the space that opened up before him.

He addresses him curtly: 'The Russians are proclaiming left and right, in our rear, the stunning victory they won against you, since for no reason you let them sleep on the field of battle.'

Oudinot begins to protest, but Napoleon stops him.

'War is a matter of opinion; the reputation of armies is everything in war and equals real strength.'

How haven't they understood this yet, these old soldiers? If the Russians fall back before me, it is because they are afraid of me, of my reputation, of the opinion they've formed of my forces.

If they knew that the horses lack forage, and the men have been feeding themselves on whatever they can find for a month! Luckily, the country is rich, the fields full of vegetables, the cellars of provisions and alcohol. The men drink so much they lie by the roadside, in the sun!

AS THE DAYS PASS, the storms grow more frequent. The weather, in the middle of August, is increasingly erratic. It rains prodigiously for three days; the ground turns to mud. It is impossible to move.

Napoleon dictates a letter for Barbier his librarian, who for more than ten years has found all the books he needs, compiled his campaign library and written reviews of new publications.

The Emperor would like to have some amusing books. If there are some good new novels, or older ones that he does not know, or memoirs that make agreeable reading, you will do well to send them, because we have moments of leisure here that are not easy to fill.

No women, no theatre, no court, no ceremonial. Rustic castles, cities with unpaved streets. No dignitaries to hand over the keys and put themselves at my service. A country worse than Egypt! The austere life of a soldier-emperor.

He likes to see himself in this light. He muses on it for a few moments as he drinks a glass of Chambertin, bottles of which the quartermasters have managed to bring out. His only luxury, this wine. This is the one moment he relaxes, savouring the two or three mouthfuls more often than not mixed with water.

Then it's back to the war, and Berthier – who he has to berate, whose constant reservations irritate him. 'We have to go up to ten or twelve leagues from Vitebsk to find forage for the horses,' the marshal complains. 'The inhabitants who haven't fled have everywhere taken up arms. In looking for food, we are exhausting horses that need rest and exposing them, as well as the men, to being captured by the Cossacks or massacred by peasants, which often happens.'

Napoleon doesn't want to listen. They have to organize their foraging, he has already said that. But most of all they have to set off again, catch the enemy, fight them and so force them to peace.

He leaves Vitebsk for Smolensk, and reaches the banks of the Dnieper. He follows the river, riding until nightfall. Everything here – rivers, distances – is immense.

He hears a cannonade. Some aides-de-camp ride up at a gallop and report that Murat's cavalry has attacked a Russian division at Krasnoe and taken some cannon, the first trophies of the campaign. Prisoners have revealed that the Russian troops are concentrated on Smolensk, the 'holy city', they said. So that is where the battle will take place.

He goes back to his tent, pitched in the middle of the square of the Guard.

It is 15 August 1812. This Saturday he is forty-three years old! He holds a review of his Guard, who cheer him.

No *Te Deum* in a cathedral, no dignitaries coming to present their compliments. But has he ever had that? It seems to him that he has been waging war for ever. In a moment he will set off for the advance posts, which have already reached Smolensk.

Standing, he writes a few lines:

My friend,

   I am writing to you from my tent, since I am on the road to Smolensk. My health is extremely good. The news you give me of the little king is extremely interesting. He is very lucky to have you at his side. Farewell, my friend, ever yours.

   Your faithful
   Nap

He looks at Smolensk, its brick walls, its domes, the hills flanking it rising up above the left bank of the Dnieper on which the town is built. That bridge, there, marks the junction of the St Petersburg and Moscow roads.

He listens to the reports. The city is being defended. Some Cossacks actually managed to surround Marshal Ney, who had the collar of his uniform ripped by a bullet fired at point-blank range.

He observes the movements of the Russian troops on the bridge through his telescope. Some are returning to the town; others are leaving. Are the Russians preparing another retreat?

He asks Caulaincourt's opinion, but he can guess what he will say. The grand equerry thinks the Russians are going to pull back.

He observes the town for a long time; at nightfall, fires start to be lit.

'If this is how it is, by abandoning one of their holy cities the Russian generals are dishonouring their arms in the eyes of their own subjects,' he says.

He walks about outside his bivouac.

'This puts me in a good position,' he continues. 'We will drive them back a little more for our peace of mind. I will fortify the town. We will rest and, with this as a base of operations, the country will get organized and we will see how Alexander feels about that turn of events. My army will be more formidable and my position more threatening than if I had won two battles. I will establish myself at Vitebsk, raise Poland in arms and later, if needs be, choose between Moscow and St Petersburg.'

He sees how the faces of Caulaincourt, Berthier and his aides-de-camp light up. This is what they all want, what they all hope for. Probably it is the wisest thing to do. But is it still possible to be wise?

Suddenly two enormous explosions set the sky ablaze. The Russians must have blown up their munitions depots. The entire city is burning, lighting up the night. The whole horizon seems to be on fire.

He is fascinated by this spectacle, enthralled.

'An eruption of Vesuvius,' he says. 'That's a fine spectacle, isn't it, Monsieur Grand Equerry?'

He claps Caulaincourt on the shoulder; the man shudders.

'Horrible, sire,' murmurs the grand equerry.

Haven't they learnt anything about war?

'Bah,' Napoleon exclaims. 'Gentlemen, remember the Roman emperor's saying, "The body of a dead enemy always smells sweet."'

HE ENTERS SMOLENSK on Tuesday 18 August. Dead bodies everywhere among the burning rubble. The smell of smoke mingles with the stench of corpses starting to rot. He rides slowly, issuing orders. The dead are to be removed, the wounded collected, the fires extinguished and an inventory made of supplies in the town.

He establishes himself in the governor's house. It's stifling. The smell of death has impregnated all the rooms. He tosses his sword onto a table.

'The campaign of 1812 is over,' he says wearily.

He sits down, stretches out his legs. They feel heavy, swollen in his boots. He starts to write.

My friend,
   I arrived in Smolensk this morning. I have captured this town from the Russians after killing three thousand of their men and wounding more than triple that. My health is extremely good.

The heat is extreme. My affairs are going well. Schwarzenberg has beaten the Russians two hundred leagues from here.

Nap

He feels better after night has fallen, cooler. So, Prince Schwarzenberg has defeated the Russians. Good Austrian ally!

'This gives a dash to the alliance. These cannon will resound in Petersburg, in the throne room of my brother Alexander. It sets a good example for the Prussians. Perhaps their honour will be pricked.'

But he is anxious too. In Sweden, Bernadotte has approved the signing of an Anglo-American alliance. This Frenchman is preparing to betray him! The dispatches from Spain announce victories for Wellington: Marmont has been beaten; Joseph has abandoned Madrid. But misfortune does, admittedly, have its uses.

'The English are occupied,' he tells Caulaincourt.

'They won't be able to leave Spain to skirmish in France or Germany. That is what matters to me.'

But it would only need a defeat for everything in his rear to go up in flames. Prussia, Germany and in France itself, people are watching, waiting for their chance. Can he allow himself to stay another season in Russia and not conclude this campaign with victory and a triumphant entry into Moscow?

He stands up. He is going to ride round Smolensk towards Valutino, where the troops have engaged Barclay's rearguard and can surround them. He looks at the maps, consults his aides' reports.

'Barclay is mad,' he says. 'His rearguard is ours if Junot just moves forward.'

He gallops towards the site of the battle and observes the troop movements. What is Junot doing?

He is not attacking. He lets Murat charge on his own, who is forced to fall back. The Russians are going to escape again.

Napoleon returns to Smolensk in a sombre mood. He remembers Junot's courage, his loyalty, his intrepidity so long ago at the siege of Toulon.

'Junot does not want any of this any more,' he says. 'He is making me lose the campaign.'

He should punish him ruthlessly: demotion, dismissal, humiliation.

But it's Junot, my first aide-de-camp when I was wandering round the streets of Paris in a faded, tattered uniform.

He knows there are so many generals like Junot, who are tired of fighting, even if they are brave, even if they still charge heroically.

But can I make peace? Who wants it?

He wishes to meet Count Orlov, an officer of the Imperial Guard who has come as a mediator to obtain information about Russian officers taken prisoner.

'The war is merely political,' he says. 'I have nothing against the Emperor Alexander. I want peace.'

But who can afford to dream of a peace that is not preceded by a defeat?

ON SUNDAY 23 August in terrible heat, as he has just written to Marie Louise, he walks about the square in front of the governor's house. He cannot afford to retreat. War, as he said to Oudinot, is a matter of opinion. If he doesn't win victory, if he doesn't enter Moscow, it will be a defeat.

He sends for his marshals.

He sees them on Monday 24 August. Will they dare speak? Murat claims the Russian army can be caught and beaten. The others say nothing. But he knows what their silence means. They want to defer until 1813.

As if they could wait! He has considered this option himself, and hesitated. But now he has made his choice.

'Within a month we shall be in Moscow.'

He stares at each of them in turn. They lower their eyes. They must agree.

'In six weeks,' he goes on, 'we shall have peace.'

Then, bidding them return to their units, he says (but will they understand?), 'Danger itself is driving us towards Moscow. I have exhausted the objections of the prudent.'

HE LEAVES SMOLENSK on Tuesday 25 August at one in the morning. He rides for part of the night and almost all the following day. The villages are empty. He doesn't see a single cart or peasant. The houses of Durogobouje, a little town on the Dnieper, are in flames. Who started these fires — his own troops or the Russians?

He rails against the indiscipline and chaos he sees on the roads. The officers' baggage-laden carriages are sometimes obstructing the artillery.

'I shall have mine burnt if it is not in its rightful place,' he says.

He plods forward on horseback, ordering chasseurs of the Guard to stop any carriages driving outside the column and set them on fire. An officer tries to plead his case. The carriage belongs to M. de Narbonne, he says, the Emperor's aide-de-camp, who is going to lose everything he owns and perhaps will be wounded tomorrow.

'It would cost me far more if I didn't have any artillery tomorrow,' Napoleon replies.

He passes through Slavkovo, Rouibkoi and Viasma, where Murat's squadrons have repulsed the Russians, but which ones? Perhaps it was their advance guard; perhaps they are getting close to a battle?

He writes to Marie Louise:

I am here, in a fairly attractive town. There are thirty churches, fifteen thousand inhabitants and plenty of stores of brandy and other things the army can use. It has rained a little, which has settled the dust and made it cooler. My health is extremely good; my affairs are going well. Farewell, my friend, ever yours.

Your faithful husband,

Nap

I have learnt that the little king is his high-spirited self again, kiss him twice for me.

HE WALKS ABOUT Viasma. He has ordered the skirmishers of the Guard to enter the town first to find out the cause of these fires that are reducing cities and villages to rubble. They have seen Cossacks lighting fires. The few inhabitants who have stayed confirm that the rearguard of the Russian army prepared the fires.

'What sort of people are these who burn their houses to stop us spending a night in them?' he exclaims.

But he is worried.

What is this war becoming? What does Alexander, this Emperor who I call my brother, want? Smolensk, his holy city, is burnt; his country is in a fine state. He would have done better coming to terms. But he has preferred to give himself over to the English again. Will they rebuild these burnt cities for him?

They continue to advance. The town of Gzhatsk is in flames, but a few houses have escaped the fire. Napoleon examines the surrounding area and then, when it's dark, takes up quarters in the town. A Cossack who has been taken prisoner is brought in for interrogation. The Emperor has him approach, gives him a few gold coins, then questions him. The Cossack declares that General Kutusov has taken command of the army in place of Barclay de Tolly. The nobility, explains the Cossack, have forced the Emperor Alexander to make this appointment, which has delighted the Russian army.

Napoleon gets to his feet, smiles. 'At last,' he says.

'The new general cannot continue this system of retreat that public opinion condemns. He has been put in charge on the express condition that he fights. The system of war followed up till now must therefore change.'

Napoleon raises his voice, takes several pinches of snuff.

'Kutusov will give battle to please the nobility,' he continues, 'and in a fortnight Alexander will have neither a capital nor an army left. He will then be able to make peace without incurring the reproaches and censure of the grands seigneurs, whose choice Kutusov is.'

HE IS DETERMINED but on edge. He doesn't feel the elation that has always borne him up on the eve of a battle. Sometimes he is even gripped by anxiety. And then there is Berthier, who comes to beseech him not to continue advancing towards Moscow but to pull back to Smolensk or Vitebsk! He doesn't want to see Berthier any more. He doesn't want the marshal to share his meals.

They must do the opposite: push on, fight Kutusov and smash the Russian army.

On Saturday, 5 September 1812 he has his tent pitched a little way from the village of Borodino, where Murat's cavalry has just driven back the Russian advance guard. Kutusov's army is there, on the other side of the river Kalatsha. This runs between two plateaux, hemmed in by steep banks, and then flows into the river Moskva, which he can see in the distance.

At night, when the cold is bitter and it's raining, he saddles up and tours the advance posts, and does the same all day Sunday until he has drawn up his plan. Eugène will be on the left, attacking Borodino and the great redoubt on the other side of the Kalatsha river. Ney and Davout will be in the centre and will launch the attack on the hills known as the Three Arrows. Poniatowski's Poles will assault the right.

And I will be with the Guard, ready to intervene.

At six in the evening, on that Sunday, 6 September 1812, he assembles his marshals. He listens to their reports. The attacks will be difficult, they say; the Russians have fortified their redoubts. They fight well. Davout insists that instead of a frontal attack they should attack on the right wing, reinforcing Poniatowski.

No one shares Davout's opinion.

Napoleon gets to his feet. He is with the majority, he says. The plan he has presented, therefore, is adopted.

HIS HEAD IS heavy, his legs swollen. He sends for Doctor Mestivier who, after a long stay in Moscow, had returned to Paris and then come out again with the army.

'Well now, Doctor,' Napoleon says, 'the thing is, I'm getting old. My legs are swelling; I barely urinate. No doubt it's these damp bivouacs; my skin is drenched.'

He coughs. His pulse is feverish. His urine only comes in drops and it hurts.

But he sends Mestivier away. He will see about it after the battle.

He goes into his tent and suddenly sees, at the back, a portrait of the King of Rome painted by Gérard which M. de Beausset, one of Marmont's aides, has just brought from Paris.

The wave of emotion he feels is so strong and his tiredness so great that he clings to the frame of his iron bed.

Staring at the portrait, he asks for a quill and piece of paper and begins to write.

> My good friend,
>   I am very tired. Beausset has given me the portrait of the little king. It is a masterpiece. Thank you so much for your attentiveness; it is just like you. I will write to you tomorrow in more detail. *Addio, mio bene,*
>   Nap

He would like to go to bed, but he grabs the portrait of his son, takes it out of the tent in the muggy dusk and stands it on a chair. Some grenadiers come up and bow as if it were a holy image.

Napoleon murmurs to General Rapp, who is standing near him, 'My son is the most beautiful child in the world.'

IV

IN HIS TENT PITCHED in the middle of the regiments of the Guard. He wakes with a start.

It is two in the morning on Monday, 7 September 1812. His body aches. He feels heavy. His legs are still swollen. He coughs. His head is held in the iron grip of a horrible migraine.

This cursed cold! But one doesn't stop for that.

He hears the buglers sounding reveille from one end of the French lines to the other. He has already witnessed the dawn of battle so many times.

'It is nineteen years now that I have been waging war and I have fought many battles and laid many sieges in Europe, Asia and Africa,' he repeats.

He has already written this in a letter to Marie Louise. He is thinking of her and his son, whose portrait emerges from the dark again, lit up by the torch held by the duty aide-de-camp.

He gets up.

Outside the night is dotted with bivouac fires. The Russians' seem innumerable, and a solemn murmur, like a threnody, rises up from the valley and drifts across the plateau. The Russians are praying before the battle.

Around him he makes out the soldiers of the Guard putting on their parade uniforms. They pass around bottles of schnapps in silence. It must be the same in all the units.

He has seen these dawns so many times.

And so often his whole destiny has hung on the outcome of the battle that is about to be joined. But each time he has won – at Marengo, Austerlitz, Jena, Friedland, Wagram – and he's been waiting three months for this moment. Yet he knows this morning that he does not hold all the cards. The rules of the game, which he has always laid down and imposed on the enemy, have slipped from his grasp. It is not he who has chosen the place and time of this engagement but old Kutusov, who he defeated at Austerlitz but who is also the conqueror of the Turks.

So, the battle is beginning when the Grand Army has been worn down by three months marching through this sun-baked, dust-choked country. It's been a month since any supplies were distributed to the men; they've been living off the land. He hasn't even managed to find out exactly – he who always wants to know the state of his units down to the last soldier – how many men he has at his disposal. Perhaps barely 130,000, if Berthier's calculations are to be believed! But what does Berthier know, when thousands of stragglers are spread over the countryside and roads, easy targets for the Cossacks?

He walks through the Guard camp. The men are formed up. The artillerymen of the Guard are preparing their guns.

He approaches. He has 587 cannon. But Kutusov probably has more; he is likely to field over 600 cannon, 120,000 men, perhaps, not counting the Cossack horsemen who swirl about the Grand Army and can fall at any moment on its rear during the battle.

They are what I have to think of; they are what I have to anticipate. At all times I have to have a reserve unit able to confront an attack by this cavalry on our flank or rear while we're advancing.

I must not engage the Guard in the main battle. I need to win without them, to keep them as a last resort to pit against the unexpected.

He mounts.

Above the rhythmic hum of the Russians praying, he hears the voices of the officers reading out the proclamation that he wrote yesterday in his tent.

He listens, murmuring the words himself.

'Soldiers!

'Here is the battle you have so desired! From now on victory depends on you; it is necessary for us. It will give us an abundance of good winter quarters and a prompt return to our country! Conduct yourselves as you did at Austerlitz, Friedland, Vitebsk and Smolensk, and let the most remote posterity proudly quote your conduct on this day. Let it say of you: He was at the great battle under the walls of Moscow!'

He looks at the Russian bivouacs. He must be victorious,

destroy Kutusov's army, enter Moscow and impose peace on Alexander. Then the game, once again, will be won.

If he loses it . . .

He cannot lose.

AT SIX O'CLOCK, when day is breaking, he gives the order to the artillery to open fire. He watches the aides gallop off. And suddenly the cannonade erupts, filling the Kalatsha valley, rolling between the edges of plateaux, sending showers of earth shooting into the air around the great redoubt and the Three Arrows.

The first lines of infantry, Eugène's, launch an attack on the village of Borodino, which is already in flames, and the great redoubt. Then, on the right, Davout, Junot and Ney's soldiers make for the great redoubt, and Poniatowski's Poles try to take the Three Arrows. The Russian cannonballs plough bloody furrows through their lines. Smoke gradually covers the battlefield, driven by a light breeze that blows from west to east and thus hides part of the Russians.

The sun slowly appears, piercing the fog and smoke.

'It is the sun of Austerlitz,' he cries.

Will this be another Austerlitz?

HE STAYS SITTING there, motionless on his horse. One aide-de-camp appears after another. They announce the capture of Borodino and the Russian counter-attack. General Plausonne, commanding the assault, has been killed in the village with most of his officers. Davout has taken the great redoubt, only to be dislodged by the Russians. General Compans has been killed; Davout, whose horse has been brought down, is still unconscious. The Three Arrows, the great redoubt, Borodino and the village of Semionovskaya have changed hands several times. The Russian general Bagration, he is assured, has been killed defending Semionovskaya.

Every time a name is flung at him, he merely tightens his grip on the reins. Montbrun, Damas, Compère, all generals, are dead. And Caulaincourt, the grand equerry's brother, also a general, is cut down leading his troopers in a charge. He turns towards Caulaincourt. Tears are rolling down the grand equerry's face. He has heard the aide-de-camp announce the death of his brother.

'You have heard the sad news. Go to my tent.'

Caulaincourt does not move, just salutes, half lifting his hat.

'He died like a brave man,' says Napoleon.

How many have fallen? Dozens of generals, it seems, hundreds of colonels, tens of thousands of men – this is what he senses, and still the Russians are not giving in. They are not scattering; instead they are counter-attacking with bayonets. Their artillery-men are being hacked to pieces on their guns.

'These Russians are getting themselves killed like machines,' he calls out. 'We won't storm the redoubts; they don't advance our cause. They are citadels you have to destroy with cannon.'

It will not be another Marengo or Austerlitz or Jena or Friedland or Wagram, he foresees.

'We will win the battle,' he says through clenched teeth. 'The Russians will be crushed, but it won't be conclusive.'

HE IS SOMBRE as the day progresses. The cannon have fired 100,000 rounds, and the Russians are still resisting.

Murat's and Ney's aides-de-camp insistently repeat the mar-shals' demands: the Guard must be sent into action. They will smash the Russian front, who will then flee. Then the generals appear, plaguing Napoleon with their cries: The Guard! The Guard!

He doesn't even turn his head.

'That's the last thing I'll do. I will not demolish it,' he says. 'I am certain I'll win the battle without them taking part.'

They insist. What do they know of the whole picture? They see the battle at the points of their sabres. But I must grasp the whole.

'What if there's another battle tomorrow? What shall I wage that with?' he says.

Do they know that, just as I had feared, the Russian cavalry and Ouvarov and Platov's Cossacks have carried out a diversionary attack on our rear, falling on the baggage transports of the division that led the attack at Borodino?

Can I run the risk of being outflanked, surrounded?
I must win without the Guard.

BUT THE GREAT REDOUBT is holding out. He sees the French cannon on the Three Arrows, the hills that have finally been captured, bombarding the great redoubt which is still not giving in.

Taking matters into his own hands, Marshal Lefebvre orders the Guard to advance.

For a moment, he lets himself go.

'Advance, you bloody fools!' he yells.

But then he immediately stops the movement.

You win a battle with a cool head; you don't give in to an impulse.
Eventually the great redoubt falls.

NAPOLEON GOES FORWARD and joins the front ranks of the skirmishers, who are making their way along the Moscow road. The Russians are withdrawing in good order. They still hold a redoubt and a little breastwork that covers the road.

Napoleon orders his escort to stay back. He is in the front line. The bullets whistle past.

Why not die, like the forty-seven generals who have fallen and the hundred or so colonels?

The ravines and slopes are covered with thousands of dead from both sides. How many – 50,000, 60,000? He is used to this macabre accounting. He just has to see the ditches filled with corpses that the robbers have not yet been able to strip of their uniforms for him to estimate that three quarters of these dead are Russians. And how many wounded – 30,000, 40,000? Never has a battle cost so dear.

He will not launch an attack on the remaining Russian entrenchements.

'The affair is over,' he murmurs.

NIGHT FALLS. He looks at the Russian masses marching away in good order. Cannonballs are falling among them, but still they reform their lines.

Step up the fire, he orders.

'They want more, do they? Then let's give it to them.'

He has won the battle. He is on the banks of the Moskva, on the road that leads through Mojaisk to Moscow. But he has not destroyed the Russian army and the battle of the Moskva is more like Eylau than Friedland.

A cemetery of tens of thousands of men!

He returns slowly to his bivouac.

The screams and yells of the wounded rise up from all directions. The hunched silhouettes of the robbers come and go like scavengers. The corpses will soon be naked.

How can I sleep?

I must pursue Kutusov, enter Moscow, and there finally, having taken the capital as security, obtain peace.

Now I must write so that people know that victory is mine.

My good friend,

I write to you from the battlefield of Borodino. I defeated the Russians yesterday; their entire 120,000-strong army was engaged. It was a warm affair; in two hours victory was ours. I took several thousand prisoners and sixty guns. Their losses can be reckoned at 30,000 men. I have had a good many killed and some wounded . . . I wasn't at all exposed myself. My health is excellent, the weather a little cool. Farewell, my friend, ever yours,

Your Nap

He reads it through. He knows what the Court and his entourage are like. They whisper among themselves, try to catch the Empress showing some agitation or distress. Then the damage spreads. He must only write what people have to know and believe. And who knows, anyway, if one of these letters won't be seized by a band of Cossacks and sent on to Petersburg and London?

He ought to think about that too. War and victories are matters of opinion. Kutusov may write to his Emperor that he won the battle. Didn't General Beningsen do that after Eylau? And then the poison spread through Europe.

He must pre-empt a lie that would destroy the effects of the battle.

He dictates a letter to the Emperor of Austria.

My Brother and very dear Father-in-Law,
    I hasten to inform Your Imperial Majesty of the happy outcome of the battle of the Moskva, which took place on 7 September in the village of Borodino. Knowing the personal interest Your Majesty is good enough to afford me, I thought it fitting to inform him myself of this memorable event and the good state of my health. I estimate the enemy's losses at from 40,000 to 50,000 men; they had from 120,000 to 130,000 men engaged. I have lost between 8,000 and 10,000 killed and wounded. I have taken sixty guns and a great number of prisoners.

He stops dictating. It's the reverse – there are so few prisoners. The Russians get themselves killed rather than surrender. On the Mojaisk road, aides-de-camp of Murat, who is in the advance guard, report that there are only a few stragglers, the enemy hasn't abandoned a single cart and the Russian cavalry and infantry are continuing to fight in Mojaisk.

But one can't say that.

HE LEAVES HIS TENT. He is going to walk around the battlefield. He tells the officers surrounding him, 'Of all actions recorded in ancient and modern history, the battle of the Moskva is the most glorious, the most difficult and the one that confers most honour on the Gauls.'

It is no lie. He has seen the infantry charging, bayonets fixed, without firing a shot under the hail of grapeshot. It is said that, before he died, Bagration cried out when he saw them, 'Bravo, bravo!'

He mounts and adds, 'The Russian army at Austerlitz would not have lost the battle of the Moskva.'

But these Russian corpses he sees piled on top of each other, in the ravines, around the redoubts, on the plateau, are those of men who have fought with furious determination. They have fought well.

He passes slowly among the troops who are bivouacked on the battlefield and turning the soil to bury the dead.

They cheer him. He gets off his horse. He has to talk to these men.

'Intrepid heroes, it is to you that glory is due,' he calls.

He goes up to a group of men, questions them. 'Where is your regiment?'

'It's there,' replies an old officer.

'I asked you where your regiment is. You must join it,' Napoleon repeats.

Suddenly, he understands. These few dozen men are all that is left of a regiment. The hundreds missing are bodies lying in ditches and on the walls of their redoubt.

Suddenly he feels a pain in his side. He coughs. His voice grows weak, husky.

'Peace lies in Moscow,' he says, straining to speak. 'When the Russian nobility see us masters of their capital, they will think twice. If I free the peasants, that will put paid to all these great fortunes. The battle will open my brother Alexander's eyes, and the capture of Moscow those of his senate.'

His voice goes. He cannot make himself heard any more.

With a wave, he indicates that they must take the Mojaisk road to Moscow.

THE COLD IS starting to turn bitter, the nights damp. He feels feverish, but they have to get to Mojaisk.

On the square of the little town, which has been deserted, but not burned, by its inhabitants, he enters a house that stands open with all its doors ripped off. The quartermasters have filled the stoves.

The room is hot. He tries to dictate. In vain. Not a sound comes out of his throat.

He sits down, bangs his fist violently on the table. Paper and ink are brought to him and he starts to write, tearing the paper into little squares on which he scribbles a few lines so fast that Berthier, Méneval and the aides find them hard to decipher.

He hits the table again. He has already written a fistful of notes. Do they think he's going to stop doing anything because he cannot speak? Is he going to submit his destiny to a loss of voice? As long as he's alive, he will try to make his mark on history.

He writes, more slowly, a message to Marie Louise. He will only talk about what may concern her.

Everything else? The two bridges I want thrown over the Moskva, the exact numbers of losses, the supplies I want brought in, my questions about Kutusov's army – will he defend Moscow, or will he withdraw deeper into the bottomless abyss of the Russian land, and will Alexander sign the peace if I am in the Kremlin? This all obsesses me, but how can I communicate it to anyone? And what would Marie Louise understand of it?

My friend,
I received your letter of the 24th. The little king, from what you tell me, is very naughty. I received his portrait on the eve of the Moskva. I showed it and the whole army thought it admirable: it is a masterpiece. I have a bad cold after being out in the rain at two in the morning visiting our positions, but I hope I'll be rid of it tomorrow. Otherwise, my health is extremely good. You can, if you wish, receive the Prince of Benevento and Rémusat, I have no objection to that. Farewell, my friend, ever yours,
Nap

He is better. He can talk, even if every word he says irritates his throat. But does he want to?

He listens to the aides' reports. Why isn't Kutusov or Alexander proposing an armistice or peace? Why do the Russians keep withdrawing in an orderly fashion, without thinking of defending Moscow? After Smolensk, do they want to abandon their other holy city, this third Rome?

AT TEN IN THE morning, on Sunday, 14 September 1812, he rides alongside the Guard as it slowly trudges up a hill. He sees the soldiers stop. He goes up to the crest of the hill – the Hill of Birds. Suddenly, shouts ring out: 'Moscow! Moscow! Moscow!'

It is a beautiful day. The sun blinds him at first. Then, lit up by its golden light, he sees the domes, the spires, the palaces.

An aide-de-camp arrives at a gallop. The city is empty. A Russian staff officer has requested a suspension of arms. The officer has commended the wounded to the Emperor's mercy.

The silence emanating from the city grips Napoleon.

He appoints General Durosnel governor of Moscow. Durosnel must take over the public buildings and instill a respect for order.

But this silence that hangs over the city worries him.

He rides slowly to the town gate. Aides-de-camp arrive. They haven't encountered any deputation of town dignitaries. Moscow is a desert with the only inhabitants to be seen a few hairy, filthy wretches dressed in sheepskins, convicts no doubt who've escaped from prison.

Napoleon walks a little way past the gate.

He is in Moscow and he feels no joy.

PART TWO

*I am in the dark
about everything*

14 September 1812 to 5 December 1812

V

HE RETCHES ON ENTERING the inn in the Dorogomilov suburb where he is to spend the night of 14 September 1812. He looks for a moment at the quartermasters and chasseurs of his escort who are bustling about, pouring out vinegar and alcohol and burning it to get rid of the rotting smell that fills the rooms.

He is furious. He cannot suppress this dull anxiety that gnaws away at him.

Where are the representatives of this town? Even in Cairo they presented themselves to him; they recognized his victory, his authority. He was able to have talks with them.

But how can one negotiate the peace if there is no one to listen or respond?

He goes back outside. The cold is bitter. But above all he is struck by the silence, which is occasionally rent by a few explosions.

He goes towards Grand Marshal Duroc, who has come back from a reconnaissance to the centre of Moscow. The soldiers accompanying him are pushing in front of them a few inhabitants who speak French. They look bewildered. They don't know anything. They ought to have left the town like most of its inhabitants, they explain. Some couldn't bring themselves to, to protect their property. A group of people start gesticulating. They are French and Italian actors who have been performing for years in Moscow. Why would they have followed Kutusov's army?

Their anguish and their fear are contagious. They will be protected, says Napoleon.

He questions Duroc. All the town's authorities have disappeared. Criminals have barricaded themselves into the Kremlin and are firing on Murat's advance guard.

'All those wretches are drunk,' Duroc adds, 'and refuse to listen to reason.'

'Open the gates with cannon,' Napoleon exclaims, 'and drive out everyone who's in there!'

He goes back into the inn and begins dictating orders and listening to reports from officers who have carried out patrols in the city. The streets are empty, but here and there drunken individuals slip into a house and fire on the soldiers.

'So this is how the Russians make war!' he says. 'Petersburg's civilization has deceived us,' he cries. 'They are still Scythians.'

ON TUESDAY 15 September he wakes at dawn with the same feelings of rage and anxiety. As he gets dressed, he listens to the reports from the previous night. The bazaar caught fire at around eleven o'clock. This large square flanked by porticoed galleries containing lots of little shops has been entirely destroyed without anyone being able to fight the fire in the dark.

He questions Marshal Mortier and General Durosnel at length. Their features are hollow with tiredness. Their faces and hands are still black with smoke. They have not found any fire engines, they say. Inhabitants and the soldiers have looted the shops and houses. Two other fires have broken out in the remoter suburbs.

Would the Russians dare burn Moscow?

He imagines this possibility for a moment, then rejects it. No doubt it is the soldiers' bivouacs that have set fire to the wooden houses.

They must send out new patrols. Marshal Mortier, commander of the Young Guard, will replace Durosnel as town governor.

HE IS IMPATIENT to visit the town. But, from the first streets he rides down, the silence and emptiness irritate and unnerve him. He only sees a few silhouettes behind the windows of houses, and then drunkards staggering all over the place, who run away as the cavalcade approaches. Where are the crowds of Milan, Vienna, Berlin?

Eventually he makes out the Kremlin. He spurs his horse to get there quicker. For the first time since entering Russia he has a sense of satisfaction. He tours the fortress walls, then enters this separate city in the heart of a city. He looks at the church domes for a long time. He could stay here with the army, at the centre of the Russian empire. Kutusov's troops would have to hibernate too.

*But Moscow would be in my hands and, when spring came, like
a ship breaking free from the ice that has imprisoned it, I would
move again, and shatter the Russians with a Grand Army that
would have recovered all its strength in Moscow. And Alexander,
faced with this threat, would be forced to negotiate even before
spring, on my terms.*

HE MUSES ON this possibility all day. He investigates the town's
resources. It is overflowing with provisions, he is told. Elegant,
luxurious palaces rub shoulders with hovels; there's an abundance
of shops.

He visits the room the Tsar occupied. He will not sleep in
his bed. He calls for his camp bed. He will retire early to write
to Marie Louise. These letters are also a way for him to form
opinion in Paris. He sends for Caulaincourt. He wants to be
informed immediately of the arrival of the couriers who every
day come from Paris. Have these men been attacked? How are
their equipages changed? Can't they go any faster? Gaining a
day out of the fortnight the journey takes could be decisive. He
must be informed as quickly as possible of what is happening in
Paris and the Empire. And he must govern as if he were in the
Tuileries.

Hence he wants a conscription of 100,000 men in France and
30,000 in Italy. 'The battle of the Moskva should not weaken our
zeal,' he says. 'This instruction must go in the portfolio for the
Paris courier tomorrow.'

He is alone now. He writes to Marie Louise,

My friend,
    I write to you from Moscow, where I arrived on 14
September. This town is as large as Paris. There are 1,600 spires
and more than a thousand fine palaces; the town is adorned with
everything. The nobility has left, the merchants have also been
forced to leave; the people have stayed. My health is good; my
cold has gone. The enemy is withdrawing, so it seems, to Kazan.
This fine conquest is the result of the battle of the Moskva.
    Ever yours,
    Nap

He goes to bed, falls asleep. Then there are sounds of voices. He wakes up immediately. In the glow of the candlelight he looks at Caulaincourt and Duroc, who are standing a foot from his bed. And suddenly he notices through the window that other glow, staining the whole night red.

They are burning Moscow, he thinks immediately.

It is four in the morning on Wednesday, 16 September 1812.

He walks quickly to the Kremlin's terrace, from where one can see the whole town. He feels as if all the anxiety that has been building up in him for days has exploded and turned to rage.

He listens to Caulaincourt's acount. The first fires broke out a long way from the Kremlin, around nine in the evening, but the north wind stirred up the flames and spread the blaze to the centre of town; then other fires broke out and soon the whole town was in flames. The Guard has been called out; patrols have been sent to all quarters and incendiaries killed, caught with torches in hand. Often they are drunk and so dogged that to take their torches one has to kill them or cut off their hands. Fire-raising tools and fuses have been found everywhere. The inhabitants have confessed that orders were given to the police by Governor Rostopchin to set fire to the whole town during the night. All the fire engines have been destroyed or taken away.

Napoleon watches the town burn. He stands motionless on the terrace for a long while as a fierce wind drives embers across the sky.

This wooden town burns more than Troy or Rome can ever have done! He is fascinated. It is like an ocean on fire.

He issues orders. They must protect as many buildings as possible, save the bridges over the Moskva, try to get provisions under cover. Arrest and shoot all incendiaries on the spot.

The Russians want to drive me out of Moscow, burn everything that might be of any use to us and leave us naked in the coming winter.

They are Scythians, barbarians. What sort of war are they waging?

He cannot tear himself away from the spectacle. A coppery smoke fills the sky and keeps on rising, erupting with sparks and firebrands. Sometimes there are explosions and then whirlwinds spin off.

The Russians, Caulaincourt explains, have left charges and shells in the stoves of some of the palaces.

Napoleon watches the wreaths of pearly smoke that form and add to a sort of pyramid whose base covers the whole town. Above that appears the moon.

No fiction, he murmurs, no poetry could match this reality.

He turns towards General Mouton, who is standing near him.

'This presages great misfortunes for us,' he says.

Then he collects himself. An emperor does not confide in others.

He waves the people standing around him aside and goes down into the Kremlin courtyard. It is nine in the morning. The wind has turned to the west. The houses near the Kremlin are starting to burst into flames. He smells the sulphur; he inhales the air that burns his throat and skin and eyes. He stops. Soldiers of the Guard are flanking two men in uniform with blackened faces. They are *boutechniks*, policemen.

Interrogate them.

He walks back and forth in front of them. Their answers are translated. They confirm the fire was prepared on Governor Rostopchin's orders. Policemen were entrusted with lighting it, quarter by quarter.

Suddenly the arsenal, close to the Kremlin, blazes up. He sees soldiers of the Guard trying to stop the bridge over the Moskva in front of the Kremlin catching fire too. Their bearskins are burning on their heads. The air is becoming unbreathable.

The Russians may have combined this fire with an attack on Moscow. He cannot stay shut up in the town. He must leave it.

He gives more orders. He will never let himself be caught in a trap. He leaves the Kremlin, marches through the rubble of the western district. He pushes on in the suffocating heat, a handkerchief over his mouth, walking over a land of fire under a sky of fire. Firebrands fall all around him. He walks along the Moskva. The fire is like a red dusk that sets the whole horizon ablaze.

He crosses the Moskva on a stone bridge and mounts a horse.

The horse rears. On either side of the Mojaisk road the fire rolls its wall of flames. The suburbs are destroyed. Soldiers are wandering among the smoking ruins, ducking into the cellars, looting the charred houses.

What will become of the Grand Army when it is given over to its instincts like this?

He takes up quarters in the Petrovsky palace, two leagues from Moscow. He wants to be alone. He walks about the park. He looks at the horizon. Moscow carries on burning, despite a thin rain which starts to fall.

HE TURNS IN on himself. One plan after another runs through his mind. Sometimes, in this palace, the finest he has lived in since the start of the campaign, he goes to the table on which the maps are spread out.

He calls Berthier, Eugène de Beauharnais and Murat over. At first he doesn't speak. What are they thinking? He stares at them. Murat is the only one who appears contented. He claims that the Cossacks in Kutusov's rearguard have such respect for his gallantry that they have decided not to kill him.

Berthier, Prince of Neufchâtel, dreams of getting back to his chateau at Grosbois, organizing hunts there and seeing his mistress, Madame de Visconti. As for Eugène, the most faithful of all, he is tired of this war too, so far from his family, from Italy.

What about me? Do they think I don't have any dreams?

He turns towards the portrait of the King of Rome, which he has had put in the room.

He paces back and forth, hands behind his back, head bowed, without looking at them.

'We can,' he begins, 'when the fire is put out, remain in Moscow. The supplies are in the cellars and not all the houses will have been destroyed.'

He looks at them. None of them dares reply.

'We can,' he continues, 'return to Smolensk or even Vilna.'

Berthier and Eugène nod approvingly.

'We can also,' he continues, bending down over the map, 'march towards St Petersburg and force Alexander to flee or sign a treaty of peace. As we've done with the Austrian Emperor in Vienna and the King of Prussia in Berlin.'

They lower their eyes.

He will have to choose on his own.

FIRST HE RETURNS to Moscow, even if the city is still in flames.

With his escort he slowly makes his way through the smoking ruins of the destroyed parts of town. He must see everything; one must always measure what the enemy is capable of.

The Russians, he is convinced, are going to use the fire to make the people rise up against him. He will be the Antichrist. He must fight this slander without wasting a moment, and try to catch the incendiaries in their own trap.

He writes to Marie Louise, because she will speak to the people around her and she will write to her father. The Court of Vienna must be waiting for a moment to turn against him too.

'The Austrians and the Prussians are enemies in our rear,' he says to Berthier.

He writes to Marie Louise:

I had no idea of this town. It had five hundred palaces as fine as the Élysée, furnished in the French style with incredible luxury, several imperial palaces, barracks, magnificent hospitals. It is the governor and the Russians who, in their rage at being defeated, set fire to this beautiful town. These wretches have taken their premeditation to the degree of removing or destroying all the fire engines . . . Only a third of the houses are left. The army found riches of all sorts because in this chaos everything is pillaged. Privates have large quantities of provisions and French brandy.

You should never listen to Paris gossip.

Write often to your father, send him extraordinary couriers, recommend him to reinforce Schwarzenberg's corps so it does itself honour.

I sometimes contemplate Gérard's portrait, which I find very fine.

You cannot doubt that I love you very much and my happiness consists of being near my good Louise.

Kiss the little king three times, love me and never doubt,
Nap

IT IS ALREADY two in the morning but there is no question of succumbing to sleep or tiredness. He must hold all the reins tight now that the fire has died away thanks to heavy rain, the wind dropping and, as he writes to Marie Louise so she will repeat it, the fact that, 'We have shot so many incendiaries that they have given up.'

First he must try to conclude peace by turning the Russians and, if possible, the Tsar against those who have destroyed Moscow.

He receives Deputy Chief of Staff Toutolmin, director of the foundling hospital, whose charges have stayed in Moscow. He has come to ask for French help. Napoleon unrolls in front of him the poster that Governor Rostopchin has had put up outside his house at Voronovo, a short distance from Moscow. He reads it out, glancing at Toutolmin as he does so. ' "For eight years I have embellished this country seat and lived here happily in the bosom of my family. The inhabitants of this estate, to the number of 1,720, are leaving at your approach and I am setting fire to my house so it won't be soiled by your presence. Frenchmen, I have abandoned to you my two houses in Moscow with furnishings worth half a million roubles; here you will find only ashes." '

Napoleon goes up to Toutolmin.

This criminal behaviour of Rostopchin's is even more barbaric, he says, because the civilian population has nothing to fear from the French. Destroying cities, is this the way to make war?

Does the deputy chief of staff, he says leaning forward, remember Pugachev, the man who wanted to liberate the serfs?

'I have not sought to unleash the hurricane of a peasant revolt,' Napoleon murmurs.

He walks about the room. He is prepared to allow an envoy of Toutolmin's to pass through the outposts to give the Empress an account of the state of the hospital, since she is the patron of this institution.

He goes back towards Toutolmin and says brusquely, 'When you send your envoy, please write to Emperor Alexander, for whose person I have the same esteem as ever, and tell him that I want peace.'

He watches Toutolmin depart.

One must always try. Peace now, when he is in Moscow, would be the best solution. The terms don't much matter. If it is signed, it would appear to Europe as the crowning of his military victory, whereas if he had to leave Moscow without having been able to negotiate with the Tsar in any conclusive way, that would be considered a failure.

'Europe is watching me,' he says to Caulaincourt.

He falls silent for a few minutes, then suddenly asks, 'Do you want to go to Petersburg, Monsieur Grand Equerry? You will see the Emperor Alexander. I will give you a letter and you will make peace.'

One must be able to overcome one's pride. *I have often castigated Caulaincourt. Today I need him.*

Caulaincourt refuses, declaring the mission useless.

What do people know of what's possible and impossible before they've tried it?

'Just go to General Kutusov's headquarters then!'

But Caulaincourt demurs.

'Well then, I will send Lauriston; he will have the honour of having made peace and saving your friend Alexander's crown.'

I SHOULD TRY everything to obtain peace. But how can one believe it's possible? The fire of Moscow is living proof of the Russians' determination. Does Caulaincourt imagine that I think for one moment that a mission to Alexander has a good chance of succeeding? But even if I were convinced it was doomed to failure, I would attempt it all the same, since peace would be the best solution. And because it costs me nothing to try, just a little pride. And who baulks at that when one's fate is at stake?

HE RECEIVES JAKOVLEV, one of the few Russian aristocrats to have stayed in Moscow. The man is old. He confesses that he wanted to leave Moscow but could not carry out his plan. He speaks perfect, elegant French. He knew Marshal Mortier in Paris when he was there.

'I am not making war on Russia,' Napoleon begins, 'but on England. So why the vandalism of a Rostopchin?'

He speaks at length, then suddenly breaks off.

'If I write one, would you take a letter and can I be sure that it will be given to Alexander? If so, I shall see you're given a pass, for yourself and all your family.'

Jakovlev nods.

'I'd gladly accept Your Majesty's offer, but it is difficult to vouch for the letter arriving.'

It makes little odds to me whether Jakovlev remains in Moscow or not. I have to take this chance of getting in contact with Alexander again.

He dictates a letter to the Tsar without pausing.

Monsieur my brother,

The beautiful and superb city of Moscow is no more. Rostopchin has had it burned. Four hundred incendiaries have been arrested in the act; all have declared that they were setting fire to it on the orders of this governor and the minister of police; they have been shot. The fire seems finally to have stopped. Three quarters of the houses have burned down, a quarter remain.

This conduct is atrocious and without purpose. Is its aim to deprive us of some supplies? But these supplies were in the cellars that the fire could not reach. Beside, how can one destroy one of the most beautiful towns in the world and the work of centuries for such a paltry end? If I supposed that such such things were done on the orders of Your Majesty, I would not be writing him this letter, but I consider it impossible that, with your principles, your heart, the correctness of your ideas, you would have authorized such excesses unworthy of a great sovereign and a great nation.

One must always, when one cannot crush an enemy completely, leave him the possibility of fleeing and saving face, so that instead of being compelled to fight to the death, he agrees to negotiate.

I must hold out my hand to Alexander, whatever sort of man he is – which, as I have said so many times, and know for a fact, is a false one.

Napoleon resumes:

I have waged war on Your Majesty without animosity; a word from you would have stopped my march before or after the last battle, and I should have even wished to sacrifice the advantage of entering Moscow.

If Your Majesty retains some part of your former feelings, you will take this letter in good part. At any rate, you can only be grateful to me for having informed you of what is happening in Moscow.

I HAVE DONE what I had to without illusions, but without hesitation either. Now to work, day and night.

The couriers arrive with the portfolio from Paris, the parcel of letters from Warsaw and that from Vilna. Nothing's going right in Spain any more. Wellington entered Madrid on 12 August. The Austrians and Prussians, at news of the slightest reverse here, would turn into 'our most dangerous enemies'.

Bernadotte, that Judas, signed a treaty of alliance with Alexander on 30 August – against me! What does he hope? That the Tsar and the English will put him in charge of France? That jealous maniac is perfectly capable of imagining that. Haven't I become, as Madame de Staël from her refuge in Stockholm says, 'the enemy of the human race'? And she is there organizing, so our spies say, the crusade of the 'free world' against me! With this Russia where peasants are sold at auction like slaves in ancient Rome!

There you have my enemies.

And my only resources are my will, my mind, my work.

He dictates dispatches and decrees, sometimes all night.

Nothing must escape my authority.

On 15 October 1812 he finalizes a decree concerning the organization of the Comédie Française. For a few minutes, as he talks, he forgets where he is, in this Kremlin on which, on 13 October, the first snow has fallen.

'Actors are grouped in companies, and the production of receipts is divided in twenty-four parts . . .'

He finishes dictating the decree, then goes over to the window. It is beautiful, the weather as fine as at Fontainebleau. He would like to think that this will last, that Caulaincourt was exaggerating in his description of the climate yesterday. But snow fell the day before yesterday.

'Let us make haste,' he says. 'In twenty-four days we must be in our winter quarters.'

HE GOES DOWN into the courtyard of the Kremlin to preside over the parade, as he does every day. Then work, again.

He wants the wounded to be evacuated to Smolensk. From there they will be moved to Vilna, then France, escorted by NCOs who, once back in their barracks, will train the newly conscripted recruits. An inventory must be made of all vehicles, the units reorganized. Every evening he receives the marshals and generals. They listen to an Italian singer, Tarquinio, a soprano, who has been forced with his troop to stay in Moscow. The fire and looting have made them destitute.

He gives instructions for them to be given assistance, but he quickly stops the performance. It is not the time for songs. He questions the officers. Caulaincourt explains that for the first time relays and couriers from Paris have been attacked. The daily link with the capital of the Empire is no longer secure.

This is the most serious news.

He listens to Murat, who is still parleying with the Cossacks and seems like the crow in the fable, faced with foxes.

'These talks have no aim but to terrify the army about their isolation from France, the climate and the winter,' says Napoleon.

Murat is taken in by them.

'Those people don't want to negotiate. Kutusov is civil; he'd like to be done with this, but Alexander doesn't; he is stubborn,' continues the Emperor.

He studies the maps. If they leave Moscow, they will march south first. The corps must make biscuits for two weeks. All vehicles without horses must be brought to the Kremlin.

HE HAS MADE his decision. Now it just has to be put into practice. The time of departure must be kept secret until the last moment.

On Sunday, 18 October 1812 at midday, in the courtyard of the Kremlin, he is reviewing III Corps, Marshal Ney's. It is beautiful. The band is playing a merry air. Suddenly an aide-de-camp races up. It is M. De Béranger, an officer serving under Murat, who announces that the Russians have attacked at Vinkovo.

Napoleon listens to the report. The French bivouacs have been taken by surprise. The Russians have taken twelve cannon. Only a charge by Murat enabled them to be repulsed.

'I have to see everything with my own eyes,' bursts out Napoleon. Without Murat's presence of mind and courage, everything would have been captured and his position compromised. But I cannot rely on him. He trusts too much in his own bravery and relies on his generals, who are negligent. At all events, we must expunge the affront of being taken by surprise like this. People in France mustn't say that a reverse has forced us to withdraw.

He leaps down from his horse, goes back inside the palace.

'What stupidity by Murat! No one was on guard. This upsets all my plans. It spoils everything.'

HE REMAINS ON his own. It is no longer time to wait. Tomorrow he is leaving Moscow.

He should write something to Marie Louise – peaceful, reassuring.

My good Louise,
I write to you just as I am about to mount to go and inspect my advance posts. It is hot here, very beautiful sunshine, as fine as it can be in Paris in September. We have not had any cold yet. We have not yet experienced the rigours of the northern climate.
My intention is soon to take up my winter quarters and I hope to be able to have you come to Poland so I can see you. Kiss the little king for me twice and never doubt the feelings of your tender husband,
Nap

IT IS SEVEN in the morning, on Monday 19 October. He goes up to General Rapp, who seems concerned.

Does he think I'm not? I look at these thousands of carriages full of loot – pictures, vases, furs, relics, furniture, barrels. Is this my army? And these 100,000 men, apart from the Guard, are they still

*soldiers exactly, weighed down with flasks and packs full of their
booty, their bodies swathed in ill-assorted clothes?*

What can I demand of these men?

He cheerfully remarks to Rapp, 'Well then, Rapp, we are
going to withdraw on Poland. I will take up good winter quarters.
I hope Alexander will make peace.'

'The inhabitants predict a hard winter,' says Rapp.

Napoleon walks away.

'Bah, enough of your inhabitants!' he calls out. 'Look how
beautiful it is!'

HE JOINS MARSHAL BERTHIER.

He demands in a harsh voice that every vehicle takes two
wounded. 'Any vehicle found on the road without wounded will
be burnt. The vehicles must be numbered, under penalty of
confiscation.'

Berthier murmurs that there may be between 20,000, 30,000,
perhaps 40,000?

He doesn't reply. He dictates a new order to be transmitted to
Marshal Mortier, who is to stay in the Kremlin with 10,000 men
after having evacuated the crippled and wounded.

'On the twenty-third of October, at two in the morning,
Marshal Mortier will set fire to the Kremlin palace.'

He looks at Berthier, then starts dictating again as he walks.

'When the fire has taken in several parts of the Kremlin,
Marshal Mortier, Duke of Treviso, will start on the Mojaisk road.
At four, the officer of artillery given this mission will blow up the
Kremlin. On the road he will burn all the vehicles left behind,
and do as much as he can to bury all the corpses and smash all
the muskets he can find.'

There.

The Guard swings into motion.

He takes his place in the middle of them, straight-backed in
the saddle.

It is nine in the morning, on this Monday, 19 October 1812.

He is leaving Moscow.

VI

HE LOOKS FAR AHEAD. He'd rather not see what he can't avoid seeing at the side of the road, grenadiers of his Guard who have already come to a halt. They have only been marching for a few hours. They are searching through their packs, jettisoning things that are too heavy. The mud banks are already covered with books with gilt bindings, statuettes, dresses and carpets.

He mustn't let anything show of what he feels: his anxiety, rage, uncertainty.

Yet it all gnaws away at him. Has he been right to take the southern road towards Kaluga in order to inflict a defeat on Kutusov? And where is the Russian commander-in-chief? All they see from time to time, looming out of the fog, are Cossacks who fire a few rounds, wield their lances and then scatter like a swarm of flies when the squadrons of the Guard charge. But each time they kill or wound a few men who are left lying on the ground.

Should they get to Smolensk as soon as possible, where there are magazines full of supplies? The army needs everything: bread, munitions, shoes, uniforms, shredded linen for the wounded.

What if the depots are empty, because the supply commissaries are incompetents and brigands?

And what if the Russian troops coming up from the south, under Generals Tormassov and Tchitchakov, join up with those commanded by Wittgenstein coming down from the north? I would be surrounded, trapped in Russia as all of Europe, my Europe, rose up!

But I have to remain impassive, pay no attention to these carriages already tipped over on the side of the road, these artillery caissons bogged down because the ground is like glue, the fact that the short cut I have chosen to get to Kaluga and so evade Kutusov's reconnaissance missions is narrow and riddled with potholes.

And after long freezing fogs in the morning and rain during the day, there's the cold as night falls.

THE ROOMS IN the Troitskoye palace, the first halt for a few hours, then at Fominskoye and in a house in Borovsk, the following stages, are dirty, freezing and damp. Napoleon gives orders that any carriages that can't move be burned. He sees soldiers cutting up their horses. Some grenadiers plunge their arms, even their heads, into the animals' open stomachs to find the livers, searching through the entrails. Others fill buckets with the blood, which they drink still warm.

He can't fail to see this, or the anxiety on the faces of Caulaincourt, Rapp, Berthier, Eugène and Lauriston. They surround him, with questioning looks in their eyes.

He takes Caulaincourt by the arm.

'I see it will be indispensable for me to get closer to my reserves,' he says. 'I may drive off Kutusov and make him evacuate Kaluga and its entrenchments, but the Cossacks will still hamper my communications.'

Caulaincourt agrees and, in a distorted voice, starts talking about the weather that's going to turn, the coming snow and cold, the movements of peasants and partisans all the couriers report when they arrive. The whole country as far as the border of the Grand Duchy of Warsaw is rising up. They can't forage safely any more. Couriers are attacked. Isolated soldiers are killed. Rumours are spreading: the peasants impale their prisoners or throw them into vats of boiling water and oil.

He mustn't reply or let any of his feelings show. He simply says, 'We shall be without news of France, but more vexing is that in France they will be without news of us.'

There must be the greatest circumspection in what they write, he requests. Any letter might be seized.

He writes to Marie Louise with this in mind.

My good friend,
    My health is good, my affairs are going well. I have abandoned Moscow after blowing up the Kremlin. I needed 20,000 men to guard the town. Destroyed as it was, it hampered my operations. The weather is very fine.
    I share your desire to see an end of all this; you shouldn't doubt how happy I will be to embrace you.

Kiss the little king from me; write to your father that I beg him to think of Schwarzenberg: have him supported by the corps from Galicia and reinforce him. When you write to the Empress, show me on bended knee before her.

Farewell, my friend. You know how much I think of you.

Ever yours,

Nap

He hears the cannon. He immediately goes out. There's fighting around Maloyaroslavets, to the south. He rides towards it, listens to the scouts' reports. Marshal Davout and Eugène de Beauharnais have been attacked by General Doctorov, at the head of Kutusov's advance guard. They saw them off, took a few prisoners, but the Cossacks are everywhere, harassing the troops.

Napoleon returns to Borovsk. He questions an officer prisoner. The man has a victor's calm. The Emperor Alexander has announced, he repeats, 'This is when my campaign begins.'

The man doesn't answer any question concerning Kutusov's movements. Are the Russians falling back after having been defeated at Maloyaroslavets? How is one to pursue them with an army whose men and horses are exhausted?

Napoleon cannot stay still. He marches about the room, studies the maps, then goes out into the doorway. The night is grey with fog; one cannot see more than a few feet in front of one.

'This is becoming serious,' he murmurs. 'I always beat the Russians, but that doesn't end anything.'

He falls silent as he walks around the tiny, rank-smelling little room, then suddenly he grabs his hat.

'I am going to see for myself if the enemy has taken up positions or is, as everything suggests, retreating. That devil Kutusov won't join battle. Bring up my horses; let's go.'

He bumps into Berthier, who is blocking his way. It's not dawn yet, the marshal says. They don't know the position of the different units. The Cossacks can appear at any moment.

One of Eugène's aides-de-camp arrives and confirms Kutusov's troops are retreating. Napoleon listens, waits a few minutes. But he cannot stay in that smoky room. He wants to act. He mounts his horse without worrying about who's following.

HE IS RIDING when suddenly some riders burst out of the fog, yelling, and surround his escort and aides-de-camp. He hears Rapp shout, 'Stop, sire, these are Cossacks!'

'Take the picket's chasseurs and get forward,' Napoleon cries.

He looks around. Berthier and Caulaincourt are on either side of him, their swords drawn. He draws his own.

They fight in front of him. He hears the clash of swords, shouts, the Cossacks' hurrahs. Eventually the squadrons of the Guard arrive, just as the fog is lifting. Then he sees thousands of Cossacks in the plain, probably Platov's, who have attacked the Guard's bivouacs and artillery park and taken prisoners and guns. They must have emerged from the groves of trees that here and there form dark clumps on the plain.

He must be serene, cheerful even. He laughs and jokes with Lauriston and Rapp. He senses the grenadiers looking, not taking their eyes off him.

He must appear heroic and invulnerable.

'Long live the Emperor,' they shout. But the voices quickly die away. He makes his way back slowly through the camps. The men squat round their fires, hunched over — turned inwards, he senses. Indifferent to one another, enemies even. Isolated by the mounting cold and tormenting hunger. He sends for Dr Yvan, the doctor of the Guard who has served him for years.

He looks at him fixedly. He wants, he says, turning his back on Yvan, a phial of a powerful poison. He wants to carry it on him. He mustn't run the risk of being taken prisoner.

He turns to face Yvan, who is stammering. He says it's an order to be carried out immediately.

It is Sunday, 25 October 1812. He has almost been killed or captured. But destiny has left him alive. Onward march, then.

He gives the signal to set off. He has made his decision. They will get to Smolensk as quickly as possible. They're giving up the southern road and picking the Mojaisk, Borodino and Viasma road again instead.

THERE'S A FROST at night now but the days are still merely grey. He rides in the middle of the Guard, then gets into his coach, then walks for hours with the soldiers, like a soldier, leaning on

Caulaincourt or Berthier's arm or steadying himself with a big stick.

He sees it all.

The dead on the slopes and the road, the wounded abandoned, the broken carriages that he orders to be set on fire.

Suddenly he recognizes the plateaux with the earth still ploughed up, the ravines out of which thousands of crows flick into the air. The ground is covered with debris and dead. Arms stick out of the ground; horses' carcasses rot. The rain has left the ground waterlogged and the buried corpses have been partly exposed. This is the village of Borodino.

It is barely fifty-two days since the battle of the Moskva was fought.

He wants the army to quicken its pace. Every soldier walking through these rotting corpses is a man losing his energy, a man succumbing to despair. He looks at Caulaincourt. His brother is down there too. He hears a murmur starting up among the men. He wants to know the cause. They say a French grenadier has been found with both his legs blown off but still alive: he's probably been sheltering in horses' carcasses and eating their flesh.

They have to block everything out; they have to push on.

He turns around. The column stretches for as far as the eye can see. The carriages are jolting about, toppling over, burning, the soldiers looting them whenever they can. As they pass an abbey moans can be heard: wounded that have been there since the battle.

He stops and orders that the wounded be loaded onto the Guard and Emperor's household coaches.

He sets off again. He hears shouts. The coach drivers are whipping up their horses so that the wounded they've been forced to pick up will be thrown off into the road by the jolting.

He turns his head away and murmurs, 'The army isn't a fine sight today.'

But he has to know. Ignorance is no use for anything. He leaves the road, goes up onto a hill. He wants to watch the troops and convoys passing. How many men does he still have? There were 100,000 when they left Moscow. Ten days later there may be only half left.

A MAN WITH an insolent expression is pushed in front of him: Count de Wintzingerode, an aide-de-camp of Alexander who has been caught dressed in a civilian coat at the gates of Moscow inciting French soldiers to desert.

What, a man born in Würtémberg, a French subject, putting himself at the service of the highest bidder, a secret agent, a spy – not a soldier, a military agitator. A traitor, Napoleon yells. He cannot contain himself any longer. All the rage that is in him, that has been growing every time he looks at the road, the soldiers, the wounded and the dead, now explodes. This man should be shot.

He looks at Caulaincourt, Berthier and Murat.

They condemn me.

He calls the gendarmes himself.

'As you wish, sire,' says Wintzingerode, 'but never as a traitor.'

Napoleon kicks the frozen ground. He looks up and sees a castle a little way from the road. The building is big and beautiful. He orders two squadrons of the Guard to go and forage there and then set fire to it.

'Since these barbarian gentlemen see fit to burn their cities, we should help them,' he cries.

HE CALMS DOWN suddenly. Flames envelop the chateau. He returns to the road. He will not have this Wintzingerode shot. He goes up to Caulaincourt, pulls his ear.

'Is it because of Alexander that you take such an interest in him? Come now, we won't do him any harm.'

He slaps the grand equerry's cheek.

He stands in his stirrups. Ahead, the fields are white. Snow has fallen. The cold is going to enfold what's left of the army, and the snow is going to shroud it.

He leans towards Caulaincourt, and asks what he thinks.

'Our retreat will have set everybody against us,' the grand equerry says.

In Russia, Austria, Prussia.

'And the cold,' Caulaincourt goes on, 'is going to bring great hardship.'

He listens. *We must move faster, outrun the cold, reach Smolensk and cross the Berezina, the Dnieper's tributary, before the Russian troops from the north and south join up and pull the trap shut. Then the army will be able to reform in Vilna or behind the Niemen.*

At which point perhaps he'll be able to return to Paris after putting the army in its winter quarters.

He must start to raise this as a possibility. Because he cannot stay here, buried under the snow, when the Empire might be in danger.

He thinks of his departure from Egypt.

One must know how to choose.

THERE'S A FROST on Sunday, 1 November 1812. He writes a few words to Marie Louise: 'I am moving closer to Poland to establish my winter quarters there. That'll mean a hundred leagues less between us. My health is perfect, my affairs go well.'

That's what he must say and write.

Who can imagine, apart from those who are at my side, what is happening here?

Even the best units are breaking up; it's every man for himself, and yet they still have to fight. Marshal Ney must take command of the rearguard. These Cossacks are like the Arabs. They have to march as they did in Egypt, with the baggage in the centre and fixed bayonets forming a wall.

But I see those muskets that have been thrown on the ground because the soldiers' hands freeze on the metal.

The first flurries of snow have begun, and the temperature has fallen to freezing.

I see the men lying on the side of the road, the ones who have toppled, asphyxiated, into fires because they've got too close to the flames, and all the wounded who've been abandoned and, among the scattered loot, seem to form a long, black trail.

ON 6 NOVEMBER 1812 Napoleon reaches Mikhaeliska, a village of little, half-destroyed houses already full of men, the ones who've been keeping ahead of the advance guard to find shelter and to loot any supplies before the main column arrives.

Snow is falling in big flakes and at the same time there's a thick fog. The sky seems to have disappeared.

Suddenly, just as he is entering a hovel, a trooper appears, pushing through the crowd of soldiers, slipping between the carriages. It is a courier. He hears him shout, 'The Emperor! The Emperor!' The man finally gets to him and gives him a portfolio full of dispatches.

Correspondence from Paris. Napoleon starts to read.

He mustn't wince; he mustn't let his face show anything.

On the night of 22 and 23 October, General Malet, who had been imprisoned in 1808 for a Republican conspiracy and put in a mental asylum, escaped. Claiming that the Emperor was dead in Russia, he requisitioned a cohort of the National Guard. He presented a forged *senatus consultum*, declaring the fall of the Imperial regime and the establishment of a provisional government with General Moreau as president and him, Malet, as representative. With his accomplices, General Lahorie, former head of Moreau's staff, Guidal, a friend of Barras who is conspiring with the English in the south of France, a marquis and an abbé, they managed to arrest Savary, the minister of police, and Pasquier, the chief of police. Luckily the military commandant Hulin challenged the conspirators and his deputies arrested them; they were tried and shot on 29 October.

Napoleon looks up. He had thought the Empire was weakened by his absence from Paris. But that ministers, that Frochot – the prefect of the Seine, who had allocated a room in the town hall to Malet's provisional government – should have let themselves be gulled like this, revolts and astonishes him.

He reads Savary's summing-up assuring him that Paris didn't even notice the event, that order was restored by ten in the morning.

He passes the letters to Caulaincourt, then starts to walk about in front of the fire that has been lit on the beaten earth floor and whose smoke is filling the room.

'The news of my death,' he says, 'made everyone lose their heads. The minister of war, who always vaunts his devotion to me, didn't even put on his boots to run to the barracks, make them swear an oath to the King of Rome and haul Savary out of prison. Only Hulin had any courage.'

He kicks the logs, sending sparks flying into the air. The flames spring back up, fiercer.

'The prefect and the colonels' conduct is incomprehensible,' he continues. 'How can you put your trust in men whose earliest education does not guarantee feelings of honour and loyalty. The weakness and ingratitude of the prefect and the colonel of the Paris regiment, one of my old comrades whose fortune I have made, fills me with indignation.'

He goes outside. The snow flakes are bigger and falling faster. Everything is covered. Men stagger past. His face is stung by the cold.

And the people who betray him are in Paris, in the warmth of their gold-encrusted palaces.

'I cannot believe this cowardice!' he cries.

He starts walking. He wants to leave this village, get to Smolensk as quickly as possible. Perhaps he will be able to get the army into order there. And then, if it can fend for itself, he will leave to return to Paris, restore order and be at the heart of the Empire once again.

'With the French,' he says, 'it's like women: one mustn't be away for long periods. You never really know what intriguers will be able to persuade people to believe and what will happen if they don't have any news of me for a while.'

He marches along among a pack of isolated soldiers. The slopes are covered with dead and wounded. Men are gathered around a horse that is still moving as they start to cut it up. Its belly is torn open. A woman has plunged her arm in to pull out the heart or liver.

He cannot accept the prospect of being surrounded and completely cut off from all contact with Paris.

'That's what might happen if the Russians have any common sense,' he says.

An aide approaches. Viceroy Eugène, he explains, has had to abandon Vitebsk. The artillery is lost. Shoeless and exhausted, the horses have not been able to pull the cannon on the black ice.

So, Wittgenstein's troops have occupied Vitebsk. And, to the south, Tchitchakov's troops must be only thirty or so leagues away. If we don't get through before they join up, we'll be trapped. We must prevent that.

He takes shelter in Pnevo castle, as icy as a windswept square. He dictates a dispatch to Marshal Victor, ordering him to counter-attack Wittgenstein's troops.

> In a few days, your rear may be overwhelmed with Cossacks: the army and the Emperor will be in Smolensk tomorrow, but worn out by a march of 120 leagues without stopping. Assume the offensive; the army's safety depends on it. Every day's delay is a calamity. The cavalry are on foot; cold has killed all the horses. March, this is the order of the Emperor and a matter of necessity.

NOT GIVE IN. Fight.

All the officers still with mounts are to form up in a special squadron. The generals will serve as captains, the colonels as subalterns.

Fight. *Write then, to prove to everyone watching that I am alive.* A courier is going to leave and try to get to Paris.

He writes to Marie Louise:

> My friend,
>   I am angry that the minister of war sent an aide-de-camp to inform you about that affair of the blackguards who tried to assassinate Hulin. I'm afraid that would have upset you, even though I know your firmness of character.
>   As you can see, I am drawing closer. Tomorrow I will be in Smolensk, that's to say over a hundred leagues nearer to Paris. The weather is starting to break; snow's coming. I read your letters with as much pleasure as you can have reading mine.
> I hope I will soon hear from you that my son has his first teeth and has recovered his good humour.
>   Farewell, my good Louise. Kiss my son twice and, most of all, never doubt all the love I feel for you. Ever yours,
>   Nap
>   7 November, at one in the morning.

Outside, death everywhere.

He starts marching again. Then the sun lights up the sky and he sees Smolensk's spires glinting in the distance.

ON MONDAY 9 November he enters Smolensk. The army must regroup here.

He tours the town, where the destruction wrought by the battle in August is still everywhere, and, like then, the streets are full of dead. But these are no longer Russians. They are his exhausted soldiers who lie here dying; they're men who have fought each other to break into the supply warehouses and strip them; they're men who have been killed by looters. He catches sight of the looters sometimes, coming out of the cellars where they've holed up and which no one dares go into; you would be risking your life.

He takes quarters in one of the few undamaged houses. But how can he rest? The Russians have attacked in the north. General Augereau has capitulated in Ljachewo. He must move westwards quickly, try to cross the Berezina and reach less devastated country, milder conditions.

Here everything freezes. The temperature is minus twenty-five degrees.

One of Kutusov's proclamations, found on a dead Russian soldier, is brought to him. It is dated 31 October. He reads it. 'Let us hasten to pursue this impious enemy . . . Extinguish the flames of Moscow with the blood of your enemy. Russians, obey this solemn order. Then, appeased by this just vengeance, your fatherland will withdraw satisfied from the theatre of war and, behind its vast frontiers, it will adopt a majestic attitude between peace and glory. Russians warriors, God is your guide!'

Does God give the Russian peasants permission to boil French soldiers? But indignation does nothing. They must fight and get through.

EVERY DAY HE inspects the environs of Smolensk. Everywhere there are dead, burning carriages, horses cut to pieces, men bartering with one another, exchanging the jewels they have stolen for a bottle of brandy.

He inspects those depots that still contain some supplies. They must set aside flour for Ney's rearguard when it reaches Smolensk.

But they can't wait for Ney.

On Saturday, 14 November 1812, at eight thirty, Napoleon gets ready to leave Smolensk.

Before leaving his room, he writes, while standing up, a note to Marie Louise.

My good friend,

I have received your letter of the 30th. I see that you have visited the salon. Tell me what you think; you must be a connoisseur since you do not paint badly yourself.

The cold here is quite keen, eight degrees. It's a little early in the morning. My health is extremely good. Kiss my son; tell me that he has his first teeth.

Addio, mio bene,
Nap

VII

HE PLUNGES HIS BATON furiously into the snow covering the road that leads out of Smolensk. He will not let himself be stopped; he will not let himself be imprisoned here, on this exposed plain swept by the northern wind. He will not fall like these men he sees staggering along in front of him, who veer off the road and collapse on the banks. He will break through the noose that the Russian troops are trying to tighten around him. He will not let himself be cut to pieces like these horses who hold up their heads as they are disembowelled. Never.

He feels like a block of ice.

The wind steals through his velvet cap and the black fox skin over it. The wind scatters the skirts of his fur-lined greatcoat, even though he has secured it at the waist with a thick belt. The wind turns everything to ice: limbs, faces, emotions. He doesn't want to feel anything. Every moment, Caulaincourt or Murat or Duroc or Berthier or Mouton, who are marching at his side, pass on another piece of bad news.

Leaving Smolensk, the Cossacks attacked and pillaged the convoy that contained the trophies from Moscow, the huge Ivan Veliki cross from the Kremlin that I wanted to go to the Invalides. They've taken the map caisson too! So I haven't got any maps any more. But I am still marching.

He raises his head. In front of him he sees some cavalry of the Guard and a few generals, some of whom are still on horseback. That's what's left of the special squadron. It has only taken three days for it to be reduced to this handful of men. He turns round. Between 700 and 800 officers and subalterns are marching behind him, in good order and complete silence, carrying the eagles of the regiments they belonged to. Behind them comes the Imperial Guard.

And then what remains of the regiments, a handful of men in each. Some units like Davout's are intact, marching in this throng of stragglers, looters, roasters, men whose only thought is to grab a bit of flesh from the horses and find somewhere to bivouac. Men who are no more than wild animals, not soldiers.

How many men are there around me now, trying to escape the snow, the Cossacks and the Russians? Thirty thousand? Fifty thousand probably, with Marshal Victor and Oudinot's corps which are on the Berezina where we must cross the river at Borisov. Because there is a bridge there.

He mounts. The Russians are in Krasnoe, on the road that, via Orsha, Tolotchino and Krupki, leads to Borisov.

HE HEARS SHOTS. There's fighting at Krasnoe. They must get through. The Russians are beaten aside in hand-to-hand combat. *I am through.* The screams of the wounded rise up from the houses in Krasnoe where they have been abandoned.

Now there's a hill to be climbed. The last of the horses lose their footing and keel over, taking their riders with them. No one can push the few guns they still have left to the top. They're abandoned, burnt.

The ground is like an ice mirror. On the other side of the hill they have to let themselves slide, because no one can keep upright on that black ice. But they have to push on.

I'll crawl if I have to.

It is Thursday, 19 November 1812. Where is Marshal Ney? Has he got to Smolensk with the rearguard he is commanding? Has he been caught, killed? Or has he managed to escape the Russians, cross the Dnieper?

'I would give the three hundred millions in gold in my cellars in the Tuileries to save that man!' Napoleon exclaims.

He falls silent. He paces back and forth through the rooms of a Jesuit convent near Orsha where he is spending a few hours. Everything is frozen. The wind carries gusts of snow as sharp as knives.

From time to time men stagger into the convent and collapse by the fire. The Cossacks are everywhere. Any stragglers the peasants get their hands on, they strip, then slit their throats or torture them.

He listens impassively.

The Russians are in Borisov, someone calls out. Wittgenstein and Tchitchakov's armies have almost joined up. Tchitchakov's soldiers are occupying Borisov, holding the only bridge over the Berezina. Kutusov and Tormassov's troops have also got within a few leagues of the river.

He doesn't move.

The trap is closing.

In a muffled voice, his head bowed, he says that all his papers must be burnt.

Then he straightens up.

'This is becoming serious,' he tells Caulaincourt.

He stares at him. They hear shouting. Ney has managed to get through. He is coming to join the Emperor with several thousand men formed up in squares, someone yells.

'Forward march!' says Napoleon. 'We have waited too long.'

If Ney has managed to extricate himself, how can I fail to?

OUTSIDE IT IS still dark. But the days are so short, a few hours barely, that they can't see when night starts and finishes any more.

He orders what's left of the grenadiers, chasseurs and Guard to form up in a square. In these men he still has a resolute force.

He goes into their midst. He looks fixedly at each of them. He recognizes some of his veterans. Their faces are black; chips of ice hang in their beards.

I have been marching for days in their midst. My marshals, my generals march with me. And not a voice is raised against us. We are united.

He grips the guard of his sword.

He starts to speak, raising his voice so that it can be heard over the wind. His lips are frozen hard. The temperature must be minus twenty-five.

'We have the elements against us,' he says, 'this premature, rigorous winter none of us could have foreseen.'

The Russians are waiting for us on the Berezina. They have sworn that not a single one of us will get back across that river.

He draws his sword, brandishes it. His voice booms louder.

'Let us now in turn swear that we shall rather die, sword in hand, than not see France again.'

They yell, 'Long live the Emperor!' They raise their caps and hats on the tips of their sabres and muskets.

We will get through.

HE CALLS BACLER D'ALBE. They only have a single map, but Bacler d'Albe can remember the details. They must look for a ford in the Berezina, since the Russians hold Borisov and the only bridge. Unless, that is, Oudinot's men retake the town. This is the order to give him. The army's safety depends on it. What's left of the army; over 30,000 horses have perished. Three hundred cannon have been destroyed. The regiments have been reduced to a few men. Cold and hunger are killing them. The Cossacks have severed all communications.

'It is two weeks since I received any news, any courier,' he says, 'and I am in the dark about everything.'

I only know one thing: we must get through. We will get through.

First he must reassure the others. He hears Count Daru and Grand Marshal Duroc chatting in low voices as he drowses in a smoky room in the monastery at Tolotchino.

What are they saying?

'We were thinking of a balloon,' Daru explains. 'To take away Your Majesty.'

'My word, the position is tricky. So you're afraid of being prisoners of war, are you?' he asks.

'Not of war,' Duroc replies. 'They won't give Your Majesty such a good ending.'

He brings his hand to his chest and feels the sachet of poison which Dr Yvan has given him. But this is not the moment to die.

'Matters are serious, it's true,' he carries on, getting to his feet. 'It's becoming complicated. Kutusov is close; Minsk has fallen. Yet if the commanders set an example, I am stronger than the enemy.'

He holds out his arms so that Constant can put on his fur-lined greatcoat.

'I have the means, more than I need, in fact,' he continues, 'to get through the Russians if their troops are the only obstacle.'

On Wednesday, 25 November 1812 he learns that Marshal Oudinot's troops have driven the Russians out of Borisov.

He sets off immediately. The cold, suddenly, is less bitter. In the distance he sees the Berezina, which is a hundred metres or so wide, in full spate and carrying blocks of ice. A few hours ago they could have crossed the frozen river, as Ney crossed the Dnieper. Now they need a ford, a bridge.

The Russians have burnt the one in Borisov.

In the distance, in the fog, he makes out the silhouettes of Cossacks. He hears their hurrahs; he sees them falling on scattered groups, looting coaches.

They must get through, quickly, before Kutuzov arrives or Wittgenstein and Tchitchakov attack. So they must build a bridge, several bridges. He grows impatient. The army, like a routed mob, is gradually piling up on the left bank of the Berezina. Destiny is measured out in hours – minutes – here and not in days and weeks.

He paces along the river bank. He looks at the flowing water that could have been, should have been, frozen over.

It will be said that none of the elements favoured me.

He walks onto the burnt bridge. He stops at the edge. The blackened beams hang in the water. Can destiny come to a standstill here? He recognizes General Corbineau, who served in Spain for a long time and who has just thrown back Wittgenstein's troops with his division. Corbineau comes up to him. He knows a ford in the Berezina, he explains. He has just crossed it. At that point the river is hundred metres broad, the bottom only two metres. A peasant they have arrested has revealed the crossing opposite the village of Studienka.

Suddenly Napoleon remembers. It was there, on 29 June 1708, that the King of Sweden Charles XII crossed the Berezina, after his campaign in the Ukraine.

Such is destiny.

He gallops towards the ford. They must throw over two bridges, one for the infantry, the other for the artillery. He feels he is going to manage to escape the trap, that he won't get himself surrounded by four Russian armies.

But this is the decisive moment, the one when all his energy must be concentrated on the action he has been considering for days.

They must, he says, mislead the Russians: bear down on Borisov, make them think the army is going to cross there and in the meantime build the bridges.

He sends for General Éblé.

I know this old officer, originally an artilleryman like me, now in command of the pontoon train of the Grand Army. He has distinguished himself in Germany and Portugal. Jérome had appointed him minister of war in his kingdom of Westphalia, but he preferred to join the Grand Army. I saw him in action during the attack on Smolensk.

Everything now depends on him and his men. The water is freezing. Napoleon knows. The engineers are hungry. But they must build these bridges. They have the fate of what's left of the Grand Army in their hands.

He reviews them. They are still soldiers.

He sees them start to work, plunging into the river, skidding around on little rafts, arms in the water as they hammer in the piles and trestles.

He stays on the bridge all day, talking to them, handing out wine in person. At two in the afternoon, Thursday, 26 November 1812, the first bridge is finished.

Napoleon stands at the head of the bridge. Oudinot's men, who are still in military formation, have to cross first. They shout, 'Long live the Emperor!' They are going to drive Tchitchakov's Russians back on the right bank to allow the others to cross. Davout's corps crosses, band leading. Marshal Victor must remain on this bank to hold off Kutusov, and General Partouneaux's division must sacrifice itself at Borisov to stop Wittgenstein advancing on Studienka.

NAPOLEON IS CALM. He will not be taken prisoner. He stays at the head of the bridge as, on that Friday, 27 November 1812, the Guard crosses to the right bank.

He sees Marshal Lefebvre's carriage coming but inside he recognizes a woman, the French actress Louise Fusil, who did not want to stay in Moscow where she lived.

'Don't be afraid,' he says in a composed voice, 'come now, don't be afraid.'

But he knows everything can change in a matter of minutes.

The bridge on which the artillery is crossing has already broken, been repaired, then broken again and been repaired again. The Russians are attacking; they're about to bombard the bridges. These 15,000 stragglers and isolated soldiers and scavengers are in no hurry to cross, even when the bridges are clear, preferring to roast their bit of horsemeat and camp on the east bank. How will they ever manage to get across?

He sees the remains of the cavalry crossing the river near the bridge with an infantryman on the crupper of each horse.

He stays for a long while like that as night suddenly falls and the wind picks up. It's pitch black; the cold has never been as bitter, perhaps minus thirty. The Berezina is going to freeze again, and the Russians will cross even if the bridges are blown up.

He slowly withdraws and crosses to the west bank.

I have done my duty.

I have got the surviving soldiers out of Russia.

Now that what's left of the army has escaped the worst and crossed the river, I have other duties: to form another army and prepare for the next campaign.

He tells Caulaincourt, in a hut in Zapivski, half a league from the Berezina, 'In the present state of affairs, I can only impose myself on Europe from the Tuileries palace.'

He must return to Paris.

HE MUST NOT think of the Berezina's east bank any more, where the horde of stragglers and isolated soldiers and people who cannot take any more or didn't want to keep rank is going to rush the bridges. The Russian shells have started falling. He can hear them.

He doesn't want to hear them any more. He must look ahead, to Paris, to his departure.

In a few days, he will be able to communicate with Vilna, with Mainz, and with Paris again.

He writes to Marie Louise:

My good friend,

I know that fifteen couriers are waiting for me three days from here. So then I will find fifteen letters from you. I am very sad to think of how upset it will make you being without news of me for so long, but I know that in exceptional circumstances I can count on your courage and character. My health is perfect, the weather very bad and cold. Farewell, my sweet friend; kiss the little king twice from me. You know all the tenderness of your husband's feelings,

Nap

He cannot say anything else to the Empress for the moment. But he must impress public opinion so that rumours do not upset it, inflame it and lead it astray. And he will have to appear suddenly, like a saviour, gathering all energies around him.

He must prepare for that. Inform Maret, who is in Vilna, of the army's state. No equivocation with this minister, who must act!

'The army is numerous but scattered in an appalling manner. It will take two weeks to bring them back to their colours, and where will they get this two weeks? Cold and privation have broken this army. We will be making for Vilna. Will we be able to hold it? If we are attacked in the first eight days, it is doubtful we will be able to remain there. Provisions! Provisions! Provisions! Without those there are no horrors this undisciplined mass will not inflict on that town . . . If you cannot furnish us with 100,000 rations of bread in Vilna, I pity this town.'

HE WON'T BE there himself.

He must leave in the next few hours. But it must be a secret.

On Wednesday, 2 December 1812, he sends for one of his aides-de-camp, Anatole de Montesquiou. He likes this dedicated young man who fought well at Wagram and whose mother is the governess of the King of Rome. He hands him a letter. It is for the Empress.

'You will leave instantly for Paris. You will give this letter to the Empress.'

Napoleon shuffles round the tiny space that serves as his room. It is all that could be found in the small town of Sedlicz.

'You will announce the capture of ten thousand Russian prisoners and the victory of the Berezina, at which we took six thousand Russian prisoners, eight flags and twelve cannon.'

Napoleon is silent for a long time. It is Oudinot's, then Victor's troops, who gained this success. Victor's soldiers crossed the bridges last, clearing a path through the hordes of stragglers. Then Éblé, at nine in the morning on Sunday 29 November, set fire to the bridges. The Berezina was already washing down hundreds of corpses, and the Cossacks flooded onto the east bank, covered with dozens of thousands of abandoned men. That is how it is.

Now he asks Montesquiou to wait. He is going to dictate the 29th Bulletin of the Grand Army, which Montesquiou should give to Arch-Chancellor Cambacérès to have printed and published in the *Monitor*.

'I am going to say everything,' Napoleon murmurs. 'It's better they know the details from me than from private letters.'

He starts to dictate:

'The army's movement was at first perfectly executed, but then the cold suddenly increased: the roads were covered in black ice, more than thirty thousand horses died in a few days . . . We had to march on, in order to avoid a battle, which our lack of munitions made undesirable. The enemy, who saw on the roads the traces of the appalling calamity that had struck the French army, sought to take advantage. It enveloped all our columns with its Cossacks, that despicable cavalry that, like Arabs in the deserts, snapped up the trains and carts that strayed . . . Men whom nature has not formed firmly enough to be above the vagaries of fate and fortune seemed shaken, lost their merriment and good humour and only dreamt of misfortunes and catastrophes . . . The army needs to re-establish its discipline, repair itself, remount its cavalry . . . The Emperor has marched in the midst of his Guard throughout . . . Circumstances demanded that officers who still had a horse remaining were gathered together to form a special squadron, commanded by General Grouchy under the orders of the King of Naples. It never lost sight of the Emperor.'

He stops dictating for a few moments.

That is the past. Everyone must know that I am going to take all the Empire's affairs back in hand.

'His Majesty's health was never better,' he adds.

A few wretched madmen, like Malet, have announced my death. Some have believed them.

Here I am.

He hands the text of the bulletin to Montesquiou. The aide-de-camp must set off immediately with an escort.

He watches him ride off.

Montesquiou will arrive in Paris a few days before me. The newspapers will publish the 29th Bulletin of the Grand Army. People will be overwhelmed; they'll start talking. I will appear suddenly and everyone will regroup around me.

ON THURSDAY 3 December, in Molodetchna, the cold is so bitter that near the house where he is going to spend the night he sees blacksmiths with rags wrapped round their hands, because even standing over their forge their fingers may freeze while they're shoeing horses.

Fourteen couriers' dispatches are waiting for him. He goes through them quickly. France is calm. Public opinion has confidence in the Emperor. But he must get back to Paris quickly, before the wave of bad news, mourning and death breaks. He turns to Caulaincourt. His hand is resting on the Empress's letters.

'These difficult circumstances,' he says, 'shape her judgement and give her an aplomb and a thoughtfulness which will attach the nation to her. She is the wife I needed, sweet, good, loving, like all German women. She pays no mind to intrigues; she is an orderly soul and only concerns herself with me and her son.'

He bends down, and starts to write.

My good friend,

 I sent Anatole de Montesquiou to you yesterday, who will give you news of this country. I thought that you would be very pleased to see someone who can talk to you about what interests you. Here is the regular courier who is going to leave in an hour. I will reply to twenty of your letters, because I expect twenty couriers in an hour.

 Addio, mio bene,
  Your Nap

I mustn't say anything about my departure, my imminent arrival. I can't have any trouble travelling through Poland, Prussia and Germany, so I can fall on Paris like lightning.

78

He calls Berthier, that old comrade-in-arms, efficient chief of staff so often rudely handled but indispensable.

He is going to stay here at Murat's side, whom I appoint to command the army in my place.

Berthier starts crying. He has never left the Emperor, never, he repeats.

That is how it is. Murat will need him.

Napoleon assembles the marshals. Murat, Ney, Mortier, Davout, Lefebvre, Bessières. Berthier's face is pale; he sniffs and bows his head.

Caulaincourt crosses his arms.

They are all going to agree to me going, whatever they think.

They know that I am not going for base reasons. They have seen me facing the roundshot, in the midst of the Cossacks. They have accompanied me through the deserts and snow. They have seen me march and lie down like a soldier, and here, in this hamlet of Smorgoni on 5 December 1812, I have the same quarters as them, not much better than a grenadier.

I am not leaving to flee the war, to desert in the face of danger.

I may be accused of anything, except cowardice or lack of courage!

I am leaving to reform an army of 300,000 soldiers. It's not the Russian armies that have defeated us. We defeated them at the Moskva, Krasnoe and on the Berezina, just as we defeated them at Austerlitz, Eylau and Friedland. The cold, and the winter so premature and harsh that it even took the peasants by surprise, and inflicted heavy losses on the Russians — prisoners have confirmed that — only they forced us to retreat.

In spring, we will mount another campaign. A victorious one.

HE TAKES BERTHIER to one side.

'We will put it about that I have gone to Warsaw with the Austrian corps and VII Corps,' he murmurs. 'Five or six days later, depending on circumstances, the King of Naples will issue an order of the day informing the army that, having had to go to Paris, I have entrusted him with command.'

Then he calls in each of his aides and marshals in turn. Each has his mission. Lauriston to Warsaw, Rapp to Danzig. He looks at them hard. He doesn't want any trouble, any hesitation. He will monitor them from Paris.

Then he checks with Caulaincourt that everything is ready for their departure at ten in the evening, on this Saturday, 5 December 1812.

Caulaincourt will ride with Napoleon in a carriage drawn by the six finest horses in the Imperial stables. Count Wonsowicz, who will serve as interpreter, Roustam and two outriders will ride alongside the carriage.

He wants Grand Marshal Duroc, Count Lobau, a servant and a worker to come after in a barouche.

My secretary Baron Fain, Minister of State Daru, Dr Yvan, Constant my valet de chambre *and Bacler d'Albe will follow in another carriage. I will be escorted by 200 Guardsmen. The relays and horses must be prepared.*

It must be kept absolutely secret.

A few hours before leaving, on this Saturday 5 December, he writes to Marie Louise:

My friend,

I have received your letter of the 24th. I am very upset by all your anxieties and the fact these will last a fortnight; and yet my health has never been better. You will have seen from the bulletins that, without going as well as I would have wished, my affairs are not going badly at present.

The cold is very fierce. In a few days I will make a decision about your trip, so that we can see each other again soon. Be hopeful and do not concern yourself.

Addio, mio bene, ever yours,
    Nap

In a fortnight at the most, he will open the door of her room.

PART THREE

*I have made a great mistake,
but I shall have the means
to redeem it*

5 December 1812 to 15 April 1813

VIII

QUICK, QUICK, QUICK! He urges on Caulaincourt, who is sitting next to him. He urges on the postilions. Now the carriage is moving, he would like it already to be under the porch of the Tuileries and for him only to have to climb the steps. Quick! What are these horses doing? Why are these postmasters taking so long? He pushes Caulaincourt out, and then follows. But he stumbles immediately. Furs cramp his movements. He wears fur boots, a fur-lined coat and gloves, and a cap pulled down over his eyes and ears. But he is still cold. He shivers. He looks at the riders in the escort, who are having trouble: their horses are slipping on the sheet ice; their legs tremble. The cavalrymen's arms and legs are frozen. What temperature is it? Minus twenty, minus thirty? Caulaincourt's face is dotted with little bits of ice – under his nose, on his eyelashes, around his eyelids.

Quick, quick, quick.

THEIR FIRST RELAY post is at Ochmiana, around midnight, Saturday, 5 December 1812. Barely two hours from Smorgoni and the escort has already been reduced to a few men. Who could bear this cold? There's no sign of the carriages with Duroc, Constant, Fain and the others. They are sniped at from the hills surrounding the town. The country is infested with Cossacks. And it will be like this until they leave Russian territory. Then they will have to cross a bit of Prussia and be at the mercy of ambushes if anyone finds out that the Emperor is driving through the night almost unprotected.

He remembers his return from Egypt, when he had to evade the English cruisers prowling the Mediterranean by the coast. He had managed to get through.

Now he will get across Europe. He will get back to Paris, he is sure of it. Things are much easier for him now. He is convinced of it.

Quick.

HERE IS VILNA. A freezing dawn. The carriage has stopped in the suburbs; the Emperor could be recognized in town. It's even colder. Minister Maret finally arrives. He hosted a ball yesterday evening when a night's drive away men are dying of cold and hunger. Does Maret understand that when that famished throng bursts into the city, it will be like a towering wave breaking and that the Cossacks will be behind it?

Quick, quick.

They speed off again into the day that is so short and sombre it is like a night of shame. There is so much snow on the road that the wheels skid and sink in, and they can only move slowly. Then it is dark already. The carriage is like a block of ice. They cross the Niemen at Kovno. They have a hot meal. Then they set off again. But they have to push the carriage, which is held fast by the snow. And the cold presses down on them even harder. The ice is thicker on their faces, their skin burns and is stretched taught.

Is this where my destiny is going to come to a halt?

All these decisions, these challenges, these dangers, just to be trapped by the snow on the borders of Russia and the Grand Duchy of Warsaw?

At the relay in Gragow, he castigates Caulaincourt. They must find a way of going faster.

At last! Caulaincourt has bought a covered sleigh from a certain Count Wybicki. Render all my thanks to him.

Napoleon gets in. With a shake of his head he cuts short Caulaincourt's apologies that they're leaving the carriage and the Emperor's essentials behind because, he explains, the sleigh will go faster, but there is a danger that the discomfort, after a few hours, may be unbearable. They will be even less protected from the cold than in the carriage.

Quick. At last the sleigh sets off, skimming over the snow, hurrying towards Warsaw, which is only two or three days away.

HE HAS THE impression, now they are on the Grand Duchy of Warsaw's roads, that the hardest part is over. He is driving through country that has given him a triumphal welcome. He has presided over court balls at Warsaw, organized parades. He has a son with a Polish mother, Marie Walewska. Marie! He wonders for a moment whether he could spend a night with her. Then he suppresses this fleeting desire. He must arrive at Paris only a day or two after the publication of the 29th Bulletin of the Grand Army recounting the Russian campaign.

'Our disasters will cause a great sensation in France,' he says, 'but my arrival will balance out the regrettable effects.'

He needs to talk. What can he do with all this dead time travelling? Sleep? The cold and his impatience barely allow him any time to drowse. And besides, he cannot stand the thought that a surprise, of whatever sort, will brutally yank him out of his sleep. He is on his guard and often, with a slow movement, he touches his saddle pistols lying near him.

'The Russians,' he says, 'must appear a scourge to all people. The war against Russia is a war entirely in the calculated interest of old Europe and civilization. We should only see one enemy in Europe from now on. That enemy is the Russian colossus.'

He knows the song Caulaincourt starts singing.

According to him – but he is only one of a choir – I am an ambitious schemer who wants to establish universal monarchy, who imposes an onerous fiscal system on all Europe, who has established a finicky inquisition in Germany, who suppresses nations.

Me!

He reaches for Caulaincourt's ear under his cap. Not finding it, he gives the grand equerry's cheek and neck a friendly slap. This man hasn't a very agile mind – he let himself be fooled by Alexander and he is Talleyrand's friend – but he is a good barometer of the ready-made ideas going round establishment Europe.

'England pushed me into it,' Napoleon resumes, 'forced me into everything. People say, and you are the first, Caulaincourt, that I abuse my power. I admit this reproach, but it is in the general interest of the continent. If I triumph over England, Europe will be eternally grateful. Europe doesn't see the real dangers it faces. All anyone does is criticize France! They only want to see her armies, as if England wasn't everywhere as well and much more threatening.'

He falls silent for a moment, tries to look out of the sleigh.

But the canvas has frozen and the windowpanes are covered with ice. Better to talk. Say that Europe has not accepted the new France.

The kings use passions to fight the wisest, most liberal laws; that is the driving principle of the coalition against me.

But everything will change again.

'It's a new era; it will lead to independence.'

He sighs.

'I am no more an enemy to the pleasures of life than anyone else. I am not a Don Quixote who needs to search for adventures. I am a creature of reason who only does what he thinks has utility. The only difference between me and other rulers is that difficulties stop them whereas I love overcoming them – when it is proved to me that the goal is grand, noble and worthy of me and the nation I govern.'

He is less cold. Talking warms one up.

'Winter is what killed us,' he murmurs. 'We are victims of the climate. The fine weather deceived me. If I had set off two weeks earlier, my army would be in Vitebsk. I would be laughing at the Russians and your prophet Alexander.'

The sleigh slows; they are approaching Warsaw.

'Everything has contributed to my reversal,' he says. 'I have been badly served in Warsaw. The Abbé de Pradt, rather than representing me as a grand seigneur, has been afraid, and played the arrogant wretch.'

HE SUDDENLY ORDERS the vehicle to stop. He has recognized, despite the ice, the Praga bridge over the Vistula.

They are in Warsaw. Caulaincourt explains that the plan is to stop for a few hours at the Hôtel d'Angleterre in Elm Street.

Napoleon wants to walk through the Krakow suburb on foot, along the broadest of Warsaw's streets. It is too cold for the few passers-by to linger, even if his green velvet fur-lined coat with gold frogging and big sable cap attract people's attention.

'I held a great review on this street once,' he says, walking fast.

He is not nostalgic at all. He feels happy to be in Warsaw. Life moves on. He moves on with it.

He goes into the little low room on the ground floor of the Hôtel d'Angleterre. Caulaincourt wants the shutters to be kept half shut so that he can remain incognito. A gawky maid endeavours to light a fire of damp, green wood. Smoke fills the room.

What are they waiting for? He wants to eat, see de Pradt and the ministers of the Grand Duchy of Warsaw and then set off again.

Finally the Abbé de Pradt arrives with his hypocritical face, his courtier's servility. He tries to justify his failure to raise more Poles to fight against the Russians. He claims his appeals have been met by the greatest resistance.

But the fact is, de Pradt has been trying, like so many others, to maintain a 'stupid popularity'.

'What do the Poles want, then?' Napoleon asks. 'It's them we're fighting for, and I'm spending my funds. If they don't want to do anything for their cause, it's pointless having such a passion as they do.'

'They want to be Prussians,' de Pradt murmurs.

'Why not Russians?'

The Abbé de Pradt fills him with indignation. This diplomat was afraid of the Russians throughout the campaign. He thought he could keep them happy by not prompting the Poles to intervene. He must be dismissed.

'Carry out the order on the spot,' Napoleon tells Caulaincourt.

He only stays at table a few minutes.

'Affairs feed one,' he murmurs. 'Displeasure satisfies one's appetite and that abbé has made me angry.'

He receives the Polish ministers.

What are these men who complain incessantly? What are these lamentations?

They seem to be worried on my behalf, contemplating the risks I am running!

'Rest is only for "*les rois fainéants*",' he jokes. 'Tiredness does me good.'

As for his army, they mustn't worry about that. Within three months he will have an army as big as that with which he entered the campaign. The arsenals are full and, when he returns to Paris, he will make Berlin and Vienna see reason, if these capitals dare to show signs of unrest.

'I carry more weight on my throne in the Tuileries than at the head of my army.'

Horses are put to the sleigh. Let's set off, cross this part of Prussia, reach the Rhine, and France!

NIGHT HAS FALLEN, denser than ever. The cold and wind get in everywhere, under the bearskin, under the fur-lined coats that Caulaincourt bought in Warsaw. Napoleon's fury mounts. He curses de Pradt, the Poles, Prussia's devious policy. He listens to Caulaincourt speaking on such and such's behalf.

'You see things like a young man; you don't understand, you understand nothing about affairs of state.'

And, in a low voice, he adds, 'There is but a step from the sublime to the ridiculous, and posterity will be the judge.'

He drowses for a few minutes but the cold is too bitter. He must soliloquize, debate, think aloud.

'People are mistaken,' he begins. 'I am not ambitious. I am too old for sleepless nights, fatigue and war. I love my bed and rest more than anyone, but I want to finish my work. In this world there are only two alternatives, command or obey. The conduct of every Cabinet towards France has proved to me that it can only count on its own power, and, consequently, on its army. So I have been compelled to make France strong, and maintain large armies.'

Suddenly, he is worried. They have entered Prussian Silesia, which they must cross at full tilt. Suddenly, a massive jolt. One of the sleigh's runners has broken. They have to stop at Kutno.

A little crowd forms round the sleigh, which is joined by the second sleigh carrying Constant and Duroc. The sub-prefect approaches, bows. It is pleasant to be recognized like this, in the depths of the night and of Europe, to see admiration and enthusiasm, happiness even, in the eyes of the prefect's wife and sister-in-law, two pretty Polish women. *I'd like to have time to look at them, charm them, but I have to dictate letters to Maret although Caulaincourt's fingers are paralyzed with cold, and when I try to write I can only trace incomprehensible signs my fingers are so numb and clumsy.*

THEY SET OFF again. It is already Friday, 11 December 1812. He berates Caulaincourt. When will they get to Posen? When will they have the dispatches from Paris?

Then he grows calm.

'I make myself more disagreeable than I am,' he says, 'because I have remarked that then the French are always ready to eat out of your hand.'

He laughs.

'They lack seriousness and consequently that is what they find most imposing. People think me severe, harsh even. So much the better. It saves me having to be. My firmness is taken for insensitivity. Since we owe the order that reigns partly to this opinion, I am not complaining!'

He rubs Caulaincourt's cheek with the tip of his glove.

'Come now, Caulaincourt. I am a man. I too, whatever certain people may say, have compassion and a heart, though it is the heart of a sovereign. If the tears of a duchess leave me cold as marble, I am touched by the sufferings of the people. I want them happy and the French will be. Prosperity will be universal if I live another ten years.'

Will he live? He's about to enter his forty-fourth year. He no longer suffers from the fatigue, dizziness and flu that exhausted him at the time of the Moskva battle. He feels vigorous and happy, despite the cold. He is on his way to Paris, to Marie Louise and his son.

He wants to talk about them. Marie Louise is gentle and good, he says. A German woman, Caulaincourt.

Then he goes on: 'Universal prosperity in ten years, that's it. Do you think I don't like pleasing too? It does me good to see a contented face, but I am obliged to be wary of my natural disposition because people would abuse it. I felt this more than once with Josephine, who was always asking for things and even ambushed me with tears which made me agree to things I should have refused.'

Josephine is not the only one I have given in to.

'Fouché too, who is nothing but an intriguer, who has a prodigious mind and a flair for writing but is a thief who grabs everything he can. He must have millions. He has been a great revolutionary, a man of blood. He thinks he can make amends for his wrongs by becoming the protector of the Faubourg St-Germain. As for your friend Talleyrand, he is a man of intrigue and great immorality, but plenty of intelligence and admittedly the most capable minister I have had.'

He stops. The sleigh is bumping over cobbles. It's Posen. At last a courier, letters!

The portmanteaux containing the dispatches are in a room at the Hôtel de Saxe. Quick. He pushes Caulaincourt out of the way, tears off the ribbons fastening the packets of envelopes, opens them, and then tells Caulaincourt to carry on while he starts to read. Looking through the letters, he exclaims. France is fine. Almost too fine.

'In the present circumstances, this sense of security is unfortunate,' he murmurs, 'because the Twenty-Ninth Bulletin of the Grand Army will shatter it. Anxiety would have been preferable. It would have paved the way for misfortunes.'

He holds out his hand. Quick, more dispatches.

He reads the Empress's letters aloud, repeating the passages that concern the little king.

'I've got a good wife, haven't I, Caulaincourt?'

He starts walking about the room, picking up the dispatches again and commenting on them. He has kept aside a packet, from the Black Cabinet, containing correspondence opened by the spies who work in the post office. He laughs.

'What imprudence! Are men so mad as to confide in letters which they must know we can open and read?'

Then he grimaces with contempt. Among them are impudent comments by courtiers, people he has showered with rewards.

'I don't have enough esteem for them to be what's called malicious and avenge myself.'

Come on, quick, let's leave.

THEY CONTINUE IN the sleigh. The snow is thick, covering the countryside between Posen and Glogow. The cold is only slightly less bitter.

'If someone stopped us, Caulaincourt, what would they do to

us? Do you think they'd recognize me? Do they know that I'm here? You're pretty popular in Germany, Caulaincourt; you speak the language.'

The Prussians would quickly realize that he is the Emperor and not a secretary by the name of Rayneval travelling with M. de Caulaincourt.

'Fearing I'll escape or there'll be terrible reprisals if they give me up, the Prussians will hand me over to the English.'

He laughs.

'Can you imagine, Caulaincourt, what you'd look like in an iron cage, on a square in London, chained like a wretched negro who has been condemned to be eaten by flies because he has been covered in honey?'

He laughs again for a long time, then suddenly grows sombre.

'But a secret assassination here, an ambush, would be easy.'

He touches his pistols. Are Caulaincourt's to hand?

He falls silent. They arrive at the relay. They have to wait. The night is icy. There are no more than two gendarmes for an escort.

'It's the first scene of the cage act,' he says.

Then here the horses are. They set off again. He has never been this cold. He has to talk, escape from this painful, interminable night by looking towards the future, already prepare for it in his head, by thinking and talking about it. And this new game he is about to undertake, this France like a chess board on which he is going to gather his pawns, stimulates him. He would like to strike the first blow now, so that it can end as checkmate this time.

'I will be in the Tuileries before anyone knows about my disasters or dares try to betray me,' he says. 'My cohorts form an army of more than one hundred thousand men. Well-trained soldiers commanded by battle-hardened officers. I have money, arms; the wherewithal to form good cadres; I shall have conscripts and five hundred thousand men called out on the banks of the Rhine within three months. The cavalry will take longer to get together and train, but I have what generates everything – money, in the cellars of the Tuileries.'

HE GROWS IMPATIENT. The sleigh is only moving slowly. The high winds have banked up the snow into huge mounds. He curses.

'The nation needs me,' he says. 'If it meets my expectations, everything will be quickly repaired.'

He tries to see the road, then huddles down under his fur-lined coat.

'People say I love power! The prisons have never contained fewer prisoners! No humiliations, no hatred, no more parties, thanks to me. As First Consul and Emperor, I have been the people's king, I have governed for it, in its interest, without letting myself be deflected by the clamour and advantage of certain people. They know it in France, and so the French people love me. I say the people meaning the nation, because I have never favoured what many people understand by the word "people" – the rabble.'

He shrugs his shoulders.

'They call this my tyranny; they say I am a tyrant because I do not want to let a few intriguers, a few crazy women, draw attention to themselves by indulging in conspiracies that I don't give a fig for. Salons are always hostile to the government. They criticize everything and never praise anything. The bulk of the nation is fair. It sees that I am working for its glory, for its well-being, for its future. If it were all for me, what could I be lacking? What can I personally desire? I have given Europe the law. I have distributed crowns. I have given millions, but I don't need money for myself. No one is less occupied with personal interests than me!'

It is Monday 14 December, midnight. After Görlitz and Bautzen, they arrive in Dresden. They wander through the city streets looking for the French minister's residence, but the windswept town is deserted.

Two hours! Two hours before finding the building in Perna Street. And he must immediately set to work, start dictating, so that the dispatches can go. He must be the first to inform the Emperor of Austria of his return to Paris, in order to convince him that everything is going well, that he has not been defeated. He writes to Marie Louise's father.

Despite quite heavy fatigue, my health has never been better . . .
I will be in Paris in a few days; I will stay there during the
winter to attend to my most important affairs.

I have full confidence in Your Majesty's sentiments. The
alliance we have contracted forms a permanent system . . . Your
Majesty will do all you promised me to assure the triumph of
our common cause and lead us promptly to a suitable peace.

*I must bind the Emperor Francis, my very dear father-in-law, into
this alliance. And words can be bonds.*

The King of Saxony arrives. Napoleon has been in bed for an
hour. The King sits in his room.

*A few words to reassure him, show him I'm still the power that
makes the law in Germany.*

Then set off again and arrive in Leipzig when the day is
ending.

THE AIR IS MILDER; there's almost no snow in the town. He feels
cheerful. These houses, after the Russian hovels, these hills, these
bell towers – it's a world and landscape he recognizes. He slowly
paces about the square and the garden for an hour, dines with the
French consul in the Hôtel de Prusse and then sets off again.

In Weimar the carriage fitted with runners that the King of
Saxony had given him in Dresden breaks. He has to get into
a post-cart. Further on they change vehicles and horses. The
postmaster of Eisenach is slow harnessing them; he seems evasive.
He has to threaten him. His wife cries, begs.

When will they get there?

He tries to calculate the remaining distance to the Rhine, to
Paris. How many hours, how many days?

It is Wednesday 16 December. It seems that he has been living
on the road for months when in fact it's only been eleven days.

Then suddenly a rider. They stop the carriage. It is Anatole de
Montesquiou, back from Paris, who has seen the Empress, who
has handed over the text of the Bulletin. Everything is fine, he
says.

At last the Rhine, Mainz, capital of the French *département* of
Mont-Tonerre! Napoleon is home.

And here is a familiar face, old Marshal Kellerman, who stammers emotionally. What a pleasure it is calling him the Duke of Valmy.

I am home.

St-Avold, then Verdun, where they have supper on Thursday 17 December. They set off again. Suddenly, a crash. The axle tree has broken, five hundred feet from the relay stage. They must walk.

I am going to have to struggle every last metre of the way.

But I am home.

He takes deep breaths of the light, mild air. This, winter? Better than a Russian spring.

At Château-Thierry he takes his time for the first time. He is going to see Marie Louise and his son again in a few hours. He spends a long time dressing, choosing the uniform of the foot grenadiers, but, laughing, puts on his fur-lined coat and cap. Because the only transport left is an open carriage, one of those yokels' carts that rattle about, but it gets them to Meaux.

The rest, if necessary, he will cover on foot. But the postmaster gives him an old carriage with two huge wheels, a post-chaise, that keeps out draughts. They set off again.

THE POSTILION WHIPS up the horses, which break into a gallop. Napoleon leans forward. Paris. In the distance, the Arc de Triomphe. The postilion drives through the arch without receiving the order, but he is entitled to because only the Emperor has this privilege.

'That augurs well,' says Napoleon.

Already they're turning into the Tuileries. It is quarter to midnight on Friday, 18 December 1812. They left Smorgoni on the 5th. It is so far away: Russia, the Berezina, Moscow, the Moskva. Another world that is already unreal.

The sentries look enquiringly at each other. Who are these officers? Dispatch bearers, probably. They let them pass. Slowly the carriage drives up to the peristyle. A porter in a nightshirt comes forward, a light in his hand. He is terrified by the bulky, fur-swaddled silhouette of Caulaincourt, whom he has trouble recognizing. At last he identifies the Emperor's grand equerry.

Napoleon sits in the darkness at first. Then he gets out. They look at him. He walks slowly. A cry: 'It is the Emperor!' Running, laughter, voices echoing under the vaults.

Napoleon abruptly pushes his way through those around him and joins Caulaincourt, who is walking towards the apartments of the Empress's ladies-in-waiting. The women are hesitant, anxious. Who is he?

Napoleon brushes past him.

'Good evening, Caulaincourt; you need rest too,' he says.

And he goes into the Empress's quarters.

IX

He looks intently at them, smiling, and then enters the room.

They are all there, in the salon of his private apartments. It is eleven o'clock, on Saturday, 19 December 1812. They have come for the Emperor's levee.

He sees the surprise and incredulity on their faces. He is in Paris; it's really him! They imagine him in the depths of Europe, buried under the snow with the remains of his Grand Army. They were overwhelmed by the 29th Bulletin, which was published three days ago on 16 December. They see that he is, as the Bulletin said he was, in good health, just skin a little cracked from the cold, eyes swollen, reddened by the icy wind which blew almost the entire thirteen days the journey lasted.

He is amused by their terrified, servile expressions. Everyone there, the ministers – Cambacérès, Savary, Clarke and Montalivet – and the others, the chamberlains and officers of his household, accepted the myth of his death when General Maret put it about. Not a single one of them thought of his son. All of them were ready to rally round a provisional government.

He must get to the bottom of this affair; find out how to prevent his son being removed from the succession.

He saw him this morning before going into the salon.

My son, this little boy dressed as a man?

It is only when he saw him walk towards him that he gauged how much time had passed, that this campaign of almost six months to Moscow had not been a nightmare you forget when you wake up. And yet that was the feeling he had had this morning, seeing Marie Louise and then going into his study.

Everything has stayed in its place.

Last night he rediscovered Marie Louise's body, who froze at first with a sort of dread, as if she couldn't recognize this man rushing at her. Then she was that 'good German woman' again, so sweet and tender. The simple fact of touching her soothed him and erased all the exhaustion of the journey, even the memory of what he had experienced with hundreds of thousands of men between Vilna and Vilna, the town where, in June and December 1812, the Russian campaign began and finished.

Will Murat, Berthier and Eugène manage to hold Kutusov's troops, who must be as exhausted, bruised and decimated as those of the Grand Army? If Murat hangs onto Vilna, then in the spring Napoleon will be able to take his revenge on the Russians; that is what he is thinking of.

He is going to wind up the springs of the Imperial machine, levy hundreds of thousands of men and give them muskets and cannon. In April 1813 everything will be ready. Until then he will have to try to preserve the alliance with Austria and manage, if possible, to stop Prussia from entering the war on the Russians' side.

Here's what I must do.

HE PASSES AMONG the assembled dignitaries. He stops in front of each of them. He questions them on the state of their department. Then he asks, 'Why did you forget my son? Why did you think me dead? Why didn't you think of my heir?'

He looks around for Frochot, prefect of the Seine and state councillor, who, at the request of the conspirators, gave them a room to assemble their provisional government.

'We need an example,' he says, 'not of the man, whom I wish to spare, but of the state councillor. It is time people learnt, if they have forgotten, what it is to abide by one's oath. We must fix the principles of this.'

Then in a harsh voice, walking away a little, he adds, 'Timid, cowardly soldiers lose nations their independence, but pusillanimous magistrates destroy the laws of the empire, the rights of the throne and the social order itself.'

He will repeat this in the Senate, which he intends to convene tomorrow, Sunday 20 December. But, starting from today, he wants to preside over daily councils, councils of the ministers of finance, of home affairs and, obviously, the State Council. He will receive the diplomatic corps on 1 January 1813. Then, in a few weeks, on 14 February, the Legislative Body will be convened. He wants to see the whole Empire working. He must raise 350,000 men before spring. He is thinking of 150,000 from the class of 1814, 100,000 in the classes of 1809–12, 100,000 others from the National Guards.

He has already thought of all this. It is now only a question of putting it into practice in the forthcoming weeks.

He observes the ministers and dignitaries. The directives he has just given seem to have reassured them. Men need to act; they need to know a leader is at the helm, guiding them. Now he can talk to them about Russia, the disasters of the campaign. What use would it be trying to dissimulate? Soldiers' private letters are going to start reaching France. And people will know what the men went through over there, and the dead will be counted.

He begins to speak in a calm voice.

'The war I am waging against Russia is a political war. I have waged it without animosity. I would have wished to avert the misfortunes it has brought about. I could have armed the greater part of the population against itself by proclaiming the liberation of slaves ... Many villages asked me, but I refused to take a measure that would have condemned thousands of families to death ...'

Then he walks slowly up and down in front of the dignitaries.

'The success of my enterprises depended on eight days. It is the same with everything in this world. The moment, timing is everything.'

He indicates that the levee is over, but detains Decrès and Cessac, with whom he wants to begin talking about the first measures to be taken to reform the artillery and cavalry.

He sits down at his desk.

'Well, gentlemen, fortune has dazzled me! I let myself be carried along rather than following the plan I had made. I have been in Moscow; I thought I would sign the peace there. I stayed there too long. I thought I could achieve in one year what should only be executed in two campaigns. I have made a great mistake, but I shall have the means to redeem it.'

He must start today. He issues his first orders. Then, when Decrès and Cessac have gone out, he says to Caulaincourt, 'The terrible Bulletin has had its effect, but I see that my presence gives even more pleasure than our disasters cause pain. We are more afflicted than discouraged. This state of opinion will be known in Vienna and everything will mend itself within three months.'

HE WALKS ON the terrace of the Tuileries with Marie Louise. She leans on his arm, tender, light and frivolous. He only listens to the chirrup of words. He asks her, 'How is your dear papa Francis?' He needs the alliance or at worst neutrality of Austria. And he must use Marie Louise to influence the Emperor Francis.

For the news the couriers bring every day is bad. The crowd of soldiers who escaped the Berezina have flung themselves on Vilna's magazines. The town has been looted, apparently. And it only took one Cossack's hurrahs for these men to flee and start sacking Kovno in the same way! And the Guard – *my Guard* – sacked the houses and storehouses as well, and then fled when the Cossacks appeared. Only a few thousand men managed to cross the Niemen with Ney, to find Yorck's Prussian army corps defecting to the Tsar, thereby exposing Macdonald's men to the Russians and forcing them to withdraw. Then it was Schwarzenberg's Austrians who started talking to the Russians about the possibility of an armistice.

And Murat has left the army, returned to his kingdom. He is negotiating with Metternich, betraying Napoleon like another Bernadotte in the hope of keeping his throne – perhaps he is dreaming of wearing the iron crown of the Kingdom of Italy!

'I presume you are not one of those who think the lion is dead,' he dictates to Murat. 'You have done me all the harm you could since my departure from Vilna. The title of king has made you lose your head. If you want to keep this title, you must conduct yourself differently to how you have up until now.'

I SENSE THE nation around me ready to defend itself. The conscripts are joining their colours, the arsenals are filling with arms. The whole of France is a workshop. But there is a handful of traitors at the top.

In the salons of the Faubourg St-Germain, for instance, where they make fun of the 'wooden leg' dances I have asked Hortense to organize so there will be no change in Parisian and Court life. But there's betrayal nearer me too.

He goes through the letters that the agents of the Black Cabinet, who spy on correspondence, have been able to seize.

It doesn't even surprise him to discover that some are from the pallid Talleyrand, a man who still attends privy councils. He writes to his uncle, the former archbishop of Rheims, an émigré and relative of Louis XVIII and his companion in exile at Hartwell, where the small court around Louis XVI's brother lives in England. Talleyrand offers his services and declares that the Russian campaign is 'the beginning of the end' for the Empire, and that it will all end in 'a return to the Bourbons'.

Unworthy Talleyrand!

Napoleon feels a sharp current of rage. He wants to prosecute Talleyrand, exile him to his estates, but Savary and Cambacérès speak up for the former bishop of Autun. Why make a scandal? they say. It is enough to keep him under surveillance.

Napoleon hesitates. Putting Talleyrand on trial would indeed be interpreted as a sign of trouble at the top of the Empire.

It will be enough, once again, to express my contempt and anger to this individual.

He sends for Talleyrand.

'You are trying to betray me! You *are* betraying me!' he cries.

But Talleyrand rejects the accusations, barely looks at the intercepted letters, claims he didn't write them; they're forgeries intended to ruin him.

'I know you,' yells Napoleon. 'I know what you are capable of; you have stolen more than anybody in the world!'

And now the Bourbons!

Napoleon drives him out of his study. He hears him telling the dignitaries waiting in the next room, 'The Emperor is charming this morning!'

But the man is affected. He takes to his bed, the victim of an attack.

Let his masters weep, Alexander especially, who now thinks himself invested with a divine mission to bring me down and liberate Europe.

And who has convinced him of these absurdities? Émigrés, who hate what is new, who want an Emperor of the Reaction to pit against me. The informers mention Madame de Staël, whose services and

*even admiration I have refused, Joseph de Maistre and Stein the
Prussian.*

*All of them hovering around the Tsar, pushing him to go further,
to Paris, while the English are paying.*

*And Bernadotte, out of jealousy and in the hope of succeeding me,
joins the coalition. Austria must not fall into it.*

MARIE LOUISE COMES towards him holding the little king by the
hand.

She is more and more tender. She doesn't want him to leave,
even to go to his study. So he has to work in the middle of the
night. In public she is often awkward and curt, even when he is
at her side at official ceremonies, at the Invalides or the School
for Young Girls of the Legion of Honour. She does not know
how to smile or give; she can't find the right words.

But, in a tête-à-tête, she is sweet and loving and full of
laughter. And she is the daughter of Francis, Emperor of Austria.
Would Francis dare to wage war against his daughter's husband?
Against the Empire his son might inherit?

Napoleon writes to him.

I have never encountered the Russian army without beating it.
My Guard never went into action. It did not shoot one round
and did not lose one man to the enemy. But in the terrible cold
storm bivouacking became unbearable for my men; many went
off in the evenings to find houses and shelter; I had no cavalry
left to protect them. The Cossacks picked up several thousand.

*This is what Francis must think of the Russian campaign. Isn't it
true, anyway, that I have always defeated the Russians and in the
next campaign, with my new army, I will drive the enemy back
beyond the Niemen?*

He continues to dictate.

As for France, it would be impossible to be more satisfied with it
than I am: men, horses, money – I am being given everything.
My finances are in a good state.

The consequence of which should be that I shall make no
overture towards peace.

Your Majesty now knows my affairs and views as I do.

I presume that this letter and the feelings I confide in Your Majesty will remain between him and me; but he can, in consequence of the knowledge he has of my dispositions, act as he sees fit in the interests of peace.

If Austria wants to play intermediary between the Russians and me, why not?

But who can be sure of the Austrians? They will crumble like the Prussians if I weaken. I need to fight. My sword is my army. And my shield Marie Louise of Habsburg and the King of Rome, and the Austrian blood that flows in their veins.

Napoleon sends for Régnaud de Saint-Jean-d'Angély, secretary of state to the Imperial family. He wants, he says, a search to be made of all works since Charlemagne on the conventions to be followed in the case of the coronation of a presumptive heir.

What better way to prepare for the future than to set up a regency council, and make the king of Rome a crowned heir in advance? Will Francis then have the sacrilegious audacity to wage war on his daughter and his grandson?

BUT THERE WILL be war against the Russians, and probably against the Prussians too, so Napoleon goes hunting because he wants to keep his agility and stamina and he can feel his body growing heavy. The cold is very sharp, this Tuesday, 19 January 1813, in the forests around Grosbois, Berthier's chateau.

The marshal has returned from Poland, crushed. Berthier blames himself for having supported the choice of Murat as head of the army. They should have chosen Eugène de Beauharnais from the start, he says. What can the viceroy of Italy do now? The army hasn't more than 30,000 men, all that's left of more than 400,000 who crossed the Niemen in June 1812. Berthier laments. Napoleon takes him to task. What's the use of wanting to alter the past? Things that have happened are beyond remedy. As for their consequences, these must be endured.

'It is a torrent,' he says. 'We must let it flow. It will stop of its own accord in a few days.'

He wants to accept what he cannot refuse and change what can be changed.

IN GROSBOIS FOREST he suddenly does an about-turn. They will ride to Fontainebleau. He had the idea a few days before. But he didn't want to tell anyone.

Most of the palace's rooms are empty. The furniture has been removed in the Emperor's absence. The salons and bedchambers are icy, no fires. Servants are few and far between. But one whole wing of the palace is lit up. This is where Pope Pius VII has been living for the past few months.

This is whom he wants to take by surprise and surround with marks of affection and respect in order to reach an agreement, a new concordat.

Napoleon walks towards him along the long cold galleries and embraces him.

We must achieve an agreement. I will not leave the palace until I get it.

He wants to appear in the eyes of Europe and French opinion not as the Antichrist damned by Christian leaders but as an emperor who is the Pope's ally.

Marie Louise is happy at Fontainebleau, in the small circle that gathers every evening despite the cold apartments for 'games and a little music'. But she mustn't just be the loving wife. She must also write to Francis. On Monday 25 January Napoleon wants the concordat to be signed in the Empress's apartments.

He observes Marie Louise. She has a radiant expression on her face. He reads the letter she has written to her father.

'We have been in Fontainebleau for six days, where the Emperor today has settled the affairs of Christianity with the Pope. The Pope seems very content. He has been very happy and in good spirits since early this morning and he signed the treaty a quarter of an hour ago. I have just come from his apartments; I found him in very good health. He has a very attractive face, very interesting; I am convinced that you will learn of the news of this reconciliation with as much pleasure as I.'

NAPOLEON IS ECSTATIC. Of course the Pope considers this accord just a draft document to be agreed on by the sacred college of cardinals. But he must move faster than this assembly.

On Saturday, 13 February 1813 Napoleon has the concordat

published in the press. And in France and Italy all the churches salute the event with a *Te Deum*.

This is what matters! Let them call me the Antichrist, a pagan king, now!

He receives Metternich's envoy, the Austrian Bubna, with irony, challenging him scornfully about the armistice Schwarzenberg has signed at Zeyes with the Russians.

'You are trying to get your auxiliary corps out of the game; you have changed tack!'

But if that were true Vienna must openly break with him; Francis must dare to confront both his daughter, who perhaps one day will be the regent, and an emperor on the best possible terms with the Pope.

Here is something they must know in Vienna, he says — and he repeats it to the Legislative Body — 'I desire peace but I will only make an honourable peace.'

He feels master of the game again.

'God has given me the strength and joy to undertake great things,' he says. 'I must not leave them imperfect.'

He leafs through the *Monitor* containing the text of the concordat.

'The clergy is a power that never stands still,' he adds. 'Your enemy if it is not your friend, its services are never free. The clergy must concern itself with reconciling us with heaven, consoling us when we grow old, and leave power in this world to us: the king in the temple, the subject at the gate.'

X

HE IS SITTING IN HIS study in the Tuileries. He doesn't look around as Molé enters, but carries on looking at the changeable sky that wavers between winter and spring, at times bright blue and at others low and dark and showery.

This is what he feels himself, this alternation between enthusiastic energy, with more will power than ever, and abrupt, crushing waves of weariness.

He has presided over great parades and reviews in the courtyard of the Tuileries and the Carrousel all through February 1813. He has watched the provisional regiments of barely draughted conscripts march past. He has walked through the ranks of the Young Guard. He trusts these men but, despite their uniforms and new muskets, are they soldiers yet? They are very young to go into battle.

But it is not this that suddenly checks his momentum and makes him stop dictating here, in the middle of the night, in this study, with his secretary. He is preparing the forthcoming campaign, organizing the plantations of beet that will allow them to forego sugar from the colonies, explaining that he doesn't want to see so many cooks in his suite on the next campaign. 'Fewer dishes and plates, no large dressing case, and this as much by way of setting an example as reducing the bother.'

But suddenly his voice fails him.

He has already done all of this. He's already said it; he's already seen it. He has the feeling that he is repeating himself, retracing his steps, but that he doesn't have the lightness, the aggression and the eagerness of before. He still has the energy, but it feels like a habit.

He has hunted two days running in the Bois de Boulogne. He has gone to a masked ball at Hortense's — a ball that he ordered should be thrown. But he has felt no joy. Living and conquering seem like starting all over again. He is a machine. He goes because he has gone before. He makes campaign plans to sweep aside the troops that will be matched against him — Russian, Prussian too, probably. The itineraries he marks on the maps of Germany occur to him almost effortlessly.

He knows these hills, these rivers and these towns. He has already travelled these roads countless times. He has defeated every possible army. Will he be able to do better than at Austerlitz, Jena, Wagram?

HE INVITES MOLÉ to sit down. He appreciates this ambitious man, scion of one of the most illustrious political families under the monarchy. Molé is a flatterer, Napoleon knows that. Presenting the budget in the Senate on 4 March 1813, Molé spoke of the marvels that would have astonished a prince of the time of the Medicis that have been achieved in 'twelve years of war and by just one man'.

Me!

Napoleon is not taken in by toadies. He pushes aside the dispatches lying on the table.

There isn't one that doesn't contain bad news. The Russians have entered Warsaw. Prussia is agitated, rises up against me, signs a treaty with Alexander and declares war on 17 March 1813. Bernadotte is allying himself with the English against me, against his country! Eugène, to whom I have entrusted the army, is evacuating Berlin, Hamburg and Dresden.

He has written to Eugène:

I do not see what compelled you to leave Berlin . . . You must finally begin to make war. Our military operations are the object of ridicule to our allies in Vienna and our enemies in London and in St Petersburg because the army constantly leaves a week before the arrival of the enemy infantry, on the approach of light troops and on mere rumour.

My army! I can remedy this situation.

He gets to his feet and goes through to the map room, followed by Molé.

'My intention is to take the offensive vigorously in May, recapture Dresden, free the fortresses on the Oder and, depending on circumstances, clear Danzig and drive the enemy back behind the Vistula.'

He can also draw the enemy into the steep Saale valley, turn their army and cut it off from the Elbe.

He sees these troop movements. He has the landscapes of these places in his mind's eye. He has done all this before. And now he has to start again. He can; he must. It is a stone he is rolling to the top of a hill. He is Sisyphus.

HE GOES BACK to his study, and sits down at his desk again. Does Molé know that the Pope, this fine fellow, he murmurs sarcastically, has decided to retract, to withdraw his signature from the concordat signed two months ago?

The Pope has written that his infallibility did not preserve him from an error for which his conscience reproaches him. And naturally this pontifical letter will be spread around Paris by those black cardinals who are hostile to me, and who will find all the accomplices they need among the staunch believers of the Faubourg St-Germain!

But tomorrow, 25 March, the concordat will be made law anyway. And on 30 March the Regency Council will be organized with the Empress presiding over it, and Cambacérès as her advisor.

'What do you think, Molé?'

'His Majesty wants to protect France from a surprise, a coup such as Malet's . . .' Molé hesitates, then continues, ' . . .while he is leading his armies. The public has been expecting to see this important law for a long time.'

Napoleon stands up.

'All this is very little,' he says. 'I am under no illusions, believe me. If I write a will, it will certainly be broken after my death. Would a *senatus consultum* be any more respected?'

Molé protests. 'Learning of your death,' he murmurs, 'the stunned parties would need time to collect themselves; everything would depend on the alacrity and energy with which the regency's governance could take advantage of that first moment of hesitation.'

This is the moment my life has reached. They are talking about my death and succession, not to secure my power, as before, but really to examine what will happen when I am dead.

Napoleon makes a weary gesture.

'Bah! The King of Rome must be twenty years old and a distinguished man – everything else is irrelevant.'

But will I be able to live until my son reaches manhood?

He remains silent, then starts walking.

'What is good about this regency,' he says, 'is that it conforms to all our traditions and all our historical memories. It will be entrusted to an empress whose bloodline has already sat on the French throne.'

He shrugs his shoulders.

'There are what I call the *tricoteuses* who loathe the Empress, dredging up the same slanders they showered on the unfortunate Marie Antoinette. As long as I'm here those dregs won't make any move, because they learnt what I am like on the Thirteenth Vendémiaire, and they know I am always ready, if I catch them red-handed, to crush them.'

He remembers when he had to confront the crowd as a second lieutenant. He has never liked disorder, the shouts of the rabble. He is a soldier. He has re-established an etiquette, a precise ceremonial everywhere. It is a constant effort to maintain respect for these rules. And he imposes on himself this rigour that forges one's character.

'Sire,' Molé says, 'nothing stirs in your presence; no one would dare. But when you're not here, as you have found out only too clearly, everything is poised to start again.'

'I know and I take it very seriously. They are more daring since the disaster of Moscow and they will continue to be.'

He sighs.

'But we will have to fight another campaign and get the better of those wretched Russians, forcing them to return to their borders and not think of leaving again.'

He bows his head. This duty he sets himself, this necessity he has to face up to, doesn't give him any enthusiasm any more. But it is his duty. That's all.

'Do not delude yourself, sire,' says Molé. 'For the first time we won't see you leave without profound sadness and much concern. We believe you are needed at the head of your armies, but we fear that you don't know how much you are needed here too.'

He knows.

Napoleon sighs.

'What do you expect, my dear sir?' he says. 'The truth is, I have no one to put in my place anywhere, neither in the army nor here. I would probably be only too glad if I could wage war with my generals, but I have made them too accustomed to only knowing how to obey; there isn't a single one who can command others, and all of them only know how to obey me.'

He goes to the window. He thinks of the army lost at Vilna through Murat's fault. The King of Naples has not been able to make himself obeyed, to impose himself on anyone, he says. Indiscipline reached its nadir after my departure. Twelve million was looted from the army's coffers in Vilna by my troops, since when it has been impossible to put them to good use.

He walks back towards Molé.

'Poor human nature, always imperfect,' he says wearily. 'How many transgressions is one forced to punish that derive solely from the habits or organization of the man who commits them! Do you think Murat ever writes to his children without wetting the page with big tears? Impressions are too powerful for him. Instead of dominating them, he is bowled over.'

He walks slowly to the window.

'Don't think that I don't have a sensitive heart like other men. I have had to develop a strong habit of self-control so as not to let any emotions show. From my earliest youth I have striven to mute the chord that now produces no sound for me. Without this work on myself, do you think I would have done everything I have done? The hours fly by and in my position losing a moment could mean losing everything, even what I have won.'

He clasps his hands behind his back.

'I must march, act, advance,' he says.

'Sire,' murmurs Molé. 'Your Majesty must come back as soon as possible.'

Napoleon pulls out his watch, smiles. 'Come now, enough chat. It is late, I am going to bed.'

SLEEP? HOW? He feels a storm brewing that could sweep everything away in its course. He is calm, but he sees everything so clearly that it is becoming painful. The clouds are gathering. He knows he will enter this campaign under the most difficult circumstances, with young recruits who have never come under fire. The prefects' reports say that the new *senatus consultum*, which authorizes the mobilization of 180,000 extra men, has been seen as a curse in the countryside. The people aren't rebelling, but they are crushed.

Anyway, he only has to attend a ceremony or go to the Opéra with the Empress to see that people greet him with a sort of dread. He is the 'Ogre', in the words of the underground pamphlets printed in England, the 'bloodthirsty Antichrist'!

Do they want him to give in, to step aside for the Bourbons? Hasn't Louis XVIII just restated his rights to the French throne? But what has he done to be entitled to reign? What country would he be king of? A France humiliated, defeated, driven out of its conquests and subjected to the law of an Alexander or a King of Prussia!

Is this what I have fought for? Is it for this that so many soldiers have died since 1792, when I was nothing? I have only defended and increased the inheritance I was given.

Do they think I am ready to give it up now, when Europe's sovereigns are reforming coalitions and turning popular feeling against me, despite the fact I embody the new Europe they are the enemies of?

He gets to his feet.

This year, 1813, is my biggest challenge. If I bring it off, I will establish my Empire, and when the time of my succession comes, my son will benefit.

But if I am defeated . . .

He does not want to think of that.

If he is defeated, then he will just have to face it, use every event to try to regain ground, like a regiment that has to pull back in good order and save whatever can be saved.

ON 30 MARCH 1813, in the council chamber, he receives the Empress with great pomp and ceremony, amid dignitaries in full dress, 'sashes over coats', and the princesses in long décolleté dresses. He leads Marie Louise to a seat next to him. She will swear an oath confirming that she has been invested with the responsibilities of the regency.

She starts to speak in a monotonous voice, with the guttural accent she has not yet lost.

'I swear loyalty to the Emperor,' she says. 'I swear to conform to the acts of the Constitution decreed or to be decreed by my husband the Emperor, in the exercise of the authority which it will please him to entrust to me in his absence.'

Will she really be able to resist those who, if I am beaten, will seek to keep their power by betraying me?

He is under no illusions. He looks at these dignitaries. How many of those obsequiously lowering their eyes now would remain loyal to him to the point of accepting that the Empress and the King of Rome would rule?

But perhaps, thanks to this appointment, Austria won't enter into a coalition, or will hesitate to do so and so will leave him time to win?

HE INSISTS Marie Louise write to her father. He monitors this correspondence. 'The Emperor asks me to give you all his best ... The Emperor is very affectionate towards you,' he makes her write.

And Marie Louise, with touching naivety, does what he asks.

'Not a day goes by,' she adds for her father, 'without him telling me how much he loves you ... The Emperor tells me to assure you of his friendship, and also to write to you often. You can be very sure, my dear papa, that I do not need to be told that twice!'

It would be a 'monstrosity' to see Francis declare war against an empire of which his daughter is the regent!

But how long will 'good papa Francis' resist the storm driving him forward?

NAPOLEON READS THE dispatches, the reports of French agents. Germany is rising up. Wittgenstein's Russian troops have been met by delirious crowds in Berlin. The professors in all the universities have stopped teaching. 'Lessons will resume in a free country,' the philosopher Fichte has said, 'or else we will die winning back our freedom.'

He remembers that young man, Staps, who had wanted to stab him at Schönbrunn and whose hatred and fanaticism had surprised him. Because he knows the sovereigns.

Most of them are cowards. They will follow and use the passions of the crowds, and if I cannot defeat their armies, they will all rally against me. Like Bernadotte and that fool Murat, who is clumsily trying to obtain Vienna's support, while the Austrians are raising two armies, one in Italy and one in Germany, so they can attack if the moment is right.

How many times already have I had to beat their archdukes? And will I have to start all over again?

He receives Prince Schwarzenberg, who has been appointed ambassador to Paris again. On this Tuesday 13 April St-Cloud's park is full of the noises of spring. The windows of the large reception room are open.

Napoleon leads Schwarzenberg to one of them. He speaks of the successes won by the prince and his corps during the Russian campaign. He says nothing of the armistice concluded with the Russians.

The prince listens and seems embarrassed. He does not venture any answer to Napoleon's questions.

Would the Emperor Francis accept a gift of the Illyrian provinces to reinforce our alliance, Napoleon asks. Austria would then touch the Adriatic again.

Schwarzenberg still holds his tongue, as if he were afraid of wounding me by relaying the words of Metternich, who wants to impose himself on all this as an 'armed mediator'.

What else can he do but appear to turn a blind eye, call Prince Schwarzenberg 'my dear friend', take him by the arm, lead him back through St-Cloud's long galleries, and declare himself delighted by this conversation of almost four hours in which nothing has been decided?

HE WATCHES Prince Schwarzenberg walking away.

Perhaps he was too conciliatory?

Perhaps Schwarzenberg thought I am afraid of war?

I only fear impotence, being in a position where I would be unable to fight. But that will only happen when I die!

Even if I were alone, I would fight.
And I am not alone.

He is going to set off to join the armies in Germany. He has already left France so often by this road that goes through Sainte-Menehould and on to Mainz.

Fleeing with his Austrian wife, Louis XVI took this road, and it was on it that he was recognized and arrested.

I am leaving the regency to my Austrian wife, the niece of that unfortunate beheaded queen, and I am not leaving to flee but to fight.

HE LEAVES THE palace of St-Cloud on Thursday, 15 April 1813 at four o'clock in the morning.

At eight in the evening he dines in Sainte-Menehould. He drives through Metz at seven in the morning on Friday the 16th, and he arrives in Mainz at midnight the same day.

He has been driving for more than forty hours.

PART FOUR

Death is drawing near us

16 APRIL 1813 TO 9 NOVEMBER 1813

XI

HE IS SITTING DOWN, writing. It is six in the evening on Saturday, 17 April 1813.

My good Louise,
  I reached Mainz on the 16th at midnight. I have not received any letters from you today. I am longing to hear how you are and what you are doing. Tell me that you have been sensible and brave. I have a great deal of work as you can imagine. Grand Marshal Duroc has not arrived yet.

He gets up and walks to the window. On the main square of Mainz young soldiers are drilling. One of them must have seen him because they lift their muskets and shout, 'Long live the Emperor!' He steps back, waiting for the cheers to die down. The drums sound, their rolls approaching and receding on the wind that has been gusting hard all day.

HE HAS NOT gone out since he arrived yesterday at midnight. He has listened to his aides-de-camp, read the dispatches from Ney and Eugène de Beauharnais, then consulted the maps with Bacler d'Albe. The Russians and Prussians have advanced everywhere; Torgau has fallen; they have been received as victors and liberators in Dresden.

And my ally the King of Saxony, Frederick Augustus, has fled, prompting a rapprochement with Austria, which is simply waiting, its arms at its feet, for me to be wounded so it can finish me off.
He picks up his quill again.

There is plenty of wind here.
  Kiss my son on both eyes. Write to Papa Francis every week; give him military news and tell him of my attachment to him personally.

This may make Austria hesitate for a moment, a few days or a few weeks, time for me to beat the Russians and Prussians.

He goes over to the maps. It is starting to grow dark. Roustam comes in and lights the chandeliers.

The shadows lengthen on the floors. With a wave he asks for the candles to be brought nearer the table. Bacler d'Albe has marked the enemy units on the map.

If I had a few thousand more cavalry, the game would be simpler.

But he has no trump cards, and he has to play with the little that he has.

He walks about the large room, his hands behind his back. This campaign, this game, is all or nothing. If he wins, he scoops the pot, all the stakes that have been on the table since he came to power. If he loses, they will take everything. England will win the war it has been waging against France since 1792.

All or nothing. These are the stakes of this year 1813.

He sits back down and continues writing to Marie Louise,

I don't want you to have stomach ache any more. Be cheerful and then you will be healthy. Political matters will give you a certain amount to do.

Seeing you and spending my life with you is very sweet to me.

Farewell, my dear Louise; love me as I love you, if that is possible given the levity of your sex. Ever yours. Your husband, Nap

The drums have fallen silent; the wind has dropped. He is not going to sleep. Too many orders to dictate, too many thoughts going round his head, too many decisions to take. He calls in Fain, his secretary. He shows him the letter he has received from Frederick Augustus of Saxony, the ally who does not want to provide troops, who is abandoning his capital Dresden. He begins dictating: 'Monsieur my brother, Your Majesty's letter has grieved me. You have no friendship for me any more; I blame the enemies of our cause who are in your cabinet. I need all your cavalry and all your officers. I have spoken my mind with the frankness Your Majesty knows me for. But whatever the outcome may be, Your Majesty may count on the esteem you have inspired in me, which nothing could shake.'

This is what I can write, if I choose. But I have to restrain myself, order France's ambassador in Vienna, Count Narbonne, to do nothing that could displease Francis's court. I know perfectly well what Metternich and 'Papa Francis' want: to rob me without taking any risks. Pull their chestnuts out of the fire. Prepare and then wait for my defeat.

All or nothing.

It is the armies that will decide everything once again: all or nothing.

ON WEDNESDAY, 28 April 1813, he has installed his headquarters in a house on the main square of Eckartsberg, not far from Erfurt and Weimar. More than 200,000 men are concentrated here, in the Saale valley, in driving rain that soaks their uniforms.

Napoleon stands in a little room, bent over the maps. The aim is to debouch from the Saale valley, reach Leipzig, then Dresden, and drive the Russians and Prussians back eastwards, towards the Vistula. And then go down the Elbe towards Hamburg and threaten Berlin.

Saxony is a crossroads which, when one controls it, allows one to dominate all of Germany, north and east. Leipzig and Dresden are the two points Napoleon rings with a circle.

ALL OR NOTHING.

The cannon begin to roar, merging with the sound of thunder and the storm that won't stop. They are fighting at Weissenfels.

The troops, he says, have to advance along both banks of the Saale. General Souham's division is made up of young recruits who have never seen fire. Will they hold out against the Russian cavalry and cannon? On Friday 30 April, when he is riding through their lines in conquered Weissenfels, he learns they have captured the hedges and houses with the bayonet.

'They taught the old moustaches,' Marshal Ney says as he approaches. 'Give me plenty of these youngsters; I'll lead them where I want. The old moustaches know as much we do; they think; they've got too much composure. Whereas these intrepid children don't have their difficulties. They always look ahead, never to left or right.'

He is among them. He hears the rolling shouts of 'Long live

the Emperor!' He sees the beardless faces, flushed from running, fighting, shouting, trembling, that turn towards him. These young men are lifting their muskets. These young men are going to get themselves killed. Because the game is only beginning.

All or nothing. He cannot lose it.

HE MUST ADVANCE on Leipzig. He will pass through Lützen. 'If you hear cannon near this town,' he writes to Eugène de Beauharnais who is further to the north, on the Elbe, 'march on the enemy's right.'

His thoughts have never been so clear. The troop movements emerge before his eyes on the map. If he had cavalry, he could destroy the Russian and Prussian armies of Barclay de Tolly, Wittgenstein and Blücher.

But one must play with what one has.

And first of all stop the Austrians entering the game. He writes to Marie Louise again that night,

> I am surprised that Papa Francis says that peace depends on me. Three months ago I told him that I was ready for that and I received no answer. Let him see that this country will not let itself be mistreated or have shameful conditions imposed on it by Russia or England, and that if I have at present a million men in arms, I will in the future have as many as I wish . . .
>
> Have your letter sent by the Austrians so that it is not suspect.
>
> My health is very good. It rained a great deal yesterday, but it didn't do me any harm; the sun is shining now. I am mounting up. Kiss my son twice. *Addio, mio bene*. Ever yours,
> Nap

HE GALLOPS ALONG the crests of the hills surrounded by his staff. He wants to be with the advance guard. These young soldiers must see him, learn who he is and how he defies danger. And how the cannonballs don't hit him.

What if they do? Why not? It is a challenge he throws down to destiny.

Nothing is trembling in me. Let them hit me if they want. I will accept it. But if I don't die, then I will carry on and never give in.

He hears the whistle of a cannonball; clods of earth fly into the air in the middle of his staff. When the smoke clears, he sees a man's body being wrapped in a coat.

Bessières! Marshal, Duke of Istria, one of those I loved, who I put in command of the cavalry of the Guard.

'Death is drawing near us,' Napoleon says, riding away.

He stops, after galloping for a few minutes, in the bailiff's house in Lützen. Night falls. It is Saturday, 1 May 1813. They will fight tomorrow. Before lying down, he takes up his quill.

My good friend,
    Write to Papa Francis that he should not let himself be carried along by the hatred his wife feels for us; this would be fatal for him and cause much misfortune. The death of the Duke of Istria afforded me great pain; it is a very sensitive blow. He had gone forward to the skirmishers for no good reason, out of curiosity. The first cannonball killed him dead. See something is said to his poor wife. My health is extremely good. Tell the vicereine that Viceroy Eugène is in good health.
    Farewell, my friend, ever yours,
        Nap

Bessières fell near him, a few feet away.

But why worry Marie Louise? All the Court, all Paris, would know that the Empress was trembling for me, that I am therefore in danger, and in the shadows some General Malet would be hatching another plot.

He dictates a short letter to Arch-Chancellor Cambacérès.

I have moved my headquarters to Lützen today. The first shot fired today caused us a great loss: the Duke of Istria was struck by a cannonball through his body and was killed stone dead.
    I am writing in haste so that you may inform the Empress and let his wife know, to prevent her finding out from the newspapers. Make the Empress understand that the Duke of Istria was very far from me when he was killed.

DIE?

On this Sunday, 2 May 1813, when fighting has begun in the villages to the south of Lützen, he is wondering about dying.

Why not, since this game is all or nothing, and he has to play with all his cards? When he launches himself at the enemy advance guard, among the young recruits who are starting to break up, his life is a trump card.

He is on horseback, in the soldiers' midst, among the cannon-balls and whistling bullets. He shouts at the conscripts scattering through the lanes of the village of Kaja that they have already taken, lost, retaken and lost several times, 'Follow me, men; the battle is won. Forward march!'

At the same time he gives orders to his aides. The entire right wing of the army has to pivot, with this village of Kaja as the axis, and they will turn the enemy army. He orders the artillery to follow the movement, to crush the Russians retreating under the salvoes of cannon fire. He observes the retreat of the enemy units, still under fire. They are beaten, but they are not destroyed.

'I would be able to conclude matters very promptly if I had sixteen thousand more cavalry!' he cries.

But this is victory, and the open road to Dresden.

HE VISITS THE advance posts after night has fallen and the firing stopped. The soldiers cheer him. The shouts of 'Long live the Emperor' roll along the lines.

He turns towards his aides-de-camp.

'Nothing equals the valour, goodwill and love of all these young soldiers,' he says. 'They are full of enthusiasm.'

By the light of the bivouac fires he looks at the officers who surround him. They are gloomy although the victory is won, and Lützen will be considered, he is convinced, a model battle.

He stops, dismounts near a bivouac fire. He dictates his proclamation to the army. It is now, here, that he will find the words that will touch these young troops. 'Soldiers, I am satisfied with you! You have fulfilled my expectations. You have made up for everything with your goodwill and bravery. You have added new lustre to the glory of my eagles; you have shown all that French blood is capable of. The battle of Lützen will be set above the battles of Austerlitz, Jena, Friedland and the Moskva.'

He mounts up again. He hears the groans of the wounded.

The battle has been murderous. How many — 1,000, 10,000, 20,000 — dead and wounded on each side?

Suddenly he is overwhelmed by tiredness. All these victories and none of them ends the game!

He reaches Lützen, goes into the bailiff's house.

The couriers from Paris have arrived. He leafs through the newspapers and grows furious. Is this how they report the war? He dictates a letter to Savary, minister of police.

Since all the newspaper articles that talk about the army do so without tact I think it would be better if they didn't talk about it at all! It is a great mistake to imagine that one can introduce ideas this way in France; it is better to let things go their own pace . . . It is truth and simplicity that are needed. One statement — this is true, this is not true — is enough!'

He is exhausted. He has to hold everything in his hands. Everything. Not let go of anything, because it would take one dropped thread for everything to give. He needs a couple of hours sleep. He sighs. One last task. He has himself brought a piece of paper, a quill.

My good friend,
    It is eleven in the evening; I am very tired. I have won a complete victory over the Russian and Prussian army commanded by Emperor Alexander and the King of Prussia. I have lost ten thousand men killed or wounded. My troops have covered themselves in glory and have given me tokens of love that touch my heart. Kiss my son. I am in very good health. Farewell, my good Louise. Ever yours,
    Nap

HOW MUCH HAS he slept? He doesn't know when he started working again, studying maps, dictating orders to his aides-de-camp.

The whole left bank of the Elbe is now in the hands of the French troops. General Lauriston has occupied Leipzig. Dresden can only fall in the days to come. Afterwards they will be able, depending on the reaction of the Russians and Prussians, either to go back up towards Pseilein, or continue eastwards.

On the map he underlines the names of Bautzen, Würschen, Görlitz and Breslau.

What worries him is that, by advancing like this on the Vistula, he has his whole right flank exposed. He is going to be very close to the Austrian border, and how can he trust Metternich and the Emperor Francis?

He writes to Count Narbonne. The ambassador has been coldly received by the Emperor. The Viennese court's sole hope is for a French defeat. And Metternich imagines that he will be able to impose his views on the Russians and Prussians.

So they will have to fight against Austria too.

HE GOES OUTSIDE. The bivouac fires are still burning in the brightening dawn. The sky is bright but it's cold. He gallops over the battlefield. He stops for a moment, catching sight of the huge ditches into which peasants surrounded by soldiers are throwing the bodies of the dead.

He spurs on his horse. He rides along the marching columns. The soldiers cheer him.

They are alive. Their comrades are dead. Marshal Bessières is dead. I am alive.

Death didn't want me. I do not fear it. I defy it. What does it matter to me to be alive if I do not fight?

AS NIGHT FALLS, he makes a halt in the little town of Borna, sits at the desk the quartermasters have put up. He starts to write:

My good friend,
    I have received your letter of 30 April. I see with pleasure what you tell me about my son and your health. Mine is extremely good. The weather is very beautiful. I am continuing to chase the enemy who is fleeing in all directions and in all haste.

He could stop there and write what he wants to, what he wrote yesterday – 'I think the little king has completely forgotten me. Kiss him twice on his eyes for me' – but he has to try everything still possible to avoid war with Vienna.

Papa Francis is not behaving very well. They want to turn him against me. Send for M. Floret, the Austrian chargé d'affaires and tell him, 'People want to turn my father against us. I have sent for you to ask you to write to him that the Emperor is in a good position; he has a million men in arms and so, if my father listens to the Empress's gossip, I foresee him storing up a great deal of misfortune for himself. He does not know this nation, its attachment to the Emperor and its energy. Tell my father on my behalf, as his beloved daughter, who takes so much interest in him and the country of my birth, that if my father lets himself be led astray, the French will be in Vienna before September and he will have lost the friendship of a man who is very attached to him.'

Write to him yourself to the same effect, for his own interest more than mine, because I have seen them coming for a long time and I am ready.

Addio, mio dolce amore,
    Your Nap

He has done what he ought.

HE ENTERS DRESDEN on Saturday 8 May at eight in the morning, as the sun fills the town with a hazy light. A cannonade can be heard in the distance, and smoke is rising above the Elbe. The Russians and Prussians have burnt the bridges on their retreat to Breslau, along the Austrian frontier. They are withdrawing in order.

Suddenly, in the middle of the road, a few metres from the city gates, he sees a solemn deputation coming towards him bearing the keys of the city. He looks at these men with contempt.

A few days ago they were fêting Frederick William of Prussia and Tsar Alexander. They were enthusiastically offering hospitality and tributes to those they thought were their conquerors. And now here they are, sheepish and trembling in front of me.

'You would deserve to be treated as a conquered country!' he calls out. 'I have the figures for how many volunteers you have armed, clothed and equipped against me. Your young girls have strewn flowers under the feet of kings, my enemies.'

What is left of these garlands and petals? Dung on the paving stones!

His horse stamps its feet. The notables tremble. But one must also use men's cowardice.

'But I want to pardon everything,' he carries on. 'Bless your king, for he is your saviour. Let a deputation from among your number go and beg him to return his presence to you. I only pardon you for love of him. I shall see that war causes you as little harm as possible.'

I need Frederick Augustus, King of Saxony. I need his cavalry and infantry. He must return in triumph to Dresden, his capital. I will dine with him. I will forget he fled the town, refused me the support of his troops and waited for my defeat, and that he only comes over to me now, like the inhabitants of Dresden, because I am victorious.

HE INSTALLS HIMSELF in the royal palace, in the heart of this wealthy, beautiful city, during a mild spring that is already like summer.

'People say you are as fresh as springtime,' he writes to Marie Louise. 'I would very much like to be with you. I love you as the most beloved of women. *Addio, mio bene,* Nap'.

He rides along the banks of the Elbe. He reviews the engineers throwing a bridge over the river in this hot weather. He watches them working, stripped to the waist. He remains motionless. He thinks of the bridges over the Berezina, of all the men who died there. General Eblé and almost all those engineers only outlived their superhuman efforts by a matter of days.

Sometimes images from the past like this come back to him with such vividness that he can only tear himself away with the greatest difficulty. At those moments he would like a cannonball to come and blow off his head.

He crosses the river as soon as the bridge is over. The Prussians and Russians have retrenched in Bautzen, on the banks of the Spree. He studies their position from a distance, then returns to Dresden.

ON SUNDAY, 16 May 1813, he receives Count Bubna, a general and diplomat who is Metternich's envoy. He listens to him as he walks slowly about the sunlit salon of the royal palace. Little by little the shadows lengthen; night draws in.

He lets Bubna talk, setting out at length Metternich's conditions for the establishment of peace. Vienna wants to be a mediator.

'Armed?' asks Napoleon.

He stops in front of Count Bubna, whose face is now lit by the chandeliers.

There's no mystery about this man, nor the proposals he is putting forward. The aim is to strip me and force me to submit. They don't want peace. They want my abdication.

He guesses this. But can he extricate himself from negotiations?

'I have admired my father-in-law ever since I first met him,' he says. 'He arranged my marriage in the most noble way and I am wholeheartedly grateful to him. But if the Emperor of Austria wants to change course, he would have done better not to have made this marriage, which I ought to regret now.'

He has dared say this, question his marriage with Marie Louise. He walks away from Count Bubna.

'What affects me most deeply,' he goes on, 'is the fate of the King of Rome. I do not want to make Austrian blood more odious to France. The long wars between France and Austria have caused resentments to take root. You know . . .'

He walks back towards Bubna.

'. . . that the Empress, as an Austrian princess, was not at all loved when she arrived in France. Barely has she begun to win over public opinion with her amiability and virtues than you wish to force me to proclaim manifestos that will irritate the nation. Admittedly, I will not be reproached for having too loving a heart, but if I love someone in the world, it is my wife. Whatever the outcome of this war may be, it will influence the fate of the King of Rome. It is in this respect that a war against Austria is odious to me.'

As Bubna is leaving the salon, Napoleon goes up to him,

Has this man understood my determination?

'I am resolved to die, if I must, at the head of all France's noblest men, rather than become a laughing stock of the English and let my enemies triumph.'

DIE?

This word keeps coming back to him this year, 1813. These are the stakes: all or nothing.

He remains standing in the grand salon lit by dozens of chandeliers for a long time, then, leaning on a little table, he writes a few lines to Marie Louise.

> I saw General Bubna this evening and I told him what I
> thought. I hope they will think twice. In any case you shouldn't
> be too affected. They will all get a due thrashing, all of them.
> Farewell, my friend. Love me as I love you. Ever yours,
>   Napoleon

HE HAS TO leave Dresden, go where the advance guards are, pass through villages and towns that have been set ablaze by roundshot and reduced to ashes. While still riding he asks for Grand Equerry Caulaincourt to join him on a hill which rises up from the Spree. The Prussians and Russians have entrenched themselves east of Bautzen, in the ravines and on the green hills.

He turns towards Caulaincourt.

'You see Alexander,' he says. 'Knowing his views, we will end up coming to an understanding.'

He draws on the reins so his horse does not shy away from Caulaincourt's. He studies the hills the men will have to climb under grapeshot. And he will be with them.

If it all could only stop!

'Moreover my plan is to offer Alexander a fortune to free him from Metternich's intrigues,' he adds. 'If I have sacrifices to make, I'd rather they benefit the Emperor Alexander, who fights me fairly, and the King of Prussia, in whom Russia takes an interest, than Austria, who has betrayed our alliance and who, under the title of mediator, wants to claim the right to dispose of everything, after taking what suits her.'

Caulaincourt bows. His face has lit up like someone who has heard what he wanted. They are all like that around me: Berthier, the generals, perhaps even Duroc, my grand marshal of the palace, the most faithful of all. They are weary. They want peace. They want to enjoy their properties – perhaps at any price. They are afraid of dying without having enjoyed their accumulated wealth.

'I am waiting,' says Napoleon.

Caulaincourt hurries off.

THE WEATHER IS turning on that Wednesday, 19 May 1813. Rain is falling when Caulaincourt arrives bringing Alexander's response. There will be neither armistice nor peace. The Tsar refuses them both.

'All these people will be more accommodating when I win a new victory,' Napoleon says.

He gives orders all night. They will force the enemy to withdraw troops from its right by attacking on the left. But the main attack will be on the right, while Marshal Ney crosses the Spree and cuts in front of the enemy's rear.

The rain is torrential now. He wakes up. They will fight in a storm on this Thursday, 20 May 1813. He is with the advance guard, in the hail of canister shot and cannonballs. He enters Bautzen. He sleeps on the ground for half an hour or so in the very heart of the battle. He spends the night in front of his maps. And, on the morning of Friday 21 May, he is in the saddle again, galloping towards Würschen. He does not leave the advance guard. He needs to be there, with the men who are most exposed. He remembers often telling his generals that a leader should only take risks when they are necessary for leadership, and that in all other circumstances the officer should protect his life.

Risking his own at this moment is necessary.

When he looks at his escort and staff, he sees the incomprehension on their faces. Why is he running towards the roundshot like this? they are wondering.

He must know what destiny wants.

The battles of Bautzen and Würschen have been won. It is six in the evening. He has his tent pitched in front of an isolated tavern still full of traces of the Emperor Alexander who spent all day there.

The band of the Imperial Guard play as night falls.

He writes,

My friend,
    I have had a battle today. I have taken Bautzen. I have dispersed the Russian and Prussian army, which had been joined by all its reinforcements and reserves from the Vistula and was in a superb position. This has been a fine day. I am a little tired.

I have been drenched two or three times today. I embrace you and beg you to kiss my son for me. My health is good. I have not lost anyone of distinction. I reckon my losses at three thousand men killed or wounded.

 Addio, mio bene,
  Nap

BUT IT IS not over. *Will it ever be over?*

 We must pursue the Russians and Prussians, who are not breaking up. And I haven't any cavalry!

He gallops to the advance guard and climbs the hills with his voltigeurs as the cannonballs fall all around. His group of richly uniformed horsemen attracts the attention of enemy gunners. A chasseur of the escort is killed.

'Fortune bears a grudge against us today,' Napoleon calls out.

But he continues to go forward, followed a few paces behind by Caulaincourt, Grand Marshal of the Palace Duroc, General of Engineers Kirgener and Marshal Mortier.

He turns around. They are not caracoling their horses like conquerors, but riding like men who submit to a law imposed on them. He carries on advancing.

Suddenly a cannonball whistles, strikes a tree. It is as if destiny had just drawn a menacing line around him. He waits for the mud to fall back down with the sound of hail as his horse rears. He recognizes Caulaincourt's voice, which seems to come from a long way away.

'Sire, the grand marshal of the palace has been killed.'

These few words open a wound from which memories come gushing out like blood.

Duroc at the siege of Toulon, close to me. Duroc who, when we were alone, used the tu *form. Duroc who introduced Marie Walewska to me. Duroc from whom I hid nothing. Duroc in whom I had absolute confidence. Duroc dead after Bessières, after Lannes.*

 Will destiny leave me alone, like an island, living in the middle of an ocean of dead?

He dismounts.

The cannonball struck the tree, ricocheted, killed General Kirgener, then tore Duroc's innards apart; he has been taken to a house in the village of Makersdorf.

Duroc is white as a sheet. Napoleon sits next to him, grasps his right hand. It is already frozen. He stays like that for more than a quarter of an hour, his head resting on his left hand.

Duroc stammers, 'Ah, sire, go away – this sight affects you.'

Napoleon gets up heavily, leans on Caulaincourt's arm, murmurs for the last time, bending down towards Duroc, 'Farewell then, my friend; we will see each other again soon.'

HE REMAINS SITTING stock-still in front of his tent pitched in a field. General Drouot asks him for orders for the artillery. Ney announces that the enemy has been defeated.

'Tomorrow, for everything,' he says.

He wants to see Duroc again. He goes back to the house. He kisses the dead man's face.

This is a whole chapter of my life dying with him.

He does not sleep. This death oppresses him like a fatal omen, like a curse too. He is not 'meant' to die. He must go through with his life seeing everyone close to him die. He is not 'meant' to know the rest of a brutal death on the battlefield.

So be it.

He is with the advanced posts again, entering Görlitz. He is even ahead of the infantry. Suddenly Russian cavalry burst out on the road. They are only a few hundred metres away. Napoleon calmly turns his back on them. He directs the movement of an approaching artillery unit, guides its cannon into position. Berthier shouts that the Russians are advancing.

'Well then, we will advance too,' Napoleon replies calmly.

What risk is he running? Death?

What is that? The end of the game.

THAT EVENING HE stays in a little farm that has been looted. He has only a dark, miniscule room. What matter? He cannot think of anything except Duroc's death. He must share his pain, confide a little.

My good friend,

You will have learnt of the fatal cannonball that in one fell swoop robbed me of the grand marshal and General Kirgener. Imagine my grief! You know my friendship with the Duke de Frioul. Grand Marshal Duroc has been my friend for twenty years. I have never had reason to complain of him; he has only ever given me matter for consolation. It is an irreparable loss, the greatest I could suffer. I have ordered that until I find a replacement the grand equerry will perform his job. *Addio, mio bene.* My affairs are going very well. Ever yours,

Nap

HE HAS ESTABLISHED himself in Neumarkt, between the Oder and the Neisse. He looks at these great Eastern European skies that stretch their long white trails of cloud over limitless expanses. It is mild. He walks about in front of the opulent house that is his headquarters.

In less than a month he has made the Russians and Prussians withdraw 350 kilometres. He has always defeated them, but he has not destroyed them. He hasn't enough cavalry to pursue them. They are defeated, hard-pressed. Kutusov is dead, he has just learnt, and illness had in any case prevented the Russian marshal leading his armies.

What shall I do now, when we are moving into summer and I know Poland's desert wastes?

He looks around him; he sees Caulaincourt, Berthier. He hears what they're saying.

They want peace. Caulaincourt may even be prepared to want defeat so that the war may end. And this is whom I am sending to meet the Russian and Prussian plenipotentiaries who have come to ask for an armistice under Metternich's mediation. I could try to destroy their armies. But where are my dragoons, my cuirassiers, my Polish lancers? Buried under the Russian snow!

He has Berthier bring him the returns of the different units. Losses have been heavy. The conscripts can't take the continual marching. Out of a nominal 47,000 men, III Corps only has 24,000 soldiers. Ammunition is growing scarce.

He sends for Caulaincourt. 'I am ready,' he says, 'to sign an armistice convention that will be valid until 20 July. Peace negotiations should start during this period in Prague.'

Caulaincourt is glad, brimming with enthusiasm even. And this is the man who has replaced Duroc! There you have the men around me now. The best are dead. The Caulaincourts are left.

On 4 June 1813 the armistice is signed at Pleiswitz.

Before leaving Neumarkt to return to Dresden, he dictates a letter to Clarke, the minister of war.

> This armistice interferes with the course of my victories.
> I decided on it for two reasons: my lack of cavalry, which prevents me from dealing decisive blows, and Austria's hostile position. That court, under the most amiable, the most tender and, I would even say, the most sentimental pretences, wants nothing less than to use fear of its army assembled at Prague to intimidate me and reap advantages by the mere presence of these 100,000 men, and without any real hostilities.
> If I can, I will wait for the month of September to strike major blows.

He does not believe in the peace.

Who really wants it? It will only be built on the defeat of my enemies or my capitulation.

But I must act as if peace were possible. So many people want it and desire blinds them.

A last letter to Marie Louise before leaving Neumarkt.

> My good friend,
> I received your letter of the 28th in which I see that you are very afflicted. I hope that the news of the armistice for two months that the Mainz telegraph will have informed you of has given you pleasure.
> My affairs are going well. My health is good. Look after yourself. Kiss my son twice on the eyes and dearly love your faithful
> Nap

I will go to Dresden during the armistice to be closer to you.

XII

HE WALKS HIS HORSE along the road that leads from Neumarkt to Dresden, holding the reins distractedly and letting himself be jogged about by the horse's swaying gait. His thoughts come and go.

He hears shouts. Some soldiers are running down the hills, sliding down the embankments. 'Long live the Emperor!' they cry.

He does not respond to their cheers. They are like a distant murmur that disturbs his thoughts. Since the armistice was concluded, he has been hesitating. Perhaps he was wrong not to pursue the enemy to the Vistula. Perhaps he let himself be convinced involuntarily by these unbridled peace-mongers Berthier, Caulaincourt and all the others riding behind.

Every evening, at each post stage, they urge him to return as quickly as possible to Dresden, take a carriage and spare himself such exhaustion. They don't like riding from three in the morning to nightfall any more, bivouacking wherever they find themselves, then taking his dictation for another few hours.

They all want peace so they can rest. And they turn their fatigue into high politics.

He refuses. He returns on horseback. The dawns are cool. The days long. He sees the soldiers and they see him. Sometimes a town's inhabitants surround him cheering. For instance at Görlitz on Tuesday, 8 June 1813, when, as dawn was breaking and he was just about to leave, a suburb caught fire and he gave orders to the troops to fight the blaze, and then had 6,000 francs distributed to the disaster victims.

HE STOPS AT Bautzen. The houses are still full of wounded. The whole town seems to be moaning.

In the little room where he has set up his study for the night, he is given a report from Marshal Soult and General Pradel, the grand provost of the army. More than two thousand soldiers have been found with wounds to their right hands, self-inflicted according to the report. Pradel demands all these men be made an example of.

He has seen these young soldiers, courageous but often distraught. He pictures the firing squads he is being asked to assemble. A crackdown is only just when it is useful. He sends for Larrey, the surgeon-in-chief. He knows the devotion and honesty of this man. He asks him what he thinks.

'Sire,' Larrey cries immediately, 'these children are innocent. You are being misled.'

Napoleon listens, his face leaning forward. According to Larrey, the soldiers are wounding themselves involuntarily with their muskets and often their comrades too when they fight in squares. Larrey speaks with conviction; produces witnesses and evidence.

Napoleon stops in front of him.

'My orders will be communicated to you,' he says.

Then he walks a little way and adds, 'A sovereign is very lucky to have to deal with a man like you.'

He orders that Larrey be granted 6,000 francs in gold, a State pension of 3,000 livres and a miniature set of diamonds.

HE MUST SEE everything, know everything, decide everything.

How many men like Larrey can he still turn to? Lannes, Bessières, Duroc and so many others dead. Then there is the dispatch he has just received which reports that, while governing the Illyrian provinces, Junot has been suffering fits of dementia.

He remembers. It was the siege of Toulon.

He was a captain, Junot was a sergeant.

When a shell covered an order I was dictating to him with mud, this young unknown had said laughing, 'So much the better. We didn't have any sand to dry the ink.' Junot, in the days of poverty in Paris, sharing what he had with me; Junot with me at St Jean d'Acre; Junot, whom I assured, when I left Egypt, 'of my tender friendship'.

Those were my words. And now Junot is mad, appearing at the ball he organized at Ragusa with decorations as his only clothes! Junot in full governor's uniform driving his carriage instead of the coachman!

Junot raving. He must be locked up, sent back to his home in Burgundy.

Junot worse than dead. Demented.

NAPOLEON REMAINS SITTING in a chair for most of the night, until he stands up and looks around as if he were coming out of a dark tunnel. He starts dictating orders and dispatches in a clear voice.

'War,' he writes to General Bertrand, 'can only be waged with vigour, decisiveness and constant will; one must neither grope around nor hesitate. Establish harsh discipline and, in action, do not hesitate to trust your troops.'

To horse now! It's five days now that they've been on the road. To horse, to horse! On Thursday, 10 June 1813, he finally reaches Dresden again.

He writes to Marie Louise,

> My good friend,
>   I have reached Dresden at four in the morning. I am lodged in a suburb in a little palace belonging to Count Marcolini that has a very beautiful garden, which I find very agreeable. You know how sad the King's palace is. My health is extremely good. Give my son a kiss. You know how much I love you.
>   Nap

HE SLEEPS FOR a few hours and when he wakes up it seems he's been asleep for days and days.

He immediately goes out into the suburb, Friedrichstadt.

Soldiers mill about idly. Do they think they're at peace?

He carries on into the town. Groups of people stop and stare when they see him. There are no cheers, but they seem transfixed, watching him pass with a mixture of astonishment and dread.

He sees the King of Saxony, who rushes towards him.

'The most insane rumours have been circulating,' the sovereign says. 'People thought Your Majesty was dead. They claimed that a dummy looking like you had been put in a carriage to cover up your death.'

Napoleon smiles. Dead? Sometimes it seems to him that part

of his life is dead, and that he is looking at another part of himself carrying on riding, giving orders, fighting, hoping. And sometimes he doesn't understand anything, and he is absorbed by a sort of reverie as if he were drowsing, absent from life.

He walks about the salon a little, turning his back on the King of Saxony, who goes on talking about the rumours of negotiations between the Russians, Prussians, Austrians and English.

The king's informants in Austria and Prussia tell him that London is preparing to pay Russia over a million livres and Prussia over 600,000 to bind them to a treaty which would prevent them ending hostilities with the Emperor without London's permission. England would thus assume the right to dictate conditions and choose the moment of peace. Austria is prepared to sign this treaty, but Metternich wants to play his own cards and not hand Europe over to England or Russia. So he is putting himself forward as a mediator. But what will be the use of these peace negotiations in Prague if England dictates the rules?

Napoleon turns around. He should say, 'It's a show they're putting on to fool me! And they think I am fooled! I am playing along to gain time.'

AND THIS TIME he mustn't lose the game. Every day he inspects the troops, directs parades and reviews. *Dresden must become my army's stronghold*. The grenadiers must clear the outskirts of trees. Create military camps on the hills. Fortify the gates. Erect palisades.

He is in the saddle from dawn until late at night.

'I was on horseback from midday until four in the morning yesterday. I caught a lot of sun,' he writes to Marie Louise.

When he returns to his study, the dispatches and letters have been put on the table.

He reads them as he walks around the room; sometimes he lets out a roar of anger. He dictates an official letter to the regent, Empress Marie Louise.

Madame and dear friend,

I have received your letter in which you informed me that you received the arch-chancellor while in bed. My intention is that, under no circumstances and on no pretext, will you receive anyone in bed. That is only permitted to persons over thirty years of age!'

His anger does not lift. All these dispatches irritate him.

Savary, the minister of police, sends report after report on the state of public opinion. The people want peace, according to him. Draft evaders are in the tens of thousands and could represent a menace to order and stability in the west and south. Hostile gangs are supposed to be forming in the forests. Savary is afraid it's the Jacobins, but my spies point to the activities of the Chevaliers of the Faith, royalists plotting here and there, creating secret societies.

Savary, like all those who have had their fill, wants me to lay down my arms! He wants peace, like all that pot-bellied, complacent lot, and who cares what the conditions are!

He writes to Savary:

The tone of your correspondence does not please me. You bore constantly with your need for peace. I know the situation of my Empire better than you . . . I want peace and no one is more interested in it than me; your speeches about it are therefore useless. But I shall not make a dishonourable peace or one that would bring us a fiercer war in six months.

Savary is going to try to convince me just like Caulaincourt and Berthier.

Don't reply to this. These matters do not concern you; do not involve yourself in them.

Angrily flinging up his arms, he bursts out, 'The minister of police seems to be trying to make me peaceable. It's totally fruitless and it wounds me, because it presumes that I am not peaceable.'

He adds, still louder, 'I am not a swaggerer. I do not make war a trade and no one is more peaceable than I!'

HE GOES OUT almost every evening for a few hours. He must show himself. He hosts a big dinner, then takes his guests to the theatre, with him leading the way with the Queen of Saxony on his arm. Sometimes he goes to the opera, or the little theatre he has had fitted out in his palace, the 'little Marcolini house' as he likes to call it.

He has requested that French actors be invited to come to Dresden.

'I desire that this should make a noise in Paris, and so in London and Spain, by making people think we are amusing ourselves in Dresden. The season is little suited to comedy,' he adds in a bitter voice, 'so you need only send six or seven actors at the most.'

Among them, Mesdemoiselles Georges, Mars and Bourgoing. He knew them when they were so young and so beautiful. Sometimes he receives Mademoiselle Georges after a performance. He chats with her, jokes and laughs, and for a few moments his carefreeness transports him far from Dresden. Then everything comes crashing back down. Her face and body are heavy. And he is weary.

In any case, he often falls asleep in the theatre and then wakes up with a start and looks around to see if anyone has noticed.

But one night in his apartments in the east wing of Count Marcolini's palace he can't sleep. The windows are open. It is hot. Sometimes he can hear soldiers singing, and the hooves of a mounted patrol echoing on the paving stones. Often a storm breaks.

He goes back to his study, leans over the maps prepared by Bacler d'Albe.

If Austria enters the conflict, it will pour hundreds of thousands of men onto the battlefields. We will have to hold Dresden and the Elbe line.

He straightens up.

The Austrians will be in the south, the Russians and Prussians in the centre, and Bernadotte in the north. For all the dispatches confirm that Bernadotte has landed in Pomerania with 25,000 Swedes. He is accompanied by Moreau, who has returned from the United States to contribute to my downfall – Moreau who couldn't bring me down in the time of Cadoudal. And at Alexander's side, in his service, is Pozzo di Borgo, my enemy from Ajaccio days. The Tsar has sent him to buy

Bernadotte, promising him the throne, my throne, when I fall! They are all here, all my enemies since the start of my life!

And England is paying them in pounds sterling, just as yesterday it was paying the assassins to stab me! Just as today it is offering Murat power in Italy and money if he abandons me. And the prize fool is tempted!

And they would like me to believe in the possibility of peace!

How could he sleep, when they are preparing his execution? Do they imagine he is going to let himself be strangled? He will do what he must up to the very last moment. Besides, nothing has been decided, even if he has never had to face such a difficult situation.

But here is a challenge worthy of my life!

All or nothing. These are the stakes.

HE RELAXES, SITS down. This is the moment when he can write: 'It is very hot here, there's a thunderstorm every night. Kiss my son twice. I would very much like you to be here, but it is not appropriate. *Addio, mio amore*, Nap'.

Then he pulls himself up; he can never let himself go for long. He is someone who should also reprimand, flatter, instruct. Even Marie Louise. She is complaining about the severe official letters he has sent her, so he must console her.

You must not be distressed by what I write to you, because it is to educate you and for the future, for you know I am pleased with you and that even if you did something that didn't suit me, I would find it very straightforward. You can never do anything that makes me angry, you are too good and too perfect for that, but if I see something I don't agree with, I shall carry on telling you without it upsetting you.

He puts down the quill.

Perhaps it was a mistake marrying a descendant of the Habsburgs, this Austrian?

Tomorrow he is seeing Metternich, the enemy, the trusted counsellor of the Emperor of Austria, *my wife's father.*

What a destiny my life represents!

HE HAS PUT the letter from Emperor Francis that Metternich has given him on the desk. He looks hard at the Austrian diplomat, this man with the haughty bearing who was the principal architect of the marriage with Marie Louise. He has respected the intelligence and cunning of this prince.

But perhaps Metternich is only one of those men who confuse lies with high politics.

Napoleon walks slowly towards him.

'So you want war,' he says in a calm voice. 'That is fine; you will have it. I have wiped out the Prussian army at Lützen; I have beaten the Russians at Bautzen. You will have your turn. We shall rendezvous in Vienna.'

He stops in front of Metternich.

'Men are incorrigible,' he goes on. 'The lessons of experience are wasted on them. Three times I have restored the Emperor Francis to his throne; I have promised to stay with him as long as I live; I have married his daughter. I said to myself then, "This is folly," but it is done.'

He raises his voice.

'I regret it today.'

He does not look at Metternich, who is talking of peace, *the fate of which, apparently, is in my hands.*

'To assure such a peace,' Metternich goes on, 'you must return to confines compatible with general stability or you must succumb in the struggle.'

'Well then, what do people want of me, that I dishonour myself?' he retorts in a loud voice. 'Never! I will know how to die. Your sovereigns, born on the throne, can let themselves be beaten twenty times and always return to their capitals, but I can't! I am aware of what I owe a brave people who, after unprecedented reversals, have given me fresh proofs of their devotion and the conviction that I am the only one who can govern them. I have repaired the losses of last year; look at my army now.'

'It is the precisely the army that desires peace,' murmurs Metternich.

'No, it's not the army; it is my generals who want peace. I don't have any generals any more. The cold of Moscow has demoralized them.' He gestures scornfully, then laughs. 'But I can assure you that next October we will see each other in Vienna.'

He walks about the room. He should be gripped by complete certainty, but he has to force himself to give a confident laugh.

'Fortune can betray you,' says Metternich, 'as it did in 1812. I have seen your soldiers; they are children. When this army of adolescents you are leading has gone, what will you do then?'

Napoleon bows his head and walks towards Metternich, his teeth gritted.

'You are not a soldier!' he cries. 'And you do not know what goes on in a soldier's mind. I have grown up on battlefields. You have not learnt to despise the lives of others and your own when it is necessary.'

He thinks of Lannes, Bessières, Duroc. It is painful remembering the death of his closest comrades, remembering all those dead stretching their arms through the snow of the Moskva.

'A man like me pays little heed to the lives . . .' he begins.

He breaks off and hurls his hat into a corner of the room. He despises Metternich, who pretends to be concerned with the fate of men and yet, for all his hypocritical mask and pitying words, sends them to their deaths by the hundreds of thousands, and calculates the profits he can gain from it.

'A man like me,' cries Napoleon, 'pays little heed to the deaths of two hundred thousand men!'

That's the truth of leaders in war, the honest, inhuman truth of those who govern that a Metternich will never confess.

He picks up his hat.

I have nothing in common with these people. I thought I could make them my allies. But they are simply predators.

'Yes,' he says, walking about the salon, 'I have committed a very great folly in marrying an Austrian archduchess.'

'Since Your Majesty wishes to know my opinion,' says Metternich, 'I will be very frank and say that Napoleon "the conqueror" has made a mistake.'

'So the Emperor Francis wants to dethrone his daughter?'

'The Emperor only knows his duty,' says Metternich.

This is what well-born princes are like. They give their daughters to a conqueror and then abandon her!

Napoleon stops Metternich, who has carried on speaking.

'By marrying an archduchess,' he says, 'I wanted to unite the past and present, Gothic prejudices and the institutions of my century. I was mistaken and I sense today the full extent of my mistake.'

He leads Metternich to the door.

'I do not hope to attain the goal of my mission,' Metternich murmurs.

Napoleon claps him on the shoulder.

'Well then, do you know what will happen? You will not make war on me.'

'You are lost, sire,' replies Metternich. 'I had a presentiment of it when I came; now I am going, I am certain.'

NAPOLEON IS ALONE in the salon. He has spent all that Saturday afternoon, 26 June 1813, with Metternich.

There will be war, of course. How could a Metternich accept my existence when I am weakened? Past, present — one or the other. I thought I could marry the two; it was a mistake.

He sends for Caulaincourt. He has the armistice extended until 10 August in order to delay Austria's engagement.

Caulaincourt is again advocating accepting all the Austrian demands. Cede the Grand Duchy of Warsaw, abandon Germany and even Italy. And even that wouldn't be enough, since England controls the timing and conditions of peace. But Caulaincourt and the others are so keen to negotiate that they don't see anything any more.

'You are asking me to drop my breeches myself so that I can be given the lash,' cries Napoleon. 'It is too much; you want me to be ruled by a rod of iron. Do you think I don't like rest as much as you? That I feel the need for peace any less than you? I will not baulk at anything reasonable to achieve peace, but do not suggest anything dishonourable, since you are French!'

But are they still? I am told that Caulaincourt started his discussions with the plenipotentiaries by saying, 'I am as European as you could possible be; get us back to France by peace or war and you will be thanked by thirty million Frenchmen.'

Traitor!

But who else can I use? And what does it matter, because

everything will be decided on the battlefield? Let Caulaincourt talk, negotiate, sell me. As long as I have an army, let them come and take me!

Go on, Caulaincourt, an armistice until 10 August, find out what they want from me!

HE WRITES TO Marie Louise,

My good friend,

I have talked for a very long time with Metternich; it tired me. Metternich seems a terrible intriguer and to be leading Papa Francis very badly. That man hasn't enough sense for his position.

A thousand amiable thoughts,
Nap

ON THE SURFACE everything is calm. He rides through the countryside. The days are hot and stormy. He visits the troops' bivouacs, the fortresses, and reviews the Saxon troops.

Who can tell if they won't turn their muskets against me?

In this game of all or nothing I have the cards but their real value in the game is uncertain. Where is the enthusiasm among those who surround me?

Here is Fouché, whom I have summoned to Dresden to entrust with the government of the Illyrian provinces in place of that poor madman Junot.

I am seeing him on 2 July 1813. Since yesterday he has known, like me, that ten days ago Wellington gained a dazzling victory at Vitoria and changed everything: no more talk of keeping Spain but of how we can defend the Pyrenees border.

I have instructed Marshal Soult to go and take command and I have withdrawn all powers from my brother Joseph. And here is Soult's wife, who imagined she'd be swanning around Dresden with a large retinue, coming to protest. Her husband is tired of waging war in Spain, she says.

'Madame, I did not ask to hear your angry outbursts. I am not your husband, and if I were, you would behave differently. Bear in mind that women are meant to obey; go back to your husband and do not plague him any more!'

Look at what I have to say! Look at the state of mind of my marshals and their wives!

And now here is Fouché, advising me to give in like Caulaincourt and Berthier. How can he fail to understand that they don't want to obtain certain parts of the Empire but everything that constitutes the Empire, and me and my dynasty as well?

'For me, it is a question of the Empire's safety,' he explains to Fouché. 'It is unfortunate, Your Grace, that a fatal disposition to discouragement dominates the best minds. The question is no longer the relinquishment of this or that province. It is our political supremacy that is at stake, and on that our existence depends.'

But Fouché and most of the others probably already think that they can save their possessions, their titles, even their jobs by getting rid of me. Who knows how far their agile minds have gone? These men of the Revolution have seen so many thrones fall, why not mine? But I have no one else but them to govern, lead the army and negotiate.

THE WAIT FOR war is always a long one. Napoleon spends most of his evenings at the theatre. But neither the inescapable workings of fate in *Oedipus* or *The Game of Love and Chance* nor the late-night conversations with Mademoiselle Georges distract him for long.

He does not want to overlook any possible trump card.

Hence, for example, he wants Marie Louise near him; it might add another grain of sand into the discussions taking place in Prague from which he neither expects nor wants anything, except to gain time.

He writes to Marie Louise,

My friend,

I want to see you. You will leave on the 22nd; you will sleep at Châlons. On the 23rd you will stop at Metz, on the 24th at Mainz, where I will come to see you. You will travel with four carriages on the first leg, four carriages on the second, four on the third. You will bring the duchess, two ladies, a prefect of the palace, two chamberlains, two pages, a doctor . . . Prepare all this. Count Gafarelly will be in command of the escorts.

Farewell, my friend. There will be time for you to have more news of me before you leave. Ever yours,

Nap

He reaches Mainz on Monday 26 July, at eleven in the evening. He left the previous day at three in the morning. He has driven day and night.

He takes Marie Louise by surprise. She can barely open her eyes and her face is puffy from tiredness and a cold. In fours days, she apologizes, she has barely been able to sleep ten hours. She has a migraine. He takes her arm and shuts himself away with her for what's left of the night.

HE IS AT work by dawn the next day. He dictates dozens of letters and orders. Then he has to receive the minor princes of the Confederation who have arrived to form a curious court, which he must divert, organizing dinners and spectacles.

Often at table the silence will suddenly make him start. He realizes that he is sitting there, opposite Marie Louise, with everyone respectfully waiting for him to speak, and his mind is full of troop movements and sentences he has to dictate.

He says a few words but doesn't hear the reply before he retreats inside himself again.

He walks out with the Empress on his arm. He doesn't want to worry her. She is not responsible for her father and Metternich's politics. He accompanies her on a tour of the Rhine, to Wiesbaden, Cassel, Biberich. It is hot. He listens to the women's voices, joyful and high-pitched. And in his mind he hears the dull roll of drums and the roar of cannon.

But he smiles. He must appear carefree, sure of himself.

On the eve of his departure for Dresden, Saturday 31 July, he tells Marie Louise, 'Peace would come if Austria did not try to fish in troubled waters. The Emperor is deceived by Metternich, who has sold himself for money to the Russians. In any event, he is a man who believes that politics consists of lying.'

She seems overwhelmed. She is going to write to the Emperor again.

'If they want to impose shameful conditions, I will make war on them,' he says. 'Austria will pay for everything. I will be sorry for the pain I will cause you but one must resist injustice.'

Suddenly, however, he changes his tone. She must, he says in an urgent voice, on her return to France, visit the arsenal of Cherbourg. He will attend to the organization of her trip.

Paris and London must know that, once the continental coalition is defeated, he will have done with England and that he is already equipping himself with the necessary naval strength. He sees the panic-stricken look in Marie Louise's eyes.

Everyone has to believe – they have to – that all this is possible.

HE LETS HIMSELF go in the berline driving towards Dresden. It is pouring with rain on this Sunday 1 August. He makes a stop at Würzburg to see General Augereau, who also speaks of peace, of the troops withdrawing to the Rhine and so giving up the fortresses on the Elbe!

Where will I find a resolute general?

In the berline, he writes,

My good Louise,
    I have been very sad all night. I had become accustomed to be with you; it is so agreeable! And then I found myself all alone. Let us hope that we will be back together for a long time within a month.
    Farewell, my good friend; love me and take good care of yourself. Your faithful husband,
    Nap

HE REACHES DRESDEN on Wednesday, 4 August 1813. It is nine o'clock in the morning. The rain has stopped. He goes to his study. From the garden of the Marcolini palace rise the sounds of summer and the smell of wet earth and leaves after the over-night storm.

He reads the first letter. He gets to his feet and goes to the window. Below him spreads a gleaming vault of trees, their every leaf covered with droplets of rain. He stands there, leaning out of the window, for a long time, then he returns to the desk and reads the piece of news again.

Junot has thrown himself out of the window of the chateau in Burgundy to which he had retired. He is dead.

Lannes, Bessières, Duroc, Junot and so many others before them. He remembers Muiron, fallen so long ago to save his life on the bridge of Arcola, taking bullets instead of him.

He was twenty-two. I am going to be forty-four in a few days.

He stays in the Marcolini palace all that day.

HE DOES NOT sleep. He is up at dawn. He wants to know what stage negotiations in Prague have reached. The French plenipotentiaries, explains Maret, minister of foreign affairs, have not even been received. Caulaincourt is at Metternich's feet in vain. We can't find out what they're asking of us.

'Everything,' Napoleon murmurs.

So they must catch them in their own trap, ask to be officially notified of their proposals.

And accept them. Why not? What are they risking? Being embroiled in long discussions.

He is under no illusions. England would ask even more. The treaties it has signed with Prussia and Russia and the money it has given them put it in control. And Austria has thrown its lot in with them.

So, what now? Wait and prepare for war.

He visits Dresden's fortifications. On 10 August he presides over a great review of 40,000 men to celebrate his birthday because he is sure that by 15 August they won't be thinking about marching past but fighting.

My good friend,

The army celebrated my birthday today; I had a very fine parade of 40,000 men. The King and Princes of Saxony took part. This evening I am going to a Court banquet and afterwards fireworks. Luckily the weather is beautiful. My health is extremely good. I suppose you will leave on the 17th for Cherbourg. I want you to enjoy yourself. You will tell me what you have seen. Farewell, my friend. Ever yours,

Nap

And what he has anticipated happens.

An envoy of Caulaincourt breathlessly announces that Metternich has declared the congress of Prague will close on Wednesday 11 August, at midnight. And Metternich has refused to read Napoleon's responses to his propositions.

So, you gentlemen of the peace-at-any-price school, do you need more proof?

He turns towards Maret.

'The question of peace or war has not turned on the concession of some part of our territory that does no damage to the Empire's strength, but on the jealousy of the powers, the hatred of secret societies, the passions fomented by England's machinations.'

He takes a few paces about the salon.

'I haven't received the news that Austria has declared war on me, but I assume I will get it today.'

THE NEWS ONLY arrives on Thursday, 12 August 1813.

In a harsh but dispassionate voice he berates the mad pretensions of Austria and its infamous treachery.

I am the husband of the Emperor's daughter and the King of Rome is his grandson, but what does that matter to these people?

He dictates a few lines to Cambacérès: 'I wish the Empress to make her journey to Cherbourg and not to know anything about this until her return.'

Then he takes up his quill, on 12 August, and tells Marie Louise, 'Don't tire yourself and take it gently. You know how precious your health is to me. Write to me in detail. My health is good. The weather is very beautiful. The heat has got up again. *Addio, mio bene*, two kisses to your son. Ever yours, Nap'.

They will all know soon enough — her, my son, the French — that war has started again.

XIII

HE IS FORTY-FOUR TODAY, Sunday, 15 August 1813. He is out in cold thundery rain, riding past the columns of soldiers leaving Dresden by the gates and suburb of Prina to march east towards Bautzen, Görlitz and the Spree, Neisse and Katzbach rivers, the latter a tributary of the Oder.

He stands for a while at the start of the bridge which crosses the Elbe on the outskirts of Dresden. Night has fallen and the downpour is growing even heavier. He feels the water running down his hat, soaking into the felt and drenching his coat. He shivers. He has been in situations like this so often – on the banks of the Italian rivers, along the Rhine, the Vistula, the Niemen. How many bridges he's crossed, how many rivers he's ridden along in torrential rain!

And now it's starting all over again, on the day of his forty-fourth birthday. Is this why he feels no enthusiasm, just a dogged determination to fight, against the whole world if necessary?

He crosses the river. There are no cheers. These soldiers march with their heads bowed, drenched by the rain. They are hungry. Again. He has told Quartermaster-General Daru, 'The army isn't being fed. It would be an illusion to think otherwise. Twenty-four ounces of bread, an ounce of rice and eight ounces of meat are insufficient for a soldier. At present you are only giving them eight ounces of bread, three ounces of rice and eight ounces of meat.'

They march and countermarch and, by the third day, when they have not yet fought, they are already straggling. Berthier and the surgeon Larrey have reported thousands of sick. The stormy weather, hot and cold alternately, wreaks havoc on the men's empty stomachs and their lungs.

HE STOPS AT Bautzen. He won a victory here just a few weeks ago, on 20 May. What use was it?

He does not even change his clothes. He wants to examine the maps. He knows every detail. And yet he needs to study them again. Facing him there are probably 600,000 men. To the north Bernadotte, in the centre the Prussian Blücher and the Russians, to the south Schlumberger and his Austrians. Against the traitor Bernadotte he pits Oudinot and Davout, who is to leave Hamburg, which he holds. These two must take Berlin. In the centre he deploys Macdonald, Ney, Lauriston and Marmont in a line. *I will drive into Bohemia, brush aside Schwarzenberg, march to Prague and let Austria feel the weight of its infamy.*

He hears shouts and exclamations. An aide-de-camp rushes up. The King of Naples has just arrived.

Napoleon looks at Murat approaching. It is as if, behind the magnificent uniform, blue, cinched with a gold-spangled belt, the hat topped with white ostrich feathers and an aigrette, the King of Naples wishes to hide the embarrassment his whole posture expresses.

He knows that I know. He knows my police. He wanted to betray me. But the English didn't offer him enough, or else he was afraid he was choosing the wrong camp by leaving me. He is here. He will command the reformed cavalry, 40,000 troopers who will be the spearhead of this army of 440,000 men I have assembled.

He invites Murat to sit down.

'I have here,' he says, sitting down opposite the King of Naples, 'three hundred and sixty-five thousand rounds for harnessed cannon, the equivalent of four battles like Wagram, and eighteen million cartridges.'

He speaks forcefully, but he senses that he is not managing to transmit this energy to Murat, who is worried about the enemy forces.

The King of Naples is uncertain, like them all. He talks to me about Bernadotte, Moreau, and Jomini too, that tactician who has deserted Ney's staff and gone over to the Russians.

These three men know my way of fighting. They can guess what I will do. They are going to try to evade me, as Kutusov did so often, and wear out my army with lengthy manoeuvres where it will be dissolved in the mud by tiredness and sickness.

He senses this. But what can he do?

He gets up, goes to Murat and says in a harsh voice, 'What is unfortunate in this situation is the lack of confidence the generals have in themselves: the enemy's forces seem considerable to them everywhere I am not.'

And I cannot be everywhere.

'One must not let oneself be scared by chimeras,' he adds, 'and one must have more firmness and discernment.'

He dismisses Murat. On the battlefield, among the cannonballs, the man will forget his hesitations and temptations. He will fight.

Constant, his valet, enters and puts logs in the fireplace.

I am forty-four.

He writes,

> My good friend,
>   I am leaving this evening for Görlitz. War has been declared. Your father, deceived by Metternich, has sided with my other enemies. It is he who wanted war, out of outlandish ambition and greed. Events will decide. Emperor Alexander has arrived in Prague; the Russians have entered Bohemia. My health is extremely good. I want you to be brave and in good health.
> *Addio, mio bene.* Ever yours,
>   Nap

HE RIDES THROUGH the night and the rain. They cross a bridge without a parapet. Suddenly someone near him shouts; he sees Colonel Bertrand, one of his aides-de-camp, trying to check his horse but not being able to and falling into a ravine.

He doesn't stop. He remembers his fall in the wheat on the banks of the Niemen. He spurs his horse. He must leap over bad omens, fight them, dominate the future in spite of them.

As he rides he listens to his aides, who report that Blücher is withdrawing. His troops have retreated over the Katzbach river. The enemy, as Napoleon had foreseen, is refusing to join battle.

At Lowenberg, he rereads the dispatches received in the last few hours. Davout has been victorious in the north, at Lauenburg, but Oudinot is marking time opposite Bernadotte.

'I cannot confirm my line of thought,' he murmurs, walking about the little room where they have set up his study.

He goes out; it is midday. Now all nature streams and gleams in the sun. But the horizon is black. It will rain again.

He eats lunch standing up, reading the dispatches. Suddenly he smashes his glass on the table. The 10,000 Bavarians and Saxons under Oudinot have deserted! And, in the south, Schwarzenberg's army is heading towards Dresden, trying to take it from the rear while he is advanced but unable to engage Blücher.

Dresden must hold. It is the centre of my system.

He asks General Gourgaud his opinion, this officer having just returned from the town.

'Sire, I think Dresden will be taken tomorrow if Your Majesty is not there.'

'Can I depend on what you tell me? Will you hold out until tomorrow?'

'Sire, I will answer for it with my life.'

HE ISSUES ORDERS in the rain that has started again. About turn. They are going back where they came from. The columns surge back onto the roads and he overtakes them, galloping towards Dresden.

He crosses the bridge over the Elbe in the midst of a throng of troops. All this smacks of panic, defeat almost. Can it be possible? He dismounts, sees General Gouvion St-Cyr and reassures him, 'The reinforcements are coming. I am leading them.'

The soldiers recognize him as he gives the corps commanders their orders in the middle of the bridge. As fusillade and cannonade herald the arrival of the Austrians and Prussians marching in tight columns preceded by fifty cannon firing grapeshot. They are almost 250,000 and we are 100,000. *We will prevail.*

He has studied every square metre of the countryside around Dresden. He gives the order to Murat's cavalry to charge on the left flank, to General Victor's infantry to push into the breach opened in the enemy army and to Ney to attack. Twelve hundred cannon pound his men.

All of this in the rain and mud.

He inspects the advance posts. The enemy is falling back. They must give pursuit. He returns to Dresden for a few moments. The King of Saxony clasps him in his arms. Napoleon pushes him away. He is shivering; his teeth are chattering and he wants to vomit. His hat is so soaked that it hangs down on his shoulders. He feels he is walking in icy water because his boots are full of it. He can barely stay upright. Constant undresses him. They warm his bed. He gets in, but the cold and fever don't abate. He dictates all the same. Fain reads him the dispatches. Victory at Dresden is certain. There are 10,000 prisoners, generals among them, flags. Certain Austrian soldiers say that the French General Moreau was killed by a cannonball when he was at Alexander's side.

He opens his eyes. Moreau! He feels nothing. Destiny has removed from his path this man whom he had spared in the past and yet had never stopped hating him.

I don't hate. I fight and I scorn.

But does one scorn a dead man?

He grows colder and colder. He wants a scalding bath. Gradually, he stops trembling. He goes to bed. He gives orders not to be woken. But at five he is already up.

A letter to Marie Louise, on this Friday 27 August, before returning to the advance posts.

My friend,

I have just won a great victory at Dresden over the Austrian, Russian and Prussian army commanded in person by the three sovereigns. I am mounting to pursue them. My health is good. Bérenger, my orderly officer, has been mortally wounded. See that his family and young wife are informed. Farewell, *mio bene*. I will send you flags,

Nap

HE CANNOT GALLOP. He feels his body so weakened that sometimes he thinks he's going to slip out of the saddle. He stops near the hamlet of Pirna. It is a beautiful day; troops pass and cheer him. Yesterday's victory has transformed them. He wants to eat here, in this field, so he can watch them pass and be seen by them.

He sits down, swallows a few mouthfuls. And suddenly his forehead is dripping with sweat. He slumps forward and vomits, thinking, they've poisoned me. The English, Metternich, perhaps those in their pay around him, they all want him dead. This would allow them finally to organize Europe as they wish, with a subdued France.

People gather round him. He gestures for them to step back. He needs air. He does not want to die like this, like a Roman emperor fallen victim to a conspiracy. He wants to die on a battlefield, like Muiron or Duroc or Lannes or Bessières, or so many young men.

To die at forty-four when those soldiers were barely half that age. He straightens up. He must go back to Dresden, Caulaincourt keeps saying. The Emperor must receive treatment; he cannot continue with the pursuit. Others think he should be taken to Pirna, which the Young Guard has reached, and from there he will be able to direct the movements of the troops.

He must live, he thinks. Live first, so as to be able to die as a soldier if necessary.

He says, 'Dresden.'

He closes his eyes. He is picked up and carried to a coach. It sets off against the tide of armed men flowing eastwards.

HE IS IN his study, lying down.

He has just been brought a bundle of dispatches. Blücher has beaten Macdonald, who has lost 3,000 men, 20,000 prisoners and 100 cannon. And how many eagles? General Vandamme's corps, which had set off in pursuit of General Schwarzenberg, has been surrounded at Kulm, and Vandamme has been taken prisoner with his soldiers. Ney has also been defeated, at Dennewitz, by the Prussian General Bülow. What has become of the victory of Dresden?

He has trouble getting up – and he has already been in bed for a day!

He receives Daru. The quartermaster-general of the Grand Army has hard times written across his face. Ammunition is beginning to run short. The men, he admits, are poorly fed. Dysentery and flu, in this climate, are laying them low before the battle even starts.

'Dire,' murmurs Napoleon.

He gets to his feet, refusing Daru's help, and goes to the window. The rain is still falling.

'My expedition into Bohemia is becoming impossible,' he says.

He can barely take a few steps. He wants to be left alone. He forces himself to stand upright, leaning on the window.

I feel the reins slipping away and I can't do anything about it. Everywhere Saxon, Bavarian, German contingents are deserting. Betrayals are starting to reach all the way up to me. They tell me that Murat, although he may be fighting, is still negotiating with the English. The generals, apart from a few, are gorged on esteem, honours, wealth. They have drunk from the cup of pleasure; now all they ask for is rest. They are ready to purchase it at any price. The sacred fire is going out. These are no longer the men from the early days of the Revolution or our finest moments.

He is walking about now, straining all his muscles so as not to stumble.

'Only a thunderclap can save us, which means that all that's left is to fight.'

His strength gradually returns.

'That's war. Couldn't be better in the morning, couldn't be worse in the evening,' he says to Maret as he consults the latest dispatches.

They are dire, as he anticipated.

Bavaria has signed an armistice with the Allies. No more Saxons, no more Bavarians. A column of Russian cavalry has got as far as Cassel and driven Jérôme out of his capital. No more Würtembergers!

But what other response is there but to fight?

'One can stop on the way up,' he says, 'but never on the way down.'

On Tuesday 31 August he paces about his bedchamber.

Some lines of poetry learnt on garrison duty in Valence, when he was a young lieutenant full of rage and energy, come back to him. He repeats them several times:

> 'I have served, led, conquered for forty years
> Held in my hands the fates of this sphere
> And I have always known that at every turn
> The fate of States depends on a single event'

He can, he wants to, he must create this event again.

HE IS AT the head of his troops once more. He crosses the Spree, trying to catch Blücher, who refuses to fight.

He stops after days of riding. He goes into an abandoned farm. He sees the chasseurs of his escort dismount along with his aides-de-camp, who come up and await his orders.

But he has nothing to say. Exhaustion overwhelms him. He slumps down on a bale of straw and stays like that for a long time, looking through the roof smashed by cannonballs at the clouds gliding across the blue sky.

An aide approaches, waits for a few minutes.

I see him but don't hear him. I must make an effort to listen.

Blücher's and Schwarzenberger's troops are converging on Dresden, the officer says. Bernadotte has crossed the Elbe to the north. Blücher is preparing to cross the river further south. Murat is in full flight.

Napoleon listens. He straightens up, issues orders in a brisk, resolute voice. They must abandon the Elbe line so as not to be surrounded and fall back around Leipzig. They must fight; they will fight. This may be the thunderclap that will change the fate of the campaign.

But first he must reassure Paris, dictate letters and send multiple copies since partisans are intercepting couriers in the army's rear.

Just like in Russia.

He pushes this thought aside.

All these ministers who are panicking need shaking up.

He dictates,

Monsieur the Duke of Rovigo, Minister of Police,

I have received your coded letter. It is very good of you to concern yourself with the Stock Exchange. What does a drop matter to you? The less you meddle with such matters, the better. It is natural that in the present circumstances there is more or less of a fall; so let them get on with it. The only way of making this worse is for you to meddle and give the impression that you are attaching importance to it. As for me, I attach none!

EVERYTHING WILL BE decided here, swords in hand.
But they must not betray me! Let them give me the men I need.

He dictates a speech for Marie Louise that she will have to give as regent to the Senate to explain why the Emperor needs 160,000 men from the class of 1815, and 120,000 from the classes of 1808–14.

She will say, 'I have the highest opinion of the courage and energy of this great French people. Your Emperor, your country and your honour are calling you!'

Will they accept, will they understand?

What else can I say?

He thinks for a moment that if he died now, his body disembowelled by a cannonball, his son and Marie Louise might reign. Perhaps his death is in fact the only way to guarantee his dynasty? The Emperor of Austria and Metternich would be happy to see a Habsburg descendant on the throne of France. And the dignitaries of the Empire would gather around the King of Rome to protect their titles and properties.

Should I die? To assure the future?

HE HAS INSTALLED himself in the little castle of Duben, in the middle of the Leipzig countryside. He has had his iron bed and a table, on which the maps are spread out, set up in a vast room with narrow windows that look out on a landscape often veiled by rain.

It is the middle of October 1813. Everything is silent around him. Everyone is waiting for him to speak, give orders.

He is sitting on a sofa. Sometimes he goes to the table, consults the maps. Often he takes a piece of paper and mechanically lets his hand form big letters. Then he drops the quill and goes and sits back down again.

He glances at Bacler d'Albe.

A dispatch is brought in. Bavaria's defection is confirmed. German contingents are deserting everywhere and going over to the enemy.

He looks round for Berthier. But the marshal is sick, unable to move.

He gets up, goes to the table, where the dispatches are piling up unread.

He knows what they say. He has 160,000 men against probably more than three times that. And of these soldiers he has to reckon on tens of thousands being sick. These are the men he has to fight with.

He could march north, take Berlin, then attack the enemy rear. He has manoeuvred so many times like that, in Italy and Germany, and this is how he has won battles, turning the situation round with forced marches. But that was in the past. What can he demand of young soldiers already exhausted by the marching back and forth and the rain? And where are the generals of the past, full of enthusiasm?

And he is forty-four himself!

Marengo was 14 June 1800. Desaix died that day.

More than thirteen years have passed since.

I cannot march north. I must fight here.

He calls his secretary. He writes to Ney, 'I have ordered my Guard to fall back so I can march on Leipzig. The King of Naples is in front there. There will undoubtedly be a great battle at Leipzig. The decisive moment seems to have come. It can only be a matter of fighting well.'

He walks around, his head bowed, then continues, 'My intention is that you should deploy your troops in ranks two rather than three deep. The enemy, accustomed to see us in three ranks, will think our battalions a third stronger.'

How long will they think that?

Long enough to win, perhaps?

The game is for all or nothing.

He dictates a dispatch for Murat: 'A good trick would be to have salvos fired in celebration of victory over the other army.'

In war, a moment of uncertainty can decide everything. He prepares to leave the room in Duben castle, then turns back. With a gesture, he indicates to his secretary that he wants to add one last sentence for Murat. 'You should also hold a full review, as if I were there, and have them shout, "Long live the Emperor!"'

It is Thursday, 14 October 1813, seven in the morning.

In the past I didn't need these tricks!

XIV

HE STANDS MOTIONLESS IN the fine cold drizzle that has been falling since nightfall on this Thursday, 14 October 1813, and watches the carriage of the King of Saxony, Frederick Augustus, driving off. The sovereign is returning to Leipzig.

He is my last German supporter. And what can he do? The King has sworn to exhort his soldiers to remain faithful to their French allies, to respect their oath and to fight honourably.

Napoleon shrugs his shoulders. Where is there any honour?

He goes back into the opulent villa in which his headquarters has been established. He stops in front of the large pictures decorating the hall. A banker's luxury! The property does in fact belong to a Leipzig financier, M. Weister, who used to come here, a few leagues from town, to this village of Reudnitz to entertain his friends.

The bankers are my enemies too. Stocks are still falling in Paris. They are betting on my defeat. London's bankers are lending to anyone who is determined to fight me. I am on my own.

He walks up and down the dimly lit room in which the maps are laid out and the dispatches are gathered.

Where is there any honour? The King of Bavaria has just betrayed me and written to his son-in-law, Eugène de Beauharnais, advising him to join the coalition of my enemies! There's their morality! Servile when I am strong, masters if I weaken.

He leans on the window sill. Through the curtain of rain he sees the bivouac fires of the armies of Schwarzenberg, Blücher, Bernadotte and Bennigsen. They almost form a circle, with a tiny opening towards the south-west, towards the road that goes to Erfurt by Lindenau and then France. But one would have to cross ditches, swamps, the river Elster and its tributaries, the Pleisse and Partha. More bridges; bridge after bridge. He thinks of the ones over the Berezina.

How many men surround me — 350,000? I do not even have half

*that! And what about the German, Würtemberger and Saxon units
serving in the French corps – what do they amount to?*

He cannot take his eyes off the crown of flickering lights that
marks the edges of the chess board on which this game of all or
nothing is going to be played. Barely a dozen square kilometres in
which, in a few hours, 500,000 men and 3,000 cannon will clash.

*All Europe against me! All the nations against the Nation. They
won't pardon me for being what I am, a French Emperor. They won't
pardon France for having beheaded a king by divine right and for
having given me the means to occupy Rome, Madrid, Moscow, Berlin
and Vienna. They want to cow us, bring us to our knees.*

So be it. I will play this game to the end.

Afterwards, nothing will be the same.

HE SLEEPS IN snatches, a few minutes at a time. And then it is
dawn already on Friday, 15 October 1813. He hears cannon far to
the south. It is probably Schwarzenberg's troops approaching. The
scouts explain that the Austrian columns are advancing preceded
by a hundred cannon. Cossacks and Bashkirs armed with bows
and arrows are harrying the French, darting out of range and then
returning to the attack. It's difficult terrain, lots of hillocks,
streams and marshes.

Napoleon mounts. This Friday will not be a day of battle but
of approach, he senses. He rides with Murat over the hills and
valleys where tomorrow the ground will be steeped in blood.
The soldiers cheer him. It is a beautiful day. He dismounts in
the village of Wachau, inspects the surrounding country. The
centre of the army will be here. The crux of the battle against
Schwarzenberg's troops.

He sets off again, gallops across the plateau.

He chooses a site behind a sheep fold not far from Wachau.
His tent will be pitched there tomorrow.

He returns to Reudnitz.

He detains Murat, stares at him. The King of Naples lowers
his eyes.

'You are a brave man,' he murmurs, 'but as a king, you think
of your crown more than mine. You are prepared to act like any
one of my allied rulers, like the King of Bavaria.'

Murat doesn't even protest.

What's the good of going on talking to him? Tomorrow will be the day of battle.

AT NINE O'CLOCK on Saturday, 16 October 1813, the cannonade starts. He has never heard it so heavy. Fighting has begun in Wachau, as he had anticipated. He gallops towards the advance posts. The cannonballs are raining down from all corners.

To die here, in this struggle of nations, me against everyone else.

He doesn't reply to Caulaincourt, who asks him to take cover. He remains perfectly still and straight-backed in his saddle.

Through his field glasses he sees men and horses fall. Skirmishers launch themselves at the enemy guns. The Austrians fall back. He advances the Young Guard. Poniatowski's Poles charge, cutting and thrusting through the Austrian squadrons.

Napoleon issues an order: Poniatowski is promoted to marshal.

Then he carries on watching. Despite the flood tide of enemies, the French are holding firm. And when darkness falls and the night sky is bright – luminous even – the battle of the first day is won.

He can make his way back to his tent.

He rides slowly. Tomorrow tens of thousands of men, perhaps 100,000, will reinforce the enemy's armies. Who can he count on? A few thousand soldiers, many of them Saxon.

He dismounts in the middle of his Guard. An Austrian officer in a white uniform is sitting outside his tent. He goes towards him. He recognizes General Merveldt. They met at Leoben, when Merveldt was one of the Austrian plenipotentiaries. That was sixteen years ago. And again after Austerlitz. That was eight years ago.

But what is the past when one is trying to bear down on the future?

'Finally this time you want to do battle,' says Napoleon.

'We want to end this long struggle against you. We want, at the price of shedding our blood, to win our independence,' General Merveldt retorts in a loud voice.

Napoleon starts walking round the tent, his hands behind his back. Has Merveldt forgotten that the Emperor Francis is his father-in-law? That the French Imperial throne is joined by blood to that of the Habsburgs?

He speaks to the Austrian general for a long time. If he could make the Austrian Emperor understand that what's dangerous for Vienna is a Russian victory or English domination of continental Europe, perhaps he could unravel the coalition. He must play that card too.

He stops in front of Merveldt. He gives orders for the Austrian to be escorted back to the advance posts so that he can testify to Emperor Francis of the desire for peace and even alliance evinced by the Emperor Napoleon, his son-in-law.

Then Napoleon walks away through the grenadiers of his Guard gathered around their bivouacs.

ON SUNDAY 17 October the sky is black and low. The cannon boom. Napoleon goes to the top of Thornberg hill from where he can see the whole battlefield. They won't fight today; the enemy are waiting for their reinforcements. He sees the stooping figures of robbers and orderlies moving over the ground covered with dead and wounded.

He returns to his tent, sits on a folding chair and leans against the wall. He doesn't move. His body is covered in sweat. He sees the terror in Caulaincourt's and his aides' expressions. And suddenly his stomach contracts; pain tears at him. He bends over and vomits. Exhaustion and agony overcome him.

He brings his hand to his stomach.

'I feel bad,' he says. 'My head is holding out, but my body is giving in.'

He does not want to die like this.

He hears Caulaincourt saying they should call Yvan the surgeon, begging him to rest, to lie down.

Rest on the eve of a battle!

'A sovereign's tent is transparent, Caulaincourt,' murmurs Napoleon. 'I must be on my feet so everyone remains at their post.'

He gets up despite Caulaincourt.

'I must stay on my feet.'

He takes a few steps, leaning on the grand equerry.

'It will be nothing. Make sure nobody comes in,' he says.

This body must obey; the pain must go back inside its cave. If death is to come, let it attack me face on, from the mouth of a cannon or the steel of a blade, not worm its way in treacherously.

He breathes more calmly.

'I feel better,' he says. 'I am better.'

The pain recedes. He is less cold.

Tomorrow he will be able to command the battle.

HE IS ON horseback at one in the morning on Monday, 18 October 1813. He inspects the advance posts, climbs the Thornberg hill. It is this battle's third day.

My Grand Army is holding out, but it is disintegrating under the onslaught. It kills more than is killed but I have no new blood to give it and the enemy has all Europe behind it.

It is the third day. Suddenly he does an about-turn; he wants to go to Lindenau, to General Bertrand. He crosses the bridge over the Elster, which must be mined so that, if they decide to retreat, it can be blown up. Bertrand and his troops will be the advance guard of the Grand Army marching towards France on this road, from Lindenau to Erfurt.

France!

If they must, they will fight on the Nation's soil.

He returns to Thornberg. He is calm. He is ready to lose this game to start another.

As long as one's alive, the all or nothing starts again and again without end. And nothing does not exist. Only death ends the struggle.

And even then ... He thinks of Duroc. Others are alive who are continuing to fight.

An aide-de-camp presents himself, his uniform torn, his face bloody. The Saxon units have gone over to the enemy in good order, turned their guns round and fired on the ranks they had just left. The Würtemberger cavalry has done the same. The Saxons are attacking with Bernadotte's Swedes.

He does not even flinch. It is the nature of things. Infamy begets infamy. He remains standing stock-still while night falls, and only then does he go to Leipzig.

THE ROADS LEADING to the town are jammed with soldiers. He forces his way through with an escort and his staff. He enters the Prussian Arms tavern on one of the outer boulevards, where his headquarters has been set up. At the foot of the stairs he recognizes Generals Sorbier and Dulauloy who respectively are in command of the army and Guard artillery.

Before they even speak, he sees what they are going to say on their faces. He listens impassively.

Ninety-five thousand rounds have been fired in the day, they say; they only have enough ammunition for another 16,000 rounds, or two hours' firing. They have to restock from depots at Magdeburg or Erfurt.

'Erfurt,' says Napoleon.

He issues his first orders immediately. Poniatowski will secure the rearguard in Leipzig, and hold the approaches to the Elster bridge. The retreat must begin straight away.

Then he slowly, calmly, dictates the Bulletin of the Grand Army.

They can hear firing in the suburbs of Leipzig, but he speaks in a composed voice, stressing the Saxons' treachery and the shortage of ammuniton.

'These circumstances obliged the French army to renounce the fruits of two victories in which, with so much glory, it had defeated a far superior force – the armies of the whole continent.'

IT IS ALREADY dawn on Tuesday, 19 October 1813. He leaves the inn and enters the town by the outer boulevards. Units are packed into the narrow streets of Leipzig, trudging slowly along. He passes without anyone cheering. He goes to visit the King of Saxony, but after greeting him he can't get near the city gates because the throng is so dense.

When he finally gets back onto the boulevards and approaches the Lindenau bridge his aides-de-camp propose setting fire to the town as soon as the troops have left it to slow the enemy's advance. It would fair enough, as punishment for the Saxons' treachery.

He shakes his head angrily. He has just seen the King of Saxony on the balcony of his palace. The sovereign refused to leave the city. He wept as he spoke about his troops' conduct. He burnt his own Guard's flag himself. After that, would one destroy his city?

They will not set fire to Leipzig.

He crosses the Elster bridge.

He dismounts and personally stations officers along the Erfurt road. They are to gather up isolated soldiers and muster them. Then he watches the soldiers marching past for a long time. They are so exhausted they don't even lift their heads.

He walks slowly away to the large mill that towers over the banks of the Elster. He sits down on the first floor and suddenly his head slumps forward onto his chest. He falls asleep.

HE WAKES UP with a start.

Murat is bent over him. The Elster bridge has just been blown up. Didn't he hear the explosion? They've destroyed it too soon. Thousands of men are still in Leipzig; others are throwing themselves into the water to cross the river. Dozens of cannon won't be able to get over. The first to escape are saying that the soldiers left in town don't have any ammunition left and that the Saxons, Bavarians and Prussians are cutting their throats.

He hunches over for a few minutes, then orders cavalry squadrons to go down to the Elster to pick up anyone who manages to cross.

Marshal Macdonald, Murat continues, has managed to swim across; he has been picked up naked. But Lauriston will have drowned. Soldiers were shouting at Macdonald, 'Marshal, save your soldiers, save your children!'

Prince Poniatowski has disappeared into the waves.

Death is taking its pick all around me, but it refuses to take my hand.

So I must continue to fight.

XV

HE STOPS DICTATING. He looks around him at this familiar room. Nothing has changed in five years. It was here, in this Erfurt palace, in this salon in October 1808, that he entertained Alexander, met Goethe and was the Emperor of Kings. Five years ago, almost to the day. But this Saturday, 23 October 1813, is no longer the time for splendour and parades. The soldiers gathering in the streets of Erfurt, waiting patiently outside the depots to try to get a uniform, a weapon, ammunition, cannon, are no more than the remnants of an army.

How many are left, properly organized in units? My Guard. Perhaps 20,000 men. The others, another twenty or so thousand, are mostly isolated stragglers – ill, crippled, wounded – making their way through the cold rain of a German autumn.

How many have I left dead in the swamps and mud of Leipzig, or drowned trying to cross the Elster, or had their throats slit in the houses of Leipzig – 20,000, 30,000? And even if the enemy has lost double that, they can refill their ranks.

I need men, again.

He resumes dictating to the minister of war: '. . . with regard to a levy of the eighty to one hundred thousand men I need. When all Europe is under arms, when everywhere married men are being levied and the whole world rushes into arms against us, France is lost if it does not do the same.'

I am sure of the rank and file's desire to fight. They didn't flee; I saw them. But the generals and marshals have lost their fervour.

Ney himself has used a light wound as a pretext to leave the army and go back to Paris. But he hasn't betrayed me.

Murat, however, before leading the charge at Leipzig, sent a messenger to the Allies with his agreement to a political arrangement. If they assure him possession of Rome, he will go over to the coalition camp. And it is my sister Caroline, his wife, and the mistress of the Austrian ambassador in Naples who are conducting the negotiations. Caroline is crazed with ambition, prepared to do anything. And a few hours ago Murat left the army as well, on the pretext of going to levy reinforcements in Naples!

I was silent when he came – sheepish and trembling but determined – to announce his departure. He fled the salon before I could say anything.

Farewell, Murat!

I MUST NOT hide this situation. I must prepare public opinion, publish a Bulletin of the Grand Army which relates the battle of Leipʒig and explains the reasons for our retreat.

He dictates a description of the premature destruction of the bridge over the Elster: 'We cannot yet estimate the losses caused by this unfortunate event. But the disorder it inflicted on the army changed the state of affairs: the victorious French army arrived in Erfurt as if it had been defeated.' He hesitates for a few moments, then carries on: 'The enemy, which had been filled with consternation by the battles of the 16th and 18th, regained courage and the ascendancy of victory through the disaster of the 19th. The French army, after such brilliant successes, has lost the ascendancy of its victorious attitude.'

HE DOES NOT go out. He does not sleep. Sometimes he goes to the window and watches the fugitives dragging themselves along, exhausted.

When an aide-de-camp brings in a dispatch, he goes slowly towards him. It can't contain any good news. They have stepped into the path of an avalanche of doom.

The Kingdom of Westphalia no longer exists. Farewell, my brother Jérôme. The last princes of the Confederation of the Rhine are joining the Allies. And after the King of Bavaria, the King of Würtemberg is doing the same. Farewell, Germany! Soult's armies are fleeing and falling back on Bayonne. Farewell Spain for ever!

He feels neither despair nor anguish. When destiny is against one, one accepts it, or one dies, or one fights. Anything else is cowardice. And he has never snivelled over his fate.

He asks for a big map of Germany and draws circles around the fortresses held by French garrisons. If these troops withdraw on Hamburg, Davout, who holds that fortress, would have 100,000 who could reach the Rhine through northern Germany.

He paces briskly about the room. In a few days he could turn the situation around with such a manoeuvre.

He imagines the coalition forces entering France, 'burning two or three of my good towns. That would give me a million soldiers. I would do battle. I would win. And I would drive them all the way back to the Vistula.'

Nothing is lost as long as my energy is still vital.

He must inspire his armies with this will.

He writes to the minister of police, who is sending ever more anxious letters, 'Your Grace, your alarms and fears make me laugh. I thought you were worthy of hearing the truth. I shall defeat the enemy quicker than you think. My presence is too necessary to the army for me to leave at this moment. When it is necessary, I will be in Paris.'

HE WANTS TO lead what is left of the army to Mainz. There he will cross the Rhine and return to Paris. He has to reassure Marie Louise. 'My health is very good. I will be in Mainz in a few days. Please give the little king a kiss from me, and never doubt the feelings of your faithful husband, Nap'.

He leaves Erfurt, galloping along the columns in the pouring rain. Aides-de-camp announce that a Bavarian and Austrian army commanded by General de Wrede is progressing parallel to the Mainz road, with the intention of giving battle.

De Wrede! That general has fought in the Grand Army since 1805! And this is the man who intends to stop me getting through! Me!

He picks up speed. Shortly before Schlüchtern, he sees a large group of Polish officers barring the road. They demand to speak to him. He rides forward. One of them approaches. He listens. These Poles want to return to their country. Them too.

He urges his horse forward.

'Is it true that the Poles want to leave me?' he calls out.

The men bow their heads.

'I have been too far away, it's true,' he continues. 'I have made mistakes. Fortune has turned its back on me for the last two years. But it is a woman; it will change! Who knows? Perhaps your bad star has dragged mine down?'

The officers look at him, astonished.

'Anyway, have you lost confidence in me? Haven't I got any spunk in my balls any more?'

The Poles protest.

'Have I lost weight?' he asks laughing.

Then, riding into their midst, he continues: 'I have been informed of your intentions. As Emperor and as a general, I cannot applaud your conduct. I have nothing to reproach you for. You have behaved loyally towards me; you have not tried to abandon me without a word, and you have even promised to escort me back to the Rhine. Today I want to give you some good advice. If you abandon me, I will no longer have the right to speak for you. And I think that, despite the disasters that have taken place, I am still the most powerful monarch in Europe.'

He pushes his horse into a gallop. He hears the shouts of 'Long live the Emperor.'

He is not yet laid low.

IT IS A long time since he has felt such determination. The Bavarians of General de Wrede have taken up a position at Hanau. There are, according to a few soldiers taken prisoner, more than 50,000 of them, including Austrians and Cossacks. De Wrede is making speeches. He is going to take the Emperor prisoner, he claims.

I have 17,000 men, but it is my Guard.

He harangues them. He gives his orders. General Drouot's artillery will advance, he says, alone, and open fire, then the cavalry will charge. They must bowl these traitors over.

The cannonade fills the narrow defile through which the road runs. He waits in the forest just a few feet from the battle. The shells fall all around. One of them lands less than a metre away without exploding. He doesn't even turn his head. He carries on chatting with Caulaincourt.

If death wants me, let her take me!

The Bavarian troops are bowled over, and he is able to continue on his way, arriving in Frankfurt on Sunday 31 October.

He stays for a couple of hours in a house in the town's suburbs. He writes,

> My good Louise,
>   I have reached Frankfurt. I am going to Mainz. I gave the Bavarians and Austrians a good thrashing yesterday at Hanau. They had 60,000 men. I took 6,000 prisoners, standards and cannon. Those madmen wanted to cut me off. My health is good and has never been better. *Addio mio bene*. A kiss to the king,
>   Nap

This victory must be exploited. While the troops march towards Mainz in a relentless downpour, he dictates what is this time an official letter to Marie Louise, the regent: 'Madame and very dear wife, I send you twenty standards taken by my armies at the battles of Wachau, Leipzig and Hanau. It is homage I am very glad to render you . . .'

He sends his orders to the minister of war. There must be a parade in Paris, with these enemy flags each carried by an officer on horseback. 'You have long known what I think of this sort of military pomp, but in the present circumstances I think it will be useful.'

Paris and France must know that I am the victor again.

Besides, has he ever been beaten? Truly beaten? At times he has not won, but what enemy general can say that he has defeated him?

He can recoup everything in another game.

HE ARRIVES IN Mainz on Tuesday 2 November. That's 300 kilometres he has covered on horseback since Leipzig.

He reads all the dispatches that have arrived from Paris. His brother Louis is in the capital. What does he want? He must put the Empress on her guard.

'That man is mad,' Napoleon writes to Marie Louise. 'Pity me for having such a terrible family, when I have showered them with benefits. I am reorganizing my army. Everything is taking shape. Give my son a kiss. Ever yours, Nap'.

HE WALKS THROUGH the streets of the town. Soldiers are dragging themselves along on crutches. The hospitals and cellars are full of the sick, he is told. Typhus is laying men low just as effectively as the bullets and cannonballs that preceded it.

He must leave to build another army.

ON SUNDAY 7 November, at ten in the evening, he leaves Mainz. No Imperial escort, just two uncomfortable carriages and an entourage of three. It is not the time for great ceremony.

He reaches St-Cloud on Tuesday, 9 November 1813, at five in the evening.

Over forty-four, he feels like a young general who has everything to conquer.

PART FIVE

I am leaving.
Let this last kiss pass
into your hearts

10 November 1813 to 3 May 1814

XVI

HE PACES ABOUT THE hall at St-Cloud, which is already growing dark as the afternoon draws to a close on Tuesday, 9 November 1813.

He sees the young woman and child coming towards him, and he stops. He could run towards them, stretch out his arms. But he remains motionless. He must not let himself be moved. He is not a private citizen. He incarnates the destiny of millions of men. He must remain unbending. If a fault opens up in him, who could stop the emotion that would sweep over him, engulfing his will?

Marie Louise leans on him, in tears. He reassures her. It has been so long since he held a woman's body. Softness and warmth after months of bitterness and cold, life after death. He bends down. The child looks at him, then smiles and laces his hands round his neck. He lifts him up and carries him to his study without looking at the approaching dignitaries. He makes out Madame de Montesquiou, the boy's governess and the Duchess of Montebello, the most assiduous of the Empress's ladies-in-waiting. He is impatient to be alone with his wife and son and away from these eyes watching him, spying on him.

This chateau is icy. These people are waiting, hoping. For what? For me to succumb or, once again, triumph?

He hears the noise of the doors being shut behind him.

He sees the dispatches on the table, the maps, the troop returns.

Tomorrow he will be back in harness. He will chair a private council and a council of ministers.

But tonight is his, just his, until dawn.

THEY ARE ALL here, around him, at the ceremony of his levee on Wednesday 10 November.

Even the pallid Talleyrand is here, that venial traitor who is in touch with the Bourbons and waiting for my downfall.

He stops in front of him.

'What have you come to do here? I know you imagine that, if

I went missing, you would be head of the regency council.' Shaking his head, Napoleon goes on: 'Take care, sir. One gains nothing by fighting my power. I declare that if I was dangerously sick, you would be dead before me.'

Talleyrand, as is his wont, does not flinch.

'Sire,' he murmurs, 'I did not need such a warning to offer up ardent prayers asking heaven to preserve Your Majesty's life.'

Napoleon turns his back on him. Every sentence Talleyrand utters is a hypocritical grimace.

But who can he still trust? He says in a curt voice, 'The coalition forces have arranged to meet on my grave, but it is up to who gets there first. They think the moment of their rendezvous has come. They consider the lion dead; it is up to whoever can finish him off.'

He lowers his head, his jaw clenched.

'If France abandons me,' he says, 'I cannot do anything, but it will not be slow to regret what it has done.'

He heads towards the dignitaries, who step aside. He recognizes among them an old man dressed all in black, Laplace, who was an examiner at the military school. The scholar sent him, just a few months previously, his latest book, a treatise on probabilities. Napoleon remembers getting it at Vitebsk and leafing through it there, in the snow, where the Grand Army had disappeared.

'You have changed and grown much thinner,' Napoleon says.

'I have lost my daughter, sire,' Laplace murmurs.

All those men dead and buried over there. Napoleon turns away.

'You are a geometrician, Laplace,' he says in a harsh voice. 'Apply calculus to this event and you will see it equals zero.'

No one dares speak. But he reads the questions and anxieties on their faces.

'Wait, wait,' he says suddenly. 'You will soon learn that my soldiers and I have not forgotten our profession! We have been betrayed between the Elbe and the Rhine, but there will be no traitors between the Rhine and Paris . . .'

But it is not here, among these resplendently uniformed

dignitaries and ministers, that he will find enthusiastic supporters. They will obey and follow him only if they think he can win and it's in their interests.

So he must re-form the army, again. He needs men. He will ask the Senate for a levy of 300,000 conscripts. More units of the National Guard must also be raised. Will they be able, with what they have, to face Blücher's 70,000 Prussians and Russians, who are advancing on the Rhine, and Schwarzenberg's 120,000 Austrians who, further south, seem to want to go through Switzerland to outflank the French fortresses defending the Rhine?

But if he had the men, would he have the necessary weapons?

'Nothing is less satisfactory than our situation in muskets,' he tells the minister of war in his first hours back at St-Cloud.

General Clarke mumbles a response. There are reserve stocks in the arsenals at Brest and La Rochelle, he says.

'A long way,' Napoleon murmurs. 'They won't arrive in less than a few weeks. And if there isn't anything else you can do, all the troops that are going to assemble will be useless for lack of muskets!'

But one must make do with what one has. He does not want to give in to discouragement, to the bad news that piles up every hour: the German fortresses Dresden, Torgau and Danzig have surrendered. Their garrisons won't be able to form an army and come from northern Germany as he had planned. He cannot count on Eugène's troops either; they will stay in Italy. *And the troops Murat was to assemble to help me will no doubt swell the numbers of the coalition.*

And everyone here, around me, knows the situation.

ON SUNDAY, 14 November 1813, he receives the senators in the Tuileries. He listens to them profess their loyalty and it's true that they vote for the levies of conscripts, but in their heads they doubt, they calculate possibilities.

Some meet up at Talleyrand's, the wits who ironically celebrate my 'ultimate victory'. They deploy an 'army of women', the Duchess of Dalberg, the Duchess of Courlande, Madame de Vaudémont, chattering conspirators who infest the salons of Paris. All of them are waiting for the Bourbons to return, I know. But that is how things are. Can I appeal to the people? So that they'll restart the Revolution I put an end to?

'Senators,' he says, 'I accept the sentiments you express. All Europe marched with us a year ago. Today all Europe marches against us. The fact is, the opinion of the world is formed either by France or England. We shall therefore have everything to fear without the Nation's energy and power.'

He wants to believe in this energy, this power.

'Posterity will say,' he goes on, 'that if great, critical circumstances arose, they were not too much for France and me.'

It must be known that he will fight, that he will not accept a peace based on capitulation. He retires to his study. A new dispatch. The English are marching on Bayonne.

He crumples the piece of paper and dictates, 'Give orders that, if ever the English reach Marracq Castle, the castle be burnt and all the houses that belong to me, so that they cannot sleep in my bed. All the furniture may be removed, if so wished, and put in a house in Bayonne.'

They'll see if the lion is dead.

FIRST SHOW ONESELF, make people believe, make them know that nothing has changed.

He presides over daily councils. He takes to the streets of Paris, visits the works being done at the Louvre, the new wine market. He walks along the banks of the Seine, through the flower market. The people cheer him. He decides to visit the Faubourg St-Antoine. He sees the workers and artisans who, when they catch sight of him, come out of their workshops and warehouses and shout 'Long live Napoleon,' and he hears them break into *'Les aristocrates à la lanterne.'*

He remembers those days in 1792, the attack on the Tuileries, the barbarism of the crowd and the impotence of the Bourbon king. He doesn't want to see that again. All his life he has sought to build something else, not to give in to the rage of the suburbs on the one hand, and escape the cowardice of kings on the other.

He feels the anxiety in the crowd milling around him. He must reassure them.

Several evenings in a row he goes to the theatre or the Opéra. He organizes reviews on the Carrousel. He wants a parade of thousands so that Paris will know the Grand Army has been re-formed. Afterwards he returns to St-Cloud. He shuts himself away in his study. No stage sets, no pretence there. Just the advancing enemy. Schwarzenberg has entered Switzerland, crossed the Rhine at Schaffhausen and, after moving on Basle, is marching on Belfort. He is now going to head back up towards the north-east, towards Dijon and Chalon-sur-Sâone, while Blücher with his Prussians and Russians are going to launch a frontal attack on the Rhine. The coalition forces have received further reinforcements and are fielding almost 400,000 men.

What can I counter that with?

He needs to escape all these questions that haunt him. He goes hunting, galloping through Satory wood, spurring his mount hard to be alone, and then walking his horse through the fog that envelops the forest. He makes his way slowly back to St-Cloud. He walks through the galleries, spends a few moments with Marie Louise; he will go to her this evening. She waits for him. But often, as soon as she falls asleep, he leaves her to go back to his apartments, where he works rather than sleeps.

THUS HE RECEIVES in the middle of the night the Count de St-Aignan, Caulaincourt's brother-in-law. The man, naturally, is a member of the peace-at-any-price party. Napoleon observes him. He is a valiant officer whom he had appointed equerry and often used as a plenipotentiary. He has been taken prisoner, and now, he says, is the bearer of Metternich and the coalition's proposals.

Napoleon gestures to him to begin and then walks around him, his arms crossed. St-Aignan speaks in lofty tones. The powers would recognize the natural frontiers of France, 'an extent of territory which France never knew under the kings'.

Napoleon stops him. What does that mean? What territory? Who could fail to see that this is a way of making the people think the Allies want to conclude an honourable peace, that they're not making war on France at all but just on the Emperor Napoleon!

He dismisses St-Aignan.

Metternich is cunning. They are even proposing a congress of peace. And they're stopping me mobilizing the people, fostering hopes of an end to the fighting and turning everyone who doesn't want to fight any more – ministers, marshals – against me. They are isolating me. That is their aim.

But I can unmask them.

On 20 November he summons Caulaincourt, Maret and General Bertrand to the Tuileries. He has decided, he says, to appoint Caulaincourt, the man of peace, minister of foreign affairs in Maret's place, who will return to secretary of state. As for General Bertrand, he will be grand marshal of the palace.

He walks a little with Caulaincourt.

'It is up to you to negotiate,' he says.

Caulaincourt is one of those who think they can conclude a treaty with the coalition forces, one of those who imagine that the European powers do not want my destruction, but only to make me see sense! That they don't want to mutilate France but respect it! When all Metternich dreams of is my fall to leave a descendant of the Habsburgs on the throne. And the English, with Castlereagh, are pushing the Bourbons towards Paris. And Alexander is dithering between enthroning Louis XVIII and Bernadotte in Paris.

How can they fail to see this, the Caulaincourts and St-Aignans?

On his desk he finds a copy of a declaration by the coalition powers that is being distributed throughout France by the enemy armies and the royalist groups who are starting to organize in the south. Thousands of copies of this *Declaration of Frankfurt* are in circulation. Here's proof of their political manoeuvre, he exclaims as he reads it. 'The allied powers are in no way making war on France but on the domination that, to the misfortune of Europe and France, the Emperor Napoleon has too long exercised beyond the limits of his empire. The sovereigns wish France to be great, strong and happy.'

He throws the piece of paper on the ground.

'What man is better suited to France than I?' he exclaims.

He learns of the proposals which the Allies are publishing with this declaration. Already there's no more talk of natural frontiers. They are taking Belgium, the left bank of the Rhine, Savoy.

They're proposing the France of 1790 without any of the revolutionary conquests.

He dictates a dispatch to Caulaincourt. This is a humiliation for him, since he is the one who is going to negotiate with the representatives of the coalition forces. The Allies are ignoring him, not answering his questions in order to gain a few days in which, they hope, the coalition forces will have advanced into France.

'I am so overcome by the infamous plan you have sent me that I think myself dishonoured just by having put myself in a position where it could be proposed to you,' Napoleon writes to him. 'You talk constantly about the Bourbons. I would rather see the Bourbons in France on reasonable terms than suffer the infamous propositions you send me.'

As he had thought, all that is left is to fight.

Spurs and boots are what I need.

HE PACES BACK and forth, hands behind his back, in his study in the Tuileries. He receives a dispatch by telegraph. His face screws up with contempt and anger. 'The masses in Amsterdam have risen up,' he says. William of Orange has just arrived in the town, and been met by cheering crowds.

These are the same Dutch who proclaimed their admiration for me! Why should one trust people? How can one?

The English are landing in Tuscany; Murat is signing a treaty with Austria and issuing a proclamation to his soldiers in which he slanders and insults me — Murat, my sister's husband, who I made king. 'The Emperor only wants war,' he writes. 'I know he is trying to prey on the patriotism of the French who serve in my army, as if there were still any honour in serving the mad ambition of Emperor Napoleon to subjugate the whole world.'

That is what Murat is saying!

And in Paris the deputies of the Legislative Body have voted by 223 to 53 to publish a report expressing the same opinions. All those politicians who, like Murat, have profited from the Empire! Murat, at least, has the excuse of having risked his life, but those snakes in the grass dare approve a text condemning 'a barbaric war'. 'It is time,' they say, 'that people stopped reproaching France for wanting to carry the torches of revolution all over the world.'

I! I who have put an end to the fires here, who have tried to introduce the Civil Code everywhere, who refused to start a peasant war in Russia.

He bursts out, 'Rather than helping to save France, the Legislative Body is contributing to hastening its ruin. It is betraying its duty; I am fulfilling mine. I am dissolving it.'

He calms down, repeats what he has just said and dictates, 'This is what I decree, and if I should be told that it will, before the day is out, cause the people of Paris to come en masse to massacre me in the Tuileries, I should decree it again; for this is my duty. When the French people entrusted me with its destiny, I considered the laws it gave me to reign: if I had thought them insufficient, I would not have accepted. Let no one think that I am a Louis XVI.'

BUT THESE DEPUTIES who rebuff me, here they are, on this 1st of January 1814, servilely appearing before me to wish me all the best! I told them on my return, 'Everyone has turned against us; France would be in danger were it without the energy and union of the French!' But what does that matter to them! They tremble. They accuse me. In their report one of them, Lainé, talks about my 'fatal ambition that has harmed Europe for the last twenty years'. And he praises the 'royal fleur-de-lis'.

Suddenly, Napoleon goes down to them and stands in the middle of their number.

'What do you want? To take power? But what would you do with it? And besides, what does France need at the moment? Not an assembly, not orators, it needs a general.'

He walks past each of them, his face contemptuous, his eyes sparkling.

'Is there one of those among you? And where is your mandate? I am looking for your titles and I cannot find them.'

He shrugs his shoulders and points to the Imperial throne on its platform.

'The throne itself is just an assembly of four pieces of gilt wood covered in velvet. The throne is a man, and that man is me, with my will, my character, my renown.'

He briskly returns to the platform.

'I am the one who can save France, not you.'

Then he abruptly steps down among them again.

'If you have complaints to raise, you should have waited for another opportunity – that I would have given you myself ... We could have explained things among ourselves, because one washes one's dirty linen in the family, not in public. But you wanted to throw mud in my face. How could you reproach me for my misfortunes? I bore them honourably because nature has provided me with a strong, proud temperament, and if I hadn't this pride in my soul, I wouldn't have elevated myself to the most important throne in the world.'

He cries, 'I am, you should know, a man who one can kill but never insult.'

Then he adds, suddenly calm, 'France needs me more than I need France. Go back to your *départements*. Go and tell France that, whatever the Allies may say, they are making war on France as much as on me, and that it must defend, not my person, but its own national existence. Soon I am going to put myself at the head of the army; I will repulse the enemy and I will conclude peace whatever it may cost what you call my ambition ...'

They are all silent. They have the lugubrious faces of the submissive. They do not accept my energy, my determination. What can I do with them?

BUT HOW CAN he not act?

The Austrians are approaching Dijon, the Russians Toul. They are preparing to cross the Marne.

'I am two months,' he tells Pasquier, Paris prefect of police. 'If I had them, they would not have crossed the Rhine. This may become serious, but I can't do anything alone. If no one helps me, I will succumb, and then they'll see if it's me the Allies resent.'

He thinks about Talleyrand, who is continuing to rally all those people preparing to join the coalition. Should he arrest the 'pallid one', have him locked in Vincennes or even shot? He gestures indifferently. So what should I do with the prefects who are not carrying out the instructions I have given them? With all of them who are distributing the manifesto Louis XVIII has just issued?

He shows it to Pasquier. The Bourbon says, 'Welcome these allied generals as friends, open the gates of your towns to them, think of the suffering a criminal and useless resistance cannot fail to bring upon you and let their entrance into Paris be received with accents of joy!'

They dare write that. And some people applaud.

He looks at Pasquier for a long time.

'Whoever refuses me his services now is of necessity my enemy,' he says.

Then, changing his tone, he asks, 'Well then, M. Prefect, what are they saying in this city? Do they know that the enemy's armies have definitely crossed the Rhine and that they number from three hundred to four hundred thousand?'

'There is no doubt that very shortly Your Majesty will be leaving to put himself at the head of his troops and marching to meet the enemy.'

'My troops, my troops,' he exclaims. 'Do people think I still have an army? Haven't almost all the troops I brought back from Germany perished from this terrible illness that has brought my disasters to a peak? An army! I will be very happy if in three weeks I can rally thirty to forty thousand men, but . . .'

He breaks off, shakes his head.

'But the most wretched odds would never make me agree to ratify what I consider dishonourable and France considers insulting.'

HE REPEATS IN a low voice, 'Spurs, boots,' when he appears before the Senate on Sunday 2 January.

He wants, he says, the senators to become extraordinary commissioners to the departments. He remembers those representatives of the people he had known in Toulon, Nice and the Army of Italy who had restored the soldiers' courage. For the Senate must decree 'a general popular levy' and since the Russians and

Prussians have entered Alsace, they must appoint 'a general of the Alsatian insurgency'.

The senators listen in emotional silence. He gets down from the rostrum and continues conversationally, 'I am not afraid to admit it. I have made war too much; I formed huge plans; I wanted to provide France with the Empire of the world. I was mistaken. I should have called out the whole Nation but, I admit, the softening of mores does not allow one to convert a whole country into a people of soldiers.'

He sits down familiarly among the senators.

'I must make up for the error of having counted on my fortune,' he continues, 'and I will make up for it. I am the one who was mistaken, and it is for me to suffer, not France. It has done nothing wrong; it has shed its blood for me, it has refused me no sacrifice . . .'

The senators flock round him, cheering.

He concludes in a loud voice that, since certain *départements* are already occupied, 'I call on Frenchmen to help Frenchmen. Shall we abandon them in their misfortune? Peace and the deliverance of our territory should be our rallying cry.'

HAS HE CONVINCED them? The police reports indicate that 'consternation reigns in Paris'. And he feels the same atmosphere in the Tuileries.

He enters Marie Louise's apartments. She comes towards him, her eyes full of tears. Queen Hortense is just as tearful, her face drawn.

He must reassure them again. 'So, Hortense, people are very afraid in Paris, are they? They're already seeing Cossacks in the streets. Well they're not here yet and we haven't forgot our trade.'

He turns towards Marie Louise.

'Be calm,' he adds laughing. 'We will still go to Vienna and defeat Papa Francis.'

He sits at the table, takes the King of Rome on his knees.

'Let's go and defeat Papa Francis,' he sings.

The boy stoutly repeats the phrase. Napoleon bursts into laughter.

Then he sends for Berthier and asks the marshal, Prince of

Neuchâtel, to take a note. He begins to dictate a plan of troop concentration on Champagne to confront the coalition armies.

'We must start the battle of Italy again,' he says.

Then he turns to the Empress and Hortense, who have remained silent, attentive.

'Well, ladies, are you happy? Do you think they will take us so easily?' *But the Allies are in Montbéliard, Dijon and Langres. The marshals are everywhere retreating, retreat, in the grip, it seems, of panic.*

What are they doing? Where is their courage, their heroism? Victor is abandoning the Vosges; Marmont has already evacuated the Sarre; Ney gives up Nancy to Blücher without a fight; Augereau claims that Lyon cannot be defended. And yet everywhere the peasants are resisting the foreign troops. Guerilla warfare is breaking out because the Cossacks are raping, looting and burning.

He dictates his orders. They must fight.

'You will feel how important it is to delay the enemy's march. Use wood rangers and the National Guards to do as much harm to the enemy as possible.'

'No preparations must be made to abandon Paris,' he thunders, 'and if necessary we must be buried under its ruins.'

He adds in a low voice, 'If the enemy reaches Paris, there is no more Empire.'

So they must do everything to make sure it never gets there.

He alone can prevent it. He must leave.

LAST DAYS HERE, in the Tuileries.

Will he come back? He is in his study with the King of Rome. The child is playing. What will be his fate?

I thought that the future of my dynasty would be assured with him. And here I am, throwing my letters and secret papers into the fire.

He looks at the flames reducing to ashes the documents that punctuate the history of his life.

Who can say if tomorrow one of these foreign rulers or one of their generals won't be here in my study, looking through my portfolios, as I did in Queen Louise of Prussia's palace when I was preparing to enter Berlin?

IT IS SUNDAY, 23 January 1814. He takes the King of Rome by the hand. Marie Louise holds the child's other hand. The three of them enter the Salon of the Marshals in which are gathered the officers from twelve legions of the National Guard of Paris. These men form a circle into the middle of which Napoleon walks.

'Officers of the National Guard, gentlemen,' he begins, 'I intend to leave tonight to go and put myself at the head of the army.'

He senses the tension in the stares that are fixed on him.

'Leaving the capital, I am confident leaving my wife and my son on whom so many hopes rest in your midst. I will set off with my mind at peace if they are in your care.'

He looks hard at them one after another.

'I leave you,' he continues, 'what it is dearest to me in the world after France, and I commit them into your keeping.'

He senses the emotion welling up in him.

'It may happen that, thanks to manouevres I am forced to make, the enemy will find an opportunity to approach your walls. Remember that this can only be a matter of a few days and that I will soon be coming to your aid. I recommend you to be united among yourselves. They will not fail to try to shake your loyalty to your duties, but I count on you to repulse all these treacherous instigations.'

He picks up his son, takes him in his arms and walks along in front of the officers.

The cries echo through the hall, making the windows shake: 'Long live the Emperor! Long live the Empress! Long live the King of Rome!'

LATER HE IS sitting next to the Empress. He stares at the child playing a few feet away.

When will he see him again?

He turns towards Marie Louise. She seems dazed. She almost fainted when the officers of the National Guard started shouting. Now she stammers, 'When will you come back?'

'That, my dear friend,' he says, 'only God knows.'

He must get up, go back to his study, where he still has to sort through papers and burn what's left of his secret correspondence and the reports from spies. But he cannot move. He would like time to stop. He would like to fix every one of his son's expressions in his mind.

Some dignitaries come to pay their respects. He pulls himself together, stands up. 'Goodbye, gentlemen. Perhaps we shall see one another again.'

PERHAPS.

If he loses the game, he won't see all those he's leaving here – his wife, son – again.

Only death will be left.

And if he wins?

He cannot imagine what will happen. But he will not be able to reconquer Europe, rebuild this great Empire and become the Emperor of Kings again. He knows that. He won't enter Vienna, Moscow, Madrid, Berlin or Warsaw again. That happened in the past, and can never happen again.

He will fight with his back to the abyss.

He throws a handful of letters into the fire. He writes to Joseph. *My elder brother. Elder, him! For my father's line, no doubt! It was one of my mistakes to think my brothers were needed to assure my dynasty.*

But he writes a few lines to designate Joseph lieutenant-general of the Empire, alongside the Empress, regent.

Even if he is incompetent, even if he has lost Spain, Joseph has not betrayed me.

Maybe.

But how many men can he still count on? Those of the people. But a leaderless people degenerates into a rabble.

He calls in his secretary, dictates his first order: see the Pope leaves before five in the morning and take him from Fontainebleau to Rome.

Then, with a gesture, he indicates that he wants to be left alone.

A few papers still to destroy. And now it's already two in the morning.

He leaves his study and walks through the Tuileries' empty corridors.

When will he come back? Who will he see again?

He tiptoes into his son's bedroom. In the dark he sees Madame de Montesquiou. She starts. He makes a sign to the governess not to move, to keep quiet.

He approaches the bed where the child is sleeping.

He looks at him for a long time in the faint glow of the night light.

He bends down, grazes his son's forehead with his lips. Then he walks away.

In the courtyard the berline and five post-chaises are lined up. Generals and orderly officers form a sombre group.

It is three in the morning on Tuesday, 25 January, 1814.

XVII

Fight. Win.

He repeats these two words to the marshals assembled in the large salon of the prefecture of Châlons, where he has just arrived. He looks at them insistently: Berthier, Kellermann, Ney, Marmont, Oudinot, Mortier. Thanks to him they are the Prince of Neufchâtel, the Duke of Valmy, the Prince of the Moskva, the Duke of Ragusa, the Duke of Reggio, the Duke of Treviso – glittering titles that they want to keep and enjoy. But are they still ready to lead troops into the attack, to charge at the head of their squadrons, risk their lives? Ney and Berthier look downcast. Victor, Duke of Belluno, talks of the fugitives already cluttering the roads, of the conscripts who have barely been outfitted with disparate uniforms, who don't know how to use a musket, who have never faced artillery fire or a cavalry charge and who besides amount only to a few thousand, against hundreds of thousands.

Fight, win, Napoleon says again.

He leads the marshals to the maps laid out on a table in front of the fireplace. He says that all along the road between Paris and Châlons, at every stage – Château-Thierry, Dormans and Épernay, where he ate lunch – crowds had gathered, shouting, 'Long live the Emperor!' He saw men of the National Guard taking up arms everywhere. And already the peasants are rising up in different places in the occupied *départements*. The pillaging and rape of the Cossacks and Prussians are provoking guerrilla warfare by the 'blue smocks'.

He stops, his back to the table, facing the marshals. Those who were with him in Italy or Egypt have to remember what it was like. They had few men, but they beat the enemy every time. Let them remember this principle. 'Strategy,' he hammers out in a slow voice, 'is the science of the use of time and space. Personally I am less sparing of space than time. Space one can always win back. Lost time, never!'

He turns, bends over the maps. There's the enemy's mistake. The coalition armies have not linked up. One, the Army of Silesia, commanded by Blücher, is moving through St-Dizier and coming down the Marne. The other, the Army of Bohemia, under Schwarzenberg, is advancing on Troyes along the Seine.

Napoleon points at the gap between the two armies. They have to defeat Blücher's and Schwarzenberg's armies in turn; go from one to the other. Some 'old moustaches' will arrive from Spain, others from the fortresses of the north and the east; Marshal Augereau, Duke of Castiglione, will advance from Lyon. We are going to win.

He feels as agile as he did at the time of the Italian campaign, when he had to race from one battle to the other and successively crush enemy armies ten times his superior.

He turns towards Berthier.

'At Vitry take two hundred thousand bottles of wine and three hundred thousand of brandy and distribute them to the army today and tomorrow. If there is no other wine than bottles of champagne, take it anyway; it's better we should have it than the enemy!'

He issues a few more orders, then dashes off a quick note for Marie Louise:

> My friend,
>   I have reached Châlons. It is cold. Instead of twelve hours,
> I spent twenty-four on the road. My health is extremely good.
> I am going to go to Vitry, six leagues from here. Farewell, my
> friend. Ever yours,
>   Nap

IT IS EARLY morning.

He mounts his horse. The wind is icy, the ground frozen.

'We shall announce to the army that our plan is to attack tomorrow,' he says. 'Fifty thousand men and me, that makes one hundred and fifty thousand.'

He gallops along these soldiers with children's faces. He knows the craggy old moustaches call them 'Marie Louises', since the regent signed the *senatus consultum* to enrol them. What will he be able to do with these young recruits? But he has confidence in them. Every time they see him, these soldiers cheer.

At Vitry-le-François, the people show the same enthusiasm. He studies his maps watched by the town dignitaries and even a crowd of peasants who have come from the surrounding countryside. They give him information, telling him how they've killed Cossacks and Prussians. Women sob describing what they have suffered.

He must win.

He issues orders and listens to the reports of the aides-de-camp who announce that the Russian troops have been driven out of St-Dizier.

These Marie Louises, he says, are fighting well.

He must go to St-Dizier.

The town's streets are filled with a crowd that presses around his horse and leads him to the mayor's house.

He listens, sitting on the edge of a table, and carefully questions the inhabitants of the villages.

'It is possible that there will be an affair tomorrow in Brienne,' he says.

He bends down over a map, but he ignores the pins aides-de-camp have stuck in here and there to indicate the presence of Blücher's troops and the Cossacks. He sees the Chateau of Brienne. So, destiny is leading him back here, to this town, to this region where he spent so many years of his childhood. This is probably where he will fight the first battle of this French campaign, where his whole life will be decided. Here in Brienne, where his destiny started to take shape, to forge its links with this Nation that has become his own, with this profession of arms.

Brienne, where destiny is going to put me to a new test.

'We are going to put our three hundred guns into play,' he says.

Then he walks back and forth in front of the officers. They must understand what is happening here, in this campaign that is beginning. 'The enemy troops are behaving horribly everywhere,' he says. 'All the inhabitants are taking refuge in the woods. There aren't any peasants to be found in the villages any more. The enemy eats everything, takes all the horses, all the cattle, all the clothing, all the peasant's rags. They beat everyone, men and women, and commit a great number of rapes.'

He lowers his head, his jaw clenched, his expression resolute.

'I wish to extricate my people as quickly as possible from this state of misery and suffering, which is truly horrible. This should also make our enemies pause to reflect: the French are not patient, they are naturally brave, and I expect to see them organize themselves in bands.'

He remembers the revolutionary uprisings, the ones he put down as a lieutenant and those he witnessed.

He dictates a note for the minster of war, General Clarke.

You have informed me that the artillery has a great number of pikes; they must be given to the National Guards assembling on the outskirts of Paris. They will be for the third rank. Have instructions printed on how to use them. Pikes should also be sent to the departments; they're preferable to forks and besides, in the towns, we're even short of forks!

THEY SET OFF again. The rain and thaw turn the forest roads into quagmires. At Mézières, he sees through the fog that has followed a downpour a curate who strides towards him, repeating his name in a breathless voice: 'Abbé Henriot. Do you recognize me, sire?'

A face from the past, of an old quartermaster from the Brienne college. Time is vanishing. Everything is joining together. The abbé offers to lead the columns through the woods.

Suddenly, in the darkness, yells, riding, shots. Cossacks.

Will I die here? Perhaps it's a sign. Here where everything started for me.

He sees a Cossack's lance; it grazes his chest. General Gourgaud wrenches it aside, fires a shot. The Cossack crumples, but the general is wounded. The lance, luckily, skidded off the cross of the Legion of Honour.

Everything won't end for me here, in Brienne.

He hears Ney's shouts.

'Forward, the Marie Louises!' cries Ney, who is leading the

grenadiers of the Old Guard flanking the young recruits. 'Forward, the Marie Louises!'

Napoleon follows them, sees them entering the steep alleys leading to the chateau. He enters the ransacked building and walks around it. He remembers when he was going to Italy to be crowned king in 1805, how he made a stop and slept here. And even then he had thought his destiny was taking him back to the places of his childhood. And now, for the third time, here he is in this place, victorious over Blücher.

But how long will it stay that way? He is concerned. He only has to read a few lines of the reports to understand that Blücher and Schwarzenberg have linked up. And he cannot do anything against such a powerful army. After a battle at Rothières, he has to fall back in a snowstorm, burn the village to allow the infantry to regain Brienne, and from there, that night, give the order to march on Troyes.

Napoleon is sombre. Six thousand men have fallen. If the enemy remains concentrated, what can he do?

And if the coalition forces attack, how can he avoid panic among the young troops? Napoleon has stayed in Brienne chateau. He dictates his orders. He goes to the window, looking towards the battlefield indicated by the line of enemy bivouac fires. The hours pass. Blücher doesn't move.

At four in the morning, on Wednesday 2 February, Napoleon finally leaves the Chateau of Brienne.

He crosses the Aube and on Thursday, 3 February 1814, at three in the afternoon, he reaches Troyes.

IN THE LITTLE lodgings he takes on rue du Temple, the news starts to arrive. He skims the dispatches.

What's the use of carefully reading these complaints Cambacérès and Joseph send him? They want him to negotiate with the coalition forces, who have convened a congress at Châtillon. He sends Caulaincourt there. But he knows what the Allies want: the amputation of France and the fall of his dynasty. Why would they make concessions when they think themselves masters in the field?

But despite these demands my intimates are all around me,

pestering me. Maret, under Caulaincourt's influence, is begging me to give in to the Allies' demands.

He takes a book, shows it to Maret.

'Read, read <u>it</u> aloud,' he says to him, showing him a passage in the *Considerations on the Causes of the Greatness and Decline of the Romans* by Montesquieu.

Maret starts to read in a hesitant voice.

' "I know nothing more magnanimous than the resolution a monarch made to bury himself under the remnants of his throne rather than accept proposals no king should hear. His soul was too proud to descend lower than his misfortune had already consigned him; and he knew that courage can steady a throne, but infamy never." '

He tears the book out of Maret's hands. *That is what Montesquieu thinks. That is what I think.*

'And I, sire,' exclaims Maret, 'I know something more magnanimous. It is to throw down your glory to fill the abyss into which France is going to fall with you.'

Napoleon walks towards him and stares at him.

'Well then, gentlemen, make peace! Let Caulaincourt do it! Let him sign everything he needs to get it, I will be able to bear the shame; but don't expect me to dictate my own humiliation.'

HE REMAINS ON his own. Just let them try to conclude peace. Then they'll find out the enemy's intentions. But why haven't they any energy or determination or even intelligence? They all want to acquiesce rather than fight.

Dispatches from Paris are brought in. The capital is seething with intrigues. The pallid Talleyrand is preparing for the arrival of the Bourbons, and is amazed and indignant at how slowly the coalition forces are advancing. As for the others, Cambacérès and Joseph, they're having masses and forty hours' prayers read.

But what is the matter with these people?

'I see that instead of supporting the Empress,' he write to Cambacérès, 'you discourage her. Why lose your head like this? What are these misereres and forty-hour prayers in the chapel? Is everyone going mad in Paris? The minister of police says and commits follies rather than finding out the enemy's movements.'

He breaks off. An aide-de-camp reports that, according to peasants, the two enemy armies are separating again: Blücher is marching on Châlons and then on to Paris, Schwarzenberg on Troyes.

Perhaps this might be a chance. He leaves Troyes, establishes himself in Nogent-sur-Seine to protect Paris.

He feels as if he hasn't had such vigour, such will to win and such agility since the war in Italy. If he can apply everyone's energies, if he is not betrayed, if people do not give in to fear, if they help him, then he can win and turn the situation around.

He must write to Marie Louise, reassure her.

> My friend,
>   I have received your letter of 4 February. It pains me to
> see you upset. Be brave and cheerful. My health is perfect,
> my affairs, although difficult, are not going badly; they have
> improved in the last week and I hope, with God's help, to see
> them to a successful conclusion.
>   *Addio, mio bene*, ever yours,
>   Nap
>   A kiss for the little king.

IT IS THE NIGHT of Monday 7–Tuesday 8 February. Berthier enters the lodgings Napoleon occupies opposite the church of Nogent-sur-Seine. Napoleon averts his eyes. He cannot look at the dejection on that face.

Marshal Macdonald, who should be holding firm in Châlons, has fallen back on Épernay, Berthier begins. The entire left wing of the army is therefore exposed. Cossacks have entered Sens and are advancing on Fontainebleau.

Napoleon gets up but, before he can even reply, an envoy from Caulaincourt brings the proposals made by the coalition at the Congress of Châtillon.

He reads, sits down. It is as if the letter were dragging down his arm, which he lets fall by his side while he holds his forehead with the other hand.

Is it possible? These, conditions of peace! And they want me to accept them.

He hands the letter to Berthier and Maret; let them read it! But each of them says that Caulaincourt should be given carte blanche.

'What! You want me to sign such a treaty! And trample my oath underfoot!'

He gets to his feet, gesticulates.

'Unprecedented reverses have been able to extract from me the promise to renounce the conquests I made,' he cries, 'but that I should also abandon those made before me, that I should violate the covenant handed on to me with such confidence, at the cost of so much effort and blood and victory, that I should leave France smaller than I found it: never! Could I do this without betrayal or cowardice? You are terrified by the continuation of the war and I am by more certain dangers that you do not see! Reply to Caulaincourt, since you wish to, but tell him that I regret this treaty, that I would rather run the most rigorous risks of war.'

He cannot speak any more. He throws himself on a camp bed. But he cannot stay there. He gets up, lies back down, asks for all the candles to be taken away, then that he be given light again.

He begins to dictate a letter to Joseph.

I have the right to be helped by the men who surround me, by the very ones who I myself have helped. Never let the Empress and the King of Rome fall into the enemy's hands.

I would rather see my son with his throat slit than brought up in Vienna as an Austrian prince, and I have a good enough opinion of the Empress to feel persuaded that she thinks the same way, as far as it is possible for a wife and mother to do so.

I have never seen a performance of *Andromache* without pitying the fate of Astyanax surviving his house and without considering it a blessing that he did not survive his father.

In the very difficult circumstances of this crisis, one does what one can and lets the rest go.

IT IS SEVEN in the morning on this Tuesday 8 February. He has not slept. An officer on Marmont's staff enters the room, gives him a letter. Marmont informs him that Prussian cavalry has arrived at Montmirail, and their infantry at Champaubert. These troops are commanded by General Sacken.

Napoleon pushes past the officer and begins studying the maps, measuring the distances with a compass.

Maret approaches with the dispatches to sign for Caulaincourt that will grant him the right to accept the Allies' proposals.

'Oh, there you are,' Napoleon says without raising his head. 'The situation is quite different now. I am at this moment about to beat Blücher. He is advancing on the Montmirail road. I am leaving; I will beat him tomorrow, I will beat him the day after tomorrow. If this movement has the success it should have, our state of affairs will change completely and then we will see! There will always be time to make a peace like the one they propose.'

FORWARD MARCH, without waiting, despite the rain and snow, despite the muddy roads, the swamps. Forward march! They must go fast and fall on Blücher's Russians and Prussians commanded by Sacken, Olssufiev, Yorck; then, that done, turn back and fall, by forced march, on Schwarzenberg's 150,000.

Madness? He reads this word in his marshals' eyes. But this is how he won the Italian campaign and he wants to conduct this French campaign in the same way. He only has around 50,000 men when the coalition field 300,000! He just has to take them by surprise, and be stronger at the point where one strikes.

Forward march, towards Champaubert, Montmirail, Château-Thierry, Vauchamps.

Filthy weather, roads where they get bogged down. He is on horseback. There are, he writes to Joseph, 'six feet of mud'. But he yells at the columns to get them to push the artillery caissons. He goes into the villages to ask the peasants to lend their horses, help with the pulling and pushing. And when they reach the battlefield at Champaubert the Marie Louises withstand the barrage of fire and cavalry charges without breaking ranks, then go on the offensive and overwhelm the enemy.

He is in the thick of the fighting and only installs himself in a farm on the corner of Champaubert's main street and the Sézanne road when night falls on Thursday, 10 February 1814.

Never, since his first victories in Italy, has he felt such joy.

He sees General Olssufiev enter; he has been taken prisoner with several of his generals. He invites him to dinner and says to the marshals, who seem worn out and half hearted, 'What does the destiny of empires turn on! If tomorrow we gain the success over General Sacken that we have had today over Olssufiev, the enemy will go back across the Rhine quicker than it crossed it, and I will be on the Vistula again.'

He looks at the sombre-faced marshals and adds, 'And then I shall make peace on the natural frontiers of the Rhine!'

He dines in a few minutes, gets to his feet, consults the maps.

'We are marching on Montmirail, where we will be this evening at ten o'clock,' he says, showing the marshals the routes they are to take. 'I will be there myself tomorrow morning before it is light, to march against Sacken with twenty thousand men. If fortune favours us like today, everything will have changed in the blink of an eye.'

Then, standing up, he writes a few lines for Marie Louise.

My good Louise,
    Victory! I have destroyed twelve Russian regiments, taken 6,000 prisoners, forty cannon, 200 caissons, captured the general-in-chief and all his generals, and several colonels; I have lost less than 200 men. Fire the cannon of the Invalides and publish this news at all performances. I will be in Montmirail at midnight, close on the enemy's heels.
    Nap

ON FRIDAY 11 February he is in Montmirail. He only has 24,000 men. They have to perform miracles. Victory again. General Sacken's Russian troops are swept aside.

Entering the Grénaux farm, where he is to bivouac, he sees bodies piled up in the two rooms that are to be his. Fighting raged here all day.

They must know in Paris, at the Tuileries, what sort of victory I have won.

'There is not a man in this routed army who hasn't taken to his heels,' he writes to Marie Louise. 'I am dying of fatigue. Ever yours. Give my son a kiss. Order a sixty-gun salute and proclaim this news at all performances. General Sacken has been killed.'

Despite his exhaustion, he cannot sleep.

'These two days change everything,' he says.

So many times in his life he has been here, on the edge of an abyss into which he could fall and lose everything. But by arching his back, clinging on, repulsing the enemy, crushing him, each time he has got away from the chasm and consolidated his power.

It can – it must – be the same now.

HE IS ADVANCING towards Château-Thierry on this Saturday, 12 February 1814. Peasants are marching with him. They are armed with forks and old muskets. They are fleeing the villages where, they say, Cossacks are raping, beating, killing and looting. They tell him how they have been setting up ambushes for the enemy soldiers, killing stragglers and isolated soldiers.

If these blue smocks rise up en masse, the coalition forces are lost. Napoleon fights with the troops all day. The Russians are beaten again.

Napoleon arrives on the banks of the Marne. The coalition forces have blown up the Château-Thierry bridge. He goes to the river's edge despite the enemy skirmishers. They must start to repair it, he says. But their pursuit is delayed.

He supervises the engineers' work, and the battle resumes at Vauchamps. Another victory.

He has a fire lit at the side of the road and watches the prisoners file past, then he questions the grenadiers and Marie Louises who come next, showing off trophies taken from the enemy. He awards crosses of the Legion of Honour, gives out rewards. Here are men who can change the course of destiny.

'What they have done,' he says, 'can only be compared to the romances of chivalry and the men of arms of those days when, by the effect of their armour and the skill of their horses, one would fight three or four hundred opponents. The enemy must have been struck with a rare terror. The Old Guard has far surpassed everything I could expect of elite troops. It was a very Medusa's head.'

He writes to Marie Louise. Let them repeat this in Paris. Let them parade the prisoners through the streets of the capital.

But while my soldiers surpass themselves, Murat declares war on me! He is a madman and an ingrate!

'The conduct of the King of Naples is infamous and there isn't a name for that of the Queen, my sister Caroline. I hope to live long enough to avenge myself and France for such an outrage and such awful ingratitude.'

HE GIVES THE order to march on Montereau to check the advance of Schwarzenberg's troops; they have been taking advantage of the French concentration on Blücher's corps to make progress.

On the way he learns that General Guyot, in command of the second division of the Guard cavalry, has abandoned two guns to the enemy.

Napoleon stops as soon as he sees Guyot, yells, leaps down from his horse and throws his hat on the ground. He lets himself be carried away by fury, then remounts, but the anger takes root in him.

He rides on despite the shells starting to fall around him into the battle under way around Montereau. He goes to the batteries, gets off his horse, aims a gun himself. The enemy return fire but Napoleon seems not to hear the explosions and the whistling roundshot. He calls out, turning towards the gunners, 'Come on, my friends, don't be afraid; the cannonball that will kill me hasn't yet been forged.'

He exposes himself to danger like this all day. He feels invulnerable, like in all the battles he has commanded.

He writes that evening,

My good Louise,
    I am tired. I have had a superb day. I have defeated Bianchi's corps, with a strength of two divisions, and the Würtembergers . . . But better than all that I have taken the Montereau bridge before they could cut it. I have advanced on the enemy, captured two Austrian flags, a general and several colonels. Farewell my friend, ever yours,
    Nap

BUT THAT EVENING, in Surville chateau, the anger is still there in him.

What are these marshals worth? Victor? Oudinot? They have

been retreating. General Montbrun has let the Cossacks invade Fontainebleau forest. General Digeon has let his cannon run short of ammunition. Marshal Augereau is not advancing at Lyon when he has battle-hardened soldiers and could threaten the enemy's rear.

Napoleon is furious.

'Everywhere,' he cries, 'I hear complaints from the people about mayors and bourgeois who are preventing them defending themselves. I see the same thing in Paris. The people have energy and honour. I am afraid that it is certain leaders who don't want to fight and will look very stupid, after the event, at what has happened to themselves.'

Here is Marshal Victor, Duke of Belluno, on the verge of tears, trying to justify himself, saying he cannot accept his being removed from the battlefield – him, one of the Emperor's oldest comrades-in-arms.

The past doesn't excuse what one does in the present. But Victor insists: he lost his son-in-law General Chataux in the fighting; he stayed with his soldiers.

'I am going to take a musket,' he says. 'I haven't forgotten my former trade; Victor will take his place in the ranks of the Guard.'

Napoleon suddenly holds out his hand to him.

'Well then, stay,' he says. 'I cannot give you your corps back, since I have given it to Gérard, but I will give you two divisions of the Guard. Go and take command of them, and let there be no more question of there being anything between us!'

He turns his back on Victor. These commanders are tired. And? Isn't he too?

Anger wells up again.

He dictates a letter to Augereau.

I order you twelve hours after receipt of this letter to take to the field. If you are still the Augereau of Castiglione, keep the command; if your sixty years weigh on you, give it up and hand it over to your senior general. The country is threatened and in danger; it can only be saved by daring and goodwill, not by pointless temporizing. You should have a core of more than 6,000 elite troops; I don't have that many, and yet I have destroyed three armies and saved the capital three times. Be the first to face the bullets.

It is not a matter of carrying on like recent times; you must get out your boots and the resolution of '93!

When the French see your panache at the advance posts and you exposing yourself to musket fire, then you will do with them what you will!

Suddenly a great wave of fatigue comes over him.

It's been days and days now that he has been on horseback, in the front line at every battle, working out his strategy, dictating hundreds of orders, eating lunch and dinner in minutes, braving the cold, the rain, the mud, trying to buoy up all the people around him, who would otherwise, as he well knows, let themselves go and take the country with them.

And now, on this Saturday 19 February, he cannot take any more. He feels as if he has carried out the task he set himself. He has beaten Blücher's Prussians and Russians and Schwarzenberg's Austrians in succession. Now he can sleep. He lies down as his valet takes off his boots. The fire burns in the fireplace in the little room in Surville chateau.

He closes his eyes.

THE NEXT DAY, at dawn, he writes,

My dear friend,

I was so tired yesterday in the evening that I slept eight hours straight. Have a salute of thirty guns fired for the battle of Montereau. When I write to you have a salute fired, you must write to the minister of war, with your signature, and say, 'in consequence of such and such advantage gained on such and such day by the Emperor'. The minister of war always needs to be informed of military affairs directly.

Farewell, my good Louise, ever yours,

Nap

He goes out. The cold is terrible, the earth frozen; it will help the enemy's movements.

Come on, in the saddle, off towards Nogent-sur-Seine and Troyes. When they stop, the couriers bring the dispatches and newspapers from Paris. In the room where he has established himself in Nogent he grows indignant. He should write the newspapers too. How can they fail to understand that one of the first principles of war is to exaggerate one's forces, not diminish them? Why don't they detail the crimes committed by the enemy, which 'make the hair on my neck stand up'? Flinging out his arm, he sweeps away the dispatches and newspapers in front of him.

'Truly,' he exclaims, 'I have never been worse served!' He takes a few steps around the room, calls out, 'No man can be worse supported than I am!'

He calms down. He contemplates a sweet box, sent by Marie Louise, on which is painted a portrait of the King of Rome. He stares at it for a few seconds. The child's hands are clasped.

Napoleon takes up his quill and writes to the Empress, 'I want you to have this engraved with, "I pray to God that he will save my father and France." This little engraving is so captivating that it will give pleasure to everybody.'

Perhaps the sight of this child will make some people want to fight better, resist.

He grows furious again. He needs to be inside the mind of every officer, every soldier, every minister.

He repeats, 'There is a remedy for everything when one has courage, patience and sangfroid. There isn't when one shapes all the facts into tableaux and lets one's imagination be shocked. That way is only fit for arousing discouragement and despair.'

HE ENTERS TROYES to cheers. An envoy of General Schwarzenberg demands an armistice.

Do they think I don't realize that they seek to delay my attack like this? That one day lost could cost me victory? While with their numerical superiority and their reserves, they have time and space? But people keep on suggesting I capitulate! They don't realize what the coalition forces are asking for: the Empire to be carved up and me to be ruined.

Here is St-Aignan, Caulaincourt's brother-in-law, who says, 'Peace will be good enough if it is prompt.'

'It will come soon enough if it is shameful,' Napoleon answers.

Some people are ready to betray me, like Murat.

Some royalists in Troyes, when their city was occupied, went to Alexander to request the restoration of the Bourbons. One of them is arrested, executed. The pardon Napoleon grants him comes too late.

'The law condemned him,' the Emperor murmurs.

He tours the fortifications of Troyes on horseback. The city has suffered from the fighting. They are burying the dead soldiers. He turns his head away. He has the feeling that victory, a reversal of the situation, is within his grasp. That is what he should think of. He mustn't let himself be preyed on by that anguish, that despair that corrodes the soul. But every moment is an effort. He grows indignant.

'I am not obeyed any more. You are all more intelligent than me, yet you constantly put up resistance, objecting with your buts, ifs and fors.'

When all that's needed is energy and intelligence!

BLÜCHER AND THE Prussians are retreating towards Soissons. He must give chase, sleep in the one room of a village presbytery, brave the cold, the rain.

At La Ferté-sous-Jouarre he listens to the peasants who come and tell of the torture and violence they have suffered.

He questions, reassures, leans over the maps. His plan is simple. 'I am preparing to carry the war into Lorraine,' he says, 'where I shall rally all the troops in my fortresses on the Meuse and the Rhine.'

That way he will cut the enemy armies off from their rear and stop them advancing towards Paris. He will defend the capital by this movement east, rather than directly. So Paris will have to hold out for a few days, a few hours even.

He is gripped with anxiety. What if Paris doesn't hold out?

He discounts this possibility. He has no other choice than to isolate the enemy from its bases and force it on to the retreat that way.

Marmont will take up position in front of Paris and hold firm while I drive east. I must explain this to people, reassure them.

He writes to Cambacérès, Clarke.

'It is enough to think that the capital today is not really

compromised,' he says to one. 'The enemy is everywhere, but in force nowhere,' he explains to another.

Then he sets off again. At Méry, the Prussians are beaten, but there is no bridging team to cross the river and give chase. A few hours are lost.

He waits impatiently, scrutinizing the dispatches. And suddenly, after reading one, he gesticulates. Soissons, a fortress on the Aisne which could slow Blücher's retreat, has capitulated for no reason. 'Infamy!' he exclaims. 'Have the general shot in the middle of the place de Grève and give this execution a great deal of importance.'

Everything has to start again. Time is slipping through my fingers. But he must react. He marches through a snowstorm. They fight in Craonne and Laon.

In Corbeny, a little village, he recognizes a silhouette among the local mayors who have assembled around him. He calls the man, who comes closer.

Once again, like at Brienne, a witness of the past: M. de Bussy, an old officer in the Regiment de la Fère. At every step I find my footprints, as if destiny is coming full circle.

He appoints M. de Bussy an aide-de-camp. He decorates an emissary who has come from the east and announced that the peasants of the Vosges have risen up. This man, Wolff, is also a veteran of the Regiment de la Fère.

He is about to give the order to leave when he is brought some dispatches from Caulaincourt, who is continuing to negotiate. He pushes them away.

'I don't read his letters any more,' he says. 'Tell him they bore me. He wants peace. And I want a grand, good, honourable one.'

ON MONDAY 7 March he enters the little village of Bray-en-Laonnois tottering with fatigue. He hesitates for a moment before crossing the threshold of the house where he is to spend the night. Wounded and dying men are lying on the floor. The battle of Craonne has been hard, uncertain.

He sits in a corner and holds his head in his hands.

In the middle of the night another envoy from Caulaincourt

announces that the Allies have rejected all the French proposals. The coalition forces will only accept a France reduced to its old limits.

Napoleon stands up and calls out, as he steps over the prone bodies, 'If we must get a whipping, it's not for me to have anything to do with it, even less when I am forced.'

So he must fight then, in Laon, advance on Rheims and learn, on Thursday 10 March, that Marmont, whom he has left outside Paris, has retreated, lost ground.

Marmont, my companion since the war of Italy! Marmont is giving up.

He must confront this, rectify the situation, say, 'This is merely an accident of war, but very unfortunate at a time when I needed good luck.'

If Marmont is giving in, after Murat, Augereau, Victor and Bernadotte, who can I still rely on?

Can I even have confidence in my brother? Perhaps Joseph wants to secure his future too, and finally take revenge on me?

What wouldn't he be capable of?

He is suddenly beset by doubt. He writes to Marie Louise,

My friend,

Don't be too familiar with King Joseph. Keep him at a distance; never let him enter your apartments. Receive him like Cambacérès, ceremoniously and in your salon . . . Be very reserved with him and keep him at a distance; no intimacy and, as much as possible, speak to him in the presence of the duchess and in the corner of a window.

He must mistrust everyone and everything. He feels them lying in wait.

Joseph could try to seduce Marie Louise. Joseph, I am told, has come up with the idea of an address in favour of peace, which he would have approved by certain dignitaries.

'The first address I am given asking for peace, I will regard as rebellion,' he says.

What is this minister of police, Savary, the Duke of Rovigo, doing then?

You tell me nothing of what is happening in Paris. There is the matter of the address, the regency and a thousand intrigues as dull as they are absurd, that could, at best, have been thought up by an imbecile ... All these people have no idea that I cut the Gordian knot just like Alexander. Let them know that I am the same today, the same man I was at Wagram and Austerlitz, that I don't want any intrigues in the state; that there is no other authority than mine and that in the case of urgent events the regent has my exclusive confidence. King Joseph is weak; he lowers himself to intrigues that could be disastrous for the state ... I do not want a tribune of the people; let no one forget that I am the grand tribune.

THERE IS FIGHTING outside Rheims. He is in the front line.

At midnight on Monday 14 March he enters the town. All the windows are lit up; the crowd has invaded the streets and is cheering him.

Napoleon is surrounded by hundreds of Rémois at the town hall shouting, 'Long live the Emperor!' He decorates the gunner who, with his firing, killed General St-Priest, the commander of the Russian army.

'He is the same pointer who killed General Moreau; one may well exclaim Providence! Providence!' Napoleon exclaims.

He receives Marmont, covers him with reproaches, and then gradually grows calm. He feels victory is within his grasp again. He has driven a wedge between Blücher's and Schwarzenberg's armies. He can get to the east now and turn the coalition forces.

'Your character and mine,' he writes to Joseph, 'are opposites. You like to coax people and follow their ideas; I like people to please me and follow mine. Today, as at Austerlitz, I am the master.'

It is reported to him that when Marmont left the town hall, he said, 'It is the last smile of fortune.'

He laughs scornfully. What do they know of fortune? You have to seize it by the mane, drag it towards you and then ride it.

ON THURSDAY 17 March he is in Épernay. The crowd cheers him. Champagne is poured for the soldiers. He decorates the mayor, M. Moët. Then he resumes his march towards the Aube, in order to take the flank of Schwarzenberg's army by surprise.

They fight for Arcis-sur-Aube; they fight at Torcy.

Napoleon sees shells explode in front of a battalion of young recruits, who surge back. He rushes forward, puts himself at their head, and when a shell falls at his horse's feet he does not move.

Die here? Why not?

The shell explodes. The horse is disembowelled. Napoleon gets to his feet in the middle of the smoke. The soldiers cheer him, launch another attack and take Torcy.

But the dead cover the ground. How many men does he still have – 20,000, 30,000?

He stays silent for a long while. General Sebastiani is near him. He trusts this Corsican from a humble family who, after conducting diplomatic missions to the Turks, has fought in Russia and Germany and now has just charged with the cavalry of the Guard.

'Well, General, what do you say to what you see?'

'I say that Your Majesty probably has other resources we do not know about.'

'Those you have before your eyes,' answers Napoleon.

'But then, how is it that Your Majesty hasn't thought of rousing the whole Nation?'

Napoleon looks at Sebastiani and walks his horse a few paces. Since the start of the campaign he has issued proclamation after proclamation to the blue smocks. But if guerrilla fighting has spread, it doesn't have the character of a general uprising as in Spain or Russia.

'Chimeras!' cries Napoleon, returning towards Sebastiani. 'Chimeras borrowed from memories of Spain and the French Revolution! Rousing the Nation in a country where the Revolution has destroyed the nobility and clergy and where I have destroyed the Revolution.'

He laughs bitterly.

Only he, with the soldiers he has left, can change the course of events.

But can he be sure of winning?

He watches the few thousand exhausted men with whom he has to face the hundreds of thousands of enemies march past.

He is going to throw the dice. He writes to Joseph.

I am going to manoeuvre in such a way that you won't go several days without any news from me. If the enemy advances on Paris in such strength that resistance is impossible, send the regent and my son away in the direction of the Loire.

Do not abandon my son and remember that I would rather know him in the Seine than in the hands of France's enemies. The fate of Astyanax as a Greek prisoner has always seemed to me the most unfortunate in history.

This idea and image obsess him. And he is afraid of his intuition and the power of his thoughts.

XVIII

At two o'clock in the afternoon, on this Wednesday, 23 March 1814, he arrives at St-Dizier. Infantrymen are lying on the ground, propped against the fronts of the houses. Their uniforms are filthy and their bodies, he can see, are broken with tiredness after days and days of marching and fighting.

How many men does he have left?

He enters the mayor's house. The marshals are already there. Berthier and Ney say in muffled voices that the battle of Arcis-sur-Aube has been costly, and that the enemy has at least 100,000 men and several hundred cannon.

'What is our strength?' he asks. And he'd rather not hear Berthier's response. Eighteen thousand infantry and 9,000 cavalry, the Prince of Neufchâtel, chief of staff of the army, repeats.

One can work miracles with a handful of men. Don't they know that, all those who have been following him since the beginning? The garrisons from the fortresses in the east will arrive. The enemy won't be able to advance on Paris without worrying about its rear, which will be exposed and which they will harry.

He begins to write.

My friend,
    I have been in the saddle every day. On the 20th, I took Arcis-sur-Aube. The enemy attacked me at six in the evening; I beat them on the same day and inflicted 4,000 dead. I took two of their cannon, and they took two from me, which made us quits. On the 21st, the enemy army arrayed itself in battle order to protect its supply routes to Brienne and Bar-sur-Aube. I have decided to move on the Marne and the enemy's lines of communication in order to push them further from Paris and to draw nearer my fortresses. I am at St-Dizier this evening.
    Farewell, my friend. A kiss for my son,
    Nap

Will this letter ever get to Marie Louise? It's almost five days now since he last heard news from her.

He turns towards Berthier and Ney.

'These Cossacks . . .' he murmurs.

They hound the couriers, driving far ahead of the bulk of the enemy troops. They seize the mail. The enemy can be informed of my movements like this, of the state of mind in Paris. But it is a risk I have to take. The 'tremblers' in Paris must know that I am fighting, that I am brimming with hope and resolve.

THAT NIGHT, AS he is making his way from his camp bed to the table on which the maps are laid out, Caulaincourt arrives. He is out of breath, his features drawn. He has almost been taken prisoner between Sompuis and St-Dizier. The Allies have stopped negotiating, he says. Napoleon exclaims, they never really wanted to.

'What the enemy wants is to loot France and turn it upside down. Alexander wants to avenge himself on Paris for his stupidity in burning Moscow. What the enemy wants is to humiliate us, but I'd rather die.'

He walks about the dark room.

'I am too old a soldier to care about living; I shall never sign the shame of France. We will fight, Caulaincourt. If the nation supports me, our enemies are nearer to downfall than I am, because the people's exasperation is extreme. I am cutting the Allies' communications; they have numbers but no support. I am rallying part of my garrisons. I am crushing one of their corps and the slightest setback may affect them deeply.'

He leans towards Caulaincourt.

'If I am conquered, better to die gloriously than subscribe to conditions that the Directory wouldn't have accepted after its reverses in Italy. If I am supported, I can remedy everything. If fortune abandons me, the Nation will have no reproaches that I betrayed the oath I swore at my coronation.'

He straightens up.

'Schwarzenberg is following me; if you come in time, you will see some fine things very soon.'

He calls Berthier. He paces, his hands behind his back.

'Send a gendarme in disguise to Metz, one to Nancy and one to Bar, with letters to the mayors,' he says. 'Tell them that we are bearing down on the enemy's rear; that the moment has come to rise up en masse, to sound the tocsins, arrest the commandants and war commissaries of the enemy, fall on their convoys, seize depots and enemy supplies, and that they must publish this order immediately in all the communes. Write to the commandant of Metz to muster the garrisons and come to meet us on the Meuse.'

He stops and stares at Berthier. The marshal, Prince of Neufchâtel, looks haggard. He stammers something but does not dare speak out in a clear voice.

I know what he's thinking, what they're all thinking. Where are we going? they wonder. If the Emperor falls, will we fall with him?

HE NEEDS TIME to rally troops. But every hour the enemy is reinforcing. And everyone is yielding. Augereau, Duke of Castiglione – what has become of the man of the Italian campaign? – is evacuating Lyon instead of bringing me his support. He is falling back on Valence. Marmont and Mortier, another two marshals, are withdrawing and are beaten at La Fère-Champenoise. The squares formed by the National Guard are holding the firmest, and they are getting cut to pieces like old grenadiers. The Cossacks, the advance guard of Wintzingerode's Russians, are right up here, at St-Dizier.

Napoleon is in the front line with the Marie Louises and the Guard, who spring into the attack. Victory is complete. But in the distance, beyond the battlefield, the bivouac fires burning in that icy March night signal other enemy troops, an enormous flood tide which is contained momentarily but will very soon burst its banks.

Napoleon ranges through the countryside around St-Dizier. The dead from the fighting just ended are sprawled on the ground, already covered with a white frost. He questions the enemy wounded. They belong to a corps that has become detached from Schwarzenberg's army, which has been marching for the last two days on Paris.

I need time, just a few days.

He hesitates, gathers the marshals around him. The choice is simple, he says. But Ney, Berthier, Mortier and Marmont all bow their heads. They don't want to talk about a choice between different strategies, but about stopping the fighting.

Let them dare say that!

They don't.

'Should we wait for the eastern garrisons, even go to meet them, while relying on – and encouraging – the peasant revolts?' he asks.

The marshals' faces are tense, dismissive.

March on Paris, then?

They approve. But no forced marches, they say; the army wouldn't survive them. They must go to the capital through Vassy, Bar-sur-Aube, Troyes and Fontainebleau. The soldiers can then get their strength back.

BUT THAT ROUTE is the longest and I need time.

He leaves St-Dizier on Monday, 28 March 1814. When he enters the village of Doulevant in the early evening he sees couriers from Paris coming towards him. He leaps down from his horse immediately. The first dispatch is from Lavalette, director of the post, a wholly trustworthy individual who has never let him down since Italy.

Only one line, which he reads and then reads again: 'The Emperor's presence is necessary. If he wants to prevent the capital being handed over to the enemy, there isn't a moment to lose.'

Here's the key to what he has so far not understood: Paris handed over!

So, their certainty of being able to take the capital without a fight is the reason why the coalition forces aren't worrying about their rear, the threat I am posing to their communications and the fact that, as prisoners attest, their ammunition and provisions are starting to run short. Paris would only have to hold out for two days for the enemy armies to be starving and, supported by an uprising of the blue smocks, my offensive against their rear would turn their French campaign into a disaster.

But if Paris capitulates, the head falls and the body can only jerk and twitch.

He reads another message: 'All the crossings within fifteen leagues of Paris are in enemy hands. In the capital the royalists are handing out proclamations. There's talk of forcing the Legislative Body to convene to demand peace. The Russians are bound to burn Paris to avenge the fire of Moscow, people are saying.'

He pictures the scene: Talleyrand, the nobility of the Faubourg St-Germain, the dignitaries – all of them manoeuvring. Talleyrand must be corresponding with the coalition forces. They will not fight although there are tens of thousands of men, and cannon, in the capital, and the gates of Paris can be defended, and they would only have to hold out for two days.

I need time.

HE WANTS TO leave for Paris immediately, but Cossacks are holding the Troyes road. He has to spend the night at Doulevant when every minute counts.

At dawn on Tuesday 29 March he is finally able to give the order to move. He marches with the Guard. On the Dollencourt bridge, he meets the couriers from Paris. The marshals have fallen back. Meaux is in enemy hands. They are refusing to arm the workers in the suburbs who are willing to fight, like the students of the Polytechnique. The manufacturer Richard Lenoir has armed his workers, but he is the only prominent citizen who has remained loyal to the Emperor. Hulin, the military commandant, one of the 'conquerors of the Bastille', declares that he has no arms to distribute. The streets are full of peasants who have taken refuge in the capital to flee the enemy advance.

I need time.

He pushes his horse into a gallop. After going flat out for hours, the animal collapses. Napoleon gets into a wicker cabriolet lent him by a butcher in Villeneuve-sur-Vanne, a small town between Troyes and Sens.

Napoleon talks to Caulaincourt, who is sitting next to him like in the sleigh when they left Russia together. If Paris holds out for forty-eight hours . . . He leans forward to see if the two carriages carrying General Gourgaud and Marshal Lefebvre, and Generals

Drouout and Flahaut respectively, are following. He has commanded Lefebvre to organize the resistance in the suburbs by arming the workers. But he needs time.

The horses are changed. A courier explains that Joseph has authorized the marshals to negotiate the conditions of their capitulation and that he has left Paris with the Empress, the King of Rome and the ministers. But there's fighting at the gates of the capital, and the enemy are not making headway; they are even falling back. Workers and students have joined the National Guard and the infantry. Only in place Vendôme and the expensive districts are there crowds sitting outside cafés, shouting, 'Long live the King.'

FASTER, FASTER, HE needs to go faster than time itself.

On Wednesday 30 March, at eleven o'clock in the evening, he enters the courtyard of the post house in Fontaines-de-Juvisy. He reads the sign on the façade, AT THE COURT OF FRANCE, and feels a pang of emotion.

A column of cavalry passes on the road. Napoleon goes out and hails General Belliard, who is riding at the front.

'What, you here? How's that? Where is the enemy?' he cries. 'Where is the army? Who is guarding Paris? Where are the Empress and the King of Rome? Joseph? Clarke? What of Montmartre, my soldiers, my cannon?'

He listens to Belliard. Is it possible that, despite the courage of the defenders, Joseph has authorized capitulation when just a few hours more would have been enough? He walks along the road, taking Belliard, Caulaincourt and Berthier with him.

'What cowardice to capitulate! Joseph has lost everything. Four hours too late! If I had arrived four hours earlier, everything would have been saved.'

He clenches his fists.

'Everyone has lost their heads,' he cries. 'This is what comes of employing men who have no common sense or energy.'

He walks on into the night, saying, 'Four hours have compromised everything.'

He turns towards Caulaincourt, who is following a few paces behind.

'In a few hours the courage and devotion of my good Parisians can save everything. My carriage, Caulaincourt; let us go to Paris. I will put myself at the head of the National Guard and the troops; we will rectify matters. General Belliard, give the order to the troops to turn around . . . Let us be on our way! My carriage, Caulaincourt; let's not lose any time.'

Belliard objects that the surrender has been signed and must be respected.

He yells, 'What agreement is this? By what right has it been made? Paris had over two hundred cannon and provisions for a month . . . Four hours too late, what a stroke of fortune! But they knew I was in the enemy's rear and, with me so close, the enemy couldn't have been very adventurous if they held out; winning the day would have been easy. There is some intrigue behind this . . . What a hurry they were all in! Joseph has lost me Spain; now he is losing me Paris. This will be the end of France, Caulaincourt!'

He strides on briskly.

'We will fight, Caulaincourt, because it is better to die sword in hand than be humiliated by foreigners. If you reflect, the matter has not been decided! The fall of Paris will signal the nation's salvation if I am supported. I will be master of my movements, and the enemy will pay dearly for the audacity that has allowed him to steal three marches on us.'

He repeats in a bitter, scornful tone, 'Joseph has lost everything! Not holding out for twenty-four hours with twenty-five thousand National Guards and fifty thousand men in the suburbs!'

Then he adds, in a voice suddenly weary, 'You don't know men, Caulaincourt, and what can be achieved in such a city by the intrigues of a few traitors, in circumstances this grave and under the pressure of the vengeance and bayonets of foreigners.'

He is silent for a long while.

It is as if he can hear Talleyrand repeating, 'Louis XVIII is a matter of principle; he is the legitimate king.' It is as if he can see all the dignitaries following the pallid Prince of Benevento to rally to the Bourbon king.

What of my son, my King of Rome, my dynasty?

'My energy irritates them,' he says furiously. 'My constancy tires them. Their intrigues will be exposed, I know everything . . .'

He enters the post house.

'Paris,' he exclaims, 'the capital of civilization, occupied by the barbarians! This great city will be their tomb.'

He sighs.

'But there are so many intriguers in Paris. Who knows what will happen tomorrow? The rank and file, the brave officers won't betray me. Marmont was raised in my camp; I have been a father to him. He may have lacked energy and done stupid things, but he cannot be a traitor.'

He sits down, his elbows on the table, his head in his hands, and then starts to write.

> My friend,
>
> I came here to defend Paris, but there was no time left. The city surrendered in the evening; I am mustering my army around Fontainebleau. My health is good. I suffer from the fact that you must be suffering.
>
> Napoleon
> The Court of France, 31 March at three in the morning

He gets to his feet. He needs . . . He turns to Caulaincourt.

'You must leave, go to Paris, go and save France and your Emperor. Do whatever you can. They are bound to impose harsh conditions on us, but I leave it to your honour as a Frenchman . . .'

He dictates an assignment order for Caulaincourt and then, as he hands it to the minister of foreign affairs, he murmurs, 'You will arrive too late. The authorities in Paris will be afraid to compromise the inhabitants with regard to the enemy. They won't want to listen to you, for our enemies have other plans than those they have declared up until now . . .'

It is my head they want.

General Flahaut, who has returned from Paris, hands him a letter from Marmont.

> I must tell Your Majesty the whole truth. Not only is there no disposition for people to defend themselves, but there is actually a formal resolve not to do so. It seems the mood has changed

completely since the departure of the Empress. The departure of King Joseph at midday, and of all the members of the government, has raised discontent to a peak . . .'

Napoleon hangs his head.

He walks out of the Court of France without a word, and gets into his carriage.

He reaches Fontainebleau on 31 March 1814, at six in the morning.

He shuts himself in his apartments on the first floor. He reads the dispatches, calls his secretary, and starts to dictate.

Nothing is lost since another day is dawning.

XIX

Never give up.

He looks through the window at Fontainebleau's park. Everything is so calm, so deserted on this Thursday, 31 March 1814. He remains deep in thought for a long while, then shakes his whole body.

'Orleans must be the pivot of the army,' he says, turning back to the map table. 'We shall concentrate all the depots there, for the artillery, cavalry, infantry and the National Guards.'

He leans forward as he speaks. He still has more than 70,000 men at his disposal. The coalition forces are over 180,000. So be it. But they have lost 10,000 men in Paris. They can drive them back, bring out the suburbs, cut off the lines of retreat, call on the blue smocks to help throughout Champagne, Lorraine, the east. With a finger he traces a line on the map and he dictates: 'The Duke of Ragusa, Marshal Marmont, will form the advance guard and will assemble all his troops at Essonne. The corps of Marshal Mortier, Duke of Treviso, will join the front between Essonne and Fontainebleau. The minister of the interior will everywhere implement a mass levy to fill the ranks of the battalions.'

He stops and goes over to the window again. The silence enveloping the chateau is suddenly devastating. Has he lost everything? Where are his wife and son? He writes, 'My good Louise, I have not received a letter from you. I am afraid lest you be too affected by the loss of Paris. I beg you to be brave and take care of your health, which is so precious to me. Mine is good. Give the little king a kiss and love me always, Nap'.

A courier from Paris arrives.

Napoleon takes the dispatch sent by Caulaincourt, who, as minister of foreign affairs, is continuing to try to negotiate. Before reading it, Napoleon tenses all his muscles as if he can hear the whistle of a cannonball.

A declaration of the sovereigns, posted in the afternoon, proves that treachery has, I fear, already made considerable headway.

I have not seen a friendly face. This gives one an idea of the opinion and character of the men who have stayed here. I have found very few Frenchmen, it grieves me to tell Your Majesty. Many intriguers want me to leave. I won't stop until I am thrown out. I hope Your Majesty does not doubt either the devotion of the minister or the indignation of the citizen revolted by so much ingratitude.

He has judged Caulaincourt too severely. *Tested, the man is loyal. He has extricated himself from Talleyrand's influence. I should trust him. How many are still with me and prepared to carry on fighting?*

He finds a second sheet of paper. It is the text of the 'Declaration of the Sovereigns', signed by Alexander. 'The allied sovereigns declare that they will no longer negotiate with Napoleon Bonaparte or with any member of his family. Consequently they invite the Senate to appoint a provisional government forthwith . . .'

He crumples the paper.

The senators are going to proclaim my fall. They will all rush to the conquerors. Every single one of them.

He finds a letter Caulaincourt has attached to his dispatch. Fontanes, explains the minister, is in the process of drawing up a text that will relieve, in the Senate's name, the soldiers 'of their loyalty to a man who is not even French'.

Me.

He feels sick.

Fontanes, who I made grand master of the university! The servile Fontanes, who lauded me to the heavens in 1804!

Here's men as they really are.

He questions the courier. The officer says that the coalition troops and the Tsar have been welcomed in the wealthy districts of Paris with cries of joy.

'You'd think they were another people,' murmurs the courier.

The women of the nobility have got up behind the saddles of the Cossacks' horses. They have kissed Alexander's boots.

These people whom I had struck off the list of émigrés, whom I showered with privileges.

*What is left for me to do, except continue the war at any price?
Because they want my deposition and my death.*

HE MUST SHOW himself, therefore, organize parades, muster the
troops, instil them with confidence.

He goes to the advance posts in Essonne. He passes in front
of the troops drawn up in the Courtyard of the White Horse at
Fontainebleau palace. Watching these men march past, the way
they stand up straighter as they approach him, he feels a sense of
confidence. These men will not betray him.

He must talk to all these faces straining towards him.

'Officers, non-commissioned officers and privates of the Old
Guard,' he begins.

He stands up in his stirrups. He looks at the dark squares that
are what is left of the Grand Army. With this handful of men, if
they want it, if he can lead them, he can still break out of this
situation they are trying to lock him into.

'The enemy stole three marches on us,' he continues. 'They
have entered Paris. I have offered Emperor Alexander a peace
purchased by great sacrifices. Not only has he refused, but he went
further: at the perfidious suggestion of some émigrés whose lives
I spared and showered with favours, he has authorized them to
wear the white cockade, and soon he will want to substitute it for
our national cockade. In a few days I will march to attack Paris.
I am counting on you . . .'

Will these soldiers reply? Everything is in the balance now.

'Am I right?'

The cries eventually ring out: 'Long live the Emperor! To
Paris, to Paris!'

His chest swells. He speaks louder.

'We will go and prove to them that the French Nation knows
no master in its own home; that if we have been that for a long
time in other people's homes, we shall remain so in ours, and,
finally, that we are capable of defending our cockade, our
independence and the integrity of our territory!'

He walks away as the shouts of 'Long live the Emperor!'
reverberate again.

HE REMAINS ALONE in his study for a few minutes. What if the attack on Paris doesn't succeed? He must take all possibilities into account.

He writes to Marie Louise.

> My friend,
> You may send a very warm letter commending yourself and your son to your father. Make your father feel that the moment has arrived for him to help us. Farewell, my friend, be in good health.
>
> > Ever yours,
> > Nap

And now the dispatches from Paris.

He reads them.

The Senate and Legislative Body have proclaimed my dethrone-ment. A provisional government has been formed, with Talleyrand as president.

So what he had anticipated has come to pass.

In the days, or perhaps even hours, to come, they are 'freely' going to call on Louis XVIII to be King of France. And they'll talk of 'the Nation's wishes'. I know them; I saw them in action on the 18th Brumaire, those chatterers! They only listen to the voice of their interests, and they only respond to military victory.

I can still win.

He calls Marshals Ney, Berthier, Lefebvre, Oudinot, Macdon-ald, certain generals and Caulaincourt and Maret into his study.

He walks briskly up and down in front of them and looks them in the eye. They are frozen, sad, lugubrious even. Haven't they heard the soldiers shouting? To Paris, to Paris! He questions them. They cannot see an end to it all, they murmur.

'An end! But that depends on us,' he replies. 'You see these brave soldiers who have neither rank nor riches to protect. They only think of marching and dying to wrest France from the foreigner's hands. We must follow them. The coalition forces are split between the two banks of the Seine, of which we hold the main bridges, and scattered throughout a vast city. Vigorously attacked in this position, they will be lost. The people of Paris are all a-quiver; they won't let them leave with giving chase and the peasants will finish them off. I have seventy thousand men, and with this mass I will throw everything that leaves Paris and tries to get home into the Rhine. What does this need? One last effort which will allow you to enjoy twenty-five years work in peace.'

He waits. The marshals are silent, then Ney starts to speak, with Lefebvre and Macdonald.

'You are asking us to march on the capital,' says the latter. 'I declare in the name of the troops that they do not want to expose it to Moscow's fate.'

Now they are all talking. He looks at them disdainfully. They all repeat 'Moscow'. They talk of the situation in Paris, the discouragement of the troops. It is time to enjoy a rest, says Lefebvre. We have titles, mansions, estates; we do not want to get ourselves killed for you.

This is what men are.

After Bernadotte, after Murat, everyone here refuses to obey me, is prepared to betray me. One does not wage war against one's officers.

'Well then, gentlemen, since this is how it is, I will abdicate. I wanted France's welfare and I have not succeeded; events have turned against me. I do not want to increase our woes. But when I abdicate, what will you do? Do you want the King of Rome for my successor and the Empress as regent?'

They do.

Ney, Marmont and Caulaincourt will go and negotiate with the coalition forces.

'Gentlemen,' Napoleon continues, 'you may now withdraw. I am going to write the instructions for the negotiators.'

Then he suddenly sinks into a sofa, slaps his thigh and calls out, 'Bah, gentlemen! Let's forget that and march tomorrow; we will beat them. One must try everything.'

But the marshals shake their heads.

So he dismisses them with a wave.

SUCH ARE MEN.

He recalls Caulaincourt.

'The marshals have lost their heads,' he says. 'They are throwing themselves in the wolf's mouth. They don't see that without me there is no more army and, without that, there is no guarantee for them. Born a soldier, I will be fine without an Empire, but France cannot do without me; it will suffer the yoke that Alexander and Talleyrand's intrigues will impose on it.'

He takes Caulaincourt's arm.

'As for me, I am decided. While you negotiate, we will fight. The Parisians will support me. What is happening in Paris is only the result of the intrigues of fifty traitors. If one has a little energy everything will be saved, and battle will settle the whole question.'

There's my plan. Play two cards.

'I am not attached to the throne,' he adds to Caulaincourt. 'But Alexander must be unmasked.'

He hesitates, then says in a lower voice, 'I do not commend my son's interests to you; I know I can count on you. As for me, you know I need nothing.'

He feels weary suddenly, exhausted even. He goes into his bedroom. He lies down. Does he still hold the cards?

HE CANNOT SLEEP. He goes to the window, opens it. The dawn on this Tuesday, 5 April 1814, is mild. The breeze blowing from the forest is laden with the smells of spring. He hears horses' hooves, the sound of voices, footsteps.

There is going to be another barrage, he can feel it. He waits. General Gourgaud enters, talking in an impassioned voice, and soon there are other officers in the room. Marshal Marmont, Duke of Ragusa, has left his troops, which form the advance guard of the army at Essonne, to go to Paris. He has manoeuvred his 10,000 men so that they have ended up right in the middle of the Austrian lines. Handed them over! Marmont has committed treachery.

'The ingrate! He will be unhappier than me,' Napoleon calls out.

He remains silent for a moment. Marmont, who he knew at the siege of Toulon, who he made his aide-de-camp, who was in Italy and Egypt, on every campaign; Marmont who he promoted to the rank of general at twenty-eight.

He gives several orders authorizing an attempt to cover the Essonne line with new troops.

'It is possible that the enemy will attack,' he says.

He dictates an order of the day for the army in a calm voice, but he often breaks off. He feels they are nearing the end of the game. A Polish officer covered in dust hands him a letter. It is from General Krazinski, who commands the lancers. 'Sire, the marshals are betraying you. The Poles will never betray you. Everything may change, but not their attachment. Our life is essential to your safety. I am leaving my cantonment without orders to rally near you and form impenetrable formations.'

He reads the letter again. He is calm, serene. He already feels so far from this game. He sees himself and he sees the players as if he had to write their history, as if he were offstage looking down from a hill through an eyeglass at the manoeuvres of one or other participant.

Yet one of the players is still him.

He receives Caulaincourt, who explains that Alexander rejected his conditional abdication in favour of the King of Rome the moment he heard of Marmont's treason. The negotiations revolved around only one argument – the army's unqualified devotion to Napoleon. Now Marmont has handed over his men, the coalition forces can demand full abdication. And the senators have given the throne to Louis XVIII.

He listens. He is a long way away.

'With a few exceptions, Caulaincourt, circumstances are stronger than men,' he murmurs. 'Everything is beyond human calculation.'

He begins walking slowly.

'Marmont has forgotten the standard under which he achieved all his promotions, the roof under which he spent his youth. He has forgotten that he owes all his honours to the prestige of the national cockade, which he is trampling underfoot in order to adopt the sign of the traitors. I was delighted to see him take up a position between my enemies and me because I believed in his attachment, his loyalty. How wrong I was! This is the fate of sovereigns. They foster ingrates. Marmont's corps can't have known where he was leading them.'

Caulaincourt agrees and says that Marmont's soldiers shouted 'Long live the Emperor', insulted their generals and that it took all Marmont's authority and lies to convince them to surrender even when they were surrounded by the Austrians.

'Ah, Caulaincourt,' he says. 'Interest, keeping positions, money, ambition; this is what motivates most men.'

He takes a few steps.

'The traitors are to be found in the highest echelons of society,' he continues. 'Those I raised highest are the first to abandon me! The officers and soldiers would all still die sword in hand for me.'

He sits down, holds his head in his hands.

'Everyone is tired now; they just want peace at any price.'

He raises his head, looks straight ahead.

'Within a year, people will be ashamed to have given in rather than fought and to have been handed over to the Bourbons and Russians. Everyone will hasten to my camp.'

He adds in a calm voice, 'The marshals think me very far from wanting to abdicate.'

He shrugs his shoulders.

'But one would have to be mad to hang on to a crown that some people are so impatient to see me abandon.'

He observes Caulaincourt, gauges the minister's astonishment. Yes, he has uttered this sentence. He is prepared to abdicate.

HE FIXES THE details of the final negotiation with Caulaincourt. They grant him sovereignty over the island of Elba, do they? So be it, since Corsica, which is a French *département*, must not be amputated from France. Elba? Choose Elba.

'It is an island for a soul like a rock,' he murmurs. 'I am a very singular character, no doubt, but one wouldn't be extraordinary if one wasn't different.'

In a louder voice, facing Caulaincourt, he adds, 'I am a splinter of rock launched into space.'

HE RECEIVES THE marshals on Wednesday 6 April.

He is sitting in front of a window. At moments he feels waves of tiredness and a temptation to close his eyes, lie down and not listen to anything any more. Then they go.

'You want rest. Have it then,' he calls out to Ney and the

other marshals as they leave. 'Alas, you don't know how much danger and sorrow await you on your feather beds.'

He stands up.

'A few years of this peace that you will pay for so dearly will harvest more of you than any war could have, even the most desperate war.'

Then he turns his back on them and sits at his desk. He starts to write.

The allied powers having proclaimed that the Emperor Napoleon is the sole obstacle to the restoration of peace in Europe, the Emperor Napoleon, true to his oath, declares that he renounces, for himself and his heirs, the thrones of France and Italy, and that there is no personal sacrifice, even that of his life itself, that he is not prepared to make in the interest of France.

All that remains is to negotiate on his own and his family's behalf.

'I can live on a hundred louis a year,' he says. 'When I had access to all the finances in the world, I never took an écu for my personal use; everything was observable and within the treasury.'

But there is his wife, his son, his brothers, his sisters, his mother and the soldiers who have remained loyal to him. He must protect them; win them the right to keep their privileges.

He feels a rush of anger. The Emperor of Austria does not seem to have done anything for Marie Louise.

'Not a mark of interest, not even a memento from her father in these painful circumstances. The Austrians have no compassion.'

He wants to be left alone.

Will he ever see his wife and son again?

He writes,

My good Louise,

My heart is heavy at the thought of your troubles.

I am very concerned about you and my son but, as you can imagine, very little about myself. My health is good. Give my son a kiss and write to your father every day so he knows where you are.

It seems that your father is our fiercest enemy. I am sorry

that I have nothing to offer you now but a share in my bad fortune. I would quit this life if I didn't think this would intensify your woes and add to their number.

Farewell, my good Louise; I pity you. Write to your father to ask for Tuscany for you, because I don't want more than the isle of Elba for myself.

Farewell my friend, give your son a kiss.

He hasn't the strength to sign.

He would like to have his wife and son by his side. What else has he got left? And this island of Elba they're giving him, is it worth the penalty of living?

He touches the little leather bag around his neck that contains the poison Dr Yvan prepared for him during the Russian campaign to escape, if need be, the Cossacks, after they had almost captured him on the Maloyaroslavets road. The ingredients, according to Yvan, are opium, belladonna, white hellebore – fit for a Roman emperor's death. An elected death, like a final coronation, an act of will, like him putting the Imperial crown on his own head at his coronation.

He thinks of Josephine, Hortense and Eugène.

In the clauses of the act of abdication their situation must be specified; they must keep everything I have given them.

So he must concern himself with money. He sends for Caulaincourt. They must send officers to Orléans, where the Empress is, to attempt to seize part of the treasury from the Tuileries which has been taken there.

Caulaincourt announces that agreement has been reached in Paris on the conditions of his abdication. The Emperor will be the sovereign of the isle of Elba and will receive an income of two million francs paid by the French government. The Empress will reign over the Duchy of Parma with the right of succession for her son.

He listens, far away, a witness to what is being played out, even though he is an actor.

He starts to write.

My good friend,

All your sufferings are in my heart; they are the only ones I cannot bear. Try to overcome this adversity. I am being awarded the island of Elba, and Parma, Piacenza and Guastalla are being awarded to you and your son. It is a concern of 400,000 souls with three or four million in revenue. You will at least have a house and a beautiful country when your stay on my island of Elba tires you and I become tiresome, as is bound to happen when I am older and you are still young.

I will go as soon as everything is finished to Briare, where you will come and meet me, and then we will go by Moulins and Chambéry to Parma and, from there, embark at La Spezia. I approve of all the arrangements you are making for the little king.

My health is good, my courage greater than everything, especially if you are content with my ill fate and you think you will be able still to be happy. Farewell, my friend; I am thinking of you, and your suffering is hard for me. Ever yours,

Nap

Will she come? Will he see them? Or will destiny deprive me of that too? He paces up and down his apartments. The park is deserted after a last parade. But that march past is already so distant, from another time, Thursday 7 April, and today is Tuesday the 12th.

Caulaincourt has brought the convention of abdication. All that remains is to sign it. But already they're all going. Berthier, who has always stayed by me, explained that he wanted to get back to Paris as quickly as possible. He will not accompany me to the island of Elba.

Who would have said that he would be one of the first to leave me? He hopes to keep his fortune, but still, his leaving Fontainebleau before my departure shocks me.

He sighs. General Bertrand, grand marshal of the palace, has decided to follow him to the island of Elba. But for every loyal servant how many ingrates and traitors?

He lies down. He has trouble breathing.

'Do they think that, useless to France, I shall outlive its glory?' he murmurs.

He has trouble speaking. Suddenly he imagines the journey to the Mediterranean coast. The insults he may have to suffer or the assassins in the Bourbons' pay. And Marie Louise and the King of Rome, who won't join him.

'Ah, Caulaincourt, I have already lived through too much. Poor France, I do not want to see your dishonour.'

The words come out of their own accord.

'Ah, my poor Caulaincourt, what a fate! Poor France. When I think of its present situation, the humiliation foreigners will impose on it, life is unbearable to me.'

He closes his eyes.

'The Empress will not want to spend the whole year on Elba,' he murmurs, 'but will come back and forth.'

No, she won't. They will detain her. She will grow weary. She is only a young woman without a will of her own. He knows.

'Life is unbearable to me,' he repeats. 'I did everything to die at Arcis. The cannonballs did not want me. I have done my job.'

He sees his valet approach. Marie Walewska is waiting in one of the galleries of the palace, explains the servant. She is alone. She wants to see the Emperor.

He shakes his head. He can't. He mustn't, because if it becomes known that he has received Marie Walewska, perhaps they will use it as an argument to stop Marie Louise joining him with his son.

But this refusal is like a surrender, another abdication.

'Life is unbearable to me,' he says again.

He closes his eyes and murmurs, 'I need rest, and you do too, Caulaincourt. Go to bed. I will send for you tonight.'

HE GETS UP, goes to his table, writes,

Fontainebleau, the 13th, at three in the morning.
My good Louise,
   I approve of you going to Rambouillet, where your father will come and find you. It is the only consolation open to you in our misfortunes. For a week I have been impatiently awaiting this moment. Your father has been misled and been bad to us, but he will be a good father to you and your son. Caulaincourt has arrived. I sent you yesterday a copy of the arrangements he signed, which assure a future for your son. Farewell, my sweet Louise. You are what I love most in the world. My misfortunes only affect me because of the harm they do you. All your life

you will love the tenderest of husbands. Give my son a kiss.
Farewell, my Louise. Ever yours,
    Napoleon

My wife and my son will be with the Emperor of Austria from now on, protected. I have done what I had to do.

Life is unbearable to me.

He sees himself, a betrayed emperor, taking the bag of poison that hangs around his neck. He pours it into a glass of water. He drinks it slowly. Then he goes and lies down.

Fire in his guts.

He calls out. He wants to speak to Caulaincourt.

He needs to hold this man's hand. He needs a man's affection.

'Give me your hand, kiss me.'

Caulaincourt is crying.

'I want you to be happy, my dear Caulaincourt. You deserve to be.'

He can barely speak. His stomach is racked, twisted, torn apart by pain.

'In a little while I shall no longer exist. Take this letter to the Empress then; keep hers in the portfolio they're stored in to give to my son when he is grown up. Tell the Empress to believe in my attachment . . .'

Cold, ice at the same time as the fire.

'I regret the loss of the throne for her and my son's sakes. I would have made him a man worthy to rule France,' he murmurs.

Waves of nausea.

'Listen to me; time is getting short.'

He squeezes Caulaincourt's hand. He does not want a doctor to be called.

'I only want you, Caulaincourt.'

Fire through his whole body.

'Tell Josephine that I thought of her.'

He must give Eugène a fine keepsake. For you, Caulaincourt, my finest sabre and my pistols, and a sabre for Macdonald.

He arches his back, his body covered in sweat.

'What a struggle it is to die, what a misfortune to have a constitution that fights off the end of a life that I am impatient to see finish,' he says in a jerky voice. 'What a task it is to die in one's bed when in war the smallest thing can end one's life.'

Suddenly he vomits.

I must keep the poison in me.

But his mouth opens and the bitter, sharp jet comes out.

He sees Dr Yvan, whom Caulaincourt has managed to call.

'Doctor, give me another stronger dose and something that can finish the job of what I took. It is your duty, a service those who are attached to me must do me.'

He looks fixedly at Yvan. He hears the doctor say that he is not a murderer.

Coward. All cowards. They want me to die for my sake and theirs — I can see it on their faces — but they don't dare do anything or take any decisions, so they'll let me vomit death back up and survive.

He vomits again. This is death slipping.

He clutches onto Caulaincourt, asks for poison again. But they pick him up and support him so he can walk to the window. He looks for his pistols, but they have taken the powder horn.

They want to let me live.

They sit him down in front of the window. Dawn breaks. He is aching all over, but the storm has passed, the fire is slowly going out.

Bertrand, grand marshal of the palace, repeats that he wants to go with him to Elba. Marshal Macdonald, Duke of Taranto, presents himself. He has come to take the convention of abdication back to Paris. Napoleon signs it. It is Wednesday, 13 April 1814.

Then, in a choked voice, he murmurs to Macdonald, 'I recognize your loyalty too late. Please accept Mourad Bey's sabre, which I wore at the battle of Mount Thabor.'

He clasps Macdonald to him.

He needs this warmth of a living being, this loyalty.

He holds his head in his hands, his elbows resting on his knees.

'I will live,' he says. 'I will live, since death doesn't want me in my bed any more than it does on the battlefield.'

He gets to his feet and, with a great effort, drinks a glass of water.

'There will be courage too in enduring life after such events,' he says. 'I will write the history of the brave.'

HE IS RECOVERING. So he must organize his life.

He will travel incognito to the port where he will embark.

'Seeing France that I love so much again,' he murmurs, 'appearing before it as an object of pity is beyond my strength.'

He repeats that they would have done better to have given him the means to die.

A letter from Marie Louise is brought to him.

He reads it walking slowly around the room. It is as if life is slowly returning to him.

'You are so good and so unhappy and you so little deserve it,' she writes. 'At least, if all my tender love can serve to make you hope for a little happiness, you would have much more in this world. I am heartbroken at this sad situation.'

He rereads the letter, hands it to Caulaincourt.

Then he writes,

My good Louise,
     I am in a hurry for us to be able to go. It is said that the island of Elba has a very fine climate. I am so disgusted by men that I no longer want my happiness to depend on them. You alone can do something about it. Farewell, my friend. A kiss to the little king, best wishes to your father. Beg him to be good to us. Ever yours,
     Nap

He goes down into the garden. The air is so mild. He walks slowly. He wants to decide on every detail of the journey. No soldiers of the Guard then, but incognito. He leans on Caulaincourt's arm.

'If you see the Empress,' he says, 'do not insist she join me. I would rather her in Florence than Elba if she arrives looking annoyed.'

He disengages his arm, walks with his hands behind his back.

'I have no throne now,' he goes on. 'There are no more illusions. Caesar can content himself with being a citizen. But it may grieve his young wife only to be Caesar's wife! At the Empress's age, one still needs baubles. If she does not of her own accord find glory in the devotion she will show me, better not to press her.'

He imagines how it might work.

'We will be able to arrange it so that I spend some months of every year in Italy with her, when they see that I am resolved not to meddle in anything and I am contented, like Sancho, with the governance of my island and the pleasure of writing my memoirs.'

Caulaincourt seems astonished.

'Like Sancho,' Napoleon repeats.

He smiles for the first time in a long while. Everything is possible in life, even that.

XX

HE IS SITTING AT his desk in the little apartment he rarely leaves. He often goes to the window, opens it, looks at the chateau's park and the forest of Fontainebleau in the distance. Sometimes he hears the wheels of a carriage crunch on the paving stones of the Courtyard of the White Horse. He thinks of Berthier, of his ministers, of all the men who have been at his side every day for years and now have disappeared before he has even left, all in a hurry to serve the Bourbons and the Count of Artois, who has just been appointed lieutenant-general of the kingdom by the Senate. How can they change cockade like this, in a few days, a few hours even sometimes?

An officer, Colonel Montholon, asks to be received. He speaks passionately of the feelings of the troops and people in all the Haute-Loire, the contempt Marshal Augereau inspires. The Duke of Castiglione has harangued his troops, demanding they adopt the white cockade. 'Let us sport this truly French colour,' he has said, 'which will put paid to the emblem of a revolution that is finished.' There is the same contempt in Paris for Marshal Marmont, who is called Marshal Judas. They could, Montholon goes on, rally the troops, fight again.

Napoleon shakes his head.

'It is too late. That would only be civil war now, and nothing could make me decide on that.'

He points to the table, which is covered with all the books, charts, maps and statistics about the island of Elba that he has laid his hands on. He wants, he says, to know everything about this 'island of my retirement'.

He ushers out Montholon, then says to Caulaincourt, 'Providence has willed this! I shall live! Who can sound out the future? In any case, my wife and son are enough for me.'

But why are they taking so long?

He writes,

My good Louise,

You must have seen your father by now. I'm told you went to the Trianon for that purpose. I want you to come to Fontainebleau tomorrow so that we can leave together and find this land of asylum and rest where I will be if you can resolve to be too and forget the grandeurs of the world.

Give a kiss to my son and believe in all my love,

Nap

Now the decision has been made, he would like to leave without delay.

What are the Allies doing? Why are they waiting to send the signed agreements, to name the commissioners who will accompany me to Elba?

'I make things awkward,' he says. 'My presence among a large number of generals and the troops may even give rise to certain anxieties . . . Why don't they have done with it?'

He looks at Caulaincourt. What does he know?

Caulaincourt finally admits that he is surprised as well. The horses laid on at the relays have been withdrawn. In Paris people talk of assassination plots. A certain Maubreuil claims to have been approached by Talleyrand's most intimate collaborator 'to rid us of the Emperor'. He is to recruit determined men. Perhaps they'll strike on the route. Here, at Fontainebleau, there's still the Old Guard.

They have already tried to assassinate me so many times. These men will do anything.

'M. de Talleyrand has been betraying me for so long,' he says. 'He has sacrificed France to the Bourbons. He has given it up to the intrigues of a coterie.'

He makes a scornful gesture.

'I have ended the era of revolutions,' he continues, 'and even pardoned their assassins. What have I done for myself? Where are my treasures, my jewels? Others are covered in gold; the uniform of my chasseurs or my grenadiers is enough for me.'

He takes a few steps, leans on the window.

'They will be astonished by my resignation, by the tranquillity in which I intend to live now. The ambition you yourself attribute to me will have no other goal than the glory of my dear France.'

He turns towards Caulaincourt.

'Since I am condemned to live, I shall write the history. I shall do justice to the brave souls who covered themselves in glory, to the men of honour who served France well. I shall immortalize their names. For me this is a debt and I will discharge it.'

HE REMAINS ALONE.

He has sometimes been unfair to those who were closest to him, he knows.

He has chosen between them to attain his political ends.

And even if he has tried to treat them gently and protect them, he has also made them suffer. Even here, when Marie Walewska came a few days ago. She waited for him for several hours, but he did not receive her. She only wanted to see him, support him.

He begins to write.

Marie,
    The feelings that motivate you touch me deeply. They are worthy of your beautiful soul and the kindness of your heart. When you have settled your affairs and go to take the waters at Lucca or Pisa, I shall see you with great pleasure, as well as your son, for whom my feelings will always remain the same. Be in good health; do not be sad at all. Think of me with pleasure and never doubt me.

He remains silent for a long while, then barely responds when Caulaincourt tells him that the allied commissioners will arrive on 19 April and so the departure for Fontainebleau can be set for the 20th. Will my wife and son be there? Caulaincourt hopes so.

With a gesture Napoleon asks to be left alone.

He has another debt to honour. He wants to write to Josephine. He begins,

I am congratulating myself on my situation. My head and mind are rid of an enormous burden. My fall is great but at least it is useful, from what they say.
    In my retirement I am going to take up the quill instead of

the sword. The history of my reign will be curious; I have only been seen in profile, but now I will reveal myself in my entirety. How much I have to say! So many men of whom people entertain a false opinion! I have showered thousands of wretches with benefits! What have they done for me, in the end? They have betrayed me. Yes — all of them.

I except dear Eugène from this number, so worthy of you and me. May he be happy under a king able to appreciate the sentiments of nature and honour!

Farewell, my dear Josephine; resign yourself as I do and never lose the memory of the one who has never forgotten you and will never forget you,

Napoleon

PS I will be waiting for your news on the island of Elba. I am not in good health.

He can admit this to Josephine. Often he has trouble breathing, as if his ribs were broken. His stomach has hurt since the night of his failed suicide attempt, and he is anxious. Despite the letters he gets from Marie Louise, he senses she will not come, that he will perhaps never see either his wife or his son again.

He picks up the letters he has received from her. Marie Louise announces that she will not be going to the springs in Tuscany but to those in Aix-les-Bains. Her father has compelled her to receive the Emperor Alexander and the King of Prussia.

He writes,

I pity you receiving such visits. The King of Prussia is capable of saying unseemly things, without meaning any harm. I am distressed not seeing you go to the baths that it would be most natural for you to visit. In any case I commend you to take care of your health and be brave enough to support your rank and misfortune with firmness and courage.

Farewell my good Louise. Ever yours,

After handing the letter to Montesquiou, he realizes that he didn't sign it. He is nervous. He wishes he could shake off this instinct that is growing stronger in him. He won't see them again.

He listens out for every sound, rushes out of his apartment. It is a courier from the Emperor of Austria. He reads over the letter. 'My brother and dear son-in-law . . .' He was right. The Emperor is taking his daughter and the King of Rome to Vienna. 'Restored to health,' he reads, 'my daughter will go and take possession of her country, which will quite naturally bring her closer to Your Majesty's residence.'

He throws away the letter.

My life is unbearable to me.

He has known this for a long time. *They are going to take away my son.*

He exclaims, 'Wanting to parade before the Viennese the daughter of the Caesars, the Empress of the French and the wife of Napoleon, and the King of Rome, the son of the conqueror of waning Austria, who was deposed by a coalition of all Europe and by the dereliction of a father – this offends all proprieties.'

May shame fall on those people who dare this. And may I be considered unworthy to be the equal of those people who steal my wife and son!

Since he cannot die, since death withholds herself from him, and since the commissioners have arrived – well, then he must go, quickly and a long way away.

ON THIS WEDNESDAY, 20 April 1814, he has been on his feet since dawn. He hears the tramp of the soldiers of his Old Guard who have come to form the guard of honour in the Courtyard of the White Horse at the foot of the horseshoe staircase.

He writes to Marie Louise,

I am leaving in order to sleep at Briare this evening. I will leave tomorrow and not stop until St-Tropez. I hope your health will hold up and that you will be able to come and join me.

Farewell, my good Louise; you can always count on the courage, constancy and friendship of your husband,

Nap

A kiss for the little king.

He goes out of the apartments and approaches the foreign commissioners, a Russian, Count Shouvalov, General Koller for Austria, Colonel Campbell for England and the Prussian Count

Walburg-Truchsess. He feels they are moved, anxious even. He dominates these men.

The Emperor of Austria does not respect his commitments, Napoleon says. 'He is a man without religion who urges my wife to divorce me. Those sovereigns who have visited the Empress have shown a lack of scruples.'

Then he calls out, 'I have never been a usurper, because I only accepted the crown at the unanimous wish of the Nation, whereas Louis XVIII has usurped it, being called to the throne only by a wretched Senate of which more than ten members voted for the death of Louis XVI!'

He walks away. He hears the carriages driving over the paving stones of the Courtyard of the White Horse.

It is time.

HE SEES HIS grenadiers standing stiffly to arms. The bayonets glint between the tall bearskins. He turns towards the officers following him, shakes their hands and then walks down the stairs with a firm step.

He goes into the midst of his soldiers. He has spoken to them so many times to send them in to battle, to their deaths. He owes them everything.

'Soldiers of my Old Guard, I bid you farewell,' he begins. 'For the last twenty years I have constantly found you on the road to honour and glory! In recent times, just as in those of my prosperity, you have not ceased to be models of bravery and loyalty. With men such as you our cause was not lost, but the war was unending; there would have been civil war and France would only have been the more unfortunate.'

He looks at them. Some of these men are covering their eyes with their hands, others are sobbing.

He feels his emotions overwhelming him.

'I have therefore sacrificed all our interests to those of the country,' he continues. 'I am leaving. You, my friends, continue to serve France. Her welfare was my only thought; it will always be the object of my prayers. Do not pity my fate; if I have consented to survive, it is to carry on serving your glory. I want to write about the great things that we have done together.'

He has to remain silent for a few seconds. He hears sobs.

'Farewell, my children! I would like to press you all to my heart; let me at least kiss your flag.'

General Petit steps forward holding the pole crowned with its eagle. Napoleon kisses the flag, clasps the general in his arms.

He sees grenadiers raising their caps. He sees the Austrian General Koller put his hat on the end of his sword and wave it.

Napoleon cannot speak. Then he continues, and says in a loud voice, 'Farewell once more, my old comrades! Let this last kiss pass into your hearts.'

He embraces the officers around him. Then he gets into the carriage, a sleeper, which instantly drives off.

XXI

HE DOES NOT SPEAK. Too many memories, too many questions choke him. He has travelled this road to the south so many times, at the most important moments of his life, going to or from Corsica as a young officer, setting off for Nice and the Army of Italy or Toulon before the departure for Egypt, taking it back to Paris when he was heading towards power, with Marmont in the same carriage, after escaping the English cruisers after Egypt. His whole life is passing before him. Marmont has become Marshal Judas.

He leans out of the window. He needs this breeze to banish all those memories. He sees the long procession of fourteen carriages, then the crowds which seem to hesitate and then suddenly cheer him. They throng the streets of Fontainebleau, Nemours and Montargis.

At Briare, when he gets out in front of the post house, the shouts ring out, 'Long live the Emperor!' The people insult the foreign commissioners whose uniforms they recognize. 'Out with the Russians!' 'Death to the Austrians!'

He bows his head. This tide no longer bears his destiny.

He wants to have supper alone.

Next morning, while the crowd is still gathered around the carriages, he writes,

My good Louise,
   I am in good health. I am going to St-Tropez, I leave in an hour. I won't stop en route; I think I'll be there in four days. I am very happy with the mood of the population, who show me much attachment and love. I have not had any news of you since the 18th. The palace courier has not arrived, which I put down to lack of horses. Farewell, my friend; be in good health. Give my son a kiss and never doubt
   Nap

AT NEVERS OFFICERS surround him, tears in their eyes. At Roanne and Tarare the crowd is closely packed, affectionate. The carriages move at walking pace through the narrow streets. He leans out of the window. All these faces turned towards him, like the days of glory. Where is his defeat? He listens without replying to those people who call out, 'What will becomes of us under a government controlled by the English? And our industry? Who will buy our cloth?'

Voices rise from the crowd: 'Keep yourself safe for us! The year will not be out before you return to France. We want it. Long live the Emperor!'

He sinks back into the corner of the carriage. Bertrand murmurs a few words which he doesn't reply to.

He has abdicated. He is only the sovereign of the island of Elba now.

At Salvigny, two hours from Lyon, he orders the carriages to stop. He wants to drive through the town at night. He does not want any demonstrations.

He walks a little way down the road on his own, out into the countryside. The stationary carriages fill the whole town street.

He wishes he were on the island already, forgetting, because he has made his decision and it is what he has to do.

But when the carriages reach the Carrefour de la Guillotière, a crowd is there again, shouting, 'Long live the Emperor.'

He leans out of the window. 'Carry on; don't stop,' he orders.

At dawn on Sunday 24 April he passes through Vienne.

He recognizes the smells of the South, the mild spring air, the light greens; it is as if he were plunging back into his childhood and youth.

He stops at Péage-de-Roussillon. While lunch is being prepared in an inn, he walks through this familiar landscape. His past life here on the banks of the Rhône seems so close, as if he experienced nothing, suffered nothing, in the depths of Germany or on the plains of Poland and Russia.

As if he hadn't slept in chateaux and palaces.

He passes through St-Vallier and Tain, and suddenly there appears on the road a carriage drawn by six horses preceded by two couriers. The convoy stops, as does the carriage. A man gets out and comes forward, his head bowed, walking with a heavy step. It is Augereau, the marshal, the Duke of Castiglione!

A man who has betrayed me, who has made his men wear the white cockade, who has issued a proclamation denouncing 'the tyrannical yoke of Napoleon Bonaparte' and my despotism, and has accused me of 'having sacrificed millions of victims to my cruel ambition' and of not having been able to 'die as a soldier'.

Now destiny places him on my road. Augereau doesn't dare raise his head and look me in the eye.

He is weeping.

'Where are you going like this? Are you going to Court? Your proclamation is very stupid; why these insults?'

Time has indeed passed since our youth. Augereau is nothing more than an old soldier who has aged by twenty years under my command. And betrayed me.

I just have to turn my back on him.

AT THE SIDE of the road a company of infantry presents arms. A captain advances.

'Did you meet that wretch?' the officer asks. 'He was canny enough not to wait for you to arrive in Valence; the troops were determined to shoot him in front of you.'

'Your general . . .' Napoleon begins.

'You and France had no great enemy. We have been sold out for petty cash!' the captain cries.

I do not want to imagine what would be possible with these men, who are still loyal to me.

He remains leaning out of the door nevertheless. Here everything speaks to his memory. He has travelled all these roads; he knows these towns. In Valence regiments salute him.

As if I had not abdicated.

Some of these men sob; others shout, 'Long live the Emperor!'

At the Loriol relay he says in a loud voice, 'My friends, I am not your Emperor any more. You should shout, "Long live Louis XVIII!"'

He is surrounded. People take his hands, shake them, kiss them.

'You will always be our Emperor.'

He frees himself.

'If there were twenty thousand men like me,' a lancer calls out, 'we would kidnap you and put you at our head.'

Napoleon turns away, gets back into the carriage.

'It is not your soldiers who have betrayed you,' cries an infantryman, 'it is your generals!'

He cannot stop himself trembling or being overcome by emotion.

'These men hurt me,' he murmurs to Bertrand.

AS SOON AS he gets out of the carriage at Montélimar he senses that the atmosphere has changed. The crowd is curious rather than supportive. The sub-prefect approaches. He is a little man who seems terrorized. All the Rhône is hostile, he says. The English have been given a triumphal welcome in Marseille. At Avignon, Orange, Orgon and Lambesc, royalists from Paris have rallied their supporters. They want to assassinate the Emperor. The monuments to his glory have been smashed. He is hung in effigy. They shout, 'Long live the King! Down with the tyrant!'

Napoleon listens. He has been expecting this since leaving Fontainebleau.

If they can, they'll kill me.

Too many men, too many soldiers still love him, he has had proof of that. But he shakes his head when the sub-prefect proposes he change his itinerary, to go by Grenoble and Sisteron.

They will simply travel through Avignon at dawn.

Put the horses to; let's be off.

But at Orange people shout, 'Long live the King.' At the relay near Avignon there's a crowd shouting, 'Down with the tyrant, the rogue!'

A band of several hundred men is waiting in town to attack the convoy, so they drive along Avignon's walls.

At Orgon a scaffold has been erected, and a dummy in a blood-splattered French uniform is swinging from it.

'That's a tyrant's fate!' the crowd shouts.

Napoleon sits motionless. He did not want to experience this – the shame, the hatred, the impotence, the speech the Russian commissioner Shouvalov gives to calm the crowd surrounding them. It has started to throw stones at the carriage and shake it, shouting, 'Death to the tyrant!'

Me, threatened by French citizens and protected by a foreign officer!

THE CARRIAGE SETS off again, and stops soon after. A rider approaches. The entire region is overrun by agents from Paris, he says, who want to kill the Emperor. Word is that they have been sent by the Prince of Benevento. A certain Maubreuil has supposedly recruited assassins and set an ambush between Aix and Fréjus.

Talleyrand wants me dead.

Napoleon gets out of the carriage, puts on a blue frock coat, a round hat and a white cockade. Then he leaps into the saddle. He will ride these roads alone. Passing through Lambesc a group hails him: 'Where's the Emperor's carriage?'

He waves vaguely, then digs in his spurs.

I will not die like this, like a hunted animal.

He gallops as far as St-Cannat.

In the past he travelled these roads on his way to glory; people shouted, 'Long live General Bonaparte!' Now he refuses to eat meals prepared for him because he is afraid of being poisoned and he has been told Talleyrand's agent has laid an ambush on the Fréjus road.

He must live. He does not want to have his throat slit by fanatics or hired killers. He looks at General Koller. He will put on an Austrian uniform and ride in the commissioner's carriage. They'll outsmart the assassins that way.

At St-Maximin, he sends for the sub-prefect.

'You must blush to see me in an Austrian uniform,' he says. 'I came into your midst completely trustingly when I should have brought six thousand of my Guard with me. All I find here is a mob of fanatics who threaten to kill me.'

He wants to set off again immediately and cross into the *département* of Var, where the royalists are apparently only meeting with a faint response. He gets into his carriage and looks at the sky, which is as limpid as when he rode from Toulon to Nice and when he landed at Fréjus on his return from Egypt.

All these memories make him nauseous.

And here is Pauline, who lives in Bouillédou chateau, near Lucques.

She is sobbing. She cannot bear to see him dressed as an Austrian like this. He tosses his clothes away, puts his uniform of a chasseur of the Guard back on, and finally clasps her in his arms, the most beautiful of his sisters. They talk on and on. They are returning to their origins – an island, Elba, so close to Corsica. She questions him, but when she speaks of Marie Louise and the King of Rome, he does not reply.

He does not want to say he's afraid he'll never see them again.

They talk about their brothers: Jérôme, and Joseph who, Pauline says, is planning to go to Switzerland, where Louis will already be. Their mother has set off with Cardinal Fesch for Rome, where Lucien probably is. Elisa may be in Bologna. Caroline . . .

He makes a gesture. He does not want Murat's wife mentioned, the woman who must have pushed the King of Naples to commit treachery.

Pauline, sobbing, says she wants to go to Elba and live with him. Pauline the faithful, when almost everyone else has betrayed him. He kisses her. At the end of his destiny he is reunited with the sister who loved him the most. As if nothing had been able to change that, almost as if nothing had taken place in their lives.

On Wednesday, 27 April 1814, at eleven in the evening, he enters the Red Hat in Fréjus.

Nothing has changed since that October in 1799 when, after landing from Egypt, he entered this room, a thin, determined, sunburnt general who had miraculously escaped the English frigates.

And today it is one of these frigates at anchor in the bay that he sees from his bedroom window that he wants to take him to Elba.

He gives the order for his baggage to be taken aboard the *Undaunted*.

A French frigate was to have taken him but it has not yet arrived and, in any case, he feels safer aboard an English vessel than on a boat where the crew may have been infiltrated by assassins recruited by the Count of Artois or the Prince of Benevento.

He walks along the dock. A crowd gathers respectfully around him.

He stands a long time at the window of his room. The sea. He has sailed these coasts so many times. If the frigate passes Corsica, will he still recognize the scent of the island?

He would like to relive all this with his wife and his son. In their company he could find peace, in these landscapes that belong to him.

He starts to write.

My good Louise,

I arrived at Fréjus two hours ago. I was very content with the spirit of the French as far as Avignon. But since Avignon I have found them very fanatical and hostile. I have been very satisfied with the commissioners, especially the Austrian and Russian generals; tell your father.

I am leaving in two hours for the island of Elba. I will write to you when I arrive. My health is good, my courage a match for anything. It could only be weakened by the thought that my friend does not love me any more. Give my son a kiss.

Princess Pauline, who is in a chateau two hours from here, wants absolutely to come to the island of Elba to keep me company, but she is so ill that I do not know when she will be able to make the crossing.

I have the Grand Marshal Bertrand and my aide-de-camp Drouot with me.

Your faithful husband,
Nap

They are taking their time leaving. He asks Colonel Campbell, the English commissioner, to assign a frigate to pick up Pauline 'in five or six days and take her to the island of Elba'. Then he writes to General Dalesmes, who is in command on Elba.

It will cease to belong to Tuscany and become my territory. I have chosen the flag: white with a red diagonal stripe topped with three bees.

Circumstances having induced me to renounce the throne of France and sacrifice my rights for the good and interests of the country, I have reserved for myself the sovereignty and ownership of the island of Elba and the forts of Portoferraio and Porto Longone. This has met with the agreement of all the powers ... Please communicate this new state of affairs to the inhabitants and the choice I have made of their island for my stay in consideration of the mildness of their manners and the agreeability of their climate. They will be the constant object of my keenest interest.

He has read so many books about Elba in a matter of days at Fontainebleau that he feels he knows everything about its history.

He walks about his room, often stopping at the window to look out at the sea.

He will be out there on that island that has been Greek and Roman; and from that land, Aithalia for the Greeks, Ilva for the Romans, he will be able to see the coast of Corsica.

A strange destiny his. From one island to another.

This one will be my island of retirement.

He sees a French frigate enter the roads.

The captain presents himself at the inn soon afterwards and requests the honour of conveying the Emperor.

Napoleon shakes his head. He does not want to sail under the white flag, he says.

'As long as his throne is only maintained by foreign bayonets and not nationalized by his conduct and national opinion, I shall have no esteem or consideration for the King of France.'

THEY HAVE TO wait for the wind to get up, and the time weighs heavy on his mind. He cannot stop asking himself questions. Will Marie Louise and his son come? When will he tread the soil of France again?

He walks about his room a little, on that Thursday 28 April, and suddenly he is gripped by nausea; the floor falls away and he vomits.

He could die here, alone. His body is covered in a cold sweat. He goes to the window. He gradually feels better.

He writes a few words to Marie Louise. 'The weather is fine and I will have a gentle crossing. I hope your health will sustain you and you will have the necessary courage. It will give me great pleasure seeing you and my son.' But will he ever see them again? 'Farewell, my good Louise. I beg you to give my son a very tender kiss and present my compliments to all the women. Ever yours. Your affectionate and faithful husband, Nap'. But how difficult it is to tear oneself away from France!

The wind is so faint that, having boarding the *Undaunted*, he disembarks at St-Raphael.

Crowds cheer.

At last, on Friday, 29 April 1814, they set sail.

He stays at the prow most of the time, or walks on the bridge. He watches the French coast receding. He leans on the rail and says to Bertrand, 'The Bourbons, poor devils, are happy to have their estates and chateaux, but if the French people become dissatisfied and find there is no encouragement for their industries, they will be driven out in six months.'

'Six months?' murmurs Bertrand.

He doesn't reply.

He spends nights on the bridge, in the mild air redolent of Corsica's plants.

And then here, on Sunday 1 May, is Ajaccio within cannon range. The past is rising up like an Atlantis. He gazes at the docks for a long time, the fortress. This is where destiny issued its first challenges, set the dice rolling.

They are becalmed off Calvi.

It seems to him that he has felt better physically since he has been breathing this air and seeing these colours and Corsican mountains.

Finally, on Tuesday, 3 May 1814, the frigate drops anchor at the entrance to Portoferraio. He takes off the sailor's hat he is wearing. He puts on his bicorne. And here he is in the uniform of the chasseurs of his Imperial Guard, with the star of the Legion of Honour and the medal of the iron crown of the King of Italy pinned to his breast.

He is still a soldier and a sovereign.

PART SIX

All France misses me and asks for me

4 MAY 1814 TO 25 FEBRUARY 1815

XXII

IT IS TWO IN THE afternoon on this Wednesday, 4 May 1814. He approaches the gangway, walking through the crew of the *Undaunted*, who salute him, their cutlasses raised. He looks at the harbour again and the sheer cliff that towers above it. On the quays of Portoferraio's port he makes out a crowd and the uniforms of the little garrison of the capital of the island of Elba. The wind coming off the land sometimes carries snatches of shouting, the high sounds of a fanfare.

Suddenly white smoke crowns the forts of Stella and Falcone whose situations he knows and whose plans he has already studied. The explosions follow one another. Between the forts he makes out several ruined windmills, which dominate both the town and the sea.

He has thought he will establish himself there, in the neighbourhood of the *mulini*, from where he will be able to see every movement on land or sea.

He gives the order to hoist the flag of the new state on the stern of the boat which will take him to the quay.

He slowly climbs down the ship's ladder and mumurs, 'I'm putting up at a good establishment here; this will be an island of retirement.'

He stands in the middle of the boat. It feels as if he is heading in towards one of those Corsican towns of his childhood, with arcaded, austere houses rising in a semicircle above the port.

He is at home here.

But if Marie Louise ever can and wants to leave the mainland with my son, how will she be able to live here?

He jumps onto the quay.

What is this masquerade? He is presented with the keys of the city on a silver platter. He is invited to stand under a golden paper canopy topped with cardboard bees.

He has entered all the most glorious cities in Europe. He has seen Moscow burn. He has been crowned at Notre Dame. And here he is walking towards the altar of a little church while the crowd shouts and cheers in the alleys outside and the drums beat and the unbearable stench of rubbish and excrement wafts into the parish church which has just been decreed a cathedral.

He barely replies to Monsignor Arrighi, a Corsican who claims he is a cousin of the Bonapartes.

He shrugs impatiently. He wants to withdraw to the town hall, where he is to stay. The crowd stamps its feet and shouts in front of the building. And there is still that rotten stink.

He will demand that the inhabitants no longer dump their refuse in the streets; he will enact laws establishing hygiene on the island.

If she comes with my son, where will she live?

He issues orders to Marchand his valet and Rathery his secretary. He wants, he starts to explain to Generals Drouot and Cambronne, and to Bertrand, grand marshal of the palace . . .

He breaks off to repeat, 'of the palace'.

He wants, he resumes, etiquette to be observed here just as at the Tuileries or St-Cloud. He will appoint chamberlains. Bertrand will preside over the dignitaries recruited from the notables of the island, who will organize dinners and balls with their wives. He will review the Guard as soon as it has landed. And tomorrow at dawn he will begin his tour of the island.

For now he wishes to be left alone.

He writes,

My good Louise,
   I have been at sea for four days in calm weather; I didn't suffer from it at all. I have reached the island of Elba, which is very pretty. The lodgings are mediocre. I am going to have them organized in a few weeks. I have no news from you. It upsets me every day. My health is extremely good.
   Farewell, my friend. You are far from me, but my thoughts are always with my Louise. A tender kiss to my son. Ever yours,
      Nap

He lies down. He hears the sound of the sea. He is back in his childhood, his boyhood. He feels full of energy.

At dawn he is already out galloping in the light May air, and as he gradually leaves Portoferraio behind on the narrow, rocky paths that hug the mountainsides he recognizes the scent of the vegetation that again reminds him of Corsica.

He arrives at Rio Marina. The earth is red. The galleries of the iron-ore mines go deep into the cliffs. He wants to know the quantities produced, the loads, the profits, the taxes paid. The face of the mine's administrator seems familiar somehow. Circumstances have so often set in his path men he has known previously that he is not surprised that Pons de l'Hérault, as he is called, took part in the siege of Toulon with him. 'But,' Pons says proudly, 'I have remained a Republican, a Jacobin.'

'All I ask is loyalty to France,' Napoleon says.

He walks away. This man deserves his trust since he has not been a courtier during the years of his glory.

HE RIDES OFF, explores the island's tracks.

They will have to build roads. Here, in the small San Martino valley, they will construct what will be both a summer residence and a hunting lodge. The place is quiet and shady. The view takes in the sea.

His palace will be here, the *mulini*.

Napoleon returns every day to follow the progress of the work. He has a tunnel dug through the cliff which provides access to a little esplanade from which one can see Portoferraio. That way one will be able to leave the *mulini* without going through the town, and also protect oneself with a few sentries from any hostile incursion.

Sometimes, while looking at a map of the island or the view from *mulini* esplanade or from the top of Monte Giove, which he climbs by a mule track, he exclaims, 'Oh, my island is very small!'

He calls Bertrand or Drouot or Peyrusse, the former treasurer of the crown whom he has made his minister of finance, to witness this: 233 square kilometres and a few thousand inhabitants!

And he has been the Emperor of most of Europe, the equal of Charlemagne! He has commanded an army of several hundreds of thousands from every nation, and now he commands no more than 1,600 men, and of those only 675 are grenadiers of the Guard and fifty-four Poles are light cavalry. There's one battalion recruited on the island and a battalion of Corsicans whom he can barely trust because they are bound to have been infiltrated by spies, enemies and perhaps even murderers.

But the countryside is exhilarating.

Past Monte Giove, he discovers a chapel and a shack in the middle of a chestnut wood: the Hermitage of the Madonna, a place of pilgrimage. He climbs the steps hewn out of the rock and is struck by the beauty of the panorama. In the setting sun he sees Corsica, *my island*, the islet of Capraia, that of Montecristo and the whole coast of the island of Elba, which stands out against the brilliant blue of the Tyrrhenian Sea.

He sits down. He could live here.

He decides to spend the hottest days there. He chooses the cell previously occupied by the hermit. A squad of grenadiers will be able to establish their bivouac below the hermitage. General Drouot will occupy another cell. And if Madame Mère comes, as she wishes to, she can occupy a house in the village of Marciana Alta, a few hundred metres further down on the slopes of Monte Giove.

IT TAKES HIM a couple of days to take possession of his territory, his new space. On Saturday 21 May he moves into Il Mulino. The rooms still smell of plaster and paint, but orderly life must begin.

He gets up before dawn, reads, dictates.

'Have the flag of the island run up in all the communes on Sunday and make a sort of holiday of it.'

'Signal my dissatisfaction at the dirtiness of the streets to the quartermaster.'

'I want the commune to cover the costs of a ball to be given in the main square. A ballroom in wood can be constructed and the officers of the Imperial Guard invited. Around this room orchestras will be set up for the soldiers to dance to and put out a few barrels of wine so they can have a drink . . .'

He stops.

It is sunrise. He goes to the esplanade and scans the horizon and Portoferraio Bay. He sees the brig *Inconstant*, the schooner *Caroline*, and the smaller vessels, the two feluccas, *Fly* and *Bee*, and the xebec *Star*, that make up his fleet. Corsica is only fifty kilometres away, the port of Piombino less than twelve. Leghorn is close, the French coast three or four days' sail.

He cannot take his eyes off these ships. Through them he can find out what is happening in France, in Europe. He can, if he wants, leave the island.

He refuses to think of that.

But he must know what is becoming of France and Europe. He wants to receive the English papers and also *Le Journal des débats* and *Le Nain Jaune*. He wants to set up a network of correspondents and informers.

All this must be put in place as quickly as possible since the first letters he receives announce that Louis XVIII has chosen as his minister of war General Dupont, the officer who capitulated at Baylen. An insult to me, to the army. And Dupont is taking his revenge. He dismisses 100,000 soldiers and puts 12,000 officers on half pay while Louis XVIII organizes a parade, flanked by the sovereigns whose armies occupy Paris!

AT SEVEN O'CLOCK, when the sun is already high, he returns, has breakfast, sometimes goes back to bed, reads the papers, writes again.

> My good Louise,
>
> General Koller, who has accompanied me here and with whom I have been extremely satisfied, is returning, so I am giving him this letter. I beg you to write to your father to do something to show my gratitude to this general who has been unfailingly good to me.
>
> I have organized rather pretty lodgings with a garden and very good air. My health is perfect, the island is healthy, the inhabitants seem kind and the countryside is agreeable enough. I miss having news of you and knowing that you are in good health; I have not had any since the letter you sent me which reached me at Fréjus.
>
> Farewell, my friend; give my son a kiss and never doubt your
>
> Nap

He remains prostrate for a moment.

MARIE LOUISE'S SILENCE and the ignorance in which he is kept about the fate of his son – the barbaric cruelty with which they keep him from his kin – disgust and overwhelm him.

What do they want? The Bourbons, the Austrians?

Informers are already assuring him that plots are being formed in royal circles to kidnap and murder him. Haven't they had solemn masses in memory of Cadoudal, Pichegru and even Field Marshal Moreau celebrated in Paris?

General Dupont has appointed the Chevalier de Bruslart governor of Corsica: a Chouan, an accomplice of Cadoudal, a man who waged guerrilla warfare in Normandy for many years and who apparently dreams of nothing but assassinating me.

Even here, I make things awkward for them. I embody France when Louis XVIII has created a military household of émigrés who have all served in foreign armies. What can my soldiers think of that and of the fact that the order of the Legion of Honour is presided over by someone who fought against them in their enemy's ranks?

HE WANTS TO dispel these thoughts, and every evening he rides around the island with an orderly officer, inspecting the forts, going to Marciana Marina or Marina del Campo, both ports a long way from Portoferraio.

He has to keep moving. He has to give audiences all afternoon. He needs to see people, to feel the life of the island and the world, to receive visitors, who are often English and respectfully question him.

He sees the astonishment on the faces of the MPs from London, Fazakerley and Vernon, when they enter the Mulini garden. The noisy bustle of this 'palace' – the etiquette, the resplendent uniforms, the throng of servants (almost a hundred), the grenadiers who mount guard, the court thus re-formed – all this surprises them. Napoleon speaks to them at length in the detached tones of a chronicler. But aren't his campaigns, his work already part of history?

'I wanted to do great things for France,' he says, 'but I always asked for twenty years. I needed twenty years to carry out my system.'

He gets up, leads them to the esplanade.

'In France,' he says, 'the tail is good, the head bad. In England, the head is good, the tail mediocre. England plays the leading role today, but its time will come; it will fall like all great empires. But France is not exhausted. I have always nursed its resources; I got soldiers from Germany, from Italy, from Spain to spare France. I levied taxes everywhere for the same purpose. You will have seen a thriving younger generation in the provinces, improved agriculture, flourishing industry.'

And he wants to change customs here, on this island. He has introduced the potato, had chestnuts planted on the northern slopes, and olive trees and vines on those facing south. He builds roads, obliges every inhabitant to have a latrine.

'I am acting, transforming,' he says.

He shows them around the Mulini, his 'hovel'. It is not a palace, but what does that matter?

'I was born a soldier. I have reigned for fifteen years and I have relinquished the throne. Well, when one has survived human misfortunes, only a coward would be unable to bear them. What is my motto here? *Napoleo ubiscumque felix.*'

WHEN THE AUDIENCES are over he rides along the paths again. He hunts and, at dusk, goes to the Hermitage of the Madonna, at Monte Giove, because he finds the silence of the chestnut forest and the cool air of the peak soothing. He stays there for a long time, watching the sun setting and Corsica standing out on the red horizon. Then he spends the night in the hermitage cell.

One morning General Bertrand comes to find him. Madame Mère has arrived. She is furious, the grand marshal of the palace explains, at not having been welcomed at Portoferraio by the Emperor.

He is touched. His mother with him on an island, like at the start of his life on that other island, which the rising sun blurs.

He rushes out. There she is facing him, at last, in her long dark dress, stiff and severe, still like a sliver of black rock but thinner and with a more anxious expression and white hair. He sees himself in her eyes. She must remember him as a child, as a young man, as the Emperor; and now she sees a man who will be forty-five in a few days and who has become fat — so much so that he seems short and massive, round as a ball almost with sparse hair.

He kisses her and installs her in the most beautiful house in Portoferraio; every evening he goes down from the Mulini to see her. They go for drives, sitting side by side, then settle down on the terrace at the Mulini. He plays *reversi* with her. She is a skilful player, but he cannot accept her winning. He cheats. He tallies up the points. And it is he who wins.

Is she fooled?

He gets up, escorts her home. He loves her voice, slightly hoarse, saying, '*Addio, mio caro figlio.*'

Sometimes he invites the island's notables to parties. He goes from one group to the next and bows to the women, who timidly perform gauche curtsies.

It is a life. His life now.

But when he is alone his throat constricts with bitterness. He doesn't miss the assembly of kings or the Tuileries gold, or even the pretty women who offered themselves to him. But he has a son and a wife. What is life worth if even they are taken from him?

He has had only one letter from Marie Louise. She announces that she is leaving for Aix-les-Bains. He is enraged. But he must control himself, try to convince her even when she is surrounded by all those who want to get her away from him, steal away his son.

He writes to her,

I think that you should come to Tuscany as soon as possible, where there are waters just as good and of the same sort as those of Aix in Savoy. This will present every advantage. I will have news from you more often; you will be closer to Parma; you will be able to have your son with you and you will not cause anyone anxiety. Your journey to Aix only has disadvantages. If this letter finds you there, only spend a season there and come to Tuscany for your health.

My health is good, my feelings for you the same, and my desire to see you and to prove it to you very great.

Farewell, my good friend. A tender kiss to my son. Ever yours,

Nap

THE HEAT OF summer sets in. Everything slows down. He often climbs to the Hermitage of the Madonna at Monte Giove, and it is only in the evening that he comes down to see his mother, who is now staying in the village of Marciana Alta.

He reads the newspapers, which are sent to Piombino and then delivered by boat in batches to Portoferraio. The *Morning Chronicle* and the *Journal des débats* are the most interesting. He also receives first-hand information about what is happening in Paris from Maret, who has stayed in the capital, and from letters to soldiers of the Guard passed on to him.

He is full of indignation. A few weeks is all the Bourbons have needed to show their true face.

They have understood nothing of the new France I built! Marshal Soult, my Duke of Dalmatia, wants to erect monuments to the glory of the Chouans! He is launching a subscription for the 'martyrs of Quiberon'! And the priests, like the aristocrats, are questioning the sale of national property! What can all the people – peasants and bourgeois – who acquired land, aristocrats' houses and ecclesiastical property, think?

He grimaces with disgust. The newspapers are full of slurs on his name. He is accused of incestuous relations with Pauline because it has become known that she spent two days on the island! They even say that, like him, and thanks to him, she is afflicted by 'vice's sickness', which she is having to get treated. And that he has been sent mad by this venereal disease!

He feels sick looking at the caricatures in which he is shown vomiting up everything he has swallowed – countries, thrones, properties, wealth – and being ill despite the 'bloodbaths' he soaks in! People who slander him and his private life as basely as this must want to kill him; they must have spies everywhere.

He starts when he reads that the pallid Talleyrand, Prince of Benevento, has had the Chevalier Mariotti appointed French consul at Leghorn, only five hours' sail from Portoferraio. He remembers this Corsican, who was prefect of police at Lucca under Princess Elisa until he betrayed her and brought out the principality's garrisons on the Bourbons' side.

Is Talleyrand, who has already tried to have me assassinated by Maubreuil, thinking of having me kidnapped because he has a premonition about what the French will think in a few months?

With the Chevalier de Bruslart governor of Corsica and Mariotti at Leghorn, the Bourbons are targeting me with a pincer movement. They are trying to suffocate me. They aren't paying the allowance of two million francs fixed by the treaty. What they want is my death!

SO I MUST fight — organize my own network, send my spies to Italy and accumulate information to enable me to defend myself and act.

And to do that I must follow public opinion; I must read.

But a few lines in the *Journal des débats* poleaxe him. This edition is a few weeks old already, but for me the death it announces happened today, at the height of summer, in 1814.

Josephine died on 29 May.

He does not move. He does not go out for two days.

His life passes before him; *all my life was intertwined with hers.*

He forgets what he read alongside the notice of her death: that she betrayed him too, playing host at Malmaison to Tsar Alexander, the Emperor of Austria and the King of Prussia. The sovereigns danced with her; she presided over dinners in their honour; she even presented Hortense and Eugène to the Tsar so that he would recommend them to Louis XVIII.

It is true that she did this, but she is dead. He had made her suffer, even though he had always tried to protect her, even though she had already betrayed him with so many other people.

He lets Bertrand come in. He says, 'Poor Josephine, now she is indeed happy.'

Then, as if to himself, he adds, 'All in all, Josephine gave me happiness and constantly showed herself to be my most loving friend. So she will always inspire in me the most loving memories and the keenest gratitude.'

He sighs, then goes out onto the esplanade for the first time in two days. He looks at the horizon.

'She was submissive, devoted and obliging too, and possessed these qualities alongside the political adroitness characteristic of her sex.'

HE GOES OFF alone, following the path that winds its way along the cliffs high above the sea.

He is forty-five on 15 August 1814.

Josephine and so many others are dead already. Why is he alive?

He welcomes his guests, the island's notables, to the Mulini. They offer their congratulations on his birthday. He is sombre, silent. Naturally he must pay his compliments to the ladies of the island and the grand marshal of the palace's wife Countess Bertrand. But after a few moments he heads towards the piano, plays a few notes. This is his way of saying he is going to withdraw to his apartments, a few modest rooms and a bathroom.

He has had a Roman mosaic hung above the bath representing a languid woman.

Why is he alone?

My good Louise,

I have often written to you. I suppose you have done the same, but I have received none of your letters since the one a few days before you left Vienna. I have received no news of my son. This conduct is very stupid and atrocious.

Madame is here and in good health. She is well settled. I am in good health. Your house is ready and I expect you in September for the grape harvest.

No one has the right to obstruct your journey. I have written to you about that.

But what if it is her refusing to come to me? She is so weak, so impressionable, that the people of Vienna have had to get round. He goes on,

So come. I await you impatiently. You know all the feelings I have for you. I shall not write to you at greater length because it is possible this letter won't reach you. Princess Pauline will be here in September.

It's your birthday. I wish you happiness. You must complain about what they are doing, preventing a woman and a child writing to me. This conduct is absolutely vile.

Addio, mio bene,

Nap

XXIII

HE FEELS THE NEED for isolation, far from the heat and the clamour of the seaside. He leaves the Mulini and moves to the Hermitage of the Madonna, and he often goes for walks on the slopes of Monte Giove alone. He stays sitting for hours at a time on the rocky platform from which one can see the whole landscape. Corsica is ablaze in the setting sun. The islets of Capraia and Montecristo are like black diamonds set in the silver sea.

In the evening he walks down the mule tracks to the house in Marciana Alta where his mother lives.

Here she is, sitting in the garden, straight-backed and perfectly still, like the axis of my life, which, after so many revolutions, comes to a halt here, with her, on an island just like that of my childhood.

He remains silent facing her.

Sometimes she asks a brief question. *But she never speaks of Marie Louise and my son.* She talks about his brothers and sisters. Lucien is in Rome, and she writes to him. He has a foundry, she says, and wants to buy iron ore from Rio Marina. Jérôme is in Trieste. Elisa has taken refuge in Bologna and the Austrian police have her under surveillance. Louis is in Rome with his uncle Cardinal Fesch. Joseph has moved to the shore of Lake Léman, at his estate at Prangins. He writes, and also passes on information through intermediaries. He says that Bruslart is recruiting a band of Corsican assassins to infiltrate Elba and kill the Emperor.

Napoleon listens to his mother. She wants to restore family ties between them all. Pauline should be coming from Naples, she repeats, and then she brings up Caroline, tries to exonerate her, and pleads for Murat.

He listens and agrees. He may need Murat. The King of Naples has betrayed him, but weak men are the playthings of circumstances.

HE GOES BACK up to the hermitage and starts to write.

My good friend,

I am here in a hermitage high above sea level, with a view of the whole Mediterranean, in the middle of a chestnut forest. Madame is in the village below.

This place is very agreeable. My health is extremely good; I spend a part of the day hunting.

I very much want to see you and my son. I will see Isabey with pleasure. There are some very beautiful landscapes to draw here.

Farewell, my good Louise. Ever yours, your

Nap

He looks around. The sun is falling into the room in broad, dazzling strips. Outside, grenadiers are dragging a mule that died overnight across the threshing floor.

He observes all this and the changing light on the horizon.

Sometimes he has the feeling that everything is the same, that it takes the same energy to have a small pump put in a stable so the mules don't risk drowning as it does to prepare a battle.

He is so constituted that he sees everything, always wants to establish order and cannot tolerate any form of confusion, chaos or negligence.

'Count Bertrand,' he writes, 'I am missing three shutters for my bedroom. Send three curtains for Madame's room; the rods are there. Send us also fire irons, tongs, shovels . . .

'I think I had asked you to write to Princess Pauline not to bring her piano teacher, but only a good male and female singer, seeing as we have a good violinist and a good pianist here.'

He stops writing.

Can he finish his life here? Under the threat of assassination, in poverty because he is getting none of the allowance he should be paid and when, already, 'All France misses me and asks for me.'

He knows that in barracks all over the country soldiers have celebrated St-Napoleon's day, despite orders, and trampled on the white cockade.

He looks at the countryside. Sometimes it seems to him that this rocky platform looks like an eagle with wings outspread.

DURING THE NIGHT of 1 September he is woken up. A boat has just dropped anchor in Portoferraio Bay, but has chosen to shelter in a creek far from the port.

He hurriedly dresses, has his white mare saddled and follows the path down to the Col de Procchio. He sees the riders coming from a long way away, the carriage, the two mules slowly trudging along.

He knew that Marie Walewska wanted to visit him, and he had given his consent to her brother, the Polish Major Teodor Walewski. But now that he is on his way to meet her, he is preoccupied. He wonders if he has succumbed to an unconsidered impulse. If Austrian spies learn of Marie Walewska's arrival, they will turn it against him; the Empress will use it for some pretext or argument.

But at the same time he is impatient and moved. Why should he refuse this visit from a woman whom he did not receive at Fontainebleau on the eve of his abdication, who is also the mother of his child? Hasn't he sacrificed enough to political calculation?

The carriage stops, a lantern is raised, and he sees the two of them: her in the full beauty of a woman of almost thirty and him, Alexander, *a child with blond curls like the King of Rome and my profile*.

He sits next to her. It has been years since he has spent any time with her.

He takes her hand, then strokes the child's head. He feels deep emotion, but at the same time (Will it always be like this from now on?) he is not entirely caught up in his desire, his affection, in the questions he asks the sleepy child.

He hears himself; he sees himself. He is witness to what he does and says.

She questions him in her lilting voice with its strong Polish accent, and he feels enveloped in memories. He takes his son in his arms and carries him to the hermitage, where he has had rooms prepared for them; he will sleep in the tent.

But why should he remain alone like this? What would be the sense of this deprivation? Life should be seized bodily when it offers itself.

He leaves the tent, goes up to the hermitage.

And when dawn brightens the sky, he leaves Marie Walewska's room and stands looking at the horizon for a long time.

While she is still asleep, he sees an officer of the Guard coming along the path from Portoferraio with a letter from General Drouot.

He reads it pacing about the platform. The entire population of the port is convinced that the Empress and the King of Rome have arrived in the night, and that they're going to stay on the island with the Emperor. The moment this rumour gets out, the spies with which the island is swarming are bound to hear of it.

He crumples Drouot's message in his fist and walks off into the little chestnut wood. He feels fettered, a prisoner forced to take account of the opinion of the population of this island, who spy and gossip like Corsican villagers.

He is no longer the Emperor who could impose his way of living on everybody, and everybody accepted. Now he fears Vienna's decisions, Marie Louise's reactions and the chatter of the Elbans, to whom he has preached virtue.

Losing power means submitting to others. He is humiliated but, if he wants to entertain any hope of seeing Marie Louise and his son again, he must be prudent.

HE HAS MADE his decision. He has dinner with Marie Walewska and applauds the dances and the Polish officers' singing. He strokes Alexander's face. And, on this last night, he goes to Marie. But he cannot agree to her staying, as she wishes, on the island. He refuses the jewels she wants to give him because Peyrusse, the 'minister of finance', has told her the Emperor's reserves are dwindling.

She listens with great dignity, her eyes full of tears.

She is, he knows, the noblest, most generous woman he has ever known.

She only asks for the right to love him.

And he rejects her.

He watches her leave for her ship as a storm breaks and gale-force winds start to blow. She is meant to embark at Marciana Marina but in the lightning he sees the ship setting sail and moving off, probably to skirt the island so that it can shelter from the wind.

Suddenly he lets out a cry and, calling for an orderly officer, tells him to get to the countess and her son and stop them embarking until the storm has died down.

He watches the rider leave in the squalling wind.

Marie Walewska has crossed the island to Porto Longone, the officer explains on his return. Napoleon sets off in the downpour. He gallops to the port, buffeted by the wind and driving rain.

At last here is the spacious harbour with the few lights of Porto Longone gleaming at the head of it. There is no ship.

He goes down to the port. They went aboard, he's told. She had the Emperor's permission, she said. And the ship immediately weighed anchor.

'Everything is in order,' he murmurs.

He walks slowly back up to the hermitage. The rain falls heavy and straight. The wind has dropped.

When he reaches the rocky platform by the hermitage, the sky is cloudless, the horizon bright.

He gives orders. He knows he will never come back here, where she was, and where she is no longer.

XXIV

HE IS PLEASED TO get back to the Mulini. It is not so hot. He hunts. He sets up a game reserve at the tip of the small promontory, Cape Stella. Looking through his eyeglass, he sees a small island twenty or so miles south, and immediately gives orders for *Inconstant* to be armed. He wants to visit this abandoned spot. He walks the islet of Pianosa, as it is called, installs a little garrison and a number of Italian families who are charged with its clearance. He wants to transform Elba, develop its iron mines, marble mines, agriculture, roads. Every evening he wants to feel crushed with exhaustion after a day spent galloping, deciding, acting.

But he doesn't forget.

'My wife doesn't write to me any more,' he says to Bertrand. 'My son has been taken from me as the children of the conquered used to be in the past to adorn the conqueror's triumph. One cannot cite another example of such barbarity in modern times.'

He has found out that the Emperor Francis is having the letters he writes to Marie Louise opened and is forbidding his daughter to reply.

What sort of people are these?

He feels he has been duped, or has deceived himself, which is worse. But he cannot give up. It is my son, my wife. So he must petition, and it hurts him to have to write to the Grand Duke of Tuscany as he does.

Sir, my brother and very dear uncle,
Not having received news of my wife since 10 August, nor of my son for six months, I am entrusting the Chevalier Colonna with this letter. I beg Your Royal Highness to let me know if you will permit me to send you a letter for the Empress every week, and if you will send me in return news of her and the letters of Madame the Countess of Montesquiou, my son's governess. I flatter myself that, despite the events that have

changed so many individuals, Your Royal Highness retains some friendship for me. If you should give me this assurance, I would draw real consolation from it.

BUT THERE IS no answer. He has been cut off from Europe.

And by whom? Talleyrand! The Prince of Benevento is intriguing at the Congress of Vienna. The newspapers are reporting his exploits. The only words on his lips are 'legitimate sovereign'. He wants 'to be a good European'. How much is the pallid, venal Talleyrand being bribed to come to an agreement with England and Austria against Prussia and Russia?

But I am the one he pursues with his hatred. The whole congress, according to my informants' letters, is chattering about getting me even further away from Europe. There's talk of the Azores because, Talleyrand is supposed to have said, 'They are five hundred leagues from land in any direction.' They are afraid of me. They concoct pretexts.

He reads this note in the *Journal des débats*: 'Word has it that agents and emissaries of Bonaparte have been arrested in Italy and that, as a consequence, he will be transferred to the island of St Helena.'

He shows the newspaper to Bertrand. 'Do you think they can deport me? I will never consent to let myself be kidnapped.'

But they are so afraid of my name, of my memory. Just my shadow terrorizes them.

HE WALKS ALONG the quay of Porto Longone. He has been staying here for a few days in the old Spanish citadel that used to guard the bay. He wants, he tells Bertrand and Drouot, the artillery in all the forts on the island to be reinforced, drill to be stepped up, and cartridges and wheat purchased in Naples.

'I have received a very tender letter from the King of Naples,' he says. 'He claims to have written to me several times, but I doubt it; it seems that the affairs of France and Italy are turning his head.'

He shrugs his shoulders.

Murat knows that Talleyrand is exerting all his energy at the Congress of Vienna to dethrone him, *so he tries to effect a rapprochement with me.* He trembles for his crown. He also senses that the émigrés who have returned to France will turn the country against them. The new minister of war, Soult, *my Duke of Dalmatia*, in his frenzied servility, has only appointed Chouans and émigrés who fought against their own country as generals. He has had General Exelmans, a hero of the Russian campaign and the French campaign, arrested solely because he wrote to the King of Naples. Soult wants to compel all soldiers on half-pay to reside in the place of their birth so he can keep them under closer surveillance. But that is nothing; they also want to restore national property, when not yet sold, to its émigré owners. That'll scare the life out of the peasants and bourgeois.

Napoleon stops, stares at Drouot and Bertrand.

'Government by the Bourbons doesn't suit France any more,' he says. 'That family only has old wigs to offer the country. But since politics has disinterred Louis XVIII, he should have slept in my bed as he found it. He has behaved otherwise and as a result he will never live in peace.'

Then he leads General Drouot aside.

'I want you to pay the closest attention to ensuring that the certificates of those grenadiers who are leaving, and are good subjects, are to their advantage.'

Drouout concurs. But he admits his concern. Their wages will be late.

The Bourbons are strangling me by not honouring the financial clauses of the Fontainebleau treaty. They are stealing my son and my wife. They want to deport me, assassinate me. And they want to stop me continuing to live here.

It is a clever trap. They want me dead.

He resumes in the same calm voice: 'Nothing will be overlooked to show my satisfaction with the brave soldiers who have given me so many proofs of their devotion. Have a model of the certificate printed here. Put my arms in the middle; remove "Sovereign of the Island of Elba", which is ridiculous.'

BUT HE MUST throw them off the scent, play the part of someone who accepts his lot and does not guess his adversaries' intentions. He must receive Princess Pauline, who is coming from Naples on the brig *Inconstant*, as if this is the capital of a kingdom.

Let the populace of Portoferraio strut about, let the artillery of the Stella and Falcone forts salute my sister's arrival!

She stays on the first floor of the Mulini 'palace' and weaves an atmosphere of fêtes and pleasure around her. As always, she organizes musical evenings and masked balls, which are entertaining and also serve as a smokescreen.

I am this sovereign of the island of Elba who amuses himself and forgets that he was the Emperor of Kings.

He dictates, 'The invitations should cover the whole island without, however, there being more than two hundred people. There will be refreshments without ice, given the difficulty of getting it. There will be a buffet served at midnight. All of this must not cost more than a thousand francs.'

Because he has to think about that too now, about money which is so short.

But the guests dance and sing and applaud the plays Pauline stages and acts with officers of the Guard. She is beautiful and high-spirited as she makes her entrance on the little stage in the makeshift theatre to declaim the lead role in *False Infidelities* or *Amorous Follies*.

And then there is her ability to surround herself with pretty women who, under her direction, emulate the piquant charms of the palaces of Paris.

When his sister introduces him, Napoleon smiles; for a few moments he forgets everything oppressing him. The Corsican, for instance, who Drouot has just had arrested, who confesses that he was paid by the Chevalier de Bruslart to assassinate the Emperor. What to do with him? Execute him? No, just dismiss him scornfully and go to Pauline's next masked ball as if it was nothing.

Then, when the ball is over, chat for a few moments with Madame Colombani or Madame Bellini or Mademoiselle le Bel. They are all amenable. They all offer themselves. He remembers Lise Le Bel, who, in the past, had spent several nights with him at St-Cloud, but he does not feel the joy he felt at seeing that little seventeen-year-old entering his bedroom. Today, at the Mulini, he sees a greedy woman trying to obtain advantages for her relatives.

He sends her packing.

He thinks of Marie Walewska and Josephine, both of whom he has banished from his life, Josephine dead. He tells Bertrand, 'My divorce has no precedent in history, because it did not affect the ties that bound me to Josephine and our mutual tenderness stayed the same. Our separation was a sacrifice imposed on me by reasons of state, in the interests of my crown and my dynasty. Josephine was devoted to me. She loved me dearly. No one ever had precedence over me in her heart; I had pride of place, her children came next. And she was right, because she is the person I have loved the most and her memory is even more vivid in my mind.'

He cannot say anything about Marie Louise, nor does he want to, since she is silent or gagged, *since those who want my death steal her from me and hide my son*.

He asks for the letters that Caroline brings over every week from Piombino or Leghorn. They come from all parts of France. He reads them over and over. They are from officers on half pay expressing their indignation, who say, 'The Bourbons aren't out of the woods yet and we don't like these gentlemen.' They relate their exploits in the Grand Army and describe the state of mind in the barracks.

Napoleon tells Bertrand and Drouot and Peyrusse what he has been saying for weeks now: 'All France misses me and asks for me.' He reads the newspapers. The divisions between the members of the coalition are obvious in Vienna. England opposes the Tsar's desire to remodel the Kingdom of Poland for his own benefit. And England refuses Prussia the right to annex Saxony.

If the coalition has broken up, that is a card to play for France, for him. And it is better to fight than to let oneself be stabbed or smothered here.

And that is what they want.

He trusts the reports he gets from Cipriani, a Corsican in his service. He has known this orphan since childhood, when he used to do little jobs for the Bonapartes. Lucien taught him to write. When he was Saliceti's quartermaster, he performed several missions, including bribing the Corsicans serving the English general, Hudson Lowe, who commanded the garrison of Capri.

The garrison had subsequently revolted and General Lamarque had been able to take the island.

He sends Cipriani to Genoa and Vienna, and the Corsican, clever informant that he is, manages to send a weekly bulletin reporting the rumours going round the Austrian capital, the sovereigns' entourages and the corridors of the congress. Every time the bulletins arrive Napoleon shuts himself away to read them with the greatest attention.

> It appears certain that, in a secret session yesterday morning, it was as good as decided that Bonaparte be abducted from the Island of Elba and that Murat not be allowed to continue ruling . . . The person who told me about yesterday's conference said that Austria had demanded that the decision about Naples be kept secret until the moment they were able to act against Murat . . .

Napoleon cannot sleep any more. He feels caught in a trap. The rope is being tightened around his throat.

Méneval, who is attached to Marie Louise, writes that his abduction and deportation to the island of St Helena are being studied and prepared by the diplomats of Vienna and London at the instigation of the Prince of Benevento.

I know Méneval, my secretary. He is not a man to deceive me or be fooled himself. And I know Talleyrand – his wish to send me away at any cost. Or to have me murdered.

How can he let himself be led to his death like this without reacting?

HE GIVES ORDERS. If they have to, they will be able to withstand a siege. *Inconstant* must sail for Leghorn and load up with 100,000 francs in wheat.

He sends for General Drouot. The hovels in front of the forts that could hamper artillery fire must be razed. He wants coastal patrols to be organized, drills to be stepped up and gunners trained in heavy barrage.

He tells Colonel Campbell, the coalition's representative on the island who keeps him under surveillance, 'This plan to deport me to an island in the Atlantic is disgraceful. It is a violation of every treaty. I will resist to my death.'

Campbell assures him that there are no plans for anything of the sort. *But what can this officer know of the Congress of Vienna? And what do even the sovereigns know of Talleyrand's manoeuvring? He is the one making sure the money I am owed is not paid. And Louis XVIII is sequestering property that belonged to the Bonapartes.*

How can he administer, defend and govern Elba when the island's annual revenue is only 470,000 francs, which barely covers the civil budget and leaves nothing for his small army and the expenses of His Majesty's household?

They are pushing me towards the abyss.

And if they want to abduct me, how long could I hold out with a handful of poorly armed men?

I am in their hands. My fate depends on my worst enemies — the Bourbons, Talleyrand — the ones who tried to assassinate me with Cadoudal's 'infernal machine' or Maubreuil on the roads of Provence.

On 7 December 1814, after night has fallen, Cipriani asks to be received. He has come from Genoa. Napoleon invites him to sit down. But Cipriani remains standing. He is certain of his information, he says. The abduction of His Majesty is now definite. It will be executed in the next few weeks, or perhaps even days. Cipriani insists on the danger; his voice is ragged, exhausted. The storm made the journey from Genoa difficult, he apologizes.

Napoleon remains impassive. Now he has taken his decision he is calm, almost indifferent.

All that is left is to act.

He hesitates for a moment when the captain of the *Caroline* gives him a letter from Vienna that bears the Habsburg seal. Perhaps Marie Louise is announcing her arrival. He opens it nervously, and reads. It is dated 1 January, 1815 Marie Louise writes, 'I hope this year will be happier for you. You will at least be peaceful on your island and you will be happy living there, to the joy of all who love you and are attached to you like me. Your son kisses you and asks me to wish you Happy New Year and tell you that he loves you with all his heart.' Not a word about her coming. The conventional coldness of polite indifference. Who dictated this letter asking him to accept his lot?

Should he live here and wait for the assassins?

No, he must flee, conquer his enemies and find them, her and his son.

This is his only chance.

XXV

He crosses the island from port to port. He questions the grenadiers on sentry duty at the entrances to the ports.

'Well then, grumbler, are you bored?'

'No, sire, but I am not having too much fun either.'

'That's not the way. You've got to take life as it comes. This won't last for ever.'

He walks away. It must be kept secret until the last moment. Colonel Campbell is watching his every movement. His spies are on the lookout. And out at sea there are French vessels sporting the white flag whose job is to prevent any attempt at flight and which perhaps are carrying assassins within their crews who will be landed on one of the island's deserted beaches.

We must be quick. But the English frigate Partridge *is moored in Portoferraio Bay. And I must leave the island without committing an act of war so as to try and keep the peace. So I need to trick everyone who's watching me.*

He repeats his motto to Campbell, *Napoleo ubiscumque felix.* He invites the colonel to the balls Pauline gives. He appears indifferent to news from France. On 21 January 1815 the memory of Louis XVI is honoured in expiatory ceremonies during which the regicides are threatened. What must Fouché think, and all the other Jacobins pretending to be penitent? But the whole country must feel humiliated and revolted by a policy that wants to erase twenty years of history. Besides, a council of war has acquitted General Exelmans. And when Mademoiselle de Raucourt, a 'bonapartiste', as they say now, and actress, is refused a religious funeral by the priest of St-Roch, there are demonstrations in Paris.

The country is ready. The country is waiting for me.

But I have to cross the sea. Now, when the nights are long.

He consults the tables of lunar eclipses.

The next one will be between 27 February and 2 March. I must leave the island then. Then let fate guide the ships. Ours and the enemy's.

HE IS JUBILANT. He feels his body light again, as if his stoutness didn't carry any weight any more. He issues numerous orders, but calmly so as not to attract Campbell's attention. The roads must be broadened to allow material stored on the east of the island to be taken to Portoferraio and Porto Longone.

'Give orders,' he tells Drouot, 'that the brig *Inconstant* is to go into the harbour basin, repair its careening and have everything done for it to take to sea. It will be painted like an English brig. I want it to be in the roads from 24–25 February and ready. It will be supplied for one hundred and twenty men for three months and provided with as many launches as it can carry. Order Pons to charter two big vessels, brigs or sloops, from Rio Marina, above ninety tons and as big as possible.'

They must load the cartridges, the horses and the men, nearly 200, and reach the French coast as fast as possible. Everything will depend on the wind.

He remembers his return from Egypt. He has absolute faith in his destiny. He cannot remain a prisoner here, waiting for his deportation or death. He is not afraid of dying at sea or being captured by an English or French ship. He will reach Paris. He can already hear the cheers that will accompany him on his way.

Afterwards destiny will play its hand again.

ON MONDAY, 13 February 1815 the officer of the guard comes to announce that a man dressed as a sailor is asking to be received. Night has just fallen. The man claims to have been sent by Maret, Duke of Bassano. He was the sub-prefect of Rheims, he says, awarded membership of the Legion of Honour in the French campaign. 'The intrepid sub-prefect' Ney had called him. His name is Fleury de Chaboulon; he has been travelling for several weeks, and he brings the Emperor news of France.

Napoleon listens to him. Fleury speaks in exalted tones. France is waiting for the Emperor. The soldiers and peasants will rise up en masse. All those who do not support the return of the aristocrats and Jesuits will join him. They are waiting for him. All France is full of hope.

Napoleon questions Fleury, and receives him again on Tuesday 14 February. But why should he reveal himself? He charges him with a mission to Murat. The King of Naples fears for his throne and so is making overtures; his help in Italy may be valuable.

Napoleon goes out into the garden of the Mulini with Fleury. He leads him to the corner of the terrace from where the view is most panoramic.

'It is not true that men are as ungrateful as people claim,' he says. 'And if one often has grounds to complain, it is because ordinarily the benefactor demands more than he gives. People say that when you know a man's character, you have the key to his conduct. But that's wrong: a person will perform a bad action even when he is a fundamentally honest man. That person will do something bad without being bad.'

So he must pardon Murat without forgetting anything he has done. *In any case, I need him. And he needs me.* Hasn't Talleyrand said in Vienna 'that Murat must be expelled because there can be no illegitimacy in any corner of Europe'?

ON THURSDAY 16 February Colonel Campbell appears, nonchalant, smiling. He has greatly enjoyed Pauline's balls to which he has been invited.

'*Napoleo ubiscumque felix,*' Napoleon repeats.

Campbell is leaving for Florence for a few days.

Oh, this joy sweeping over me that I must hide and yet is proof that destiny once again is reaching out its hand to me!

After the party Napoleon watches the frigate *Partridge* sail away towards the Italian coast.

Perhaps this is a trap, perhaps Campbell will return to take me by surprise, but we cannot miss this opportunity with the period of moonless nights coming up.

He orders the outfitters to have a complete uniform and two pairs of shoes distributed to each soldier. He reviews the Corsican battalion. He has a list drawn up of men he can trust.

On Wednesday 22 February at nightfall he starts to have the chests of cartridges and bundles of equipment loaded onto the brig *Inconstant* and the sloop *Star*.

On Friday the 24th, when he is walking along the paths above Portoferraio Bay, he sees the English frigate come back into the bay, lower its sails and drop anchor.

Is fate withdrawing her hand?

A boat glides towards land, carrying a few men, then the frigate prepares to set sail again, after having unloaded six English tourists! Campbell has stayed in Florence.

Napoleon receives the English, asks questions, listens to them, discusses his campaigns, invites them to look over the island. Then he gives the order to seal off the island. No one can leave Elba or enter it from now on.

Now the dice are rolling, and it is beyond anyone's power to stop them.

ON SATURDAY, 25 February 1815 he begins to write. He needs words of strength and enthusiasm, energy and confidence for the French people, the grenadiers and the army. And the words come.

Frenchmen, a prince imposed by a temporarily victorious enemy relies on a handful of enemies of the people who the people have condemned in every national assembly for the last twenty-five years. I have heard your complaints and your hopes in my exile. You have called for the government of your choice – that alone is legitimate. I have crossed the seas! I come among you to reclaim my rights, which are yours.

Soldiers of this great Nation, soldiers of the great Napoleon, everything that has been done without the people's and our consent is illegitimate.

These words exhilarate him. He repeatedly goes out onto the terrace. It is as if he needs to bellow them to the gathered troops. They will soon be there, he is sure.

Soldiers, throw away the cockade that the Nation has proscribed, and that for twenty-five years served as a rallying point for all the enemies of France! Show the tricolour cockade; you wore it during our greatest glory. Take up the eagles again that you had at Ulm, Austerlitz, Jena, Eylau, Friedland, Tudela, Eckmühl, Essling, Wagram, Smolensk, the Moskva, Lützen, Würschen, Montmirail ... Do you think that this handful of Frenchmen, today so arrogant, will be able to bear the sight? They will go back whence they came; and there, if they wish, they will reign as they claim to have reigned for nineteen years.

He can't keep it secret any more.

He goes up to his mother. He strokes her hair. He senses she is anxious. Throughout dinner she has watched him, surprised sometimes at his silence. Suddenly he says, 'I need to tell you that I am leaving tomorrow night.'

'To go where?'

'Paris. But first and foremost I ask your advice.'

He watches her. He trusts this woman who has never attempted to hold him back; she has taught him the opposite – how to launch himself into the world.

He hears her sigh.

'What will be will be,' she murmurs. 'May God help you. I'd regret it if I told you any different. But if it is written that you must die, heaven, which has not wanted you to die in unworthy retirement, will not want it to be by poison but with sword in hand.'

He withdraws. He reads the *History of Charles the Fifth*, then sleeps for a few hours, and then it's already dawn on Sunday, 26 February 1815. The day promises to be radiant. There will be some wind this evening which should push the little fleet north.

He looks towards Portoferraio. The loading of the ships is continuing. There is a dense crowd on the quays. He hears shouts, footsteps. Some Elbans are gathered on the esplanade behind the Mulini. He goes out to them. They press round him, fall to their knees, kiss him. But the time has not yet come to explain. He returns inside; he has to burn his papers. Then he goes down to the port to inspect the ships, including one from Marseille they have been forcibly detaining for five days; the Polish chasseurs are starting to board it as the cargo is thrown overboard to give them room.

In the evening he receives a delegation of Elbans. He is impatient. This time is over. He is already elsewhere, the sea crossed, on roads that lead to Paris.

'Gentlemen, I am leaving you. France calls me. The Bourbons have ruined it. Several nations in Europe will see me return with pleasure.'

He dines with his mother and Princess Pauline, who cries, her face haggard. He turns away when Pauline tries to give him a necklace. He takes her out into the garden, very moved. It is always up to him to console others.

ON THE QUAYS, in the gathering darkness, he drives through the crowd in a barouche. All the houses are lit up. They shout, *'Viva l'Imperatore! Evviva Napoleone!'*

He stands up. He looks at this sea of faces covering the quays of the port.

'Elbans, I pay tribute to your conduct. While it was the order of the day to deluge me with bitterness, you have surrounded me with your love and devotion . . . Your memory will always be dear to me. Farewell, Elbans! I love you. You are the braves of Tuscany.'

He jumps down into a boat.

He looks at the dark mass of the *Inconstant*, which looms at the entrance to the port. A clamour rises up, rolls over the surface of the sea and is met by the song of the soldiers already on board: *'Allons, enfants de la Patrie; Le jour de gloire est arrivé.'*

'Ah, France, France,' he murmurs.

TOWARDS MIDNIGHT on Sunday, 26 February 1815 a southerly finally gets up.

At ten o'clock on Monday the 27th, a sail appears on the horizon; it is the *Partridge*. She seems to be coming closer. They must cut the ropes of the dinghies they're towing to go faster. Napoleon gives the order to take up battle stations. Then in his eyeglass he sees the *Partridge* moving away. Destiny.

He walks a little on the poop deck.

'Campbell will be most disconcerted when the commander of that corvette announces that I have left the island of Elba,' he says.

He sits down on the bridge. In the middle of the afternoon a sailor shouts down from the crow's-nest that he has seen the sails of two ships.

These are the French surveillance frigates, but they soon disappear over the horizon. Then, at dusk, a French brig, the *Zephyr*, approaches the *Inconstant*. The grenadiers are lying down on the bridge. The captain of the ship calls out an inquiry into the Emperor's health through a megaphone.

And then it is the *Zephyr*'s turn to sail away.

It is a dark night without a moon, as he had anticipated. A steady breeze is blowing,

On Tuesday, 28 February 1815, towards midday, the French coast appears.

Napoleon is at the prow. He turns towards the officers gathered behind him, straining like him towards that dark blue line.

'I will arrive in Paris without firing a shot,' he says.

PART SEVEN

Frenchmen, my will is that of the people

1 March 1815 to 12 June 1815

XXVI

HE JUMPS DOWN ONTO the sandy beach on Wednesday, 1 March 1815. It is two in the afternoon. The sun lights up the sea held captive by the inlet of the Golfe Juan. The whole flotilla lies at anchor a few cables offshore and the first grenadiers have already disembarked; he sees them advancing in a line towards the olive trees, past the reeds that skirt the beach. The launches have started plying back and forth between the beach and the ships. It will take them several hours, he estimates, to unload the 1,200 men, the horses, the four cannon and the chests of cartridges. He cannot wait here. He must advance inland as quickly as possible, take control of the nearest towns: Cannes, Antibes, Grasse.

Destiny, once again, has opened up the way for me. Onward!

He goes as far as an olive grove, a few hundred metres from the beach. He posts the sentries himself, then orders that his tent be pitched in the neighbouring meadow. It is cold. The sun is already starting to go down. The days are still short. He calls over General Cambronne, who will command the advance guard. Everything will depend on him.

'I am giving you the advance guard of my finest campaign,' he tells him. 'You will not fire a single shot. Remember that I want to take back my crown without shedding one drop of blood.'

For that the army must rally to them. They will take the Dauphiné road to avoid the royalists of Avignon and Provence. It will be the advance guard's job to open the road without using violence. Every soldier advancing against us must hear the following words.

He takes out the proclamation to the army. He reads it at the top of his voice.

'Soldiers, come and range yourselves under the colours of your leader. Victory will march in double-quick time. The eagle with the national colours will fly from steeple to steeple to the towers of Notre Dame. Then you will be able to show your scars with honour; then you will be able to pride yourselves on what you have done; you will be the liberators of the nation!'

He goes up to Cambronne, clasps him in his arms, repeating, 'From steeple to steeple to the towers of Notre Dame – without firing a single shot.'

He watches Cambronne and the few grenadiers who accompany him as they leave. He sits down near the fire.

EVERYTHING WILL BE decided in the next few days. He watches a group of peasants and fishermen through the olive trees who observe him with a sort of indifferent curiosity. He remembers the cheering crowds on the quays of Portoferraio. If the soldiers and people don't come to him here, he will have no strength, and it will only take determination to bring him down. Then the eagle will fall.

He rests his elbows on his thighs and cups his chin in the palms of his hands. His body is heavy, his legs ache and he feels piercing pains in his stomach that sometimes shoot from his navel to his groin as if he has been stabbed with a dagger. He knows that he is not as agile as he was, that he has trouble mounting a horse and staying in the saddle for long periods; and sometimes, without realizing, he sinks into a sleep as dark as oblivion.

He is over forty-five.

He stands up. Come on, forward! He will march in the front rank. What does he risk? Dying?

Is that a risk?

A COLD WIND blows that dawn as they march towards Grasse, which he wants to avoid. The goal is Grenoble, the town where the Revolution was born.

As they march, he calls over the surgeon Émery, a doctor and devoted follower of his from Grenoble who joined him in Elba. Émery must inform the patriots of Grenoble of the Emperor's imminent arrival. If Grenoble opens its gates, if the garrison rallies to him, then the game will be won. Until then, march, march.

He turns around. The little army forms a long black column climbing the paths that snake around Grasse, through scree and brushwood, towards St-Vallier. They have had to abandon the cannon; the tracks are too rutted. He stops. He is finding it hard to breathe. The slope is steep. A mule carrying a chest full of gold coins, what remains of the exchequer, loses its footing and they have to collect the napoleons that fall out of the shattered chest. Snow starts to fall. General Drouot gives him a walking stick. Come on, forward. He pokes the stick into snow. He has marched in the sand of Palestine. He has marched in the snow of Russia and the rain of Germany. Now he must march over the scree of the Alps.

After several hours he sits for a few moments in the middle of a meadow. The snow has stopped. The sun has reappeared. Two old peasants approach, give him a bouquet of violets.

He is moved. He puts the flowers in his lapel. It is the first sign of friendship he has been given, and it is two days already since he set foot in France. But everyone who has seen him and recognized him has kept their distance. Is it possible that they fear his return or, worse, perhaps they have forgotten him?

He throws away the carcass of the chicken which he has just eaten for lunch.

It's no time for questions. Every hour counts. Either I carry it off, or I die.

HE REACHES ST-VALLIER. He stops on the main square, by a meadow. A man comes up, glass in hand. He offers him a drink.

Let him drink first! I don't want to die from poison but from a cannonball or a bullet, like a soldier.

He slakes his thirst after the man has drunk.

Forward. The path becomes narrower, overhanging sheer drops. When he was in the Tuileries he had wanted, decided even, to have a road suitable for traffic built between Grenoble, Digne and Nice. He thought his orders had been carried out. Here's the truth of it! A mule track that goes by Escragnolles and Séranon to Castellane. A few curious onlookers on the little town's square, but no cries of enthusiasm, just the stupor of the sub-prefect, even though he has been warned by Cambronne, who is still with the advance guard.

Might this country slip away from him? He feels tiredness

stealing over his body. He has to sleep a few hours at Barrême, and then set off again at dawn.

The road has widened. Napoleon rides on, then stops at the intersection of two valleys to observe Digne, the largest town he has travelled through since Golfe Juan.

He enters the town at about one in the afternoon.

Why this silence, this reserve from the inhabitants, who watch me pass without any display and follow me to the Petit Paris inn without a sound?

A few dozen people crowd round the entrance of the inn. He walks towards them.

'We must rid Paris of the mark stamped on it by treachery and the presence of the enemy,' he says.

The crowd has grown. He speaks of the émigrés who want to take back the land that has been given to those who work it. A few shouts of approval go up, but everything soon sinks back into silence.

Why do they show this reserve towards me?

But he mustn't ask himself questions; he must push on over these Durance plains swept by an icy wind that sometimes brings rain and hailstorms.

It is night already. He is overcome with tiredness. It is already Saturday, 4 March 1815. The news of his landing must have reached Paris, perhaps Vienna too. If the people don't rise up to take him to Paris, the gate of destiny will slam shut. And he will have to die, if it is possible.

He spends the night at the chateau of Malijai. He cannot sleep. Cambronne has not sent a courier with news of his progress. Perhaps he has been captured, like those dozen grenadiers who were arrested and put in Antibes fortress immediately after the landing. Perhaps in a few hours it will be the end.

He cannot believe it. He doesn't even want to think beyond the span of one useless, exhausting, sleepless night. Let's be off! He rides alongside the Bléone and Durance rivers, muddy and turbulent. In the distance appears the citadel of Sisteron, looming above the gorge where the town is clustered, huddled against white cliffs. He advances at the head of the grenadiers along a long straight road bordered with plane trees. And he sees a crowd coming to meet him. He spurs his horse a little. He cannot wait. He has to go to meet the unknown. Defy the future. Suddenly arms go up, a tricolour flag and voices shout, 'Long live the Emperor!'

At last this cry, for the first time, after too many days, too many hours of silence.

Perhaps the gate of destiny is finally going to fling itself open?

He is surrounded. He pronounces a few words. But he does not want to delay. On the contrary, he wants to go faster to reach people who perhaps will become inflamed, when in the south the population has remained inert.

NIGHT FALLS; THE grenadiers light torches to illuminate the road that winds down towards Gap. And suddenly the town appears, all lit up. Brilliant dots of light glint on the mountainside; others are moving through the surrounding countryside.

It is nine in the evening. Uproar, fervour. He sees Gap's streets jammed with enthusiastic crowds. They press round him, shouting, 'Long live the Emperor! String up the aristocrats! Death to the Bourbons!'

Peasants wave torches.

At last, at last, these people, this welcome.

He doesn't feel the tiredness any more. He jumps off his horse and goes into the Marchand Hotel. The people want to touch him.

'You are our father,' he hears. They grasp his hands, kiss them. They hail him from all sides. They denounce the laws on national property enacted by the Bourbons. He listens. Napoleon couldn't imagine this a few hours ago. Nothing is won yet, but the game is afoot.

'Citizens, I am keenly touched by all the sentiments you express to me,' he calls from the stairs. 'Your prayers will be answered. The Nation's cause will triumph again!'

The cheers ring out. 'Long live the Emperor! Long live the Nation!'

'You are right,' he continues, 'to call me your father. I only live for the honour and welfare of France. My return resolves all your anxieties; it guarantees the preservation of all property. Equality between all the classes and the rights you have enjoyed for twenty-five years and which our fathers so desired form part of your life today. My presence guarantees them.'

IF THIS ENTHUSIASM spreads, if it inflames the army, then nothing will be able to stop me.

He feels that feeling of inner peace and pride which he has often felt during his life, when what he has thought up, a plan that appeared chimerical, comes into being.

This is what he thinks of as he climbs the Col Bayard, then stops at Corps and heads on to Laffrey.

The little army is now surrounded by peasants who want to march on Paris and join the soldiers. He needs to dissuade them. He is the Emperor, a man of the Nation, but of an orderly nation and not a country in revolution. Besides, nothing is decided yet.

Here are troops on the road for the first time barring the way; it is the Laffrey pass that commands the descent to Grenoble and cannot be turned.

This is where destiny decides my enterprise.

He calls over an officer of the Guard. He is to take a message to the commander of the battalion, probably the 5th of the line. 'The Emperor is going to march on you. If you open fire, the first shot will be for him.'

He does not even wait for the officer to come back. He walks towards them alone, holding the skirts of his coat.

If I don't die here, I will go all the way to Paris.

He hears the voice of an officer give the order to fire. The muskets come up, but no shot is loosed. He walks slowly.

If I must die, let it be here.

He is only a few metres away. He sees these soldiers' faces, their insignia. It is the 5th.

'Soldiers of the Fifth,' he shouts in a loud, assured voice, 'I am your Emperor! Acknowledge me!'

He takes another step closer.

'Acknowledge me!' he continues, louder. 'If there is among you a soldier who wishes to kill his Emperor, here I am!'

A voice, a thousand voices: 'Long live the Emperor!' The soldiers rush forward, holding their muskets over their heads, some wearing tricolour cockades. He is surrounded from all sides.

He is on the verge of tears. He feels his lips trembling. The gates of destiny are wide open, revealing the future.

He orders the soldiers to fall back in. He reviews them. He says to General Drouot, 'Everything is finished now. In ten days I will be in the Tuileries.'

He stands up in his stirrups. Although he suffers more and more frequently from his heavy body, his legs, his stomach, he feels no pain now.

'The Bourbons' throne only serves the interests of a few families,' he calls out. 'The whole Nation must rise up against the return of the Ancien Régime.'

The soldiers are surrounded by a crowd of peasants shouting, 'Long live the Emperor!'

On the road to Grenoble he sees troops approaching, but they are waving the tricolour and at their head he recognizes Colonel Bédoyère, one of the best young officers of the Grand Army, a hero at the Moskva and throughout the French campaign. Why hasn't he made this man a general?

He has rallied the troops under his command to the Emperor, he explains. The garrison of Grenoble is theirs, he announces, and despite the authorities the town is waiting for the Emperor. Then he adds, 'Sire, no more ambition, no more despotism. Your Majesty must renounce the pursuit of conquests and extreme power which has brought about France's and your misfortune.'

But who has refused peace? Who forced me to wage war to defend myself? Who did they want to assassinate? What have the Bourbons just declared by royal edict? That 'Napoleon Bonaparte is a traitor and rebel' who on simple establishment of his identity must be 'rushed upon' and brought before a council of war to be shot!

To the sovereigns gathered at the Congress of Vienna, in the words Talleyrand whispers into their ears, I am 'the enemy and menace of the world, who has set himself outside civil and social relations and who must be exposed to public condemnation'.

This is what my enemies want to do with me! And Ney, the Prince of the Moskva, has promised to bring me back to Paris in an iron cage! And the Bourbons demand the help of Europe to slay the monster! Me. What does France matter to them!

He turns towards Bédoyère and points to the peasants marching towards Grenoble.

'I am not only, as has been said, the Emperor of the soldiers, I am also that of the peasants, the plebeians, France. Hence you see the people coming back to me. There is friendship between us. I have come from the people. My voice has influence over them.'

IT IS NINE in the evening on Tuesday, 7 March 1815. The grenadiers break down the gates of Grenoble. Napoleon walks through the streets, and he feels drunk with joy. He has never known this, he thinks, even in the most glorious days of the Empire – these delirious crowds, these songs, these shouts, these dances. What will it be like in Paris?

The crowd besieges the Hotel of the Three Dauphins, where he is staying. He opens the window. He sees all those faces, he hears that storm of voices.

'Citizens!' he begins. 'When in my exile I learnt of all the misfortunes oppressing the Nation, that the people's rights were unrecognized, I did not waste a moment. I landed on our country's soil and had no thought but to appear with the speed of an eagle in this fine town of Grenoble, whose patriotism and attachment to my person I was particularly aware of. Dauphinois, you have fulfilled my hopes!'

He walks through the hotel's salons. A little crowd presses round him.

The notables are back. They offer me their servile compliments and their toadying bows.

He leans towards Bertrand and murmurs, 'Until Grenoble I was an adventurer; now I am a prince again.'

WHO CAN STOP him now?

Soult, who has just declared that 'Bonaparte is nothing but an adventurer'? How many days before he comes over to me? The Count of Artois and Macdonald, who are vainly trying to rally the troops garrisoned in Lyon, all of whom wear the tricolour cockade?

He rides from Grenoble to Lyon amid enthusiastic scenes. In

the Faubourg de la Guillotière the crowd is so densely packed he can't move. Macdonald and the count have fled. The people shout, 'Down with the priests! Death to the royalists! String up the aristocrats! To the scaffold with the Bourbons! Long live Napoleon; long live the Emperor!'

He stopped the Revolution and channelled the chaotic energy that sprung from it and here it is spreading again, thanks to these Bourbons who have learnt nothing and forgotten nothing.

He enters the archbishops' palace and occupies the chambers and salons the Count of Artois vacated that morning.

What was that Bourbon, that émigré, thinking? That he could stop me?

THE NEXT MORNING, Saturday 11 March, when he opens his bedroom door, he knows he has regained power. All the town dignitaries attend his levee, as in the past. Before.

He issues his orders. He wants a review of the troops on place Bellecour. He wants the following decrees to be noted: restoration of the tricolour, suppression of the royal orders, dismissal of the King's household, annulment of all appointments made in the army and the Legion of Honour since April 1814.

He walks about the room, his hands behind his back. He glances at the secretaries writing. The dignitaries are listening respectfully.

He continues.

He banishes émigrés who have returned since 1814. He restores national property that has been given to émigrés. He sequesters the properties allocated to the Bourbons over the last year. He dissolves the assemblies and summons French voters to the Champ de la Fédération, where the nation will lay down its laws itself.

'It will be the Champ-de-Mai,' he says, hammering out the words.

Then he turns towards Bertrand and orders the Old Guard garrisoned at Metz to join their Emperor.

Whatever their commander, Oudinot, thinks, the Old Guard will obey.

He withdraws for a moment.

What about my wife, my son? Will they come to me?

He begins an official letter to 'Marie Louise, Empress of the

French at Schönbrunn. Madame and my dear friend, I have returned to my throne . . .'

Then he takes another sheet of paper. 'My good friend, By the time you receive this letter, I will be in Paris. Come and join me with my son. I hope to kiss you before the end of March. Ever yours, Nap'.

He remains motionless. Tiredness suddenly overwhelms him. And a dull anxiety starts to take hold. He will not see them again.

HE HEARS THE shouts, 'Long live the Emperor!'

He goes out of his room. The woman coming towards him is Marie-Françoise Pellapra. She is still beautiful, young. In the past, in the past . . . Here in Lyon, on the road to Italy, they had spent their first night together. Others had followed in Paris. *Am I the father of the little girl, Émilie, whom she gave birth to after being with me?* He has his doubts.

Marie-Françoise Pellapra takes his hands. He lets her talk. The past does not return. People change. He has just learnt that Bourrienne – his fellow student at Brienne, his secretary for so long and then a corrupt official in Paris and Hamburg – Bourrienne has just been appointed prefect of police of Paris by Louis XVIII. And he has tried to arrest Fouché – him, Bourrienne!

One must not look back at the past as long as one can act and go forward.

HE LEAVES LYON on Monday, 13 March 1815.

All along the road to Villefranche-sur-Sâone, he sees peasants looking at him incredulously, sometimes standing around invalids who give him military salutes, or taking five-franc pieces out of their pockets, examining his likeness, then crying out, 'It's him! Long live the Emperor!'

Who can stop me now? The streets of Villefranche, the streets of Mâcon, Tournus, Chalon and Dijon are full of cheering crowds who cling to me as I slowly push my way through.

Can Ney stop me? But the Prince of the Moskva's troops are refusing to obey the orders of a marshal in the King's service. I must extend a hand to him. I need him, his men.

Napoleon dictates a letter for Marshal Ney to Marshal Bertrand.

My Cousin,

My chief of staff is sending you the order of march. I have no doubt that the moment you learn of my arrival in Lyon you will not have the tricolour flag taken from your troops. Follow Bertrand's orders and come and join me. I will receive you as on the day after the battle of the Moskva.

He is convinced this is what Ney will decide to do. In any case, regiments are arriving, cockades on their hats and tricolour flags leading the way. It is even said that Villejuif's battalions, considered the most loyal to the King, have taken up the tricolour cockade. Exelmans, report couriers from Paris, has captured the royal artillery in the capital with some soldiers on half pay.

There's no other resistance. The mayors are rushing to assure me of their loyalty.

'You have let yourself be led by the priests and the nobility,' Napoleon upbraids the mayor of Autun. 'They wanted to bring back the tithe and feudal rights. I'll do them justice; I'll string them up!'

At Auxerre Ney asks to be received. He is sheepish, uneasy. He starts to justify himself. He presents a memo that will explain, he says, the reasons for his going over to Louis XVIII.

Men are what they do. He has come back to me. Because I am victorious? Then I just have to remain so for Ney to stay faithful to me.

'You don't need excuses,' Napoleon tells Ney. 'Your excuse, like mine, lies in events, which have been stronger than any man. But let's talk no further about the past and only remember it in order to conduct ourselves better in the future.'

He opens his arms. Ney rushes to him.

This is what men are like.

ON SUNDAY 19 March, he gets into a barouche.

He is the Emperor returning to his capital. A courier galloping alongside the barouche announces that the Bourbon King has left the Tuileries for the northern frontier. The courier hands him a letter from Fouché.

'Sire, assassins are lying in wait for Your Majesty on the outskirts of Paris. Have yourself well guarded,' the Duke of Otranto writes.

What do they have left apart from assassinating me, like Henry IV?

He gives orders. All the exits of Fontainebleau forest are to be guarded. But there is no question of him stopping before going into the chateau. He gets out in the Courtyard of the White Horse and slowly climbs the horseshoe staircase. He pauses for a few seconds.

Less than a year ago, on 20 April 1814, he was bidding the Guards farewell here; he was leaving for the island of Elba and on the road murderers were baying at the moon.

They are still there, but this Monday, 20 March 1815, at ten, he is taking back his chateau and his powers.

Has he been alive between these two moments? It seems to him that nothing has existed. So strange, his stay on the island of Elba.

His life is like this, like a succession of scenes.

He walks through the galleries. He finds his study, issues his orders. On his way to Paris he wants to review the troops at Fontaines de Juvisy.

He takes a turn in the park, then gets back into his carriage.

HE HAS SO often travelled this road between Fontainebleau and Paris, held so many reviews of troops. But he has just brought off his finest campaign. Not a blemish, because not a shot has been fired, as he had wished, thought and dreamed. The people have come out and changed everything.

Here they are, the people, as he enters Paris. Men, women and children running around the barouche, surrounding it – in front, behind. The horses are reduced to a walk.

Never, not even on the days after Austerlitz, not for his coronation, has he seen anything like this.

He sees the riders of the escort unable to push aside these women and men whose faces he fleetingly sees.

If only his son could see this with him. This 20 March is his fourth birthday! A sign of destiny. Worse pain.

He sees men and women crying, invalids waving their crutches, holding up their crosses of the Legion of Honour.

There is a sea of people in front of the Tuileries. They rush forward, carry him. He is hoisted into the air. He is passed from arm to arm to the palace, then on up the main staircase.

Yesterday, Louis XVIII was here.

He hears the shouting and cheering that doesn't stop.

It is the finest of his victories, the greatest, without a drop of blood staining the flag.

He has tears in his eyes.

He lets himself fall into a chair, exhausted.

Everything will be hard tomorrow. Everything should stop now.

XXVII

HE VISITS HIS STUDY, then his apartments. Everything is still in its rightful place, as if these rooms had been unoccupied. Only this oversized armchair, the chair of an impotent man, is a reminder Louis XVIII has lived there.

In my place.

He gives an order. The servants rush forward, take the armchair away.

He goes around the rooms again. It is as if nothing has happened in these eleven months, as if he has returned from a long campaign to find his palaces, courtiers and servants unchanged.

But he is alone. Neither wife nor son. Only these men who crowd into the reception rooms, whose murmuring he can hear. They are not leaving the Tuileries despite the late hour. They want to show themselves, set a date, make him forget what they have done.

He opens the doors. He wants to see Cambacérès, Maret, Mollien, Molé, Davout and Caulaincourt. The government must be formed tonight, so that tomorrow morning they can carry out his orders and eradicate all trace of the Bourbons.

He sees Cambacérès approach. The arch-chancellor coughs like an old man. He is bent double. He mumbles. He cannot accept a ministerial post, he says. He is racked with illness. At fifty-two he feels old. Caulaincourt and Molé are evasive as well. They are cautious.

'They have let me arrive as they let the others go,' he says to Mollien, who has accepted the treasury.

But they are afraid.

'It is disinterested people who have brought me to Paris,' he goes on. 'The non-commissioned officers and soldiers did everything; I owe everything to the people and the army.'

That night, groups of people remain in front of the Tuileries palace. He sees people dancing joyfully in the torchlight. He turns to Molé, who persists in refusing to join the government.

'I find you quite changed,' he says. 'Of us all, I am the only one in good health.'

He points to the crowd.

'Nothing has surprised me more on my return to France,' he continues, 'than this hatred of priests and the nobility, which I find as universal and virulent as it was at the start of the Revolution.'

He walks a few paces, his head bowed.

'We shall begin the Revolution again. People cannot imagine all the harm the Bourbons have done France.'

HE SIGHS. That is enough for today. But whether they accept or refuse, what does it matter, he will appoint them to the government: Cambacérès to justice, Maret as secretary of state, Fouché to the police, Caulaincourt to foreign affairs, Savary to the gendarmerie, Davout to war, Carnot to the interior.

He sits on the edge of his bed. The bath is running. Marchand, his valet, is bustling about. His former servant Constant, apparently so devoted, has not returned. He disappeared at the time of his abdication, *taking with him, so I'm told, everything he could. And Bourrienne and Berthier are driving north with the fleeing King!*

There you have mankind!

What can I do, apart from rely on those who surround me? 'I do not want to be the king of a peasant revolt.' I do not want the Revolution to be unleashed again. I owe everything to the people and the army, but I cannot give in to their passions. What system could one construct with them? Re-create the Committee of Public Safety, put Robespierre's powdered wig on my head and erect the guillotine in the place du Carrousel? I refuse. And yet I cannot govern as before. I must let liberty flourish. I will abolish censorship, establish new rules of government.

With which men? With those still here. Fouché? Yes, this head of police, this man I can't trust but who knows his business. And all the others who have used me, abandoned me and often betrayed me, but who are indispensable nonetheless.

HE LETS HIS first night at the Tuileries pass like this. And on Tuesday 21 March, at six in the morning, he is already at work.

He reads, sorts, writes, dictates, mutters. He sees Davout. He trusts this marshal, Duke of Auerstadt, Prince of Eckmühl. In Hamburg Davout defended the town long after all chances of escape were gone. He had his men fire on the white flag.

'Poor France, poor France,' Napoleon murmurs, going through the dispatches.

Europe will rise against it, he continues. *I want peace. But if I hold out my hand, who will take it?*

'So we must fight all out, and for that we must prepare an army of three hundred thousand men in three months.'

He grasps Davout by the arm.

'It is not a matter of listening to our wishes; either we win or we die.'

Everything will be decided once again on the battlefield. I am forced to make this choice; I am left no other.

He leads Davout to the window. The troops of the Paris garrison and the National Guard are lining up on the place du Carrousel. Others are taking up position on the place du Châtelet. He is to review them at one o'clock. His first great parade for months, public proof that he has resumed his place and that power is in his hands a few hours after his return.

'Government is a form of navigation,' he says to Davout. 'One needs two elements to navigate, and one needs two to steer the ship of state as well. Balloons cannot be steered because there's no pivot floating in a single element. There isn't even the possibility of direction in pure democracy, but, by combining it with aristocracy, one opposes one to the other and steers the vessel by contradictory passions.'

HE GOES OUT with Davout. The crowd cheers him. The flags snap in the chill March wind. He walks along the ranks of the troops and stops in front of two battalions of the National Guard.

'The glory of what we have just accomplished belongs entirely to the people and to you,' he cries. 'My glory is to have known you and read your minds.'

He listens to the cheering. He looks at the regiments, the thronging crowd behind the ranks of soldiers.

These are people who are faithful to him, who are ready to die for him, because they think that he'll defend their rights. And they're right. He does not want the former France. He will enforce all those laws against the Bourbons voted by the revolutionary assemblies. There will be no quarter between this dynasty and him. Since the beginning, once they realized they couldn't buy him, haven't they sought to assassinate him? And now they are goading Europe to fight a war to put an end to him.

Those who are with the Bourbons are against me.

He compiles a list of thirteen traitors. The Talleyrands, Marmonts, Bourriennes, Montesquious will have their properties confiscated and will be sentenced to exile. Anyway, they have already crossed the northern frontier with Louis XVIII!

BUT HOW MANY people have stayed completely loyal to me, how many have resisted the lure of power?

He receives Hortense, who during his year of exile has not sent him a single letter or given him any sign but, so it is said, did pay her compliments to the enemy sovereigns. Now she appears in tears with her two children.

'I would never have thought that you would renounce my cause,' he says.

Naturally she has good excuses. Who doesn't, even for the vilest betrayals? She wanted to stay at her mother's side. Josephine de Beauharnais was ill; could her daughter leave her? And before dying, he knows, Josephine danced with the Tsar and the King of Prussia at Malmaison. Hortense was thinking of her children's future, she goes on.

'You shouldn't have stayed in France,' Napoleon interjects. 'A piece of black bread would have been preferable. Your behaviour has been that of a child. When one has shared a family's elevation, one must share its misfortune.'

She cries, sobs even. *Mercy for her. For them all. If I condemned them, who would stay with me? Marie Walewska.*

She comes to see him, and he exchanges a few words with her. But his ardour has gone. He holds her in high esteem; he wants to protect her, her and her son. Who knows what the future holds? She must be free from need. But take up together again? He can't. Something is dead in him. Not just love for Marie

Walewska, but the hope without which there are no profound feelings, no attraction towards another person.

HE OFTEN FEELS weary but needs to master his fatigue. Reviews, parades, councils, official receptions, and even parties at the Tuileries or the Élysée, where he takes up residence on Monday 17 April. The Tuileries are too vast for a man on his own, as he now is.

He manages to work twelve or fifteen hours a day as in the past. And he devours the nights. He wants to see everything, think everything, organize everything, get everything moving. He must. He is the only source.

He tells everyone, 'France's destinies are here; attend to them day and night.' They must get in money to equip the army, 'I have a hundred thousand men I cannot put to use for lack of funds to dress and equip them.'

He visits major works projects in different parts of Paris because he must show himself, make people feel that his confidence in the future is the same as it was before.

He visits the École Polytechnique, the orphans of the Legion of Honour, St-Denis, the Invalides, the Muséum, David's studio, the Opéra, the Théâtre Français. He goes to mass. He dines with Hortense, Lucien, Joseph, Jérôme and his mother, all of whom have come back to Paris. He has forgotten his grievances against his brothers. They are his brothers.

He is indefatigable.

But suddenly his head becomes heavy. He feels his whole body crumple as if he wanted to retreat inside himself. He dozes off, then wakes with a start. Around him everything is silent. People are observing him. He shakes himself, walks away. His legs are leaden; his belly drags him down. The lower half of his body hurts. He is going to take himself in hand, recover his energy, mount his horse despite the pain he feels. But energy is not élan. It is as if he didn't have confidence, although destiny, he tries to convince himself, has just proved that it is still giving him his chance.

But something isn't there any more.

He receives the women from his past, one after the other, Madame Duchâtel, Mademoiselle Georges. He is temporarily distracted. He forces himself to smile, but boredom sets in. He gets up, goes back to his study. He questions his secretaries. There are no letters from the Empress.

He has seen Méneval driven out of Vienna, where Napoleon had charged him to remain at Marie Louise's side. Méneval told him the situation, hanging his head and hesitating, but he only had to say a few words for Napoleon to guess.

Marie Louise has refused to write to me. Marie Louise has been seduced by Count Nipperg. Marie Louise has entrusted my son to the Emperor of Austria to make an Austrian prince of him. Marie Louise wants a separation.

My son, lost.

He wants to forget him, hide his loss.

He tells the senators, 'I set great store on entering the walls of Paris on the anniversary of the day four years ago when the whole population of this capital gave me such touching proof of the interest it had in the affections that are closest to my heart.'

But I know my son is lost. How can I have hope now? All that's left is its small change: energy, will, determination.

That's all I have.

I don't want to think about my wife or my son any more. I don't want to know anything. They are prisoners. That's all there is to it.

He dictates a note for Caulaincourt. 'We must bring out the horror that lies behind Austria's conduct. Méneval will speak of the grief the Empress felt when they tore her away from the Emperor. She didn't sleep for thirty days after His Majesty embarked. He will stress that the Empress really is a prisoner, since she has not been allowed to write to the Emperor.'

There's the official version. I don't want to hear any other. I can't.

He looks at his son's portrait, and suddenly, despite himself, tears stream down his face.

Carnot has just come in. I must turn away to hide this emotion, this grief, from the minister of the interior.

He begins to walk with a slow, heavy tread.

'The work of fifteen years has been destroyed,' he says. 'It cannot be restored. It would need twenty years and two million men. In any case I desire peace and I will only obtain it through victories.'

He goes up to Carnot. 'I do not want to give you false hopes; I will let it be said there are negotiations, but there are none. I foresee a difficult struggle, a long war. To withstand it the nation must support me; in return for which it will demand its freedom. And it will have it.'

Carnot is an old revolutionary. Here are words he likes to hear.

'The situation is new,' continues Napoleon. 'I ask no more than to be enlightened.'

He lowers his head.

'I am growing old. At forty-five one is no longer what one was at thirty! The repose of a constitutional king may suit me.'

He sighs.

'It will suit my son even more.'

My lost son.

He turns his head. He's afraid he'll cry again.

HE MUST NOT let himself go.

He addresses a parade of National Guards at the Tuileries. There are several thousand of them. He walks slowly along their ranks. He feels them quivering with enthusiasm. Has he ever had such determined troops? He listens to the spokesman who, stepping forward from the front rank, delivers his speech. A short man, his voice is choked with emotion.

'We have welcomed you enthusiastically because you are a man of the Nation, the defender of our Nation and you will protect the people's rights.' He calls for the people of the suburbs to be armed; they are determined to hurry to the borders, 'to rush upon the aristocrats'.

That would be one path, to let the revolutionary storm break, whip it up, let oneself be borne along by it.

'Reverses have forged the character of the French people anew,' Napoleon merely responds. 'They have regained that youth which, twenty years ago, stunned Europe.'

But he cannot, nor does he want to, go beyond that.

He needs National Guards, soldiers and subalterns, but he also needs Fouché, Molé and even Soult who, Louis XVIII's minister of war yesterday, now pledges allegiance; he has made him chief of staff of the army.

I receive Benjamin Constant, the writer who calls himself a liberal who, on 19 March, the eve of my return to the Tuileries, was still comparing me in his articles to Genghis Khan, Attila, Nero — an ogre!

But I am forging ahead with drafting the Additional Act of the Constitution of the Empire, which provides for an elected Chamber of Representatives and a Chamber of Peers appointed by the Emperor and his heirs.

These are the people, Benjamin Constant, Molé and Fouché, who form important people's opinions. Without them, what can I do?

Constant says, 'All sovereignty lies with the people.' And Molé immediately protests against this dictum 'worthy of '93'. They raise the spectre of Robespierre; they point to the shadow of the guillotine.

He must reassure these people.

'We must use the Jacobins now to confront our most pressing danger,' Napoleon explains to Molé. 'But have no fear; I am here to stop them. They will not go further than I wish.'

Anyway, who will decide the future? The Benjamin Constants, Molés and Fouchés, who want elections and the assemblies to meet on 1 June? Or me, on the battlefield, in this inexorable war forced on me?

If I am the victor, all their intrigues and schemes will be swept aside and I will do what I please. If I am defeated, they will all be happy to bury me, whatever the conditions and whatever modifications I have accepted to the Constitution of the Empire. So I might as well give in. Let the elections take place. The delegates will assemble on 1 June.

He says, 'I have renounced the idea of a great Empire, of which, in the last fifteen years, I have only laid down the bases. My goal was to organize a grand European federation, a system, I had chosen as in tune with the spirit of the century and conducive to the progress of our civilization. My goal henceforth is solely to increase France's prosperity by the consolidation of public liberty.'

Let them vote then! Let Fouché intrigue to have men elected whom he can manipulate. If I return victorious from the imminent war, none of this will have any weight, and if I am defeated . . . what importance will these votes have? Where will I be? Dead, I hope. But I know death can slip out of one's grasp.

I FEEL DEATH though, both present and absent.

It is here, in Malmaison's garden where he is walking with Hortense.

He cannot look at these trees without remembering the fêtes held here, the joyful gatherings.

All that's left are shadows. Josephine is dead. Pauline, who presided over the entertainments, the balls, Pauline so insouciant and insolently beautiful, is a prisoner of the Austrians at Viareggio. Elisa is at Brünn in Moravia, also interned, like Caroline, who the Austrians are still holding with her children in Trieste. All my sisters who shone here at Malmaison in the days of glory and success! And Murat, that fool Murat, who used to swagger about on Caroline's arm, has been defeated by the Austrians after attempting to take control of Italy and keep his Kingdom of Naples. He has landed near Cannes, defeated, a fugitive, and now he is offering me his services.

Such are men.

Napoleon leaves Malmaison. He dozes in the berline that takes him back to the Élysée. He is exhausted.

IT IS JUST one of those moments when fatigue catches up with him. He has a bath. He feels anguish at seeing in the mirror what his body has become. His belly is so prominent that the tails of his shirt stick out of his trousers and it's hard doing up his waistcoat. He runs his hand over his skull and brushes a few locks forward. Now he really is the 'little shaven head' the soldiers call him.

He calls Marchand. His valet helps him dress. Then, returning to his study, he examines the reports of the spies who are watching Fouché even though he is minister of police.

But how can one trust Fouché? That man knows how to quell the royalist rebellion that has arisen in the west, encouraged by Wellington, but he is also capable of planning for my defeat to ensure a regime to suit his purposes after my fall. That is why he has influenced the elections to the Chamber of Representatives taking place at the end of May. That is why his emissaries are in contact with Metternich.

He sends for Fouché.

He has threatened the Duke of Otranto so many times already! So many times he has been irritated and fascinated by his impassivity, the heavy eyelids hiding his gaze, his complexion as pallid as Talleyrand's.

'You are a traitor, Fouché,' he says to him scornfully. 'I should have you shot.'

Fouché does not move, but simply murmurs through barely parted lips, 'Sire, I do not share Your Majesty's opinion.'

To hell with Fouché!

Napoleon's whole body quivers with anger. He shouts, 'I am being driven down a path that is not mine. I am being weakened, put in chains. France seeks me, but it can't find me any more. It is wondering what has become of the former Emperor.' He cries, 'The priority is public safety!'

Then, with a weary gesture, he signals to Fouché to go. He doesn't want any gallows, any guillotine. The sword will decide.

ON THIS SUNDAY, 28 May 1815, he strides briskly out and mounts his horse. He sees the bayonets of the soldiers drawn up on the place du Carrousel.

He is going to review them. *Everything depends on them and me.*

XXVIII

HE GLANCES AT THE results of the vote. The Additional Act of the Constitution of the Empire has been passed, with 1,532,000 in favour, and 4,802 against. He pushes the document away. More than three million people didn't vote. He shrugs his shoulders.

Cowards and waverers only make history when heroes are not in charge. If I am conquered or die, it is the mediocrities who will govern France.

He picks up another piece of paper. It bears the names of the delegates who will make up the House of Representatives. He glances through it rapidly.

There is only a handful of Jacobins, perhaps forty, and eighty deputies loyal to me. The rest, the majority, fear me, and only think of their property; they are called liberals.

He still needs them. He crumples up the piece of paper. This chamber will be no easier to win over than the one he faced on 18th Brumaire at St-Cloud.

They will stab me if they know me to be weak; they will suffer me if I am strong. And either way they will prattle and be unable to make a decision.

Now, he must choose the 177 hereditary peers. He writes down the names of the generals who are loyal to him – Drouot, Bertrand, Cambronne, Exelmans, Bédoyère – then he writes the name of Sièyes. The revolutionary spy, his ally and rival from the time of 18th Brumaire is still here. Then he adds the names of those of his brothers who have come back to Paris: Joseph, Lucien, Jérôme.

He breaks off.

Where are the people in all this? Where are those peasants, those NCOs, those soldiers who have taken me from Golfe Juan to the Tuileries? Where are those men whose prefects say they're enrolling in the army to rush to the frontiers, working unpaid on fortifications and responding to the levies with astonishing enthusiasm?

He looks for the report from the prefect of Mont Blanc *département*: '5,000 men – volunteers, recalled or retired – have left in two months, more than at any time during the Revolution.' In the Lower Rhine the 7th battalion of the National Guard has asked to be incorporated into the Grand Army to be sure of fighting.

He gets up, paces about his study. He is overwhelmed by emotion. He sends for Davout, and the moment the marshal appears, he cries, 'The French Nation is beautiful: noble, sensitive, generous, always ready to undertake everything that is great and fine.'

He remembers what he said to those two English MPs who came to visit him on Elba. 'In France, the tail is good, the head is bad.' But he has to take this head into account: La Fayette, for instance, who has emerged from the past to be elected a member of the House of Representatives. There are six hundred like him, staunch royalists, just waiting for the defeat of the people's Grand Army so they can finally govern as they please.

HE SEES THEM sitting around him on the vast stage that has been erected on the Champ-de-Mars on 1 June 1815, for the grand assembly which is to record the results of the elections.

The cannon boom. The fanfares sound. The troops march past. Facing him, sitting in an amphitheatre constructed opposite the military school, there are thousands of participants, perhaps fifty thousand, and all around, on the Champ-de-Mars, hundreds of thousands of spectators. He feels cramped in his bright red tunic and ermine-lined, gold-embroidered coat, in his white satin culottes.

He wanted all this, though; this ceremony, known as the ceremony of the Champ-de-Mai, must be a new coronation, that of a new Empire.

It is a beautiful day. They celebrate mass. He remembers Notre Dame, Josephine. Distractedly he hears the herald proclaim, 'In the name of the Emperor, I declare that the Additional Act of the Constitution of the Empire has been accepted by the French people.'

The grand chamberlain steps forward and presents him with a

copy of the act. Napoleon gets up, signs. He looks at the crowd stretching into infinity. He could have mobilized these people, swept away all these dignitaries, started another revolution. He didn't want to. He is a man of order. But he knows that his strength comes from this crowd.

He flicks back the tails of his coat, takes a few steps.

'Gentlemen, electors of the colleges of the *départements* and *arrondissements*, deputies of the armies on land and sea present in the Champ-de-Mai . . .' He looks at the crowd, then, in a loud voice, goes on. 'Emperor, consul, soldier, I owe everything to the people. In prosperity, in adversity, on the battlefield, in the council, on the throne, in exile, France has been the sole and constant object of my thoughts and actions . . . Tell the citizens that circumstances are perilous, that with union, energy and perseverance we will emerge victorious from this struggle of a great people against its oppressors.'

He raises his voice still more. 'Frenchmen, my will is that of the people. My rights are theirs. My honour, my glory, my well-being can only be the honour, glory and well-being of France!'

The cheers roll back and forth.

He waits, then cries, 'I swear to observe and to cause to be observed the Constitution of the Empire.'

The officers draw their swords and shout, 'Long live the Emperor! Long live the Empress! Long live the King of Rome!'

He distinctly hears in the uproar voices yelling, 'We will go and find them!' Behind him the dignitaries protest.

Only the people understand what I feel.

He walks forward as the standard-bearers of the army, the Guard and the National Guard present their flags at the foot of the pyramid-shaped stage.

At his feet is a bristling sea of flags, sabres and bayonets. The cannon of the Tuileries, the military school, Montmartre and the chateau of Vincennes drown out the shouts of 'Long live the Emperor.'

It is the sabre and the cannonball, once again, that will decide my destiny.

WHAT ELSE CAN I rely on?

On 3 June he is brought the results of the election for president of the House of Representatives.

He is indignant.

'They are trying to insult me! They are trying to weaken me at this critical moment,' he shouts.

They have elected Lanjuinais. He is very familiar with this man who was counsel at the Parliament of Rheims and who was elected to the revolutionary assemblies; he made him a senator, then saw him vote against the consulate for life and the Empire. *Lanjuinais even opposed sentencing Cadoudal's accomplices! He drew up the act of abdication in 1814 and was then made a peer of France by Louis XVIII. And this is who they elect. To thwart me. I could dissolve the chamber.*

He grimaces contemptuously. A pain flares up in his right side. He shrugs his shoulders.

'These men can't even unite with me, the man who alone can protect them against everything they fear. We can only defend the Revolution by cannon now, and which of them can fire one of those?'

But I need these people.

He sinks into a chair and props his head on his hands.

What can I do? Fight and win.

HE DICTATES HIS instructions to Davout.

'Give orders to Marshal Grouchy, who will be commander-in-chief of the cavalry, to be at Laon on 5 June so that we can take the field on the 10th. The Guard must be fully provisioned and ready to fight from the 10th. You will seal off all communications across the north, the Rhine and the Moselle. No carriage or stagecoach should be allowed through. You will leave Paris on 8 June. Going by Lille, you will establish an espionage office and gather the latest information on the enemy's position. Send for Marshal Ney; if he wishes to be involved in the first battles, tell him he should go to Avesnes where my headquarters will be. Transport must be got ready without people knowing, so that I can leave two hours after having given the order.'

*There. The wheels are turning again. They will grind men down
and perhaps crush me.*

The secretary hands him a letter from Murat, who again begs
to serve in the French army.

Napoleon throws it on the ground, starts to dictate.

'The Emperor cannot employ a man who, a year ago, betrayed
the French. This year you have compromised France with your
premature attack on the Austrians.'

There is nothing else to say.

But a few hours later, when he reviews the 13th regiment of
dragoons on place Vendôme, he remembers Murat's heroic
charges.

Time is cruel to men. He shrinks down in his saddle and
hunches forward as if his whole body was dragging him towards
the ground. Where is Muiron, who threw himself in front of him
on the bridge at Arcola to save his life? Dessaix, Lannes, Duroc,
Bessières?

*Death hasn't wanted me on the battlefield. It refused to obey me
at Fontainebleau. Let her not forget me if the battle I am going to
fight is lost.*

HE RETURNS SLOWLY to the Élysée on this Monday, 5 June
1815.

An officer comes towards him in the palace entrance. He hands
him a dispatch.

Napoleon reads. Everything becomes cloudy. His legs slip from
under him.

When he emerges from the darkness officers are bent over
him. And he sees the anguish in their eyes. His face is wet. They
have splashed it with water. He has fainted, they murmur.

He stands up, starts walking slowly. He realizes he is holding
the letter in his hand. He stops, reads it again.

Marshal Berthier is dead. The Prince of Neufchâtel, detained
in Bamberg by the Austrians, has thrown himself out of a window.

*Berthier, with me on every campaign, the chief of staff who
understood me before I had even finished explaining my plans;
Berthier, who only betrayed me at Fontainebleau, who fled with Louis*

XVIII and was probably trying to get back to me; Berthier, wracked with remorse, who has chosen death.

Berthier, whom my army will miss. My non-commissioned officers and soldiers want to fight, but where are my generals, where are Lannes, Duroc, Bessières, Berthier? Ney is almost mad. Soult has betrayed me, and he is not a good chief of staff. What does Grouchy amount to? Davout, the best, must stay in Paris; who shall I leave behind me otherwise?

And I have to fight all Europe, more than a million men, and all England's money!

He walks over to Mollien. He says in a weary voice, 'Berthier is dead.' Then, walking away, as if talking to himself, 'Destiny has changed for me. I have lost a helper nothing can replace.'

HE IS IMPATIENT to join the army, be on the battlefield. *Let the last test begin. But, on 7 June, I still have to give the speech from the throne to the Chambers of Representatives and Peers. They watch my every move, waiting for me to falter.*

It is like a prelude to war. He clenches his teeth. He speaks in a powerful voice. 'The army and I will do our duty. You, peers and representatives, set the Nation an example of confidence, energy and patriotism and, like the senate of a great nation of antiquity, be resolved to die rather than survive the dishonour and degradation of France. The sacred cause of the country will triumph.'

They applaud, but how many are ready to make this sacrifice? The number doesn't much matter, because what counts is the outcome of the war.

Now I must attend to every detail.

'It has pained me to read,' he dictates to Davout, 'that the men of the two regiments that left this morning have only one pair of shoes each. The stores have them; the men must be provided with two pairs in their packs and one on their feet.'

He dictates like this all day, consults maps, holds final reviews; time melts away.

On Sunday 11 June he attends a mass at the Tuileries, then receives a delegation from the Houses.

These men will outlive my soldiers.

He goes up to them, stares at them until they lower their eyes.

'I will set off tonight to put myself at the head of my armies,' he says. 'The movements of the different enemy corps make my presence there indispensable.'

He walks away then returns with an assured step. Who are they? Prattlers! When the cannonballs start falling, puncturing ribcages, what will they be doing?

'This is a serious crisis we face,' he continues. 'Let us not imitate the example of the late Empire which, threatened on all sides by barbarians, earned the ridicule of posterity by indulging in abstract discussions while the battering ram was breaking down the gates of the city.'

He crosses his arms.

'Help me save the country.'

He turns his back on them and in his study dictates, 'Hostilities will commence on 14 June.'

He swiftly consults the dispatches. The coalition armies, Russian, Austrian, Dutch, English and Prussian, are converging on Belgium.

It is time.

He goes into the dining room. His brothers Joseph, Lucien and Jérôme are waiting for him, surrounding their mother.

He must be light-hearted since they are all grave and Hortense is grimacing to stop herself crying.

When Hortense's children come in, followed by Joseph's, he embraces them.

Where is my son?

He goes to the salon. The ministers are waiting for him. They will form a Grand Council with Lucien and Joseph, which will deliberate on Wednesdays. But decisions will still be taken by the Emperor, who will be kept informed by courier every day.

He jokes and bids farewell to the wife of General Bertrand. He leans towards her.

'As long as we don't miss the island of Elba,' he says, smiling.

He goes into his study. He looks at his papers. He could, as he has already done twice, burn the most secret of them. He pushes them aside with his hand.

Nothing is ever lost. And if he should lose this time, what would be the use of destroying his secrets, since this is the last act of the last game – the last resort.

He knows that.

He gets into his berline at four in the morning on Monday, 15 June 1815.

PART EIGHT

*I offer myself as a sacrifice to the
hatred of France's enemies*

12 June 1815 to 15 July 1815

XXIX

He opens his eyes, lifts his head. The post house at Villers-Cotterêts: horses and postilions are being changed. He hears a few shouts of 'Long live the Emperor!' 'Quick, quick,' he murmurs.

They must open the campaign before Wellington's army in Brussels and Blücher's, which is marching on Namur from the south, have linked up. He will try to put the 120,000-strong Army of the North, which he has decided to command, between the two armies, then fight each of them in turn. This should allow him to occupy Brussels on 17 June, he thinks. Then he will see. He cannot think beyond that.

The coalition has assembled over a million men and I only have 300,000 soldiers to defend all our frontiers. But we must fight with the forces we have, because Europe wants to bring France to its knees.

He tells Bertrand, who is sitting opposite him, that they will cross the Sambre at Charleroi, then march towards the crossroads at Quatre Bras, where the roads from Namur to Nivelles, and from Charleroi to Brussels, meet. Whoever holds Quatre Bras holds Belgium.

Quick, let's be off.

The carriage lurches violently into motion. He lowers his head, closes his eyes. There's a searing pain in his stomach and then it feels as if scalding, thick, black blood is flooding through his entrails and all his veins are swelling as if they are about to burst. He has the humiliating, unshakeable, exhausting conviction that blood, rather than piss and shit, is going to spurt out of him.

He stifles a cry of pain. The coach jolts across the paving stones and bumps over the ruts gouged out by the rain, and the pain takes hold and spreads out through his body. He sighs. He must contain it, prevent it taking him over.

He reaches Laon on Monday, 12 June 1815 at midday.

Maps! Unit strengths!

He wants to study, investigate. What is Soult, the chief of staff, doing? What is Davout, the minister of war, doing?

'I have not found the army provisions I had been promised at Laon or Soissons,' he dictates.

The aides-de-camp bring dispatches, which he glances through. The troops are advancing too slowly. He goes out into the doorway. This horde of infantry, artillery caissons, supply wagons and baggage is his army! The men are already worn out. Their packs are crammed with four days' bread and a full complement of ammunition because there aren't enough transports for the cartridges.

He stops at the side of the road for a moment. The soldiers recognize him and shout and wave their caps.

This army is a French army. The Belgians, the Dutch and all the others, who once followed me cheering through the streets of Amsterdam and Anvers, are on Wellington and Blücher's side now. All Europe is against me, just as it was against the Convention.

He begins to dictate a proclamation to these soldiers of all ages. It will be dated 14 June.

'Soldiers, today is the anniversary of Marengo and Friedland, which twice decided the fate of Europe. We were too generous after Austerlitz, and Wagram too. We believed the protestations and oaths of the princes we allowed to remain on their thrones. But today, allied against us, they begrudge France its independence and most sacred rights ... A moment of prosperity blinds them! If they enter France, they will find their graves there.'

His chin sinks onto his chest.

If I lose, let this battle bury me.

'Soldiers,' he continues, 'we have forced marches to make, battles to fight, perils to face, but with constancy victory will be ours; the rights and honour of the country will be reclaimed. For every Frenchman with a heart, the moment has come to conquer or die.'

HE SETS OFF for Avesnes, Beaumont and Charleroi. It rains ferociously and the carriage gets bogged down; the day is airless and muggy; sometimes a cold wind drives the rain along in gusts.

He mounts his horse. Every step it takes is painful, a heavy jarring ache in his groin.

Don't feel any of it.

He stops at a mill between Charleroi and Fleurus. The sky has cleared. He slowly climbs to the top of the building. In the distance he sees the dark flood of Zeithen's Prussian army. This is who they will attack tomorrow, 16 June.

He walks slowly back down. His feet stick in the muddy ground. Every movement is painful.

A curse on this body.

He sighs involuntarily. He sees a building ahead, a roadside inn that affords one a view over the Sambre valley. It is called the Bellevue. He stands outside it for a moment. Passing troops raise their muskets and shout, 'Long live the Emperor.'

When he notices the chair La Bédoyère has brought out for him, he sinks into it and watches the men file by until their faces start to fade and their shouts recede. He wakes up with a start. The troops are still passing. He sees Ney, Soult and the officers of his staff. He gets up.

'Ney, drive the enemy back on the Brussels road and take up position at Quatre Bras.'

Then he turns to Soult. 'It is possible that an important action may take place tomorrow.'

He begins to dictate orders but then has a moment of doubt. Does Soult understand? He remembers Berthier. He never used to say more than a few words to the Prince of Neufchâtel, but Berthier always understood, intuiting what he left unsaid, filling in the gaps, seeing the orders reached the correct parties. What can Soult do?

But who else can help me? Ney looks and speaks like a madman. Grouchy is a mediocrity without initiative. Where are Berthier, Lannes, Bessières, Duroc? Dead.

He sits back down. He sees General Gérard approaching, a haggard look on his face. Napoleon gets up and walks towards him. One always receives bad news on one's feet. Gérard explains that Lieutenant-General Bourmont, his chief-of-staff Colonel Clouet, Major Villoutreys and other officers have gone over to the enemy. Gérard holds out the letter that Bourmont has left him. 'I do not want to contribute to the creation of a bloody despotism in France,' Bourmont says. 'I will not appear in foreign ranks. They will get no information from me.'

Bourmont will give them everything he knows, the orders he's received, our unit strengths, the plan of campaign. Everything. Napoleon despises this man who served in the princes' army in 1791, and fought in the Vendée.

Bourmont was Pichegru's friend. He has gone over to the English with the Army of Portugal. I had him arrested once. Then I promoted him. And now, of course, he is betraying me again.

'Blue is blue and white is white,' Napoleon says with a grimace of disgust.

NEWS ARRIVES that Zeithen's Prussians are falling back, the first battle is ending in victory: 1,500 prisoners, six cannon taken, four Prussian regiments crushed.

But who's this? Not Blücher, just one of his columns. Where's Ney? Has he taken the crossroads at Quatre Bras?

Napoleon mounts up. He is exhausted and dozes in the saddle. At Charleroi he barely acknowledges Madame Puissant d'Hensy, the owner of the beautiful house he has commandeered. He wants maps in his room and reports on the hour – or more frequently if necessary – on the movements of the Prussian troops. Has Ney taken Quatre Bras? Where is Drouet d'Erlon's corps, which is meant to be joining me in attacking Blücher tomorrow?

He feels he is talking and dictating to no avail. Soult listens, Grouchy and Ney get his messages, but they don't understand them, they don't carry them out.

I must be more specific so that they will follow my orders to the letter.

'I will be at Fleurus between ten and eleven; if the enemy are in Sombreffe, I intend to attack them. I will even attack them in Gembloux and take that position, my intention being to start tonight, and operate against the English with my left wing commanded by Ney.'

But he is still not satisfied with what he dictates. Too many secondary details.

But what can I do, seeing as they don't understand what I want, and, if they do, don't carry it out?

Where are Berthier, Duroc, Bessières, Lannes? Dead.

He does not sleep and at six in the morning, on Friday, 16 June 1815, he is pacing about the house. He wakes up his aides and dictates new orders: Grouchy to take the right wing, Ney the left, and he will take the centre.

He rides up to the advanced posts, gives the order to attack and advances with the front ranks. Then he joins the Guard in the village of Ligny. They must take the heights at Bussy. *Forward, my Old Guard!*

He watches the bayonet charge through his eyeglass. Blücher's Prussians are falling back. 'The fate of this war may be decided in three hours,' he announces. 'If Ney carries out his orders well, not a single one of that army's cannon will escape.'

WHAT IS Ney doing? Where is Drouet, who should be supporting me so that I can envelop the remains of Blücher's army? It hasn't been wiped out, although cavalry charges have cut it to pieces; Blucher himself was knocked from his horse and wounded, but his uhlans saw him and he was rescued. The Prussians have lost 25,000 men, and us 8,500.

He walks over the battlefield. Wounded and dead lie jumbled together in the burnt wreckage of Ligny, the bodies, Prussian and French, entangled. They fought with bayonets, even with the butts of their muskets.

Ligny church changed hands several times. They have won a victory. But still Blücher is withdrawing in good order.

What is Ney doing? Why are Drouet and his entire corps of over 6,000 men going back and forth, from Ney to me and from me to Ney, without doing any fighting? What are these poorly transmitted, unexecuted orders?

He upbraids Ney: 'Why such uncertainty, such sluggishness? You have just wasted three hours!'

The English have now retrenched and are holding Quatre Bras, when, a few hours ago, Ney could have easily swept them aside.

They must attack; break through this resistance. He tells

Grouchy, 'While I march on the English, you will set off in pursuit of the Prussians.'

He rides forward in the rain. Cannonballs begin to fall nearby. An enemy battery must have found them and taken them as its target. But he doesn't break into a gallop. He goes at his own pace. These explosions, these showers of stones and gun flashes, distract him from the insistent pain that returns as soon as the bombardment ceases, and he dismounts with a dull, nagging ache punctuated by brief, agonizing flare-ups.

SUDDENLY a storm breaks. Torrential rain blots out the horizon. He feels water soaking through his coat, seeping into his boots, running down his skin.

An aide-de-camp reports that the English are abandoning Quatre Bras, fighting every inch of the way. Forward! Galloping at the head of cavalry of the Guard, he forgets his body. The rain lashes down, and the shot and shell of the retreating English whistle past. He braces himself in the saddle, digging his spurs in hard. All he is now is a will: the will to reach that building on higher ground which he has identified from maps, the inn of La Belle Alliance.

Once there, he dismounts, and walks a little way down the Brussels road. Facing him, on the other side of a hillocky valley dotted with clumps of trees and hedges, rise the slopes of Mont-St-Jean. Despite the persistent rain, he can see the English; they are fortifying their position. So he has not destroyed them; he has not driven a wedge between Wellington and Blücher. That means Grouchy will have to repulse the Prussians, and then he will smash the English tomorrow.

The barrage continues. Slowly, indifferently, he walks away. Will I die here? Why not? He rides off again, against the tide of troops marching over Mont-St-Jean. He stares at these exhausted, mud-spattered soldiers, who still raise their muskets when they see him and shout, 'Long live the Emperor!'

Shivering, he turns his head away.

He has a big fire lit in the Caillou farm so that he can dry out. But then his whole body hurts. He sets out again on foot, riding being too painful, and trudges slowly through the mud to the advanced posts.

Tiredness. Pain. Determination.

He returns to the Caillou farm. But how can he sleep on a night of waiting like this?

He goes outside again. The rain has stopped. The English bivouac fires are strung out in a brilliant line along the ridge of Mont-St-Jean.

Tomorrow . . .

When he gets back to the Caillou farm at one in the morning on Sunday, 18 June 1815, he dictates in a firm voice, 'Corps commanders will rally their troops, ensure arms are in working order and allow the soldiers to make soup so that each army corps, with its artillery and ambulances, will be ready and able to take up battle formation at nine o'clock precisely.'

The Emperor commands that the army be ready to attack at nine in the morning.

XXX

HE HAS SAT DOWN on the camp bed that has been set up in a little room on the ground floor of the Caillou farm. It does not even occur to him to lie down. He won't be able to sleep, he knows. He gets up, goes to the narrow window and then walks through the rooms on the ground floor full of officers dozing on bales of straw.

Through the open front door he hears the rain still falling and smells the reek of mud and sodden ground. He goes to the threshold. In the distance drums can be heard beating the reveille. Flickering bivouac fires stand out against the downpour. It is not cold, but he is shivering. He sees soldiers go past, their clothes soaked, their weapons running with water, their bodies close to collapse, worn out by fighting and the night they have just spent without shelter from the storm.

He remains standing in the doorway. He cannot take his eyes off the murky, twilight dawn. He looks towards Mont-St-Jean. The English are up there, deployed along the crest; his men will have to climb the side of the valley under a barrage of grapeshot, and before they even reach its ridge they will have to take those clusters of buildings the English are bound to have fortified: the chateau of Hougoumont on the right, La Haie Sainte farm in the centre, and Papelotte farm to the left.

It's hard breathing, as if his chest has been crushed. Every sort of pain has racked him for several days now, and yet still he must summon up enough energy for the day ahead.

He doesn't need to look at any more maps.

In my mind everything is clear and simple. First we will attack Wellington's right, at the chateau of Hougoumont; Wellington will siphon troops away from his centre to confront the threat. Then I will attack the centre, in the sector containing La Haie Sainte and Papelotte farms. Then Grouchy and his corps, which I have had recalled, will fall on Wellington's left.

In his mind's eye he sees every stage of the battle, including the denouement, when he will march on the village of Waterloo, which lies on the plateau beyond Mont-St-Jean farm. Then he will launch his troops against Brussels. And after that . . .

He still doesn't know. And this emptiness, this blackness, is like a rising tide, swamping every phase of the battle until it eradicates the certainty that he will be victorious. He is struggling to fix this conviction in his mind and yet it keeps on being engulfed.

He doesn't know any more. He wishes he could stifle the train of thought that's taking hold of him like an instinct, a mental reflex.

This will turn out badly. You cannot win again. None of them are here any more – Berthier, Lannes, Bessières, Duroc – to carry out your orders and develop your thoughts. The enemy are too numerous; even if you win now, you will lose afterwards.

HE DOESN'T WANT to hear this voice. The drums roll. He must be victorious or perish. He looks at the sky to the east. The weather is brightening. The rain has stopped. He goes back into the farm. The generals gather around him.

Drouot murmurs, 'We cannot join battle this morning. The artillery will get bogged down.'

General Reille nods his head. 'The coolness, tenacity and superior shooting of the English infantry make them well nigh impregnable,' he goes on. 'Before we can mount a bayonet attack, we should expect to lose half our attackers. But if we can't defeat them with a frontal attack, we can with a manoeuvre.'

Napoleon listens. The drums roll; the armies are in place.

'I know,' he says. 'The English are difficult to beat when they have taken up a position. I am going to manoeuvre.'

He looks hard at the officers. He sees on their faces the same anxiety and alarm and uncertainty he feels. They are his mirrors.

'We have ninety chances in our favour,' he declares before going out. 'Wellington is a bad general, I tell you; the English are bad troops, and this will be an affair of a single lunchtime.'

He closes his eyes because the sun is blinding now. It is boiling hot; it makes his blood pump harder and harder, as if, at any moment, all his tiredness were going to come spilling out.

NAPOLEON MOUNTS UP and gallops to the advanced posts. Firing has not begun yet. He stops on a low hill at the top of which stands Ronsomme farm. He can see a large part of the valley that stretches between the two plateaux, Mont-St-Jean, where at times he can see the red tunics of the English infantry, and La Belle Alliance, where the French are deploying in battalions.

He turns to Soult and dictates a new message for Grouchy: 'His Majesty desires that you direct your movements to draw nearer to us.'

Then he requests that his camp bed be set up in this farm. He wants to try to sleep for an hour.

HE WAKES UP after a few minutes and hears drums. The army is marching past towards the farm of La Belle Alliance, which is about one and a half kilometres north of Caillou farm.

Beautiful army! Grand Army!

He crosses his arms, overwhelmed with emotion. 'So many brave men.' He dictates an order. The Guard will position itself here, between Ronsomme farm and La Belle Alliance inn. And he will stay with it, in one or other farm.

IT IS ELEVEN THIRTY. Now is the time. *They have 84,000 men. We have 10,000 less. But I have often routed a larger opponent. And if Grouchy arrives, we will be in Brussels tomorrow.* He raises his arm.

The Guard's artillery opens fire on the Hougoumont chateau. This is the first phase, the attack on Wellington's right wing.

At twelve, the infantry commanded by Jérôme launches an attack. He sees them advancing, but then, before he even hears volleys or the crackle of fusillades, he sees them crumble.

Jérôme, whom he should be able to trust! Who can he replace him with? Has he any choice? Jérôme, who is wearing out his troops by sending them on murderous frontal attacks.

They've ground to a standstill. A pretty pass this is turning into!

He looks north-east to Papelotte farm, on his right. There's a cloud of dust, the sort an army corps on the march raises. Is it Grouchy? He orders scouts to be sent out.

It is one in the afternoon and now a prisoner is being brought to the Emperor: a Prussian black hussar, one of von Bülow and Blücher's troops. He is carrying a letter from Bülow to Wellington announcing the arrival of the Prussians.

Napoleon stares at the cloud of dust. How many men are there? Perhaps 30,000, if it's all Blücher's Prussians. But what to do? Grouchy is probably giving chase. And battle has been joined here. So they must be contained. Someone must march towards the village of Planchenoit, on my right; I'll give Marshal Mouton this job, and Ney will attack Wellington's centre.

The sun blazes down; it's swelteringly hot and sultry; every inch of his skin feels as if it is being stung by a thousand fiery needles. It is one thirty on Sunday, 18 June 1815.

WHAT IS Ney doing?

He is attacking the farm of La Haie Sainte without using any artillery. His infantry are being shot at point-blank range by the English entrenched in the farm; others are in the wheat fields, splashes of red pouring fire into Ney's cavalry.

Napoleon remains motionless on his horse. He feels himself the prisoner of an omnipresent pain that grips his whole body in a vice, clamping down on his shoulders and bloating his veins in a way he has never felt before. His legs and thighs are like lead.

What is Ney doing?

Now the marshal is charging at the head of his squadrons of cavalry. Horses tumble to the ground. An aide-de-camp shouts that the marshal has had his fifth horse shot from under him! What is he looking for – death? One charge follows another. The horses are so exhausted they cannot gallop by the time they get to the English muskets and cannon that cut them to pieces.

'The wretch!' shouts Napoleon. 'This is the second time in three days that he has jeopardized France's fate.'

But he must support him and try to take La Haie Sainte and Mont-St-Jean farm on the other side of the St-Jean plateau, whatever the cost.

He senses that the situation is changing so often and so fast that it is dictating what he must do. Where is Grouchy? He turns towards Soult. Has the message for Grouchy been delivered? By how many officers?

Soult has only sent one aide-de-camp when Berthier would have sent twenty!

Grouchy may not have received the order to join me.

This is how it is.

NAPOLEON URGES his horse slowly forward towards the Guard. The bearskins are lined up, motionless, muskets on guard.

He is going to send in the Young Guard first, to check the Prussians who are only three kilometres from La Belle Alliance inn and threatening to break through the entire right flank – *as far as me*. The village of Planchenoit must be taken and held at all costs.

He watches the grenadiers take up their positions, drummers at their head.

Then the Prussian artillery lets fly. He sees the flames rising up from Planchenoit. The Young Guard has taken it. But now the Prussians are streaming forward again in their thousands. Send in the Old Guard, then.

He goes to his grenadiers.

'My friends, here you are at the moment of reckoning. It is not a question of firing now. You must engage the enemy in hand-to-hand combat and drive them back at bayonet point into the abyss whence they have emerged to threaten the army, the Empire and France.'

The grenadiers move off. He is sure they will retake Planchenoit. But how many men will be left for the main attack northwards against Wellington and Mont-St-Jean?

The day is drawing to a close. The fires burning in Planchenoit light up the dusk. A wounded aide whispers that they fought hand to hand in the village; they shot at point-blank range, just like Ligny.

He listens. Now they must stake their all; they must break through the English lines with what's left of the Old Guard.

He approaches the 6,000 men, stands in their midst, then gives the signal. The Guard marches off, drums and bands at the heart of its squares, eagles unfurled. The supporting infantry shout, 'Long live the Emperor!' They climb the slopes to the Mont-St-Jean plateau as Napoleon looks at the remains of La Haie Sainte farm, which has been taken not long before. The Guard reaches the top of the slope.

Then suddenly red uniforms rise up out of the wheat and pour long, uninterrupted volleys of fire into the column. The Guard hesitates; the Guard retreats. English cannon bombard them with grapeshot. English cavalry charges.

A shout, 'Every man for himself!'

The regiments either side of the Guard break up. The fugitives scatter in what is now darkness. The English continue attacking; Zeithen's Prussians, who have joined them, charge. The French are swamped by sheer numbers.

Napoleon is on horseback in the middle of a square of the Guard which has remained unscathed amidst the charges, the cannonballs, the bullets. He draws himself up to his full height in the saddle. Now is the moment when he should be hit; now is when he should die. He urges his horse forward to the edge of the square.

These are the best, the 1st Battalion of the 1st Regiment of the grenadiers of the Guard. It is here, with them, that I should die.

But the bullets whistle past, cutting down men who are instantly replaced, and nothing hits me. Nothing. I am defeated and alive!

The square withdraws in good order. The band plays.

He rides his horse at a walk. He looks at the dismounted horde all around him, the groups of men fleeing and fighting amongst themselves to cross the bridge over the Dyle at Genappe. He gets off his horse and the square parts. He tries to stop the headlong flight, but the tide of fugitives sweeps him away. Voices shout in the darkness, 'The Prussians! The Prussians!'

Here are the uhlans storming through the streets, sabring, galloping too fast to see me and kill me.

Napoleon rides away.

SUDDENLY he can take no more. Paying no heed to the few riders surrounding him, he dismounts. Aides-de-camp busy themselves lighting a fire in a clearing. He sinks down onto a tree stump and hides his face. This is the end without end.

He gets to his feet and repeats to himself that he must see the game through. This is life. He owes it to the 30,000 or so who must have died in the battle. How many of the enemy? Barely half that, probably.

See it through. He rides with his little escort along roads jammed with fugitives. He murmurs, 'I sensed it would turn out badly.'

My destiny has come to pass.

On Monday 19 June, at nine in the morning, he reaches Philippeville.

Another day. Another battle. Living means seeing things through to the end.

'All is not lost,' he writes to Joseph.

> I estimate that, when all the troops have been rallied, I will have 150,000 men left. The braver federates and National Guard will provide me with a further 100,000, the battalions in depot 50,000. I will therefore have 300,000 soldiers to set against the enemy immediately. I will put pedigree horses in harness to pull the artillery. I will levy 100,000 conscripts. I will arm them with the royalists' and worthless National Guards' muskets. I will institute mass levies in the Dauphiné, the Lyonnais, Burgundy, Lorraine, Champagne. I will overwhelm the enemy. But people must help me, not deafen me. I am going to Laon, where I shall probably find troops. I have heard nothing of Grouchy; if he has not been taken prisoner, as I fear, I shall have 50,000 men in three days.
>
> Tell me what effect this horrible battle has produced in the Chamber.
>
> I think the deputies will be absolutely clear that their duty in this emergency is to unite with me in saving France. Prepare them to give me fitting assistance.
>
> Above all, courage and firmness.

He gets into the carriage of General Dupuy, who commands the garrison at Philippeville.

Courage! Firmness! Joseph certainly needs to hear those words. But he can imagine them – the Fouchés, the La Fayettes, the Lanjuinais, *all those chatterers in the Chamber of Representatives – already intriguing to get rid of me as they would have if I hadn't been victorious at Marengo and Austerlitz and even Wagram.*

He rocks from side to side as the carriage jolts over the bumps in the road. His body is worn out. He hasn't slept or taken a bath for days now; he hasn't eaten for three. But it's been better not to eat anything, so as to have nothing to bring back up. Because he would have pissed and shat blood, he's sure. He shuts his eyes; his body is painful and dirty. He needs a bath. He dreams of one as he surrenders to the swaying of the carriage. When he opens his eyes again he recognizes the French countryside, and its gentleness moves and calms him. Gradually, as they drive through Rethel and Laon, he feels something like peace stealing over him. Whatever happens now, whatever the outcome of the plots that must be brewing, he won't have any regrets. He has seen his destiny through. He will not come back from another island of Elba.

He sees the squares of the Guard in his mind, like blocks of black stone gradually hacked away. He hears the explosions, the shouts. Death has refused to take him again, but struck everywhere around him, as if she just wanted him alive.

This is my destiny.

He feels neither bitterness nor regret.

I attained fortune on a battlefield, and it has thrown me off on a battlefield too.

Whatever happens, I have fulfilled my destiny.

HE OPENS his eyes. Day has broken, Wednesday, 21 June 1815. The carriage drives over the cobbles of Paris. He looks at the still-deserted streets, the shops with closed shutters. It is barely six in the morning as they pass through the suburbs.

What should I do with the people? My only loyal followers have been the peasants, the working people and the soldiers!

With them, I could have, if I'd wanted . . .

His thoughts wander.

The carriage slows, stops.

He sees Caulaincourt waiting on the Élysée stairs.

XXXI

CLIMBING THE ÉLYSÉE STEPS, he finds it hard to breathe; all this dirt and tiredness are stifling, like a heavy yoke he has to shrug off. He murmurs to Caulaincourt following behind, 'I have been dealt a fatal blow.'

Then he goes into his study. He raises his arms. Marchand, his valet, bustles about, undresses him; he hears the bathwater running. At last.

'Well then, Caulaincourt, here's an event,' he goes on. 'A battle is lost. How will the Nation bear this reverse? Will the Chambers support me?'

While the bath is filling he throws himself on a sofa. He studies Caulaincourt, then Davout, La Valette, Maret and Regnaud de Saint-Jean-d'Angély, who file, one after the other, into his study and then his bathroom.

Ten days I've been riding through the mud in driving rain, ten days sleeping wherever and whenever I can, ten days barely eating, ten days fighting. And what have they been doing for these ten days? They have been waiting.

He listens to Caulaincourt. 'The news of your misfortunes has already leaked out. There is great agitation and the deputies seem more hostile than ever. It is to be feared that the Chambers will not live up to your expectations. I am sorry to see you in Paris, sire. It would have been preferable if you had not parted company with your army, since it is that which gives you your strength and your security.'

Napoleon shakes his head. This is where he wants the last act to be played out. Everyone must assume their responsibilities! He will not let himself be sidelined as he was in April 1814, when he was being betrayed in the capital while he was still fighting, and Paris was handed over to the coalition forces. He does not want any more of that. Everyone must make a clear choice. If he is to leave the stage, then it will be in conformity with every procedure, in the full light of day and truth. If he is to fight at the head of an army, then it will be with the assent of all. He has joined together the two ends of his life.

He watches the stunned dignitaries standing around him, as the bathwater gradually washes away the grime, tiredness and tension.

Do they understand that everything concerns me in a different way now? Another game is starting, separate to my destiny — a new play, and I am both an actor and witness in it. The person they knew as me has remained with the Old Guard on the slopes of Mont-St-Jean and the approaches to the village of Planchenoit.

I am listening to their talk. My brother Lucien wants another 18th Brumaire. Carnot asks me to declare 'the nation in danger'. Fouché and all the rest are intriguing to bring about my abdication.

He gets out of the bath, splashing the dignitaries, who step back as he is dressed.

'I know the La Fayettes and Lanjuinais want none of me,' he says. 'I know I embarrass them.'

He stops. They have heard it too, and they turn their anxious, lined faces to the windows: that uproar, those shouts like a breaking storm, 'Long live the Emperor! Long live the Emperor!' It is the people.

Napoleon goes to the window. He sees an enormous crowd surrounding the Élysée, gesticulating, shaking their fists. He recognizes the workers' smocks, the grey and black dresses of women from the suburbs.

He turns back towards the dignitaries, stretches out his arm. They see that, don't they? They can hear it, can't they?

But they are talking about the Chambers and a governmental commission Fouché has formed.

'I fear,' says Saint-Jean-d'Angély, 'that a great sacrifice may be necessary.'

D'Angély! Who I've done so much for!

'If the Emperor does not decide to offer his resignation of his own accord,' d'Angély goes on, 'it is possible that the Chamber of Representatives may dare to request it.'

He even adds in a whisper that the Chamber, which has declared itself in permanent session, might go so far as to proclaim his deposition.

Lucien explodes with indignation; Carnot protests. The

Emperor must declare himself dictator. Think of the people, the army.

Napoleon looks at them. He hears the shouting, which has grown even louder. The people are there. Very true. But what is one to do with them?

'My political life is over,' he murmurs.

Then he begins to pace slowly back and forth.

'The deputies wish to do violence to me, so I refuse to abdicate. I want to be left alone to think in peace.' He stops in front of Regnaud de Saint-Jean-d'Angély. 'Whatever the deputies do, I shall always be the idol of the people and the army.'

His voice is composed. How does this concern him? He is still on stage and yet he has already left it. He sees what's happening, analyses it, speaks his mind, and yet all the while there is another voice in him, murmuring:

The game is over. Your destiny is fulfilled. Fortune is abandoning you. She no longer follows your footsteps. She has given you everything. She cannot give you any more. She has given you your every wish and now she is leaving. To act, one must be convinced of one's good fortune. And I don't feel I'm in step with my destiny any longer. I am alone, with no one to guide me. I can still extract some favours by force, but these are illusions. My time is over.

'If I said a word,' he says, 'the deputies would be cowed into submission.'

He turns back to the window. The crowd is in even louder voice. 'Long live the Emperor!'

'But if I fear nothing for myself,' he adds, 'I fear everything for France. For if we quarrel amongst ourselves, we will share the fate of the later Roman empire: everything will be lost.'

HE LEAVES his apartments. The Élysée's passages are empty. He recognizes a figure coming towards him: General Thiébault.

He was in Portugal and Spain, where destiny began to desert me.

'Sire,' begins Thiébault, 'allow me to lay at your feet a devotion that is as profound as it is respectful.'

Here's a man not toadying to the victors.

'It is France we must think of now.'

Does he understand it is not a question of me any more?

'You represent its spirit of mercy now more than ever,' the general says.

I turn away. I don't want to hear that. The other play has begun.

He goes down into the gardens and walks calmly along the avenues. The shouts of 'Long live the Emperor' break like waves on the railings, even growing louder as darkness gathers, and there is a savage fervour in the voices, a sort of fury. It is like being on a battlefield before an attack. 'Long live the Emperor!'

He approaches Benjamin Constant, who is walking down one of the avenues. The writer is respectful and attentive. *This liberal has never had any love for me, but he has independence of mind, and he is like me now, on stage but out of the game.*

'It is not a question of me any more,' Napoleon begins. 'It is a question of France. They want me to abdicate. Have they considered the inevitable consequences of my abdication? To reject me when I landed at Golfe Juan, that I could have understood, but to abandon me today is beyond me. One does not overthrow a government when one's enemies are only a few leagues away. I am part of what the foreigners are attacking now, so I am part of what France should defend. In abandoning me, it abandons itself; it admits itself defeated.'

He stops and stares at Benjamin Constant for a long time.

'Pride is not deposing me, Waterloo is, fear is – a fear your enemies will profit from.'

He listens and sees Constant turning his head towards the Champs Élysées. The din is deafening; they can make out rhythmic chants of 'Down with the Bourbons! Down with the priests! Long live Napoleon!'

The Emperor resumes walking. He could . . .

'You see,' he says. 'It's not them whom I have showered with honours and riches. What do they owe me? I found them poor and I leave them poor. But they're lit up with national feeling; the voice of the country speaks through their mouths and, if I wanted to, if I gave them my permission, in an hour the rebellious Chamber would cease to exist.'

He stares at Constant, who remains silent.

'If I wanted to,' he repeats. 'But no, the life of a man is not worth that price; I did not come back from Elba for Paris to be drowned in blood.'

HE LEAVES Benjamin Constant and stops halfway up the steps. He hears the shouts and cries rising up into the night, 'Long live Napoleon!'

What if it was his duty to go to the people, put himself at their head, dismiss the representatives, and order a mass levy? But then what? He can't see the future; a black veil covers it. He cannot fight another Marengo or Austerlitz or Wagram.

He has come to the conclusion of his destiny.

General Bertrand's wife rushes up to him. 'Why did we leave Elba?' she cries.

She walks along beside him, wringing her hands. She is the daughter of General Dillon, an Irishman – in other words, slightly English.

'Free, enlightened Englishmen are the only people who could welcome the Emperor and understand him,' she says.

He goes into his study; his desk is covered with letters. He opens them, then suddenly throws them aside without reading them. What's the use?

Hortense appears, a distraught look on her face.

'You have dined, no doubt?' he asks her, getting to his feet. 'Will you keep me company though?'

But it only takes him a few minutes to eat dinner. The food seems to have no taste. He goes through to the salon. He sees his mother staring at him; his brothers, Jérôme, Lucien, Joseph, surround her. The family. He leads them into the garden.

He cannot even hold a son's hand, a wife's arm. He is alone with those he started out with. As if nothing had happened in between, as if destiny had already taken everything back.

NIGHT HAS FALLEN. He does not sleep. From time to time shouts still echo along the Champs Élysées.

The people are with me. But everyone else – the representatives, the dignitaries – are bent on saving themselves by ruining me. It is no use talking to them of France. Anyway, haven't I already made my choice?

He gets to his feet and starts to burn armfuls of papers without even sorting through them.

Everything is in my head. My memory and my mind are my only possessions. No one will ever be the owner of these. I will never abdicate from them.

He gets to his feet. An envoy from the Chamber is here already. *It is General Solignac, whom I have always ignored, despised even, despite him being with me on the 18th Brumaire, and dismissed for embezzling and refusing to present the accounts of his army. Now here he is, bringing me an ultimatum from the Chambers. They are giving me an hour to abdicate, otherwise I will be deposed!*

He doesn't give Solignac an answer. One ignores men like him.

He walks about his study. Now here comes Lucien, waving his arms and talking of the 18th Brumaire when the situation was far more precarious than at present.

'You have all the power!' Lucien cries. 'The foreigners are marching on Paris. Never was there a time when a military dictatorship was more legitimate.'

Napoleon approaches Lucien and takes him by the arm. Desire is the key, and he doesn't feel it any more.

'My dear Lucien,' he says in the calm, almost indifferent voice of someone observing events from a distance, 'it is true that on the 18th Brumaire the only thing on our side was the nation's welfare. Today we have every right but I must not make use of them.'

Fouché enters.

I despise this accomplice in every intrigue. Terrorist, regicide, ringleader of the conspiracy against Robespierre, head of police – this minister has betrayed me in every way he could. And now he has come to demand my abdication.

'Well, let it be as they wish,' Napoleon says. 'The future will decide if they have best served France by this course of action. They will be satisfied at least.'

He turns round. 'Prince Lucien, write this down,' he says, and begins to walk about his study, calmly dictating as he goes. He is in no hurry any more. He has reached the other shore. He looks back at the raging ocean he has crossed to reach this point in his life.

'People of France, in starting the war in defence of national independence,' he dictates, 'I reckoned on the concerted efforts and goodwill of everyone, and on the support of all the national authorities. I had grounds to hope for success. Circumstances appear to have changed.'

He looks at each of the dignitaries and ministers around him in turn.

'I offer myself as a sacrifice to the hatred of the enemies of France,' he says, then breaks off. He shrugs his shoulders.

What do they understand about me?

'May they be sincere in their declarations,' he resumes, 'that their animosity has only been directed at my person. My political career is at an end, and I proclaim my son, under the title of Napoleon II, Emperor of the French. The interest I bear my son prompts me to invite the Chambers to establish the regency without delay.

'Let all of you unite for the public safety, in order to remain an independent nation.'

IT IS DONE. He watches them leave.

They are in a rush to deliver the good news. Of course they won't establish the regency. Who cares about my son apart from me? And what am I to him? Submitting to the victors, they will forget the King of Rome, and all go over to the Bourbons.

He receives reports of Fouché and La Fayette's manoeuvrings. Only La Bédoyère in the Chamber of Peers has dared speak up for him. 'Woe betide those wretched generals who have already abandoned him in their haste to accept the law of foreigners,' La Bédoyère said. 'Where are their oaths now? Is it written that nothing but base words shall ever be heard within these walls?'

Poor La Bédoyère! Too courageous for all those schemers who want to see me leave because they are afraid the people will rise up.

He listens again. The same shouts are still coming from the streets: 'Long live Napoleon! Down with the Bourbons!' He walks through the deserted palace. He recognizes the silhouette of

Marshal Davout, Prince of Eckmühl, Duke of Auerstadt, *who is coming in the name of the Assembly to enjoin me to leave the premises.*

'Where do they want me to go?' he asks, and then stretches out an arm towards the gardens. 'You hear those shouts. If I wanted to put myself at the head of the people, who know instinctively what the nation truly needs, I would soon be finished with all those who have only been brave enough to face me when they knew I was defenceless. They want me to leave, do they?'

His whole body recoils with contempt. 'Well, it will cost me no more than everything else. Fouché tricks you all; he will be the last to be tricked and caught in his own nets! Louis XVIII will be brought back by the Allies, thanks to me.'

But still, if that's what they want. He has already left the stage.

He begins to sort through the last of his papers. He wants to leave the Élysée for Malmaison; they are quite capable of surrendering it to the Allies. Carnot is announced.

This man who voted against the Empire has already come to me at a critical time once before, after the Russian campaign.

Carnot is overwhelmed. He speaks with deep feeling. 'Do not go to England,' he says. 'You have aroused too much hatred there; you would be insulted by the vulgar. Go to America without delay. From there you will continue to make your enemies tremble. If France is destined to fall under the Bourbons' yoke again, your presence in a free country will sustain national feeling.'

This man is a patriot. Like La Bédoyère, like the people shouting.

'Farewell, Carnot,' Napoleon says, clasping him in his arms. 'I have got to know you too late.'

HE RETURNS to his desk, writes an official request for two frigates to be put at his disposal at Rochefort for travel to the United States. Then, slowly, looking around him, he makes his way towards the steps.

The uproar is deafening. The crowd has seen the carriage with its six horses and is shouting, 'Don't abandon us!'

He bows his head. Is it still him they are calling for and cheering? It seems as if they are addressing someone else.

What is done is done.

He will leave by the garden gate. His aides-de-camp will take the state carriage to distract the crowd. He turns back and looks at the palace. Then he gets into his carriage and, as it makes its way towards Chaillot, he leans out of the window to see the scaffolding flanking the Arc de Triomphe, which is still being built.

He knows he will never see this again. But these avenues he is passing along, this road he is taking to Rueil, this park he is walking in, these salons, these bedchambers – all this is his whole life passing before him and gathering together at its conclusion, echoing the earliest days of his glory.

He walks past a mirror; that fat, bald, sallow-complexioned figure whose features are drawn with tiredness, is him. *Where is the thin First Consul? Dead, like Josephine, like Duroc, like Bessières, like Lannes. Gone, like my son, like Marie Louise.*

He goes from room to room. He goes into Josephine's room, then leaves and sits down next to Hortense in the garden. He murmurs, 'I cannot accustom myself to living here without her. I keep thinking she is going to appear at any moment round a corner in the park, or from behind a bank of roses.'

He gets to his feet and walks alone through the garden where he has so often walked with all those people who were constructing the Empire with him, preparing his victorious campaigns; yesterday's courtiers and devoted ministers, today they are dead or gone over to his enemies.

He feels no regret, just the weight of time, the certainty that destiny has run its course, that he cannot start again.

NOW HE MUST prepare for the future. Barbier, the librarian, must send him books on America and a catalogue of everything that has been written on the campaigns of the various armies he has commanded for the last twenty years.

Here is a goal for his new life, wherever it will be lived. To fight with his mind, to live again through the workings of his memory and thoughts, and defy idleness. He feels a surge of energy. He dictates his final proclamation to the Grand Army: 'Soldiers, I will follow your steps although absent myself. You and I have both been slandered. Men unworthy to appreciate your endeavours have seen, in the marks of attachment you have given me, a zeal of which I was the only object. Let your future successes teach them that in obeying me it was our country that you served above all else and that if I have some share in your affection I owe it to my ardent love for France, our shared mother.'

He is deeply moved.

Will my solders hear this? Fouché and the others are trying to stifle my voice, which still worries them. Demonstrations in support of me are continuing in Paris. They must be trembling.

He resumes, 'Soldiers, save the honour, the independence of Frenchmen. Remain to the end as I have known you to be for the last twenty years and you will be invincible.'

HE GOES OUT into Malmaison's garden again, where he receives the banker Lafitte.

'The powers are not waging war against me exactly,' he says, 'but against the Revolution. They have only ever seen me as the representative, the man of the Revolution.'

He sighs.

'I long to leave France. Let me be given the two frigates I have asked for and I will set off immediately for Rochefort.'

He begins to walk through the gardens with Lafitte. He trusts this man who runs the Bank of France and who, he knows, administered Louis XVIII's treasury. What can one do without money? Nothing. So he must discuss money.

'I don't yet know what is in store for me,' he says. 'I am still in good health and I have another fifteen years ahead of me. I go to sleep and wake up when I wish; I can ride a horse for four hours at a stretch and work ten hours a day. My food is not expensive. I can live anywhere very well on a louis a day. We will see.'

He sits down. He has sent Lafitte three million in gold from the Tuileries treasury, 800,000 francs in cash, and what is left of the treasury on Elba. Not far off five million in all, no? With a gesture he refuses the banker's receipt. He trusts him, he repeats. Out of this sum he will have to provide for his brothers, his mother, the Imperial household, the Bertrands and the valets. There will be 100,000 francs for Jérôme and Madame Mère,

700,000 for Joseph, 250,000 to Lucien. Not forgetting Hortense, Marie Walewska, Madame Pellapra, Madame Duchâtel.

ONE AFTER another, the women of my life come to Malmaison. Marie weeps and pushes her son — my son — towards me.

He kisses the child. He has to contain the flood of emotion that chokes him.

Here's Léon, my other son, with his tutor. It's nine years already since that night when his mother Éléonore Denuelle de La Plaigne came to me. My whole life is gathering together here, except for my wife and legitimate son.

He walks off along the avenues of the park, then returns to Hortense, murmuring, 'How beautiful Malmaison is. Wouldn't it be wonderful if I could stay here, Hortense?'

He sits down in silence.

An officer of the National Guard comes up, out of breath. Blücher's Prussians are approaching. They may try to seize Malmaison.

He laughs. 'I have let myself be outflanked.'

Then slowly he goes back inside. A prisoner of the Prussians? Never. He hands Marchand a little bottle of red liquid that Doctor Corvisart has given him.

'See that I always have it on me; attach it to my jacket or some other part of my clothes, wherever I can get to it easily.'

He sees Marchand's panic-stricken expression. He pinches his ear. He doesn't want to die if he can live another life, he murmurs. But imprisoned here, on French soil, is out of the question. He prefers death to such humiliation. He wants to choose his fate, then events can take whatever course they will.

That will be my destiny.

HE HEARS shouts of 'Long live the Emperor!' A regiment of the line is marching past Malmaison park. The drums roll, the voices swell. An officer enters and explains that Blücher's army has advanced on Paris alone, without waiting for the English.

Alone.

They could beat Blücher. Napoleon rushes to his study, examines the maps. 'France should not be brought to heel by a handful of Prussians!' he calls out to General Becker, who Fouché has put in command of the soldiers of the Guard attached to the Emperor. 'I can still halt the enemy and give the government time to negotiate with the powers.'

He takes long strides, speaking in an impassioned voice.

'And then I will leave for the United States to see out my destiny there.'

He challenges Becker: 'Give me command of the army, not as Emperor but as a general. I will crush the foreigners in front of Paris. Go and take my demand to the governmental commission and explain that I have no thought of taking back power.'

He holds out his arm.

'I promise, on my soldier's honour, as a citizen and Frenchman, to leave for America the day I beat the enemy.'

Becker agrees and hurries off.

I can still convince men of good faith.

Napoleon goes through to the library and waits.

Who will be able to accept his proposal in Paris? He paces slowly back and forth. Would the Fouchés, Lanjuinais, even Davout, agree today to what they rejected yesterday? He receives Joseph, who is going to leave France for the United States.

'If they refuse my proposal, I have nothing left but to leave,' says Napoleon.

He sends for the grand marshal of the palace and announces his intentions.

'Give the orders. When they have been carried out, come and tell me.'

BECKER is back. He says that the crowds are still cheering Napoleon's name in Paris but the governmental commission has rejected the Emperor's proposal.

'These people don't understand the state of events or public opinion,' Napoleon murmurs.

He slowly takes off his uniform, puts on a brown frock coat and blue breeches. He chooses a round hat. He looks at himself in the mirror. Here's the man of his new life.

Leave now, as quickly as possible. Hortense is crying. Some generals are protesting and furiously demanding money. 'Pay them,' he yells. Then he goes towards his family. Farewell, Mother. Farewell, son.

He goes into Josephine's room.

So far and yet so near, those days.

Then with a brisk step he goes out to the carriage.

It is five thirty in the afternoon on Thursday, 29 June 1815.

BECKER AND Savary, who are sitting facing him, and Bertrand, who is on his left, look down when his eyes meet theirs. No one speaks.

At Rambouillet Napoleon makes a sudden decision to sleep in the chateau. He feels as if he is suffocating, the air is so heavy. Who knows if assassins aren't waiting for him on the forest roads? There are so many people who dream of him being dead. He wants to see out his new life.

When he appears in the morning a crowd has gathered, pressed up against the chateau's railings, and the shouts ring out: 'Long live the Emperor!'

On the morning of Sunday 2 July crowds jam the streets of Niort, where he has spent the night. He has been recognized. They are followed by the hussars of the town's garrison.

He recognizes General Lallemand, a veteran of Italy and Egypt, who breathlessly explains that the troops of Generals Lamarque and Clausel in Brittany and the Vendée can be mustered and a front opened.

He turns his head away. These plans being put to him, these shouts he hears, these hussars who salute him with drawn sabres – all of this is already like a distant reflection of his power, a final scene. But if he let himself be caught up by this mirage, the Emperor would end up as an outlaw.

'I am nothing any more, and there's nothing more I can do,' he says.

He will leave Niort tomorrow, Monday 3 July, at four in the morning.

IN THE evening, around eight o'clock, he enters Rochefort. In the harbour he sees the two French frigates, the *Saale* and the *Medusa*, which are to take him to the United States.

Out to sea, he spies the English cruisers positioned to blockade anyone trying to leave the harbour. Their massive hulls stand out against the dusk.

Without fortune on one's side, nothing ever happens as one hopes it will.

XXXII

He takes a seat in the apartments of Rochefort's maritime prefecture. He stayed here in 1808, at the peak of his glory and power. Where is he now?

He listens to the maritime prefect, Casimir de Bonnefous. His appointee has, naturally, betrayed him, like almost everyone else.

He has gone over to Louis XVIII and received, in these very apartments, the Duke of Angoulême, who tried to lead an uprising of the west against me in March 1815. How can I trust him? He will be the docile tool of decisions taken in Paris. And what do they want to do with me? Let me reach America? The Allies haven't issued me with a safe conduct. I'd have to get past those English cruisers. Besides, why wouldn't the traitors in Paris want me to die in a shipwreck or be arrested? Talleyrand has become Louis XVIII's prime minister! And Fouché his minister of police! What is to be expected from those men whom I have long ceased to have any illusions about and who wish for my downfall? They will try to give me up as proof of their servility. And by doing so, Fouché will try to draw a veil over the fact that he has been a terrorist and regicide and hunted down royalists for me when he believed in the stability of the Empire.

I do not want to make them a present either of my death or my dignity.

But what should I decide?

There are no certainties any more; I see no straight paths leading upwards, only quagmires and the risk of ridicule and abasement, or else the failure of a desperate adventure.

He walks about a little outside the building, and immediately hears the shouts of the crowd. They are still cheering and shouting, 'Don't abandon us!'

He receives a delegation of inhabitants and soldiers. These men urge him not to leave France, but to lead the resistance. With a downward sweep of his hands he indicates his civilian dress.

'My friends, my counsel and my opinions have been scorned

and rejected. Our enemies are in Paris.' He shakes his head. 'To foreign invasion, I must not add the horrors of civil war.'

So he should leave as soon as possible. But how? And where?

HERE IS Joseph, anxious but determined. Whatever I might have thought of him in the past, he is here today, an older brother, determined to help me.

But I am Napoleon Bonaparte, accompanied by a household of sixty people! I am not a fugitive, a hunted sovereign. I have decided to abdicate in all good conscience. The law should protect me.

He receives Las Cases. Since the start of the hard times he has held this former émigré and naval officer, who fought with the Condé army but came over to the Empire in 1806, in high regard.

I have made him a state councillor. He will be my chamberlain and record what I say, if he should so choose, since his Chronological and Geographical Historical Atlas *has met with such success. I like seeing Las Cases with his son Emmanuel. Las Cases wants to follow me where I am going.*

Where am I going?

His librarian Barbier has been forbidden to send Napoleon the books he asked for about America and the campaigns of the Grand Army.

He notices a thousand worrying signs. The first white flags are beginning to appear here and there on public buildings. The largest of the English vessels, the *Bellerophon*, is entering the roads, flying the royal flag.

My enemies are drawing closer. They want to trap me.

He calls over General Gourgaud. He knows he can trust him.

This artilleryman is brutal, choleric and no diplomat, but he is loyal. During the fighting at Brienne he deflected a Cossack lance before it could hit me. He too is prepared to accompany me into exile.

'Well then,' says Napoleon, 'give the order to equip the boats for the island of Aix. I will be close to the frigates there, and in a position to embark if the winds should favour, however slightly, my departure.'

IT IS SATURDAY, 8 July 1815. Near the village of Fouras he walks over the dunes down to the beach. The whole population is gathered on the shore. The sea is rough. Will he be able to reach the island of Aix?

He turns and waves.

'Farewell, my friends.'

The wind carries off the shouts of 'Long live the Emperor.' He walks slowly forward. He is leaving the soil of mainland France. He climbs onto the shoulders of a sailor who walks into the water and carries him out to the dinghy.

The waves buffet the little boat: reaching the island is out of the question. From now on, he senses, nothing will be easy. Everything is an obstacle. He gives the order to head for one of the two frigates, the *Saale*.

He climbs the gangway ladder. The ship is still flying the tricolour. The officers salute, sabres drawn. The sailors stand to attention. But one look at Captain Philibert is enough for him to know that the man is embarrassed but, at the same time, prepared to execute a ministerial order to arrest the Emperor.

This frigate may be a prison.

He walks about the bridge, then the cabin that has been put at his disposal. As soon as the weather permits, he wants to visit the island of Aix.

He lands there on Sunday 9 July. His feet sink into the chalky soil. French soil. Perhaps this is the last time he will walk on it. More cheering. He reviews the troops and then visits the fortifications. In the past, in the other life he once had, he instigated this programme of building and redevelopment.

This could be my last fortress here.

The soldiers shout, 'Do not leave us!' Officers approach, raise their swords. 'To the Army of the Loire,' they cry.

He goes back aboard the *Saale* all the same. He needs to know what is in the dispatches that have reached the frigate. He looks through them. The government is proscribing him. And, behind the request to quit French soil as quickly as possible, he senses other intentions. They want to declare him fair game.

The new minister of the navy, Jaucourt, must have come to an understanding with the English allowing him too to be pardoned by Louis XVIII for having served me.

My life and liberty is the currency they all want to use to purchase their entry into the new circles of power. It is the same for everyone with an estate and a position to defend. The journalists, always taking somebody's coin, are already calling me the usurper in the gazettes I have received here.

They won't get me like that.

HE LEAVES the *Saale* to go to Aix. There he takes rooms on the first floor of the garrison commander's house. He cannot sleep. He listens to advice of every sort. Commandant Ponée, of the frigate *Medusa*, proposes to sacrifice himself, his vessel and his crew attacking the *Bellerophon* while the Emperor gets out to open sea on the *Saale*.

But can I be sure of the commander of the Saale?

A group of young officers offers to seize control of a large, decked whaler, sail it out to the open sea, board a merchant ship and reach the United States on that. Or they could escape on a Danish vessel moored in Aix harbour.

On 13 July Joseph is back. My brother! He clasps him to his breast. Joseph offers to serve as a decoy for the English fleet while Napoleon goes to Bordeaux and leaves France on a vessel Joseph has just chartered.

Napoleon shakes his head.

He does not fear the risks. Death is nothing. He has gone looking for it before. But he has his past life to think of, and he must give it an ending commensurate with the glory he once won.

So no shabby attempts at flight, no escapades that will end in farce.

He points out to Joseph the members of the Imperial household who are walking about in front of the house. There are four children – one of Las Cases', one of the Countess of Montholon's and two of Countess Bertrand's. There are, besides the two women, the generals, officers, servants. Nearly sixty people. He wants to leave in a dignified manner, with all these members of his household.

He embraces Joseph again. This is their last farewell. Now he will decide what path to take alone.

LAS CASES and Gourgaud have gone to Captain Maitland of the *Bellerophon* to discuss the Emperor coming aboard.

Why shouldn't I put my fate in the hands of the great people of England? Why not outstrip the manoeuvring of traitors and the plotting of police with a heroic gesture like this, one worthy of antiquity which would befit my whole life?

And if the English, when I am handed over to them, betray my trust, I will be the man of honour falling into the hands of the perjured.

It is midnight on 13 July 1815.

He remembers Plutarch and his *Lives of Illustrious Men*, which he has read so many times over the years.

This end will be of a piece with the history I have lived through.

And then, at the thought of commending himself to others for the first time in his life, at the thought of the English to whom he is going to entrust his new existence, he feels a sense of relief.

An entire lifetime of confronting, fighting, taking up challenges, incessant action. And now a second life, just using his brain and his memory. He tells Gourgaud, 'There is always a danger in entrusting oneself to one's enemies, but better to risk entrusting oneself to their honour than fall into their hands as their rightful prisoner.'

HE HAS TAKEN his decision. He is calm.

My destiny will be complete.

He takes up his quill. He raises his eyes and, through the window of his little room, he sees the sky, then the *Bellerophon* like a dark rock against the horizon.

He writes to the Prince Regent of England.

Your Royal Highness,

    Exposed to the factions that divide my country and to the enmity of Europe's greatest powers, I have ended my political career and I come, like Themistocles, to sit at the hearth of the British people. I place myself under the protection of their laws, which protection I claim from Your Royal Highness as the most powerful, the most staunch and the most generous of my enemies.

    Napoleon

He reads it through and feels satisfied. He is sure this decision will forestall Louis XVIII and Fouché's orders. They want to stop him. Going aboard the *Bellerophon* means escaping them.

He dictates instructions to Gourgaud. The general will leave first with this letter for the Prince Regent and explain, on his behalf, that, 'failing America, I prefer England to any other country. I will take the title of Colonel Muiron.'

The name came unbidden. He sees his young aide-de-camp rushing onto the bridge at Arcola and putting himself in front of him to take the bullets.

Without him, without Muiron, nothing would have come of my life. I would have died at Arcola. Muiron saved me. He is standing here in front of me as if time had not passed.

'If I must go to England,' he resumes, 'I wish to live in a country house ten or twelve leagues from London and arrive in the strictest anonymity. I would need a building large enough to lodge all my entourage . . .'

What if this doesn't happen? What if the English become jailers or executioners? What if it had been better to try to force the blockade to get to America?

In heaven's name, is a worthy fate for an Emperor of Kings to become an ordinary citizen?

He has chosen the only fitting outcome.

I MUSTN'T prevaricate any longer. The orders for my arrest will have been issued by now. I know Fouché. And, like the minister of police, the minister of the navy, Jaucourt, Joseph's old chamberlain, has plenty to beg the Bourbons' pardon for.

Napoleon asks to be woken a little after midnight on Saturday, 15 July 1815. He puts on his uniform of the chasseurs of the Guard, green with red facings. He buttons up his grey frock coat and puts on his hat with its tricolour cockade. He is going to leave his first life with his head held high, as he should.

General Becker offers to accompany him to the *Bellerophon* in person, but Napoleon refuses.

'Let us think of France,' he says. 'I am going aboard the cruiser of my own volition. If you come with me, people are bound to say that you handed me over to the English. I do not want such an accusation hanging over France.'

Becker starts to cry.

'Embrace me, General. I regret not having known you so well earlier. I would have assigned you to my personal staff.'

'Farewell, sire. Be happier than us.'

Happiness? Unhappiness?

He mulls over these words as he makes for the French vessel, the *Épervier*, which is to take him to the *Bellerophon*.

Happiness? Unhappiness?

He has experienced everything, but he has never sought happiness or feared unhappiness. He wanted to go as far as his self allowed, and not stifle the energy that raged in him like a living storm.

It is still dark when he boards the *Épervier*. The ship's commander, Jourdan, says the Emperor is wrong to trust the English and Captain Maitland. They could have broken the blockade, he insists.

'It is too late. They are waiting for me; I will go there.'

The *Épervier* approaches the *Bellerophon*, from which a rowing boat pulls away.

Napoleon salutes the crew of the *Épervier*. Farewell, France.

A few oar strokes, then he slowly climbs the *Bellerophon*'s ladder.

The topmen's whistles split the grey dawn.

Napoleon walks towards Captain Maitland. He raises his hat.

'I have come to place myself under the protection of your prince and your laws,' he says in a firm voice.

He moves closer, then adds, 'The fortunes of war have delivered me to my cruellest enemy, but I count on its loyalty.'

PART NINE

Misfortune was the only thing my renown lacked

16 July 1815 to 5 May 1821

XXXIII

As he enters the large poop cabin that Maitland has allocated him he feels a sense of peace, almost joy. Now he is merely master of his own mind. He feels free, as if choosing to hand himself over to the English has finally relieved him of the burden of responsibility. Maitland will choose the *Bellerophon*'s route, the winds will decide the course to England. Afterwards . . .

General Gourgaud will have presented my wishes to the Prince Regent. Perhaps they will let me leave for America, or else establish me in England.

If not?

He goes out onto the bridge. The sailors salute him. Maitland announces that the *Superb*, Admiral Hotham's ship, has just dropped anchor a few cables away; the admiral is proposing to pay a visit to the *Bellerophon*'s guests.

The English are not barbarians. They receive me like a vanquished sovereign who is owed respect and hospitality.

He will visit the admiral aboard the *Superb*. He sees the sailors aloft, in the ship's rigging, as if they were on parade. Admiral Hotham receives him ceremoniously and respectfully. Everything is as it should be. They eat lunch.

'If it weren't for you English, I would have been Emperor of the east,' he says. 'But wherever there is enough water to float a boat, one is certain to run into you.'

He remembers Sir Sydney Smith, his adversary on so many occasions. He speaks of his return from Egypt aboard the *Muiron*, and the hand of fortune that kept the English cruisers out of the way as previously it had kept Nelson's fleet at a distance.

He walks about the bridge of the *Bellerophon* when it finally sets sail on Sunday, 16 July 1815.

He is happy with his decision. He has not been caught in the trap that Louis XVIII, Talleyrand and Fouché clearly wanted to set for him. He leans his elbows on the ship's rail and watches the French coast disappear.

That is where my life has been.

ON SUNDAY 23 July, at five in the morning, he goes up on the bridge, which is being sluiced down. He hasn't been able to sleep at all; it is as if the creaking of the ship's hull has been echoing through his mind all night. They must be passing Ouessant.

He questions a midshipman, who points at the black spit of land arrowing out into the sea as the sky slowly turns blue.

'Cap Ouessant.'

The furthest point of my country, my life.

Napoleon hoists himself onto a gun carriage. He looks at this tip of land through his telescope. He cannot take his eyes off it. And when it disappears, in the brilliant midday light, part of him sinks into an abyss.

At dusk, on that same day, the English coast appears.

RAIN IS falling on Torquay harbour.

He looks through the portholes, then goes out onto the poop deck. He sees thousands of craft surrounding the *Bellerophon*. No cheering, but some outstretched arms. And suddenly a silhouette he recognizes. It is General Gourgaud coming aboard. The Prince Regent has refused to receive him. Gourgaud hasn't even been able to disembark from the ship that had brought him to England as a scout. But he has been able to get hold of some English newspapers. Las Cases translates the articles. They say that General Bonaparte should be imprisoned in the Tower of London or in a Scottish castle or be deported to the island of St Helena.

What is this? Napoleon goes up onto the bridge. The *Bellerophon* is slowly sailing along the coast towards Plymouth. The officers are reserved now, their faces impassive; Captain Maitland avoids looking him in the eye.

Napoleon paces urgently from prow to stern.

Is it possible? Will he be snared in a net? He senses that everything around him is changing imperceptibly. In Plymouth harbour two frigates clear a path through the crowd of boats.

The English are capable of any trap. He knew this and he tried to forget it. The truth always comes back to confront those who close their eyes to it.

He remembers the admiral in command of the Channel squadron, Lord Keith.

This officer participated in the siege of Toulon, when I blew up his ships; it was the same Lord Keith who landed at Aboukir in 1801 and forced the last French troops out of Egypt.

'I very much want to see the admiral,' Napoleon tells Maitland. 'He should not stand on ceremony. I will be happy to be treated as a private citizen until the British government decides how I am to be considered.'

But Captain Maitland doesn't reply. And the young Irish doctor on board, Barry O'Meara, who speaks Italian and is so considerate, doesn't even dare look at me any more.

At last, on Friday 28 July, here is Lord Keith. At Waterloo I saved the life of his wounded nephew, who I got under cover and seen to by my doctors. Now anger chokes me as I see him standing there so stiff and silent, only consenting to exchange a few words about the siege of Toulon and the Egyptian campaign and refusing to give any other clues. This is not about the past, but about my future.

'I am nothing any more,' Napoleon thunders. 'I cannot disturb anybody any more. Can't I live in England?'

Lord Keith doesn't answer. Napoleon must wait, and suffer the mad rages of Madame Bertrand, who tries to throw herself overboard because she wants to land in England and says she's convinced that the Emperor is going to be deported to St Helena.

He wants to die.

HE WALKS in the rain. The bridge is slippery. The horizon is a curtain of grey. He imagines St Helena. He said this name countless times in his previous life. He wanted to take possession of the little island, a port of call for the East India Company. But what could he do on that block of dark green basalt? In that equatorial climate? It would be certain death for him. Might as well die here.

AT TEN THIRTY on Monday, 31 July 1815, Lord Keith comes aboard, accompanied by Under Secretary of State Bunbery.

Here they are! Keith holds a letter in his hand which he translates as he reads it aloud. His calm voice cuts me like a blade. Prisoner of war . . . St Helena. What do the other words matter?

He takes the letter from Lord Keith's hands and throws it on the table. Then he immediately calms himself and looks at the English admiral with contempt. The British government has no right to dispose of his person. He appeals to the British people and the laws of their country. Maitland has deceived him. Admiral Hotham has lied to him.

'If he had told me that I would be a prisoner of war, I would not have come. As for the island of St Helena, that is a death sentence! What would I do on that little rock at the other end of the world? I prefer death to St Helena, and what good would my death do you?'

Let them transport him to the prison hulks of Botany Bay in Australia; that would suit him better.

He turns to the desk and points a finger at the document he took from Lord Keith.

'Your government has no right to call me General Bonaparte. I am First Consul and, if I am to be received, it must be in that capacity. When I was on the island of Elba I was just as much a sovereign as on the French throne. I was a sovereign there as much as the king was in France. We each had our flag. We each had our ships, our troops. Of course,' he laughs, 'my forces were on a reduced scale. I had six hundred soldiers and he had two hundred thousand. Finally I made war on him. I beat him; I drove him out of the country; I dethroned him. None of what has happened can change my position or deprive me of my rank among the sovereigns of Europe.'

He stares at Keith. He is going to write a protest to the British government. He starts to dictate to Las Cases.

I here solemnly protest, before heaven and mankind, against the violation of my most sacred rights, by forcibly disposing of my person and my freedom. I came aboard the *Bellerophon* of my own free will. I am not a prisoner; I am the guest of England. Once on board the *Bellerophon*, I was at the hearth of the British people. I appeal to history. It will say that an enemy who waged war for twenty years against the English people came of his own volition, in his misfortune, to seek asylum under their laws, and what more dazzling proof could he give of his esteem, his confidence? But how did England respond to such magnanimity? She feigned to extend a hospitable hand to this enemy, and when he gave himself in good faith, she immolated him!

IT IS THURSDAY, 4 August 1815. The *Bellerophon* weighs anchor and slowly moves out of Plymouth roads.

Napoleon is lying in his cabin.

They are going to transfer me to the Northumberland *out at sea, far from the crowds of onlookers, far from the British people, far from the liberals who have tried to have me called as a witness in a case to delay my deportation.*

Must he die?

He calls for Marchand and hands his valet the *Lives of Illustrious Men*. It is open at the life of Cato.

'Read.'

He pulls the curtain.

With his fingertips he can easily reach the red flask tied to his waistcoat. Perhaps this poison would have more effect than the one he took at Fontainebleau. That would be an end worthy of Plutarch.

He hesitates, sits on the bed. He goes over his life.

'Misfortune was the only thing my renown lacked. I have worn the Imperial crown of France and the iron crown of Italy. And now England is giving me another, still greater and more glorious, that worn by the saviour of the world, a crown of thorns.'

If I accept it, is there a limit to the position I will occupy in the minds of men? Who will be able to forget me?

He goes back up to the bridge. He sees the silhouette of the *Northumberland*. It would only need a single act to put an end to this second life, here, and it would be such a powerful ending too that everyone would be struck by it.

He does not fear death. But curiosity holds him back. What is there at the end of this long sea voyage? What will life be like on that extinct volcano? There is a mystery to this future, and a challenge: the challenge of imposing his memory, the image of his life, on the world at the point of his most complete destitution. What a destiny, to start as Caesar and end as martyr and prophet!

He wonders.

He asks Las Cases, 'Is it certain that I will go to St Helena? Is a man dependent on his fellow men even when he wants to stop being so?'

He walks slowly back and forth. He is calm. He sees Captain Maitland's astonished expression; he probably thought he would be prostrate in his cabin.

'At times I want to leave you,' he goes on, 'and that would not be very difficult. It is only a matter of losing one's temper a little and in no time I'll have escaped; everything will be over and you will return to your families.'

What has become of my son? I should pass on the memory of my life for his sake too, not leave it in my enemies' hands.

'It would be all the easier because there is no conflict with my inner principles. I am one of those people who believe that the torments of the other world have only been imagined as complements to their insufficient — as far as we know here — attractions. God would not have been able to desire such a counterpoint to his infinite goodness, especially for acts such as this. And what are they after all? Merely the desire to return a little quicker.'

He listens to Las Cases' arguments.

'But what will we be able to do in that godforsaken place?' he asks.

'We shall live on the past, sire; there is enough there to satisfy you. Do we not enjoy Caesar's life, or Alexander's? Well, we shall have better than that; you will reread yourself, sire.'

He looks at the horizon. Everything is played out in the mind. Ideas determine everything.

'Very well then. We will write our memoirs,' he says.

He walks away to the ship's rail, and then comes back.

'Yes, we will have to work. Work is also the scythe of time. After all, one must fulfil one's destiny; that is my great principle too. Well then, let mine be accomplished!'

HE DRAWS UP the list of those who will accompany him: the Montholons, Bertrands, Las Cases and his son. *That will be my* '*court*'. There will be twelve servants, including Marchand, the Mameluke Saint-Denis known as Ali, Cipriani and the Irish doctor Barry O'Meara.

But he must still protest to Lord Keith and to Commodore Sir George Cockburn, who was at the siege of Toulon as well, and is now in command of the *Northumberland* and will be governor of St Helena.

'I am not leaving this vessel, the *Bellerophon*, nor England of my own free will. It is you, Admiral, who is compelling me.'

But I will go aboard the Northumberland. *My decision is taken. They won't have to drag me aboard by force.*

'Oh, you will only have to give me an order,' he tells Cockburn.

My destiny is drawing to its conclusion. I shall not impede it.

THE *NORTHUMBERLAND*'S guard presents arms at the top of the ladder. He turns back. It is time for farewells. General Lallemand and Savary, Duke of Rodrigo, will not be coming on the journey. They and the other officers crowd round Napoleon, some of them crying. He embraces Lallemand and Savary.

'Be happy, my friends. We shall not see one another again.'

He remains silent for a few seconds.

'But my thoughts will not leave you,' he continues, 'neither you nor those who have served me. Tell France that I am praying for her.'

HE GOES BACK into his cabin, lies on his little iron bed with green silk curtains that Marchand has set up against the hull. The ceiling is low. He hears the sailors' clogs echoing on the bridge. He turns on his side. Near the bed Marchand has put the silver washstand and a portable writing desk with the Imperial coat of arms. The portable library's books are within reach.

This is a field bivouac – for my last campaign, without arms, without the Old Guard. My only troops are my mind. My only force is in my will.

He gets to his feet. The ship is rolling.

On Wednesday, 9 August 1815, the *Northumberland*, surrounded by a little squadron, sails south in a heavy swell.

XXXIV

HE MUSTN'T GIVE IN. He must remain himself.

He paces up and down the bridge of the *Northumberland*, his hands behind his back. He takes a pinch of snuff and leans on one of the port-side cannon. He senses hundreds of eyes on him, from the top of the rigging, the crew's quarters, the poop – everyone who can see him is studying him avidly.

There are more than a thousand men aboard this sixty-four-gun craft. And they all want to see me.

But I make them lower their eyes. I'm not the conquered Emperor; I'm still the man one cannot force to submit.

He looks eastwards. That black line on the horizon is Brittany. Farewell, France. But he does not give in to nostalgia or emotion. He is impassive. And that surprises the English watching him.

What does it matter where he is? On board this English ship, in this dining room where Admiral Cockburn is shocked when Napoleon picks up his cutlet in his fingers, or gets up after a few minutes because he has finished his meal while everyone else stays in their chairs?

Where am I?

Sometimes it seems he is back in his childhood, lost and alone in a crowd of strangers. He doesn't understand their language; he is forced to defend himself constantly against their mockery – Paille au nez, they say.

He is back at Autun. He is in Brienne. He is on board the *Northumberland* sailing towards St Helena. And he isn't giving in.

I am still myself.

They will not take his experiences away from him. He has entered Milan, Berlin, Vienna, Madrid and Moscow. He has made kings. He has imposed his will on the Pope.

What does it matter where I am?

All his past glory is his forever. And his will is as strong as the will of that boy in Brienne who had nothing but his wits.

He dictates to Las Cases every morning at eleven. The time

passes quickly. The following day Las Cases reads the text back to him.

The Italian campaigns, the Egyptian campaign. The places, the faces, the emotions, the choices I had to make, the soldiers' bravery and sacrifices. Everything comes back.

'After all, my dear sir,' he says to Las Cases, 'these memoirs will be as well known as any that have preceded them. You will live as long as all their authors. No one will ever be able to study our great undertakings or myself without referring to you.'

THE SEA is rough in the Golfe de Gascogne. Then the Spanish coast comes into sight. A vessel appears, the *Peruvian*, which Admiral Cockburn has instructed to put in at Guernsey to buy 1,200 bottles of French wine to improve their daily life. Her captain comes aboard the *Northumberland*. He has been able to get every copy of the *Moniteur* for July at Guernsey, as well as several other daily papers.

Napoleon reads the journal alone in his cabin.

He must not succumb to bitterness.

So this is how they speak of me: as the usurper, the ogre, the ferocious beast finally imprisoned. They mock me, betray me. They have banded together and now they arrest and kill 'Bonapartists'. La Bédoyère is about to be put on trial; they are already saying he will be condemned to death. Ney is being hunted. They are murdering my supporters throughout Provence.

Napoleon remains shut away in his cabin. He hears the clatter of the sailors' clogs as they run about the bridge. The sails are being hoisted. They are heading south, across the equator, to the humid, motionless heat of the Gulf of Guinea. Then will come the cliffs of St Helena.

Remain oneself.

He starts dictating again.

'I have confidence in history,' he says. 'I have had plenty of flatterers, and now the present belongs to my most rabid detractors. But the glory of celebrated men is like their life, exposed to all the vagaries of fortune. A day will come when impartial writers are motivated by a love of truth alone.'

He raises his voice. No one will be able to erase what he has been, what he has done; this will etch itself on men's memories. He must live. Never giving in, always remaining himself, he must deepen the mark he will leave on the world, combat the slanderers, impose his vision on future generations; he must equal, or even surpass, the Caesar of the *Gallic* and *Civil Wars* and the Plutarch of the *Lives of Illustrious Men*.

'In my career,' he says, 'faults will no doubt be found, but Arcola, Rivoli, the Pyramids, Marengo, Austerlitz, Jena and Friedland are granite. Envy's teeth can do nothing against them.'

HIS ENTIRE household enters his cabin, and he is surprised by such audacity. Here, crowded together, are Montholon and Bertrand, their wives and children, Gourgaud, Las Cases and his son, and behind them the servants, who fill the passageway.

I had forgotten. It is Tuesday, 15 August 1815, my forty-sixth birthday.

He goes up to the bridge. At dinner Admiral Cockburn and the English officers raise a toast. Then, in the salon, he plays vingt-et-un with Cockburn, wins almost one hundred napoleons, and then stops the game because he is sure he could clean the admiral out and refuses to do so. He takes a walk with Las Cases.

'I liked founding things, not owning them,' he says. 'My estate was glory and celebrity. The Simplon for the people, the Louvre for foreigners. They were more my domain than any private estate. I sometimes found myself thinking, to my surprise, that Josephine's expenses, on her greenhouses or gallery, were a real drain on my Jardin des Plantes or Musée de Paris.'

He goes to the gun carriage where he has got into the habit of sitting.

'It was after the victory at Lodi,' he murmurs, 'that I started to think that I could, after all, become a decisive actor on our political stage. That was the first spark of high ambition.'

Now he is forty-six and everything is decided! He looks at Montholon's and Bertrand's children, who are running about the bridge.

He has a son, and he is alone.

But as long as there are men, his destiny will be remembered. He is convinced of this, and it is what he wants.

Let the memory of what I have accomplished be my dynasty.

He grasps Las Cases by the arm and leads him to the stern.

'I never usurped the crown,' he says. 'I picked it up from where it lay in the stream. The people put it on my head and their actions must be respected!'

SOMETIMES he feels nauseous. A storm breaks when they put in at Madeira. And then they are becalmed and the sails hang slack, dead, in the humid air of the Gulf of Guinea.

Malcontented sailors, driven to indiscipline by the length of the journey, are flogged. He protests indignantly. What is this barbaric, stupid way of commanding men?

Monotonous days. Not give in. Remain oneself. Not get agitated when a huge shark that has just been caught and thrown on the bridge thrashes about and splashes one with blood.

I have seen so many men with their guts spilling out.

He remembers Duroc.

Why didn't a cannonball take me at Waterloo, or even at the battle of the Moskva?

He looks at a map, as he has done so many times on the eve of a battle. Here is St Helena, an islet of 122 square kilometres with barely 3,000 inhabitants, more than half of them slaves and soldiers, 2,000 kilometres from the African coast and over two months' sail from England!

IT IS ALREADY Saturday, 14 October 1815. The wind has finally got up. The sails billow. The lookout shouts. Land ho! Then the wind drops and in the moonlight the sea reverts to the black, smooth sheet they know so well.

My prison, the stage of my last battle, is out there, in the night.

He gets up at dawn and goes to the prow. He sees dark cliffs and then, in a cleft, a little town: a few houses with red roofs, a church spire and palm trees and on the upper slopes of the enclosed valley, cannon. This is Jamestown, the only settlement of the island.

So be it. This is how it is.

He calls Las Cases. They must work, just as any other day. He goes into his cabin, asks Las Cases to read out what he dictated the day before, and then resumes.

'I returned from the Italian campaign without three hundred thousand francs to my name; I could easily have come back with ten or twelve million and it would have been mine. I have never submitted accounts; I have never been asked for them. On my return I was expecting a substantial reward from the Nation, but the Directory pushed it into the background.'

But there is always a solution. Always a battle to fight. Until death takes you.

THE *NORTHUMBERLAND*'S hull creaks. The sails snap in the wind. The ship approaches the island. Then, on Sunday, 15 October 1815, he hears the anchor chains. They are lying at anchor. It is ten thirty in the morning. He goes up onto the bridge. The island is black, hostile. They will disembark tomorrow, the admiral explains.

'It is not an attractive place,' Napoleon says, turning to General Gourgaud.

He points to the cliffs, the mounds of rocks.

'I would have done better to remain in Egypt,' he says ironically.

Then he heads towards his cabin, his hands crossed behind his back.

XXXV

HE SITS ON THE EDGE of the bed in the stifling little cubbyhole on the first floor of Porteous House, a few hundred metres from the docks of Jamestown's harbour.

Suddenly the room is filled with scampering and squeaking. Marchand, his valet, lets out a shout, raises a torch above his head and lights up the hovel Admiral Cockburn has dared call a room. In the spreading pool of light that reveals the floor, he sees a number of huge black rats, a dozen perhaps, who don't run away but look straight back at him, their eyes red. Marchand takes a step forward and makes them scatter. They disappear into holes in the walls or through gaps in the floorboards.

Cursed island! Napoleon gets up and goes over to the narrow window.

How many nights will there be after this first night, Monday, 16 October 1815? He paces back and forth. He makes out the jostling crowd in the dark street in front of the tavern; there are no shouts, just a murmur and the sound of people milling about. He has had to face crowds so often, some of them hostile, as in Cairo or the Egyptian villages or certain German towns; he has encountered hatred and, more often, enthusiasm. But he has never ever walked through a crowd like the one kept in check by soldiers of the garrison that watched him all the way from the port to the inn.

So that's the population of St Helena, is it? There was a greedy curiosity and something base, a sort of fearful jubilation, in the eyes and expressions lit up by the torches of the sailors of the *Northumberland*. The most dignified were the blacks – slaves – who stood at the back with the people of mixed race, the Chinese and mulattoes, but the whites at the front – women with crude features, brutal-faced sailors, traders, agents of the East India Company – filled him with scorn. Rats! Yes, just like the ones slithering back in his room running between his legs.

How many more nights to live through, and die through, here?

He thinks of the cheers of the people of Portferraio when he landed on Elba and the songs and cheers when he set off again to conquer France, barely six months ago.

And now he is here – here, on this 'dreadful island' which is also a prison.

'I should have stopped earlier,' he murmurs. 'I think I should have died at Waterloo. Perhaps before. If I had died in Moscow my fame would be that of the greatest conqueror the world has ever known.'

He looks at Marchand. His valet is leaning against a wall. He has tried to turn this hovel into a bivouac, but any barn on a battlefield, any farm destroyed by cannonballs and filled with dead and wounded soldiers, would be better than this sordid room overrun with rats. War and death would be better than this island.

He studied it all day from the *Northumberland*. He saw the cliffs, the bare plains, the stunted trees bent sideways by the wind. He guessed at the sequence of rain, cold wind and oppressive heat. Then he saw the crowd of slaves and smallholders.

Here is my prison, in the middle of the ocean, among the rats. This is what they've given me!

He turns back to the bed, sits down again and asks Marchand to follow suit. The valet sits on the floor.

I have spoken with kings, marshals, ministers and scholars. I have instituted codes and laws that have changed whole ways of life. I have conceived plans of campaign that have set hundreds of thousands of men in motion. And from now on I will have no one else to talk to than this devoted young man, Marchand, my valet, and the few other loyal souls who, as has already started to happen on the Northumberland, *will fall out with one another and be racked with jealousy, because exile is a great misfortune.*

If I give any ground to the English, if I forget who I am, where I come from, what I have done; if my vigilance weakens, then everything will be swept away – myself and my dignity – and my past glory will be tarnished and soiled by such an act of submission.

That is what they want: to make me submit, to show the world that as soon as I am put among the rats I am nothing.

Now is the time when I must be an emperor; now is when I must fight a battle that can have no other outcome than death.

I must form a square. I am my whole Grand Army. I am the Old Guard that dies and does not surrender.

'They can do me violence,' he says, 'but they can never degrade me.'

He stands up again and kicks out at the rats to scatter them.

'I raised myself up from nothing to be the greatest monarch in the world. Europe was at my feet. The lampoons mean nothing. I am not afraid for my reputation; posterity will acknowledge me.'

He looks at the street.

The crowd is still there, lit by the moon now as it mills about, murmuring.

Forget these faces; forget this island. Follow my path here in my mind. Impose my ability to remain myself on my jailers and executioners in this prison. Every time they try to encroach on my person, repulse them. Stop noticing them. Don't see them, or the rats or the flies; don't feel the wind or the heat or the humidity. Remain myself.

'Crises,' he resumes, 'have slid off me like lead off marble.'

What will happen here will not hit me any harder. All this is nothing, since I have pursued my destiny in the full light of day. And it is my destiny I must serve now.

'If I had died on the throne, veiled in clouds of omnipotence,' he says, 'I would have remained an enigma to many people. But now, thanks to my misfortune, they will be able to judge me with full disclosure.'

HE TAKES UP lodgings at The Briars, an outhouse surrounded by dog roses and palm trees belonging to W. Balcombe, an agent of the British East India Company. He will have to wait for work on Longwood House, which stands in the midst of a barren plateau, to be finished.

Living there or somewhere else, what difference does it make?

Marchand and the servants busy themselves preparing his bedchamber in a room with wooden partition walls which the rats can get through. The Montholons and their children, Gourgaud, Las Cases and his son Emmanuel distribute themselves as best they can among a series of tiny rooms and tents. The Bertrands have chosen a house at Hutt's Gate, a little way from The Briars.

To work!

He resumes dictating to Las Cases and puts the other members of his entourage to work. He explores the property, and then, when he can, goes further afield on one of the horses Admiral Cockburn puts at his disposal. Sometimes the two Balcombe girls join him. The youngest, Betsy, is a merry, chatty, mischievous girl. He joins in one of her games for a few minutes, laughing, and then suddenly becomes distant, unreachable.

An English officer whose job it is to keep him under surveillance asks to be presented. He does not receive his jailers. He tells Grand Marshal of the Palace Bertrand to send him away. Let no one forget that I am the master of my own prison.

'If they try to violate my home, it will only be over my corpse, I warn you.'

The officer does not insist. It will be the same whenever he doesn't want to receive someone. People will only be given an audience if they have observed etiquette and seen the officers of the Imperial household, Bertrand, Montholon and Gourgaud, first.

I will not accept any invitations. No dinners or balls. What does this Admiral Cockburn think, that I am going to show myself to these 'rats'? Beneath these English pleasantries, I can only see 'malice and insults'.

HE SPEAKS with Las Cases. 'Do you remember,' he begins, 'on the *Northumberland*, as I did not want to stay at table shovelling down wine for two or three hours to get drunk, I used to go out and walk on the bridge? Once when I got up, Admiral Cockburn said in a scornful way, "I think the general has not read Lord Chesterfield," which meant I lacked politeness and couldn't stay at table. Cockburn is nothing but a shark. Who dares call me General Bonaparte! By what right? As if they could strip me of what I am.'

He shrugs his shoulders.

'No one on earth has the right to take away from me the qualifications that are mine.'

He takes another few steps, then adds, 'After all, they can cut and suppress and mutilate as much as they want, it will still be very hard for them to make me vanish completely! A French historian will still be obliged to deal with the Empire; and if he has any courage, he will have to restore something to me – he will have to give me my share and his task will be easy because the facts speak for themselves and shine as bright as the sun.'

He turns and resumes dictating, until he starts coughing and has to break off. The walls are damp from humidity and the room is cold, apart from when there's a sudden gust of dry, scalding wind that seems to come from the desert. Then the fog closes in. The wind is so dry that it releases a damp steam from the ground as the waterlogged soil sweats out the contents of previous downpours.

'For most of the year you never see the sun or the moon on this cursed island, only rain and fog,' he bursts out furiously, then shivers. When he walks anywhere, he is short of breath. It grows dark and he murmurs, 'Another day less.'

But then the night begins, and time seems an eternity. He reads, gets up; Marchand or Ali brings him light and something to drink. He is sweating; he can't shake off his cough; he feels he is suffocating; his left side hurts. He walks through the little rooms.

Where are these days and nights heading? What is the goal except death?

'I need to be pushed,' he says. 'The pleasure of moving forward is the only thing that can sustain me.'

Work, work then.

He dictates. He has his account of his campaigns read back to him. He reads, since some of his library has finally been brought ashore. But the English are opening his correspondence, trying to humiliate him. He protests indignantly. Petty, sordid jailers!

At table he has his little court around him. He demands that the men wear uniforms and decorations at dinner and Mesdames Montholon and Bertrand ceremonial dresses. Etiquette, respect for appearances and discipline are ways of remaining what one is. Everything has shrunk around us. No more palaces, no more chamberlains and courtiers. Let us safeguard what lies in our power.

He leaps to his feet in a rage. 'What infamous treatment they have reserved for us! These are the agonies of death! To injustice and violence they add insult and slow torture! If I was so harmful

to them, why didn't they get rid of me? A few bullets in the head
and the heart would have sufficed! At least there would have been
some energy to the crime.'

He points to the Imperial dinner service, which the
Northumberland's sailors have finally brought ashore.

'If it wasn't for you, for you women especially, I would only
want a private's rations here.'

He grimaces contemptuously.

'The sovereigns of Europe used to call me their brother. The
Emperor of Austria was my father-in-law. Now, they won't give
me any news of my son. They allow the sacred nature of
sovereignty to be polluted! I entered their capitals as a conqueror;
if I had brought the same sentiments, what would have become of
them?'

They get up from the table. Madame Montholon goes through
into what they call the drawing room. She will play the piano;
sing a few airs. The time must pass; they must make as many
inroads into the night as possible. With a wave he silences the
chattering and bickering breaking out.

*They already hate each other. They are jealous of Las Cases
because he receives most of my confidences and I dictate most of my
thoughts to him, and Gourgaud envies everyone else.*

'You have come with me for my sake, is that what you say?'
Napoleon upbraids them. 'Well then, be brothers, otherwise you
are merely tiresome! You want to make me happy? Well then, be
brothers, otherwise you are merely a vexation! I want everyone
here to be animated by the same spirit. I want everyone around
me to be happy.'

Bertrand begins to split hairs, to argue with him.

*Don't tolerate anything degrading. Even if it's just the tactlessness
of someone close to you. Don't let a single line of resistance be eroded.
Repulse everything. Be surprised by nothing. Expect the worst.*

'Poor, sad humanity,' he says, leaving the room. 'Man is no
safer on the tip of a rock than in the halls of a palace. He is the
same everywhere. Man is always man.'

He stops on the threshold of his room and sees, standing on a
pedestal table, the portrait of Marie Louise and of his son which
Marchand has put out in an attempt to create familiar décor.

They deny me my son.

He does not want to think of Marie Louise.

He says in a hushed voice, 'Men must be very wicked to be the villains I suppose them to be.'

ONE NIGHT LESS. A ship of the East India Company has brought the gazettes from the Cape. The newspapers report Bédoyère's execution and Brune's murder by royalists in Avignon.

Horror. Injustice.

'La Bédoyère was eminently French,' Napoleon murmurs. 'Noble, chivalrous.'

So many men have died for me, for the France I embodied.

'I have been abandoned more than betrayed,' he says. 'There is more weakness around me than perfidiousness. It is the denial of St Peter; repentance and tears may be imminent. That aside, who in history has had more supporters and friends? Who has been more popular and more loved? Who has ever left behind more ardent and keener regrets?'

He thinks of La Bédoyère again.

'No, it's true. Human nature could be uglier and I more worthy of pity.'

All these sacrifices, these campaigns, this glory – my whole destiny compels me to face the situation now; to resist like those squares of the Guard with which I retreated at Waterloo when death did not want me.

He goes out with Las Cases and they meet an old slave, who they question. The man was torn from his family and deported here. He works with slow, noble movements. Napoleon listens to his replies, which Las Cases translates, and then slowly walks away.

'There, that is the poor human machine,' he says. 'Not one person's exterior that resembles another, nor one interior that doesn't, and it is in rejecting this truth that we commit so many crimes. This man had his family, his pleasures, his own life, and a horrible crime has been perpetrated by making him die here under the weight of slavery!'

He stops walking and looks at Las Cases. There must be no special pleading. He is not talking about himself. He is not a slave; he will never be.

'I have been spoilt, I admit it,' he explains. 'I have always been in command. Since I was born I have always had power; I have not recognized any other master or laws. So, my dear sir, there could never be the slightest correspondence between me and this slave. No one has inflicted physical pain on us. Had they tried, we have the wit to deceive our oppressors.'

He takes Las Cases by the arm.

'Our situation may even have its attractions. The universe is watching us! We will always be martyrs to an immortal cause! Millions of men grieve for us, our country sighs and glory is in mourning. We are fighting here against divine tyranny and the prayers of nations are with us. My true sufferings are not here. If I only thought of myself, perhaps I would even be delighted. Misfortunes offer their own heroism and glory. My life was lacking adversity!'

He leads Las Cases back into the house. He must get down to work.

Opinion is everything. What I dictate here and Las Cases notes down will sculpt my public face for centuries to come.

On 10 December 1815 he enters Longwood House, which is finally finished. English soldiers salute; drums roll. His horse rears and Napoleon digs in his spurs.

He jumps off. The plateau is windswept. *So this is where they are making me live.* The buildings are wooden. Once the property of the East India Company, the farm has been enlarged. A bathroom, at last. But only attics, unfortunately, for Las Cases and his son. And the walls are already damp.

He goes out and sees sentries positioned fifty feet apart, forming two rings, one four miles from the house and the other twelve. But he will be able to ride a little, and perhaps even hunt or race the barouche Cockburn has consented to give him.

But that is not the most important thing. Since this is my final prison, my estate, I am going to mark out its limits and lay down the rules.

He sends for Gourgaud, Montholon and Las Cases. His timetable will be strict and must be respected. Dictation every morning; they will take it in turns to note down his account of his campaigns and reign. Audiences will be regulated as carefully as in the Imperial palaces. Dinner will be served at eight o'clock, the officers in full uniform and the women in décolleté dresses. Each member of his household will have a precise occupation. And the aim of it all?

To hold out, resist. Not let oneself be worn down by despair and monotony. Reject outright any measure dictated by the English that has not first been submitted to my attention – consider it a humiliation.

What do they want, these officers who watch me when I go for a walk? Am I in a cage?

ON 7 JANUARY 1816 Cipriani, the majordomo, returns from Jamestown with newspapers brought by a frigate that has just put in to port. Murat has been shot by the Calabrians, and Ney by the French!

Napoleon walks away. He wants to be alone.

Then, returning to the salon through the room called the parlour, he murmurs, 'It is terrible, but the Calabrians have been more generous, more humane, than the people who sent me here.'

But I mustn't capitulate; the opposite, I must live and work so that all I have achieved with La Bédoyère, Murat, Ney, Brune, and with all my dead comrades, Muiron, Duroc, Bessières, Berthier, Lannes and Desaix, is not forgotten or tarnished.

He questions Las Cases' son. The boy gives good answers; he knows Greek and Latin history. He went to the Lycée Napoleon.

'What a younger generation I am leaving behind me! They are my handiwork; their merits will be sufficient revenge for me,' Napoleon says. 'In work, after all, one ought to acknowledge the worker. If I had only thought of my power and myself, as they constantly repeat, if I really had had any other aim than the rule of reason, then I would have sought to hide learning under a bushel. Instead of which, all anyone saw me do was expose it to the light. And they still haven't done everything I envisaged for children. My university, as I conceived it, was a masterpiece in its arrangements and should have been in its results for the Nation.'

HE ABRUPTLY shuts himself away in his room. He has spotted a group of English officers.

It's probably the new governor, Hudson Lowe, coming to present himself. Why hasn't he sent word? What does he think? That I am innately disposed to receive him, like a prisoner on whom one can impose whatever one wants?

Everything he knows about this man renders him loathsome. He appears to have been chosen specifically to humiliate him. Hudson Lowe fought at Toulon, like so many English officers, but he also took part in the siege of Bastia. He even stayed in the Bonapartes' house in Ajaccio. Then he took command of a regiment of Corsicans who had joined the English, like Pascal Paoli. And, with these Corsicans, he fought in Egypt.

Napoleon goes up to one of the windows and sees his tall, thin silhouette, red hair and ruddy complexion.

'He is hideous. That's a sinister face, a hyena caught in a trap,' he says to Las Cases.

Then, shrugging his shoulders, he adds, 'But let us not be in a rush to judge. His mind may, after all, be able to make up for what's sinister about this face. It's not impossible.'

BUT NO. A few days is enough to assure him that this face truly expresses Lowe's character.

What sort of a man is this, who wants to reduce the space where I can walk, sets spies on me, doesn't pass on a single letter, demands that I reduce my household by dismissing four people and wants to restrict my expenses? An executioner! A man who has only commanded deserters, Corsicans, Calabrians, Neapolitans and Sicilians!

He won't see me; I won't give in to him.

'He is nothing but a pen-pusher, the likes of which we have seen on any headquarters staff: the sort who've never done anything except scribble and draw up accounts.'

Napoleon agrees to receive Admiral Malcolm, who has taken over command of the fleet and St Helena's garrison. Here is a genuine officer, not a jailer, a contemptible executioner.

'I have run a government, and I know that there are missions and instructions that one only gives to dishonoured men. The job Hudson Lowe has been given is an executioner's,' Napoleon remarks. 'He wants to lock me up. He wants to reduce me to mediocrity.'

He gives instructions that his silver plate should be sold – by weight – after the Imperial arms have been struck off. Let this show Europe what I have been reduced to by England and its representative Hudson Lowe.

'He little knows me. My body may be in the hands of the wicked, but my soul is free; it is as proud as if I were leading six hundred thousand men and on my throne, creating kings and handing out crowns.'

And a man like Hudson Lowe would claim to know who I want to – who I should – invite to Longwood!

Napoleon dictates a 'Remonstrance' in which he summarizes all his grievances about the treatment he is receiving. England has broken the law by considering him a prisoner of war and deporting him to this forsaken rock. He is persecuted here. He is forbidden to correspond freely.

'The spectacle of a great man grappling with adversity is the most sublime spectacle there is. Those who fail Napoleon in this position only sully their own characters and the nation they represent,' he says calmly. He will not lose his temper. He will not let his defences be breached, even if he feels mounting anger and contempt for Hudson Lowe and for the sovereigns who have deprived him of his son and alienated his wife's affections. Once they called him brother, now they have arranged to kill him slowly.

'It takes more courage to suffer than to die,' he says, looking at each of his entourage in turn. They are weary, he senses, afraid even.

He must keep them under control, like a troop about to scatter in a panic.

'Man only makes a mark in life when he dominates the character nature has given him,' he says. 'You have come with me to alleviate my suffering – surely such a feeling should overcome any other feelings?'

Then he draws up an inventory with Las Cases of all the silver he still owns that they can sell to Balcombe, the owner of The Briars, who will be only too happy to turn a substantial profit.

They can also obtain bills of exchange from the English banks or from Lafitte in Paris. Joseph, now safely installed in the United States, has a considerable fortune. Eugène has forty million. Can't they help the Imperial household maintain its status in St Helena? Because maintaining one's status is a form of resistance against those who want to reduce me to nothing.

'I want to provide for all my needs,' he says. 'But if, by one of these contradictions that are the true nature of injustice, the English government refuses me the means to do so, I will join the grenadiers' mess, those brave men of the fifty-third regiment. They will not withhold hospitality from Europe's finest soldier.'

HE WITHDRAWS to his bedroom.

As Marchand is helping him undress, he murmurs, 'The night's the difficult part. I'd like to work until two in the morning and then sleep. At nine o'clock I'm sleepy; I sleep for two hours, sometimes half an hour, but then I wake up. One's thoughts at night are not very cheerful.'

He coughs. His legs and stomach hurt. His eyes sting and run constantly. He finds it hard walking, doesn't ride so much; goes for drives in the barouche instead. The devil take these English who keep me under surveillance! What are they afraid of, me escaping?

He sits stock-still, drowses a little and then suddenly starts dictating a new chapter on the Egyptian or the French campaign.

At night, he dreams.

IF IT WAS all to be done again . . . What a novel my life would make. If, instead of the Egyptian expedition, I had made an Irish one. The hinges the destiny of empires turn on! How small and imperfect our revolutions are in the organization of the universe!

He coughs again; pain climbs from his stomach to his chest. He gets up and walks a little. The rats run off. He makes to pick up his hat; a huge black rat slips out of it and darts across the room.

Water drips through holes in the ceiling. Linen and clothes go mouldy.

He goes outside. The weather has changed already. Now it's

hot and windy. He looks at the plateau on which Longwood has been built, right in the middle; there isn't a single tree, no streams, no grass.

In the distance he sees the prosperous-looking buildings of Plantation House, which are surrounded by greenery. This is where Hudson Lowe has taken up residence.

A curse on that hyena, who refuses to let me go about the island as I please.

That man wants me dead. His instructions are to kill me.

I must protest, fight, never give in.

The captain of a frigate, the *Havana*, comes to pay his respects. He refuses to take a letter for Europe, but still enquires after Napoleon's wishes. To which Napoleon replies in a loud voice, 'Are people curious to know what I want? I demand either my freedom or my execution. Report that to your Prince Regent. I no longer ask for news of my son, since they have been barbaric enough to leave my first requests unanswered. I was not your prisoner; savages would have had more consideration for my position. Your ministers have basely violated with me the sacred right to hospitality; they have besmirched your nation forever.'

How many more days on this island that is too small for me, I who used to do ten, fifteen, twenty leagues on horseback every day! The climate is not ours. It has neither our sun nor our seasons. Everything here transmits a fatal ennui. The situation is disagreeable, insalubrious; there is no water. This corner of the island I have been relegated to is a desert; it has driven away all its inhabitants.

He knows perfectly well why they have chosen Longwood: so that they can keep him under surveillance, watch his every move, his every visit.

'Let Hudson Lowe send me a coffin! Two bullets in the head, that's what's needed.'

To die?

Death is going to take him here. He often feels weary. He is putting on more weight. The pot-bellied man with thin arms and legs who he sees in the mirror, that is him! *This is what life has made of me.*

Shall I die? When? How? He thinks about it every day.

He does not feel any anxiety, just a sort of curiosity.

'A man should not swear to anything about the nature of his last moments,' he says to Las Cases. 'To say where I come from, what I am, where I am going, is beyond my capability, and yet it all exists. I am the watch that exists and does not know itself. But I can appear before God; I can await his sentence without fear.'

He points to the pages Las Cases has covered with the shorthand he has devised to follow Napoleon's rapid dictation.

'I only ever wanted the glory, the might and the splendour of France; all my faculties, my efforts, my time was devoted to this end. This couldn't be a crime; I only saw virtues in it.'

He walks about a little.

'I have come from the people,' he goes on, 'and nothing I have done in my life has betrayed my origins. None of the interests of the people has been flouted by my actions as Emperor; they were the constant object of my thoughts when I reigned.'

I DO NOT reign any more. I will never reign any more. They will let me die here, as the humidity slowly eats away at me. The coalition powers have agreed to leave me to rot on this rock. The Austrian, Russian and French commissioners have arrived. The only power I have against them all is my thoughts, these phrases I dictate to Las Cases which will etch themselves on people's minds and live on there after my death. What else do I have left? I have seen everything. Even Madame Montholon's grace and Madame Bertrand's force of personality no longer attract me. People still gossip, though. But what matter!

That too is past.

He tells Gourgaud, 'You are young. Let us talk of our love affairs, of women. They would have been the delight of my life if I had had time, but the hours were too short. I had so many things to do!'

He looks at the portraits of Marie Louise and the King of Rome for a long time. He speaks about Josephine.

'She gave her husband happiness and was always his dearest friend. At every moment, on every occasion, she was compliant, devoted and absolutely accommodating. So I have always had the fondest memories and a very keen sense of gratitude for her.'

Why remember her betrayals?

But I remember everything. 'A mind without a memory is like a fortress without garrison.' And mine is full of troops.

HE DICTATES. He forgets nothing; he sees when he checks afterwards. Everything he has experienced and read is with him. He stops. It is four o'clock on 25 November 1816. He suddenly sees a group of riders heading towards Longwood. At their head, Hudson Lowe.

'Go and see what that animal wants,' he tells Bertrand,

The English have decided to arrest Las Cases and his son. Las Cases is accused of having tried to smuggle a letter to Europe, with a servant as intermediary.

Father and son leave flanked by soldiers carrying two trunks of papers.

Reckless Las Cases, who compromises my plans. If Hudson Lowe gets hold of those writings and destroys them, what will I have left?

'With this *boia* – this executioner – there is no security or guarantee. He violates every law. His eyes were shining with joy when he came here because he had found a new way to torment us. As he surrounded the house with his staff, it was like seeing savages from the South Seas dancing around the prisoners they are about to devour. My dear Bertrand, they will kill me here, that is certain!'

HUDSON LOWE is going to expel Las Cases, which the latter is perhaps not entirely unhappy about. Such are men, and how can one reproach him? Let him publish what I have dictated, since he knows about books.

He writes to him on 11 December 1816.

My dear Comte de Las Cases,

My heart is keenly aware of what you must be feeling locked up in isolation. Your conduct in St Helena has been the mirror of your life, honourable and beyond reproach, it gives me pleasure to tell you.

Your society was very necessary to me. Only you read, speak and understand English. How many nights you have made pass when I was ill. Nonetheless I wish and, if needs be, order you to request of the commander of this place to send you back to the continent. It will be a great consolation for me to know you are on the way to more fortunate countries.

Since Las Cases must and probably wants to leave, let it be with my approval.

Napoleon goes on:

If one day you see my wife and my son, kiss them. For the last two years I have had no news, neither direct nor indirect.

At all events, console yourself and console my friends. My body is, it is true, subject to my enemies' hatred. They forget nothing that may satisfy their desire for vengeance; they kill me with pinpricks. But Providence is too just to permit this to go on much longer.

As everything leads one to think that you will not be allowed to come and see me before you leave, accept my embraces and the assurance of my esteem and friendship. Be happy!

Your devoted,

Napoleon

XXXVI

Can this be possible?

He has only been living – or been buried rather – on this insalubrious island for just over fourteen months and yet, on this Monday, 1 January 1817, he feels utterly overwhelmed, as if he had been here forever. The plateau is shrouded in fog; the walls sweat with damp; the rats are busy as ever. When do they stop? They run and squeak and gnaw, skittering through his bedroom and the dining room, and when they're chased out, they simply come back, not one jot less insolent, indifferent or aggressive. How can he celebrate the start of a new year?

'I am in a tomb,' he tells Montholon and Bertrand. 'I do not feel up to a family celebration.'

Later, perhaps, after he has read and dictated. But Las Cases is not here any more and he is convinced that, one after the other, those close to him are going to leave.

Madame de Montholon is pregnant and dreams of nothing but going. Gourgaud is falling out with everyone because he can't stand the inactivity any more. He is young and vigorous. And Madame Bertrand proclaims to all and sundry that she doesn't want to spend another spring here. Only Marchand will be left. Possibly! Even some of the servants are intriguing to get back to Europe.

He murmurs to Montholon, 'I will see you around four. By then work will have banished any nocturnal thoughts.'

He begins to dictate his reflections on the French campaign, the Hundred Days and Waterloo. But he stops quickly. Does all this effort have any sense?

He says to Montholon, 'What's the good of offering all these memoirs to posterity? We are plaintiffs who bore their judge. Posterity will be quite able to discover the truth without us going to such trouble to deliver it to them.'

He returns to his room and lies down. He feels more and more keenly the need to sleep, to drift off as if it were a way of forgetting. But he gets up. He must keep on fighting. He must hold out until all his strength has deserted him. He returns to the salon, hands out presents, plays with the children for a few moments. Then he hears Gourgaud complaining. More rivalry. More stupid quarrels. He shouts at Gourgaud, 'You want to be the centre of everything here. I am the centre. If you are so unhappy, you can leave us!'

Let them all go, let them leave me. He doesn't need anyone.

'Posterity will acknowledge me,' he says, pacing back and forth. 'The truth will be known and the good I have done will be judged along with my faults. If I had succeeded, I would have died with the reputation of the greatest man of all time. And even though I didn't succeed, they will think me an extraordinary man. I fought fifty pitched battles almost all of which I won. I created a code of laws which will carry my name far into the future. I raised myself from nothing to be the greatest monarch in the world. I had Europe at my feet.'

This is what I am, what no one can take from me. I was the voice of a new age.

'I have always believed that sovereignty lay with the people. And my Imperial government truly was a kind of republic. Called to be its leader by the voice of the Nation, my maxim was careers open to talent, without distinctions of wealth, and it is this system of equality that prompted the hatred of the English oligarchy.'

He goes back into his room. What use is it proclaiming what he has done, or the principles of his Imperial regime, when he is kept under lock and key, under constant surveillance on this island in Hudson Lowe's clutches, this jailer-cum-executioner who wants to destroy him, to deprive him of everything that can bring him comfort?

He looks at the bust of the King of Rome that a sailor has brought from London.

My son. And Hudson Lowe wanted to break open the ornament to check there wasn't a message inside!

The governor even forbade a passenger on one of the ships stopping over at Jamestown reporting what he knew of Marie Louise and the King of Rome.

'The cannibals of Oceania wouldn't do that. Before devouring their victims, they would grant them the consolation of talking to one another. Cannibals would disavow the cruelties being perpetrated here. I should have died at Waterloo, or perhaps before. Misfortune is when a man seeking death cannot find it. People have been killed all around me, but I haven't been able to catch the roundshot.'

NONE OF THE attempts to make his situation known in Europe and denounce Hudson Lowe's cruelty is working. Quite the opposite! At the Congress of Aix-la-Chapelle the sovereigns approve of, even congratulate, England on its treatment of Napoleon.

And it is Pozzo di Borgo, my old enemy since the time of Pascal Paoli, Pozzo the traitor, who now serves Alexander, who is compiling the report on me. My enemies aren't letting go. It's the same cast it's always been — those who didn't want the nation or equality. They have me and they won't set me free. But perhaps this is the price of glory.

'Jesus Christ wouldn't be God now without his crown of thorns,' he says. 'It is his martyrdom that spoke to the imagination of the people. If, instead of being here, I was in America like Joseph, no one would think of me now and my cause would be lost.'

There's men for you!
But that means I have to die.

HE GOES OUT less and less.

'Gourgaud, my friend,' he says, leaning on the general's arm, 'I cannot walk any more.'

He is cold. His legs are wrapped in woollens but they are still frozen. He often vomits; his gums are swollen. Sometimes his stomach and belly hurt so much he cannot stand up. He gives up shaving. His beard covers a face that's white now, the skin almost translucent, the features finer, while his stomach seems swollen and misshapen.

He tries to carry on dictating as normal, but at times he breaks off and falls into a sleep. He asks for a hot bath, then faints. He comes round, and his eyes are blank for a few seconds. Then he starts dictating again, in a clear, firm voice. He doesn't forget a single date. He remembers the position of every regiment. He analyses the military situation during the Spanish War. His intellectual vigour is mesmerizing.

But then suddenly he feels exhausted and vomits.

ON 12 APRIL 1818 he learns that Hudson Lowe has decided to send Doctor O'Meara, with whom Napoleon could talk in Italian, back to England.

'Will the world comprehend that they have been so cowardly as to conspire against my doctor,' he asks the Irishman when they are saying goodbye. 'Thank you for all your care. Leave this place of darkness and crime as quickly as possible. I will die on this pallet, racked by illness and with no one to help me, but it will dishonour your nation forever.'

Who will stay with me?

O'Meara leaves. Madame de Montholon is going back to Europe, like Gourgaud. Balcombe, the owner of The Briars, and his two daughters come to say their goodbyes. They are returning to London. And Cipriani, his majordomo, who was such a precious confidant on the island of Elba and so adept at learning all the rumours in Jamestown, dies.

When will my turn come?

EVEN SO, he is serene. He does not want to see the English doctors in St Helena. Hudson Lowe has driven O'Meara away. Let him bear the consequences of his actions!

'The crime will be perpetrated quicker,' he says. 'I have lived too long for them. The ministry in London is very bold. When the Pope was in France I would rather have cut off my hand than rob him of his doctor.'

On his return to Europe, O'Meara must publish the confidential letters that the sovereigns have addressed to Napoleon and that Joseph has kept.

'When I had the strength and the power, those sovereigns intrigued to obtain my protection and the honour of an alliance. They kissed the dust I walked in. Now they oppress me in my old age. They have kidnapped my wife and my child.'

Old age? 1819 is my fiftieth year.

His legs are swollen, the pains in his stomach so acute that sometimes he blacks out. Hepatitis, O'Meara told him again before he left.

The condition needs treatment. But Napoleon refuses to be treated by English doctors on the terms laid down by Hudson Lowe.

I will not give in.

He vomits. He does not go out. He lies down for several hours a day. But he does not submit.

On 20 September 1819 he sees a 'little caravan' approaching Longwood. He recognizes the silhouettes of two priests and a group of English soldiers escorting them.

Their names are Fathers Buonavita and Vignali, of whom the latter is supposed to have some medical knowledge. They are accompanied by another Corsican, Francesco Antommarchi, who introduces himself as a surgeon. They are the help sent by his family, Cardinal Fesch and Madame Mère!

Napoleon receives them. So these are the men who have been sent to aid me and stay with me! Why did they choose them? Because their salaries are low? And my family is mean?

He murmurs in a bitter voice, 'The old priest is no good for anything; he just takes masses. The young one is a schoolboy. It is ridiculous to say he's a doctor. Antommarchi is a professor, but that doesn't mean he practises. I recognize Cardinal Fesch's handiwork in all this. I am enough of a figure, it seems to me, for someone to be paid thirty or forty thousand francs to treat me.'

This is how men are, even in one's own family.

HE TRIES TO get up. He dictates. He gives instructions for work in the garden and has plantations planted around Longwood. On 4 October 1820 he takes another long drive in the barouche and even gets out to visit the house of an English colonist, Sir William Doveton. The man is amiable. They eat, then it is time to go. Napoleon has trouble mounting his horse and, after a few hundred metres at a trot in the barouche, he starts shivering and vomiting.

He says to Antommarchi, 'This is not living. I have had enough; I have no illusions any more.'

He senses the fear of death, the longing to flee this cursed island, all around him, in all those who are staying with him.

He murmurs to Marchand, as he is rubbing him with a towel and wrapping him in blankets to warm him up, 'They will all go, my boy, and you alone will stay on to close my eyes.'

He forces himself to go for a few drives in the barouche. But he is weary. He takes long hot baths that calm him but leave him exhausted. And he cannot read for long any more. His eyes hurt. The light makes him dizzy.

Some mornings, however, he gets up and starts dictating again.

'My presence was indispensable when I wanted to win,' he says firmly, though short of breath. 'That was the flaw in my armour. Not one of my generals was up to a major independent command. It was not the Roman army that subdued Gaul but Caesar. It was not the Carthaginian army that made the Republic tremble at the gates of Rome, but Hannibal . . .'

He stops. He cannot take any more, and yet still he resumes. He wants to conclude this analysis of Spanish affairs. 'The Empire would have emerged victorious from this mortal combat against the kings "by divine right" if . . .'

He is exhausted and whispers to Montholon, 'There is no more oil in the lamp.'

HE GOES to bed. He doesn't want to get up again.

'What a sweet thing repose is,' he says to Antommarchi. 'My bed has become a place of delight for me; I wouldn't exchange it for all the thrones of the world! What a change! How far I have fallen! I whose activity knew no limits, whose brain never drowsed!'

He sighs, and then grimaces with pain.

'I am sunk in a lethargic stupor; I have to make an effort just to open my eyelids.'

He listens to Antommarchi urging him to get up, to go into the garden to walk a little.

'Very well,' he replies, 'but I am very weak; my shaky legs have trouble carrying me.'

He does walk, nonetheless, and refuses Antommarchi's arm. Through clenched teeth he says, 'Ah, Doctor, how tired I am!

I feel that the pure air I'm breathing is doing me good. Never having been ill and never having taken medicines, I barely know myself in such matters. The state I am in today seems almost so extraordinary that I have trouble conceiving of it.'

HE WALKS slowly back inside. It is 26 December 1820. A bundle of European newspapers has been brought from Jamestown.

He goes through them, his eyes half closed. One of them announces the death of Elisa, on 7 August 1820, at the Villa Vicentina, her estate not far from Apulée. Napoleon's sister was forty-three years old.

He hands the newspaper to Antommarchi.

'Princess Elisa is dead,' he says. 'Ah, you see, Elisa has just shown us the way. Death, which seemed to have forgotten my family, is now starting to strike. My turn cannot be far off. The first person in our family who should follow Elisa into the grave is this great Napoleon who bows under the weight of his burden and yet still keeps Europe in a state of alarm.'

XXXVII

THIS IS NOT LIVING.

He vomits. The sheets are changed. He does not shave. He is helped to the barouche. People had thought him better, the illness receding, but already he is felled by tiredness and the appetite he thought he'd recovered has disappeared. He takes some consommé and jelly and feels the black veil of pain enfolding him again.

Putting his hand on his stomach, he murmurs, 'I have a sharp, bitter pain here which, when it starts, seems to cut like a razor. Do you think it's my pylorus? My father died of that at the age of thirty-five. Couldn't it be hereditary?'

But how can one trust this *dottoraccio* Antommarchi, who knows nothing and always leaves the room?

'I do not want to suffer from two illnesses, one natural and the other caused by my doctor.'

But he is forced to take quinine and various emetics.

'Oh, Doctor, how I suffer.'

He rolls about on the floor and vomits.

'These cursed doctors are all the same. When they want to do something to their patient, they mislead him and make him afraid. But this one is stupid, ignorant, vain and without any sense of honour – get rid of him! I have made my will and I am leaving Antommarchi twenty francs to buy a rope with which to hang himself!'

He vomits again.

'I want you to have Arnott called to treat me in future.'

He lets himself be examined by the English doctor from St Helena's garrison. He gets up.

'Oligarchs are the same everywhere,' he says. 'Self-important and insolent when they are in command, and cowardly when there's any danger! The cowards, holding an unarmed man on a rock! They are all the same. I saw the oligarchs of Venice on the eve of the day they perished, and they were just as overweening as the oligarchs of England.'

HE MURMURS to Marchand, 'It will not be long, my friend. My end is drawing near; I cannot go any further.'

Marchand protests.

'It will be as God wishes,' Napoleon continues.

He tries to work and read some of the books Lady Holland has sent him. He glances through some volumes detailing his victories and conquests.

'In five hundred years,' he murmurs, 'the French will dream of no one but me. They will only speak of the glory of my brilliant campaigns. Woe betide anyone who speaks ill of me. Reading about these campaigns, I feel moved myself. All Frenchmen ought to feel brave reading this.'

He slumps backwards in his chair, prostrate, then sits up again.

'Only the Republic can give France back some energy and freedom now.'

He pushes away the meal he has been given.

'Everything repulses me; everything fills me with disgust. I can only take the lightest solids.'

He closes his eyes.

'The machine is worn out; it cannot go any more. It's over; I shall die here.'

He loses the sense of time. People have to repeat the date, the year.

It is now Tuesday, 27 March 1821. He will be fifty-two in a few months.

'IF I FINISH my career now,' he tells Bertrand, 'it would be a blessing. There have been times when I have wanted to die. I do not fear it. It would be a blessing for me to die in a fortnight. What have I to hope for? A more wretched end, perhaps.'

He tries to get up. He puts his coat over his dressing gown, dons his bicorn, and walks a little way on Bertrand's arm. He goes out to the garden in his slippers.

'Oh why, since I was going to have to lose it in such a deplorable way, did the cannonballs spare my life?'

He has dizzy spells.

'The only thing to fear is the English wanting to keep my body and put it in Westminster.'

He stops.

'Well, then they must be forced to give it back to France. After assassinating me, the least they can do is to give my ashes back to France, the only country I have loved and where I want to be buried.'

He bends over double and vomits.

'Immortality . . .' he begins, lying cautiously down on the bed in the half-light of his room.

He groans. Rats can be heard running across the floor.

'Immortality,' he continues, 'is living on in the memories of men. This idea leads to great things. It were better not to have lived than not to have left any traces of your existence.'

HE DROWSES. Suddenly, he sits up and vomits. At first he refuses the medicine he is given. What is it? A mixture of opium, quinine and an infusion of cinnamon and calomel with mercury as a base.

He grimaces with disgust.

'It is unheard of, this aversion I have to medicines,' he murmurs. 'I used to face danger with indifference. I looked on death dispassionately. And yet now, however hard I try, I cannot raise a vase containing the mildest preparation to my lips.'

His head falls back. He is exhausted. He swallows.

'*Quod scriptum, scriptum est,*' he murmurs. 'Are you in any doubt, Doctor, that everything that happens is written, that our hour is fixed.'

He opens his eyes.

'A comet,' he says, forcing himself to raise his arm to point at the sky. 'That was the sign heralding Caesar's death.'

XXXVIII

HE IS COVERED IN SWEAT. His clothes are changed again.

'Don't maltreat me,' he says, pulling away from Marchand and Montholon.

He vomits. There's that bitter taste in his mouth again, like black earth, and that colour staining his waistcoat and the sheets.

Doctor Arnott tells him again that his condition is not desperate.

'Doctor, you are not telling the truth. You are wrong to try to hide my position from me; I know what it is.'

Arnott hands him some purgative pills.

Who do they take him for?

'My machine is a little like elephants; they can be led on a string, but not on a rope.'

He sits down, then abruptly stands up again. It is Friday, 13 April 1821. It is time, he murmurs. He must dictate his will. He sends for Montholon.

'I am better today,' he says. 'But my end is near.'

He gestures: Montholon is to sit there, at the end of the bed, and note down what he says.

'I die in the Roman Apostolic Church, in the bosom of which I was born more than fifty years ago.'

He breaks off, coughs, then murmurs, 'In truth, I die a theist, believing in a God of rewards who is the principle of everything, but I am declaring that I die in the Catholic faith because I think that fitting for public morality.'

His head slumps forward. He vomits up black bile. He says weakly, 'I was born in the Catholic religion; I want to perform the duties it prescribes and receive the succour it administers.'

He sends for Abbé Vignali.

'Do you know what a funeral chapel is?' he asks calmly.

'Yes, sire.'

'Good. You will preside over mine when I have entered my death throes. You will have an altar erected in the next room and you will say the prayers for the dying.'

He turns towards Doctor Antommarchi, who breaks into a weak smile.

'Your stupidity tires me, sir. I can pardon your levity and lack of *savoir-vivre*, but a lack of courage – never. Withdraw.'

He has trouble getting his breath. He wants to be alone with Montholon. He starts dictating again.

'I want my ashes to lie on the banks of the Seine, in the midst of the French people I have loved so well. I have always had reason to praise my very dear wife Marie Louise; I retain the fondest feelings for her to the last moment. I beg her to see that she protects my son from the traps that still surround his childhood.'

He turns laboriously towards the fireplace, stretches out a hand towards the King of Rome, then continues, 'I recommend my son never to forget that he is French and never to allow himself to be an instrument in the hands of the triumvirs who oppress the people of Europe. He must never fight against France or do her harm in any way. He should adopt my motto, "Everything for the French people!"

'I am dying prematurely, murdered by the English oligarchy and their hired assassin. The French people will not be slow to avenge me.'

He remains silent for a long while. Montholon tries to go. Napoleon vomits. Marchand wraps up his feet, but he carries on shivering.

'My boy, it is time to finish,' he says. 'I feel it.'

He grits his teeth and resumes dictating.

'The two unfortunate invasions of France, when it still had so many resources, were due to the treason of Marmont, Augereau, Talleyrand and La Fayette. I pardon them. May French posterity pardon them as well.

'I thank my good and most excellent mother, the cardinal, my brothers . . .'

He has no more strength.

'Off you go,' he says. 'Go and copy out what I have dictated and the day after tomorrow, which will be my final day, we will read it through. You will dictate it and I will write it.'

MY LIFE must be in order; I mustn't forget anyone who has helped me, supported me or served me.

On Sunday 22 April he copies out the codicils. He makes his bequests. To Montholon, two million 'as proof of satisfaction for the filial care he has given me for six years and to compensate him for the losses of his stay on St Helena'. Bertrand, Marchand, the servants, Las Cases and also certain generals, the sons and grandsons of La Bédoyère and Muiron – all of them must be given proof of his gratitude. And 100,000 francs for Surgeon-in-Chief Larrey, 'the most virtuous man I have known'.

Consequently he must write to the banker Lafitte for him to pay the relevant amounts. The interest on the five million I gave him will go to the wounded of Waterloo and to the officers and soldiers of the battalion of the island of Elba.

He has more and more difficulty following Montholon's dictation, yet he has to copy out the will and the codicils in his own hand, then seal them and appoint an executor. He chooses Marchand.

He has almost finished when Marchand brings him an English newspaper in which there's another article denouncing the execution of the Duke d'Enghien and lambasting Caulaincourt and Savary, who it accuses of this 'crime'. Napoleon sits up straight and leans forward. They must add a few lines, he says. His voice is hoarse.

'I had the Duke d'Enghien arrested because it was necessary for the security, interest and honour of the French people, when the Comte d'Artois was, by his own admission, maintaining sixty assassins in Paris. In a similar situation I would do the same.'

He lets himself fall back, then slowly copies out those lines.

He vomits.

'I have written too much. Ah, the pain, the suffocation. I am about to collapse; I can't take any more. I feel an unbearable pain in the left of my stomach.'

VOMITING; hiccups. Then a few easier hours.

My son.

I must dictate what my executors should say to my son when they see him.

He calls in Montholon and starts to speak, interrupted by coughing fits and vomiting.

'My son must not think of avenging my death. He must profit from it. Let the memory of what I have done never leave him, and may he always remain French through and through, like me. One doesn't do the same thing twice in one century. I was obliged to tame Europe by arms. Today one must convince it. I saved the Revolution, which was dying; I washed away its crimes. I showed it to the world in all its resplendent glory. I implanted new ideas in France and Europe; they will not be able to go backwards. Let my son bring to fruition everything I have sown.'

He breathes more easily. The nausea seems to have gone.

'Let my son scorn all parties; let him only see the masses. France is a country where leaders have the least influence. Relying on them is building on sand. One only does great things in France by relying on the masses. The French Nation is the easiest of nations to govern when one doesn't antagonize it; nothing matches its prompt and easy comprehension. It instantly sees who is working for it and who against it. But one must always address its senses, otherwise its anxious mind wears it down. It ferments and grows furious.'

He stops. He is covered in sweat. But he forbids Montholon to come closer. He wants to carry on.

'The French people have two equally powerful passions which seem opposed and yet derive from the same sentiment, namely the love of equality and distinctions. A government can only satisfy these two needs by excessive justice . . .

'Let my son read and think about history often; it is the only true philosophy . . . But everything that he learns will be of little use to him if he doesn't have deep in his heart that sacred fire, that love of good which alone makes great things.

'But I will hope that he is worthy of his destiny.'

He collapses and vomits.

HE HAS MORE to say. He wants everything he possesses to be distributed just so. Every possession is like a unit on a battlefield; every decision in my will is a sign, a commandment, like a manoeuvre. *This is my last battle.*

He dictates, writes. His son, Comte Léon, must be endowed. It would be good if he entered the magistracy. He wants his second illegitimate son, 'Alexander Walewski, to be drafted into the service of France in the army'. Not forgetting the son and grandson of Baron du Theil, lieutenant-general of artillery, who was so generous to him at Auxonne.

Not forgetting England either.

He says to Doctor Arnott, 'There has not been one indignity or horror which you English have not taken joy in forcing on me. The simplest family communications, even those that no one has ever been forbidden, you refused me. My wife and my son have ceased to live for me! You have kept me six years in torment and secrecy. I had to shut myself away in unhealthy cramped rooms when I have ridden across all Europe on horseback!'

This bitter taste in his mouth is contempt for oligarchic England and the black blood of sickness.

'You have assassinated me, at length, in detail, with premeditation, and the infamous Hudson has been the executor of your ministers' decisions.'

He turns over and vomits.

'You will finish like the arrogant republic of Venice,' he goes on, 'and, dying here on this horrific rock, deprived of my family and lacking everything, I bequeath the opprobrium and horror of my death to England's ruling family.'

THESE ARE the last days.

A fit of hiccups sends a searing pain through his guts.

He calls for Montholon. He wants to dictate the letter that is to be sent to the hyena Hudson Lowe when the moment comes. He speaks in a voice that suddenly is clear once more. 'Governor, the Emperor died on . . . following a long and painful illness. I have the honour to inform you of this.'

That will be all.

He vomits. Marchand gives him something to drink.

The water is cool.

'If they proscribe my body,' he says, 'as they have proscribed my person, well then, let me be buried by the spring where this water flows out, so sweet and pure.'

He remembers the place shaded by three willows situated above Hutt's Gate Cottage where the Bertrands live. One can see the sea from there. And he had drunk water from the spring that wells up in that isolated hollow. 'If, after my death,' he had said, 'my body remains in my enemies' hands, you will put it there.'

WITH A GESTURE he asks for Antommarchi to be shown in.

It is Saturday 28 April.

He waits for his hiccups to die down a little. He looks at Antommarchi. There's no choice: he'll have to go through this *dottoraccio*.

'After my death,' he says, 'which cannot be far off now, I want you to open my body. I also demand that you prevent any English doctor laying a hand on me.'

He breaks off. Doctor Arnott can help Antommarchi, though.

He closes his eyes.

'I further wish,' he goes on, 'you to take my heart, put it in spirits of wine and take it to Parma to my dear Marie Louise. You will tell her that I have tenderly loved her. You will tell her everything you have seen, everything that relates to my situation and my death.'

SHE MUST know, and my son must learn, how I have lived here. How I died.

HE DETAINS Antommarchi.

'The vomiting that is now almost uninterrupted,' he says, 'makes me think the stomach is the sickest of my organs and I am close to thinking that it is afflicted by the lesion that took my father to his grave, I mean a . . .'

To learn, to know, to leave nothing in the shadows but shine a light on everything, even this death that is stalking me and I am summoning. To know everything, to understand everything, that is what I have always wanted.

HE SPEAKS in a weakened voice.

'When I am dead,' he says to his household, 'each of you will have the sweet consolation of returning to France. Some of you will see your parents again, some your friends, and I will meet my brave lads in the Champs Élysées.'

He smiles.

'Seeing me, they will all become mad with enthusiasm and glory again. We will talk of our wars with the Scipios, the Hannibals, the Caesars, the Fredericks. There will be pleasure in that . . .'

He laughs briefly.

'Unless they're afraid to see so many warriors gathered together.'

It is Thursday, 3 May 1821.

He is racked with hiccups for hours on end. In the early afternoon, turning his head towards his intimates who are gathered in the salon into which his bed has been moved, he says, 'You have shared my exile; you will be loyal to my memory; you will do nothing that may harm it.'

Then he turns towards Montholon.

'Well, my boy, wouldn't it be a pity not to die after having put one's affairs into such good order?'

XXXIX

THIS INCESSANT PAIN in the core of his body torments him.

'My God, my God, my God,' he murmurs.

He sinks into the darkness, then wakes up. Liquid is being poured into his mouth, sweet, soothing.

'That's good, very good.'

But what is it? He recognizes the colour. He tries to push the glass away. His arm falls back. He has to swallow the calomel.

'Marchand, you scoundrel,' he says to his valet.

They rub him.

'What an achievement for science! A fine consultation! Dowsing one's back in eau de cologne!'

He closes his eyes. Where is he?

It is the night of Friday 4 to Saturday 5 May 1821.

He groans; his face freezes.

'What is my son called?'

He squeezes Marchand's hand, who replies, 'Napoleon.'

It is two in the morning. He opens his eyes a little and moves his lips.

'Who retreats,' he says.

He is going to vomit; his whole body rears up. He tries to speak. A death rattle blocks his throat and two words emerge, like reefs covered by his hoarse breathing: 'Head, army.'

DEATH COMES at five forty-nine on the afternoon of Saturday, 5 May 1821.

'DEATH IS nothing,' he had said on 12 December 1804, in the full brilliance of his power. 'But to live defeated and without glory, is to die every day.'

He is still alive.

OTHER PAN BOOKS

AVAILABLE FROM PAN MACMILLAN

MAX GALLO
NAPOLEON: THE SONG OF DEPARTURE	0 330 49002 8	£6.99
NAPOLEON: THE SUN OF AUSTERLITZ	0 330 49003 6	£6.99
NAPOLEON: THE EMPEROR OF KINGS	0 330 49001 X	£6.99

VALERIO MASSIMO MANFREDI
THE LAST LEGION	0 330 48975 5	£7.99
THE TALISMAN OF TROY	0 330 42653 2	£6.99

All Pan Macmillan titles can be ordered from our website,
www.panmacmillan.com, or from your local bookshop
and are also available by post from:

Bookpost, PO Box 29, Douglas, Isle of Man IM99 1BQ
Credit cards accepted. For details:
Telephone: +44 (0)1624 677237
Fax: +44 (0)1624 670923
E-mail: bookshop@enterprise.net
www.bookpost.co.uk

Free postage and packing in the United Kingdom

Prices shown above were correct at the time of going to press.
Pan Macmillan reserve the right to show new retail prices on covers
which may differ from those previously advertised in the text
or elsewhere.